JOAN A. C
DEATH HAS

JOAN ALICE COWDROY was born in London in 1884, the third child of Arthur Rathbone Cowdroy and Marie Grace Aiton.

The author wrote a series of well-received romantic novels in the 1920's, but her career in crime fiction did not begin until 1930 with the publication of *The Mystery of Sett* which introduced one of her series detectives, Chief-Inspector Gorham. Her Asian detective, Mr. Moh, made his first appearance a year later and became a long-standing recurring sleuth in the author's crime fiction.

Joan A. Cowdroy, a life-long spinster, died in Sussex in 1946.

Joan A. Cowdroy Mysteries
Available from Dean Street Press

Death Has No Tongue
Murder of Lydia

JOAN A. COWDROY

DEATH HAS NO TONGUE

With an introduction by Curtis Evans

DEAN STREET PRESS

Published by Dean Street Press 2019

Copyright © 1938 Joan A. Cowdroy

Introduction Copyright © 2019 Curtis Evans

All Rights Reserved

First published in 1938 by Hutchinson

Cover by DSP

ISBN 978 1 912574 83 4

www.deanstreetpress.co.uk

INTRODUCTION

ON JANUARY 9, 1923 Edith Thompson was executed, along with her younger lover Frederick Bywaters, for the brutal murder of her husband Percy, in what today is generally considered one of the most notorious of British miscarriages of justice. Tellingly, the executioner at Thompson's ghastly botched hanging, haunted by the grisly details of her death, resigned from his position the next year and later committed suicide. Yet Edith Thompson received no sympathy from prominent English educational theorist and anti-feminist polemicist Charlotte Cowdroy (1864-1932), headmistress of the Crouch End High School for Girls, who branded the undoubted adulteress and supposed murderess an "abnormal woman" because she worked outside the home, earned more money than her husband and did not desire to have any children. Throughout the 1920s up to her death in 1932 (and, indeed, beyond it, with the publication of her posthumously published 1933 jeremiad *Wasted Womanhood*), Cowdroy, who ironically was herself both single and gainfully employed, passionately denounced women's suffrage and female employment in the nation's workforce as detrimental to the public welfare. She strenuously urged her sisters in the "weaker sex" to eschew personal and financial independence and take what she deemed their natural place in society as submissive wives and mothers. Such sentiments unsurprisingly have generally not endeared Charlotte Cowdroy to modern readers. At the Stuck in a Book blog, for example, Simon Thomas chose *Wasted Womanhood* as his "vilest" read of 2011, adding that Cowdroy's virulent Thirties screed castigating "single, childless woman" as public menaces made him "want to go back in time and thwack her around her unkind head with her unkind book."

Happily for vintage mystery fans, such prominent single, childless Golden Age women mystery writers as Gladys Mitchell, Lucy Beatice Malleson, Edith Caroline Rivett (E.C.R. Lorac/Carol Carnac) and Molly Thynne (reprinted by Dean Street Press) declined to follow Charlotte Cowdroy's advice and modestly put down their pens (even as Charlotte kept a firm grip on her own until grim death ungently pried it from her cold dead fingers). Another Englishwoman crime writer who declined Charlotte Cowdroy's nostrums was Charlotte's second cousin (once removed), Joan Alice Cowdroy (1884-1946). During her adult life Cowdroy remained single, supporting herself by producing a steady succession of both mainstream and detective novels, six of the latter of which detail the sleuthing exploits of Li Moh, presumably the first Asian detective created by a British mystery writer. (It was an American, Earl Derr Biggers, who gave us Charlie Chan.) Today, nearly eighty years after the last appearance in print of canny Mr. Moh, Joan Cowdroy's mysteries are being reprinted by Dean Street Press.

Like Ianthe Jerrold, who likewise has been reprinted by Dean Street Press, Joan Cowdroy was a Twenties mainstream novelist who began penning mystery stories near the end of the decade. Both women were descended from noted journalists, though Joan Cowdroy more distantly so than Jerrold. Joan's great-great grandfather, William Cowdroy, Sr. (1752-1814), founded the *Manchester Gazette*, the first radical nonconformist newspaper to service the population of the rapidly developing north England industrial city of Manchester. William trained all four of his sons--William, Jr., Thomas, Benjamin and youngest Citizen Howarth (born in 1795, his first name was inspired by the establishment in 1792 of the First Republic in France)--as printers on his paper, which after his death sadly was put out of business by the tremendous success of the *Manchester Guardian*. Citizen Cowdroy, who married Martha Rathbone of the prominent Rathbone shipping family of Liverpool (from whom cinema's greatest Sherlock Holmes, Basil Rathbone, likewise is descended), attempted to carry on the family journalism tradition, starting the *Manchester Courier* in 1817, but he died when he was only thirty-three years old, in 1828.

Citizen's son John Rathbone Cowdroy became a minister and served for many years as curate of Oxton Parish, near Liverpool, but John's son Arthur Rathbone Cowdroy (1851-1899) at a young age moved to Hammersmith, West London, where in 1876 he married native Scotswoman Marie Grace Aiton. There as well the couple's third child, Joan Alice Cowdroy, was born on September 16, 1884. Arthur, who served from the age of eighteen as a clerk and later head librarian for the Royal Society of Arts, died tragically at the age of 48 in 1899, when Joan was but fourteen years of age, from locomotor ataxia, a degeneration of the dorsal column of the spinal cord, which frequently is a symptom of tertiary syphilis.

In 1911, 26-year-old Joan Alice resided with her widowed mother, an elder sister, Dora Marion (who worked as a private secretary to a doctor), and a maid at a small villa at 23 Shalimar Gardens in Acton, West London, listing, in contrast with her sister, no occupation. It would take another eleven years--after Dora had married and her brother, Gerald Aiton Rathbone Cowdroy, had become a successful rubber planter out in British Malaya (in 1915 he wed, appropriately for a scion of a band of English newspapermen, Flora Still, the daughter of the editor of the Singapore *Straits-Times*)--for Joan, nearing the age of forty, to see Sampson, Low (future publishers of mystery writers E.C.R. Lorac and Moray Dalton) publish her first novel, *Brothers in Love* (1922). That this novel about "the devotion of one man to another" doubtlessly was inspired by the tragic lingering disability and painful death of Joan's father, this review from the *Straits-Times* makes sufficiently clear:

> We were half inclined to head this notice "A Study in Pain." The central figure in Joan A. Cowdroy's novel, a first, we believe, is a young man doomed by an accident before his birth to agonizing sufferings and to personal disfigurement which makes him almost repulsive to sensitive people, even while they willingly extend to him their pity. But, truly, it is rather the study of a beautiful soul prisoned in a racked and misshapen body, of a man capable of exquisite feeling, great tenderness, and almost superhuman courage and self-sacrifice.[1]

"Miss Cowdroy is a wonderful artist," the moved reviewer concluded, and Joan's next several novels--*The Inscrutable Secretary* (1924), *A Virtuous Fool* (1925) and *A King of Space* (1925)--received similarly favorable notices. After publishing four additional mainstream novels in the Twenties, the author in 1930 produced

1. The reviewer in the *Spectator* was far less sympathetic to the subject matter Cowdroy had chosen for her first novel, complaining that *Brothers in Love* "is concerned entirely with the physical condition of the principal character. People who like reading about sickrooms will doubtless enjoy the book; but it is decidedly morbid in tone."

her first detective novel, *The Mystery of Sett*, which introduced her series policeman Chief-Inspector Gorham. This book was followed the next year by the debut of her amateur sleuth Li Moh, who works in tandem with Gorham, in *Watch Mr. Moh!* (published as *The Flying Dagger Murder* in the US); and with that Joan Cowdroy was well launched on her criminous way. Between 1933 and her death in 1946, she would publish ten more novels, seven of them mysteries: *Murder of Lydia* (1933), *Disappearance* (1934), *Murder Unsuspected* (1936), *Framed Evidence* (1936), *Death Has No Tongue* (1938), *Nine Green Bottles* (1939) and *Murder out of Court* (1944). Most of these were headlined by Mr. Moh and Chief-Inspector Gorham, though in the remainder Gorham performed solo. I assume, though I do not know, that Joan derived her inspiration for Mr. Moh from trips to the Far East to visit her brother, who at his death in 1939 had risen to the post of Assistant Superintendent of the Rubber Control Office in Singapore. Until the death of her mother in 1935, Joan Cowdroy resided at a small villa on Essex Road in Ealing, West London, but by 1939 she was living with three women servants in the town of Newton Abbot, Devon, where, presumably, she spent the war years. Joan Cowdroy "spinster," passed away at the age of 62 on November 16, 1946 at Hopes Rest in the village of Great Holland, Sussex, having recently completed her twentieth novel in the space of twenty-four years. That Joan's work is again in print today, courtesy of Dean Street Press, is a testament not only to the enduring appeal of vintage detective fiction, but to a womanhood that was not wasted but rather lived in fulfillment of what mystery fans will know is a worthy and admirable purpose, entertaining readers, in defiance of the zealous dictates of her kinswoman and her scolding kind.

Curtis Evans

Chapter I

Chief Inspector John Gorham was stretched in a long chair one Saturday evening, reading a magazine story.

It was one of those colourful romances replete with turquoise skies, emerald shores, and translucent waters which appealed to Gorham's untutored taste, but the heroine, a young woman of gleaming limbs and hyacinth hair, had failed to capture his sympathy. With innocence that verged, he felt, on fat-headedness, she, in order to save her aged father from bankruptcy, had consented to accompany the villain alone on a lion-hunting expedition of the Yangtse River, and, when the hideous truth was revealed to her, was compelled, to escape his unwelcome attentions, to plunge desperately into shark-infested waters, and from this predicament was barely rescued in time by a naval officer to whom she had long ago given her, as she believed, unrequited love.

Here Gorham skipped a page or two and recovered her in an illustration (against a backcloth showing Shanghai), locked in the embrace of the naval officer, whose mouth pressed to hers was engaged, according to the caption, in drawing her whole soul through her lips. He glanced at the name of the author, L. V. Hyde, and dropping the magazine left them to get on with it.

It was a perfect evening in high summer, and the heat in his office at Scotland Yard that afternoon made his present refuge, in a patch of shade cast by the rose-covered trellis between his next-door neighbour's domain and his own, seem heavenly by contrast.

The grass of the small lawn was vivid green against the darkness of the monkey tree that was his special pride, and beyond the stone balustrade at the end of the garden flowed the Thames, a river of molten gold in the evening sunlight.

His friend, Mr. Moh, with whom he shared his home, stood broodingly before a herbaceous border beyond the monkey-tree, a brown spaniel, equally immobile, at his side.

Gorham whistled, and Mr. Moh picked up a kitchen chair and approached, accompanied by the dog, Feathers.

"If," said Mr. Moh with gloomy dignity, "the noble police chief is through with perusal of engrossing literature bestowed on unworthy self by sister of author of same, this inconsiderable worm has something to say."

He sat down on his chair, and Gorham grinned.

"Go ahead, old man," he said genially; "you've been looking like a death's-head ever since tea. The sooner you get it off your chest the sooner we'll all be bright and chirpy again. But don't forget I'm a policeman. I have to warn you that anything you say, etc., etc."

"Conspicuous gravity of demeanour being induced by present sorrow, and prophetic dread of further sorrow to befall, low facetiousness strikes discordant note." His tone was calmly repressive.

"All right, all right, Li Moh. Tell me all."

"In pursuit of avocation as jobbing gardener there are gardens," began Mr. Moh, omitting nothing, "to which these hands give weekly tendance. Two of these locate themselves in Pound Lane, Finnet. One belongs to your friend Mr. Hardwicke, who conveyed request through you that I should keep the front garden of his house, The Laurels, in order while he was abroad." Gorham nodded.

"I remember. Lewis Hardwicke isn't exactly a friend of mine, but I felt sorry for the poor devil. He inherited that house from his parents, lived there for years himself as a boy, and he'd had it all done up and refurnished for his fiancée, and the girl died within a week or two of the wedding-day. Very down, he was, poor chap; glad to shut it up and go to the U.S.A. for his paper. But the last articles I saw under his signature were from Spain. Did he come home between the two commissions?"

"I think not. He is abroad still. The house stands vacant; a woman cleaner goes in at intervals. But it was while working in the front garden at The Laurels that the lady asked me to go into the garden next door, where I have been regularly employed since. Do you remember Pound Lane?"

"No. It's years since I was at Finnet. It used to be a jolly, old-world sort of village, but I'm told the whole place is a mass of new streets now. Just the way every village on London's outskirts gets swamped and suburbanized in time."

"That is true. A whole new suburb lies at the foot of the hill on which the old village still exists, with the church at the top. But Pound Lane is still beyond the new building zone, and has not been spoiled. Four houses stand on the north side backing on to market gardens. On the other side is a field, high hedge-rows, and shady trees. Two of the houses are tall and gloomy, with narrow, overgrown shrubberies in front. The Laurels is smaller, painted white, and in good condition, but of similar type. But the fourth house at the corner of Chetwynd Avenue is beautiful. A trim cottage enclosed in a garden that is a dream of scented loveliness; not large, an acre all told perhaps. That is Innisfree, where I work, where work is a labour of love."

"Who lives there?" asked Gorham, as he paused dreamily.

"A brother and sister named Hyde. Authors. He wrote that tale you so earnestly perused. L. V. Hyde, a famous person it is said, by others and by himself. Of the little poems of his sister he speaks with smiling condescension, even to me, a totally unlettered person. It may be, besides these poems, Miss Hyde copies his stories. I hear the click, click, click of typewriters going—rarely two, but often one—click, click, click; click, click, click. There is a deaf servant, and a car that Mr. Hyde drives. He is often away, at golf, or in London or with friends from the Far East, where he was employed on a tea estate till illness brought him home."

Gorham, thinking of the young woman with hyacinth hair, opened his eyes with a new interest.

"L. V. Hyde in the Far East? What part?"

"Assam, I believe. But he has been to Hong Kong, Canton, Shanghai, and Singapore. To me, a humble exile from China, he has condescendingly mentioned these admired names," Mr. Moh murmured sweetly, then waved aside the subject of Mr. Hyde. "Of this celebrated person it does not become self to speak. He is seldom seen. But always Miss Hyde stays at home, and her typewriter goes click, click, click. She is the maker of the garden, a poem painted in flowers; nor, till an attack of lumbago drove her into engaging self, had she any helper. Yet this place of exquisite delights is the cause of the sorrowful mien that you derided, my Gorham."

"Ah," said Gorham with satisfaction, "I hoped we'd be coming to the point some day."

"We are there now. You recall high winds that raged last March? They snapped every branch of an almond tree in that garden just as it was blowing into magical pale blossom, snapped and broke that almond tree alone in Finnet. She who had watched its burgeoning buds with silent rapture said only that winds were freakish."

"Took it calmly, you mean?"

"With colossal calm. Other beauties in their turn wiped out the sorrow of that lost loveliness, but in May, when great waves of tulips were the garden's glory, the fairest bed of all was destroyed, the flowers hacked and crushed, the torn-up bulbs smashed. 'An act of local hooliganism', the lady said."

"Nothing was done?"

"Nothing was permitted to be done. And yesterday it was the turn of the delphiniums, Gorham. Great clumps of them that were massed at the end of a wide, paved walk, spikes of celestial shades of blue, of unutterable loveliness on Thursday, today lay chopped and bedraggled in the soil, stamped into broken limpness, the wreck of such loveliness as man's thoughts cannot create. This iniquity must be ended, Gorham. It is the destruction of beauty and life and joy! . . ."

Rarely had the Chief Inspector seen his amiable little friend stirred to such anger, but his assent was angry also. Wanton destruction always roused his civilized instincts to planning severe reprisals.

"Let's see. Finnet must come within Gray's Manor, and while Gray's away on sick leave I'm in charge myself. But I've heard nothing of this. The good lady has called in the police this time, I suppose?"

He saw Moh's mournful headshake, and exclaimed in surprise: "What? Hasn't she?"

"Again she is supine. I stood with her today to view the ruin, and she said it must have been caused by a dog. I did not"—he shrugged his shoulders—"point out that dogs rarely wear boots, or wield knives. To the wilfully deaf, speech is a waste of breath. Yet, being wrathful to see such loveliness defaced, I retorted, 'Why not elephants, madam?' But at that she turned a stony look on me and said with great coldness: 'I value your services too much to wish to part with them as yet, Mr. Moh. The gate was unlatched. It was a dog'."

"What! You've to accept the dog or the sack! D'you suppose she'd done it herself?"

Mr. Moh wrinkled his forehead, plainly worried.

"It seems incredible. Yet why does she refuse to admit the evil that strikes down her flowers? She loves them, as she loves her dog Robin. It defeats me altogether, Gorham," he said frankly. "It was as if she was not surprised . . . He paused again. "I came away, for a thought came into my mind that you might come—tomorrow, as my friend—to view the scene. On Sunday morning she goes to church. There need be no encounter—"

"I don't see what earthly good I could do," Gorham muttered uneasily. "I can't padlock the woman's gate against her booted dogs. Or take her up for destroying her own property, come to that. And you'll get the sack for a certainty for interfering when she's definitely warned you not to. Or don't you mind getting the sack?!"

"There is a group of exquisite lilies now in bud," said Mr. Moh, his face suddenly expressionless. "Jeopardy to self's employment will be gladly encountered if noble police chief can elucidate means to spare their pure heads shameful death."

"You'll pester me till I consent, I suppose," Gorham said grudgingly. "All right, I'll tool you over in the morning. But if the lady doesn't go to church, and she or her brother sail out and sack you on the spot, don't say afterwards I didn't warn you."

"Such mendacity," said Mr. Moh with great suavity, "would be inconceivable while said warning lies engraved on tablets of self's brain."

This was Gorham's introduction to the Finnet murder case. With due caution allowing ample time for Miss Hyde to walk from her house to the ancient church on the hill-top, on Sunday morning the two friends drove over to Finnet and, after passing through a network of new streets, reached Pound Lane from the far end.

It was wide and rural in character still, shaded by elms, with a steep, grassy bank and a wild growth of hawthorns facing the tall, roomy Victorian houses opposite. The luxuriance of summer mitigated if it could not conceal the shabbiness of the first two behind their narrow front gardens. Gorham exclaimed, "Hullo!" and, instead of running on to the gate of Innisfree, set in a high wall with trees showing above, pulled up abruptly in front of the third house.

"That is Hardwicke's place, The Laurels," Mr. Moh muttered, surprised. The journalist's house was more attractive than its neighbours. Whitewashed, of two storeys only, a short flight of steps led to the front door and a narrow, white-painted verandah before the dining-room windows, and the shrubs and turf of the garden below were trimly kept. But what had arrested their attention was a group of three men who seemed to be peering at something behind the screen of laurels growing beneath the verandah. One of them looked round sharply as the car stopped, and as the Chief Inspector climbed out came forward to meet him with obvious relief in his eyes.

"My word, sir! You were quick! Were you on the spot when my message came through? It's Mr. Gorham, isn't it? I'm Sergeant Norris."

"I've had no message. Came from home," Gorham explained briefly. "I happened to be passing and saw the lot of you. What's up?"

"Come and look, sir. I'd 'phoned Divisional Headquarters less than five minutes ago. Thought your coming seemed a bit miraculous!"

Tucked in between the bushes and the steeply sloping bank that carried the floor of the verandah was the body of a woman.

Gorham looked while the sergeant held one of the bushes aside with his stick and a policeman did the same on the other side. The body, naked save for a man's jacket, was tall and thin and angular. There were no visible wounds, but the appearance of the face suggested suffocation as the cause of death.

"How do you suppose she got there?"

"Tipped over that verandah railing, I think. The bushes aren't damaged in front. At the back they are."

Gorham went up the short flight of steps and peered over the two-foot railing.

"That's right, I'd say." He came down again. "What have you done?"

"I've got a hand ambulance halted round the corner in Chetwynd Avenue, sir. I thought it best not to attract a crowd here. And after notifying D.H.Q. I was waiting, on guard."

Gorham nodded in frowning thought.

"When was it discovered?"

"By this constable, sir. Twenty minutes or so ago. Come and repeat what you told me," he ordered the man.

"I was proceeding past the house, sir, and—"

"One moment. Were you on your beat?"

"The lane is part of my beat, sir, but I wasn't here exactly on duty. Passing along the corner of West Avenue—at the far end there—a man come up and asked me to take charge of a dog what he'd found astray. But as I recognized it as the brown spaniel belonging to Miss 'Ide at Innisfree"—again he pointed—"having often seen it in the village with her deaf maid, I brought him straight along, and passing this gate I saw something that looked like a bit of bare leg between two of those bushes. So I looked again to make sure, and no one being about, I dropped Robin over his gate and called up the station from the call-box round the corner, and come back and waited by the gate till the sergeant arrived, at 11.9 a.m."

"You saw no one in the road from first to last?"

"No one in Pound Lane, sir. Only a few pedestrians walking along Chetwynd Avenue."

"That's what he gave me, sir." The sergeant was gazing at the upper windows. "This house is furnished, but appears to be empty. Doors and windows locked. It belongs to a man named Hardwicke, of an old Finnet family, well-known residents here. This gentleman is a newspaper correspondent, I believe, and abroad at present—"

"On the contrary," said Gorham, interrupting this flow of information, "Mr. Hardwicke is now coming up the road."

A sunburnt, burly man in tweeds, carrying a suitcase, came briskly to the gate, opened it, and stared astonished at the group in his front garden.

"Hullo, you fellows! Is this a party, or what? Don't hesitate to make yourselves at home!"

Gorham went down the sloping lawn to meet him on the path.

"Sorry, Hardwicke. Where did you spring from?"

"Spain. Just back. Slept last night in town, and so home to find the bobbies in possession. Pleasant surprise. Don't tell me if it's a secret, but I'd love to know why."

"It's a surprise all right, but not too pleasant. Somebody has dumped a corpse in your bushes."

"The hell they have! Who?" He turned greenish, but kept himself in hand.

"That we don't know yet. Or the victim. The discovery was made by a passing constable within the half-hour." He turned back to the others. "Better cut those bushes and extricate the body. There'll be a crowd here soon."

"No, no. Cutting is wasteful. Uprooting much damn' quicker!" Mr. Moh, who had long foreseen the order, darted forward with a spade, and in a few seconds removed one of the laurels, leaving a gap that disclosed the head and shoulders, wide enough to enable two of the men to lift the body on to the grass.

"Does anyone know who it is?" Gorham asked, after a brief pause. Hardwicke and the sergeant shook their heads. One policeman frowned dubiously but said nothing, and Mr. Moh looked down at the stark thing at his feet with eyes that were devoid of expression. Every man present was familiar with the sight of death in violent form, yet none but experienced a twinge of nausea now.

The face was swollen and distorted, the body that of a woman of over forty, angular, skinny, without any redeeming beauties of shape or curve of earth-soiled limbs. The man's jacket into which the arms were thrust fell back from the thin chest, and dark bruising on the neck was clearly visible.

"Fetch a sheet and the ambulance," Gorham ordered sharply, and as a policeman strode to the gate he dropped on one knee and began gently to feel beneath the jacket.

"Death by manual strangulation twelve to fifteen hours ago I'd say, at a rough guess. And dumped behind those shrubs within an hour of death. The doctor may narrow the time down more definitely, I hope." He got up. "There's a hint of damp about the coat, specially the left shoulder, that was uppermost. What weather did you have here last night, Norris?"

"There was the beginning of what looked like developing into a heavy thunder-shower between ten and eleven," the sergeant stated after thought, "but it passed over and the moon came out. There was a heavy dew on the grass early this morning, though."

Gorham went over and felt the ground where the body had lain.

"Um, soil here bone dry. That goes towards confirming the rough estimate of time, but not much moisture would penetrate below those laurels, in any case. Crime couldn't have taken place here. Much too exposed. But the ground's too hard to retain footmarks. Strip that coat off before deceased is taken away."

He paced the path and steps and verandah while the sergeant and the remaining constable removed the coat, his glance scrutinizing every inch of the plain cement without result.

As he returned to the group of men all staring downward he became aware of an odd intentness, marked in the case of Mr. Moh.

"Are you sure none of you recognize her?" he repeated sharply. "How about you, Li Moh?"

"Deceased resembles a person I have seen in this lane occasionally, while pursuing avocation of gardener," Mr. Moh admitted with childlike candour. "You would like name of said person?"

"You think it's she? Of course, man! We want her identified as quick as possible."

"Individual alluded to had employment as daily help at last house in Pound Lane, called the Burrs. Self has seen same, ungainly walk, wearing brown tweed coat, an orange wool cap—no, not cap—beret, with a green metal feather sticking up and American cloth shopping-bag in hand, but no speech exchanged. The name is Shields."

"Hi, you there! Move along, please!" came the voice of the policeman returning with a canvas sheet, and addressing a milkman who had abandoned his bicycle to hang with absorbed interest over the gate. And, waiting till this uninvited hearer had moved reluctantly but obediently away, the young constable who had found the body stepped forward eagerly.

"That's right, sir; Ellen Shields. Used to live with her mother and sister in a flat over a baker's in the High Street, and went out by the day. And still come over, though the mother's dead and she didn't live here any more. It's her, I'm certain."

"Then why the dickens couldn't you tell Mr. Gorham so straight off?" demanded his sergeant wrathfully.

"Well, sir, I thought I knew her, but with no clothes on—"

"Exactly. Some difference, what!" broke in Lewis Hardwicke. "I knew Ellen Shields myself. In fact, she made some chair-covers for me, and damned badly, too. Mrs. Manstead, next door, employed her. I didn't connect her with—this—till Mr. Moh spoke. But now I'm sure he's right. Oh, look, have her taken away out of this, for God's sake, Gorham, and then come in and have a drink! This is a cheerful homecoming for the wanderer, I'm damned if it isn't."

"All right, but wait for us, old man," Gorham said soothingly. "We shan't be long now."

Hardwicke waited moodily on the steps while the body was covered and conveyed to the ambulance at the gate, and meantime the Chief Inspector conferred apart with Norris; and Mr. Moh, with mournful tenderness, planted the uprooted laurel temporarily in a side bed.

"Great dubiety exists as to whether laurel of such mature age can survive uprootal, but best chance should be given," he murmured aside to the laurel's owner when the deed was done. But Hardwicke wasn't bothering much about a mere bush just then.

"Remember helping my mother to shove those bushes in," he grunted, and let the subject lapse.

The ambulance moved off at last; a single constable was stationed at the gate to keep back spectators who had begun to drift up, and the two police officers joined Hardwicke at the front door. But as he inserted his key in the lock Gorham laid a detaining hand on his arm.

"One moment, old man. Before we go any further, there's a chance we mustn't overlook. I realize how rotten all this is for you, but you must see the obvious alternatives for yourself. It's unthinkable that she was murdered where she was found—so she was either conveyed here dead or—the crime was committed in the house itself."

Hardwicke exploded in quite natural wrath.

"Upon my soul, Gorham, this is getting beyond a joke! Not content with mucking up my front garden with corpses, you dare to suggest that the wretched creature passed out in my house!"

"Well, be a good chap and stop here while we make sure she didn't, anyway," Gorham said with firm cheerfulness.

He submitted with an ill grace, but it did not take more than a cursory glance over the rooms above and below stairs to assure the police officers that there had been no intruders or disturbance in the place since the cleaner's last visit.

She had faithfully fulfilled her trust, for the rooms were fresh and spotless; though, with its bright, unworn carpets, its suites of furniture arranged in conventional order, which bore no stamp of human usage, the absence of those little intimate touches which turn inanimate things into possessions bearing the impress of their owner's personality, the whole place was like one of the show-houses in an exhibition. Gorham remembered the bride-to-be who had selected these furnishings and had not lived to use them, and felt sorry for Hardwicke, but the light film of dust on polished surfaces of tables and chairs proved conclusively that the crime had not been committed inside the house.

"Better wait and get what information we can now we're here," he murmured, as they reached the hall again and the sergeant showed signs of hesitation as to his next move, and they entered the dining-room, where Hardwicke, profoundly relieved, promptly produced a siphon, whisky, and glasses from the interior of a sideboard. This room, in which Hardwicke had retained much of his family stuff, looked much less bleak than the bedrooms.

"Well, you're satisfied, I hope?" he demanded. "Say when."

"Thanks. Oh yes, there's not a trace of any strangers coming in here. You looked round the back garden, Mr. Moh?"

"Intensive scrutiny reveals utter blamelessness of premises at rear of domicile, and side gate guarding same is padlocked on inside and immovable. This wretched being," explained Mr. Moh, "being directed to confine activity to front garden, that at back has reverted to impenetrable jungle; no blame allocated to self for such."

"That's all right, then." Gorham settled himself in a comfortable chair.

Chapter II

"Now we're here, Hardwicke, I'll be grateful if you'll tell us what you can about deceased. Have you known her long?"

Hardwicke frowned, perching himself on the corner of his dinner-table, glass in hand.

"I've never, so to say, known the woman at all." He growled, and waved to the sergeant to take a seat. "But she's been around here, working for various people for years—since I was a lad. I'm sure my mother never employed her, for she wouldn't have stood her dithering ways for a second. Shields was one of those women who wear glasses and amble in and out of houses doing everything badly. Intelligent in her own fashion, I suppose. Or at any rate thought she was. Read books and aired her views on them. The type my mater used to call neither fish, flesh, fowl, nor good red herring. No good at domestic work, but would do it if you called her a help—and had to, because she couldn't have held down an office job for an hour.

"Let's see, when I remember her first she was companion-help to Mrs. Manstead, next door. Sat at table and poured out tea." The gleam of a reminiscent grin lightened the gloom of his eyes. "Lord, I'd cause to remember the first time I noticed her. Might be eighteen years ago, or more. My mother dragged me in one Sunday afternoon to a sort of party the old lady was throwing—her birthday or something. Well, this female was installed behind the tea-tray, and suddenly she gave a loud squawk, picked up the pot, and started to scutter out of the room; tripped over a chair and measured her length on the floor, emptying the boiling water from the pot—into which she had omitted to put any tea—all over my ankles. Which, being a perfect little gentleman at that time, I had to swear blind didn't hurt."

"Um. Did she remain with this lady—Mrs. Manstead?"

"I can't give you dates, Gorham. I was away a lot in France and Germany, and afterwards covering spots of trouble here and there for my paper, so I was only at home for intervals, but I believe she stopped with old Manstead for some years, and afterwards came back at times when Mrs. M. was hunting for a new help. There's been a long procession of them, I'd say, so probably she was frequently there, off and on. I seem to remember, too, that in some of the Mater's letters she spoke of Shields being employed at Innisfree by Miss Hyde, who was a close friend of hers. But after the Mater's death five years ago I rather lost touch with the neighbours she had been friendly with. But Mr. Moh said she'd got in with the Hubberds at the end house. I've been away a couple of years, and can't vouch for that, though it's quite likely. You see, everyone who knew Mrs. Manstead must have seen her at some time or other, and when they were hard-up for domestic help probably thought of her as a *pis aller*. Shields was very much the female *pis aller*, I'd say."

"Yes, I get the idea," Gorham said thoughtfully. "It looks as if Mrs. Manstead would be our best informant. Norris, go next door and ask if it would be convenient for the lady to give me an interview."

"You won't get much satisfaction out of her," Hardwicke exclaimed with a malicious grin when the sergeant had gone. "She's over eighty, and as deaf as a post—one of those old ladies who don't take the slightest interest in anything but their own stuffy comforts. I bet if any of her domestic slaves tried to worry her with their troubles they'd be shut up, damn' quick."

"Well, when did you last see Shields yourself to speak to?"

"Oh—two years ago. Met her in the street one day when I was refurnishing this house, and she said she was out of a job, and looked as if she was on her uppers, I gave her two chair-covers to make. She made the damn things so badly it would have been simpler to have given her a couple of quid to leave 'em alone. She spoke to me again in the street a week or two later, but by that time the mess she'd made of the job didn't matter, and I cut her comments a bit short."

Gorham understood the elliptic sentence. Between those two meetings the girl for whom the house was being prepared had died. Probably Shields had ventured on some clumsy word of sympathy. But he was wasting time.

"What about these people, Hubberd, who are said to have employed her last?" He glanced at his watch. "Know them personally?"

"Only as neighbours. Used to drop in at The Burrs sporadically in the dim past. Ordinary sort of married couple. Chap used to be in the Orient somewhere. No children. You say they're still there?"

He turned to Mr. Moh, who, having declined any refreshment, was sitting on the edge of a chair in the doorway like an image of patience, his glance fixed on the blue jacket that the Chief Inspector had examined and laid on the table.

"Same still in residence, with addition of brother of Mrs. Hubberd, and second married couple, actor and wife named Hughes, who share roof of Burrs."

"You don't mean poor old Hubberd is finally landed with that rotter Bob Dent?" Hardwicke exclaimed. "He was always being shipped off somewhere in my time, *and* landing back again! Hughes—seem to remember meeting them there. Flamboyant-looking female and fellow like a film star. Theatrical people—that's right—more often resting than not. Didn't know they'd joined forces, though. Probably for economic reasons. The Hubberds were always deuced hard-up. He had some job connected with a local race-track—not much—and Ethel was no manager. Quite a decent pair really, though given to scrapping in public latterly. Tempers frayed by constant living on the edge of their means, which develops a tendency to snarl at your nearest and dearest, I've observed."

"Any of these people likely to be connected in any dubious way with deceased?"

"Great Heavens, no man! She wasn't the sort anyone would—well, *de mortuis*, etc., and in the circumstances one doesn't want to be unkind, but if you were thinking of a sexual motive for this murder, it's sheerly ludicrous." His grin showed signs of a dawning, if tardy, shame. "Look here, if I've been giving you the impression that any of these people are scallywags, cut it out. They're just the normal mixture of middle-class citizens you'd find in any section of any street in London if you sheared it in half."

"Don't worry. I shouldn't dream of taking your judgment for gospel," Gorham assured him cheerfully. "It's merely useful to get names and so on in a new case. Hello, here's Norris back. Well?"

"The house is closed, sir. And the old lady has been away for a month, at Littlehampton. Spends two months there every summer, I'm told."

"Well, that's that. We'll have to deal with her later. Now for the last house of the four in Pound Lane, Hardwicke—Innisfree."

"Oh, for Heaven's sake leave Innisfree alone, Gorham. The little lady there is the most retiring soul alive. My mother was devoted to her, but I've scarcely met her myself. Writes children's verses, I believe, and lives like a hermit among her flowers. Her brother, the author, L. V. Hyde, lives there too. Came home from India or somewhere at death's door, and she nursed him like a Trojan. That was years ago, and the fellow is as strong as a horse now; making pots of boodle too; can't pick up a magazine that hasn't his name in it. One of those noisy fellows. Shouldn't say success had improved him. At least, if it has, God help what he was before. Still, that's only my personal view," he added hastily. "A lot of people like heartiness, and being thumped on the back by well-known fellows. He's always been the centre of an admiring crowd when I've run across him at the Burdock. Personally, I can't bear it, and always make a point of thumping back, good and hard, to teach 'em, at the risk of being thought jealous. Where was I? Oh, cataloguing contents of Innisfree. There used to be a niece, a jolly kid. Does any of that still apply, Mr. Moh?"

Sergeant Norris was watching Mr. Moh with worried curiosity. He had not met him before. He was certainly a Chinese, and apparently a jobbing gardener. Why he was in the heart of this investigation was not clear to Norris. But both Hardwicke and Gorham treated him as an equal.

"All is precisely as celebrated Mr. Hardwicke states." Mr. Moh spoke suavely, almost as if an image were emitting words. "Mr. Hyde, Miss Hyde, still inhabit Innisfree, complete with deaf but capable servant and spaniel dog. Also garden. But niece now dwells with husband in distant part of far-flung British Empire."

Gorham stood up.

"Then I don't think we need trouble you any more, Mr. Hardwicke, or—yes, one more question: have these neighbours of yours cars?"

The innocent query seemed to be the last straw to Hardwicke's already strained temper. In spite of the coolness with which he had carried on during this whole affair, which had so hideously intervened on his home-coming, he was obviously deeply disturbed in mind, and if his sunburnt skin masked recent changes of complexion, his hands were none too steady, and his second splash of whisky had been as liberal as his first.

"Don't be an infernal idiot, Gorham!" he exploded. "Of course we've all got cars. You must have spotted Hubberd's garage, and Hyde's too round the corner in Chetwynd Avenue! I've got one myself, come to that, though it's laid up at Turner's by the station. But how the hell does that affect this damnable affair! As you're kind enough to swear she wasn't put out here, in my sweet house, it stands to reason her body was brought here from a distance. You're barking up the wrong tree absolutely. It's insane to imagine she could possibly have been strangled in any of these houses which are swarming with inmates. My neighbours are normal British citizens, not transatlantic murder gangs! Do you suppose, if one of them was seized with a sudden impulse towards murder, the others would sit by twiddling their thumbs while he got on with it? Can't you see that the simple fact of the corpse being dumped down in my garden in Pound Lane automatically washes out every inhabitant of the lane as a suspect at once? The last thing you could expect of a murderer is that, having collected and scragged his victim elsewhere, he would then deliberately cart her home in order to concentrate suspicion on his own immediate neighbourhood!"

"Quite, quite," Gorham said mildly. "There's no question of suspicions, yet, my good chap. You forget that some of these blameless neighbours of yours may be wanted as witnesses to deceased's habits, etc. All I wished to get at from you was the sort of witnesses they would make." He picked up the coat as he spoke, and, ever obliging, Mr. Moh glided from his corner, took the coat from his hand, and retreating to the hall rolled it into a neat parcel.

"Sorry I spoke," Hardwicke muttered, and with truth.

He had badly wanted to examine that coat, and he ruefully realized that his outburst of temper had shut the door on any confidential information from the police officers.

After a warning to keep what he knew to himself, which struck him as sarcastic in view of the fact that he had given information and received none, and thanks for his refreshment, Gorham and Norris departed, and he flung himself moodily into a chair.

"Suppose I shall have to lug that damn' suitcase of mine back to the station and put up at my club," he growled to Mr. Moh. "Pretty thick home-coming, what?"

"Now that deceased person has been removed, when displaced laurel returns to former position all will be smoothed out, and painful episode can be erased from memory," Mr. Moh said, attempting consolation.

"Don't you believe it!" Hardwicke snorted. "Once bobbies get their foot inside a place they're as clinging as germs. They'll be digging up my grass and making pests of themselves looking for clues for months to come. Had they turned up anything before I appeared?"

"Only what was obvious to meanest intelligence at sight: that she had been lowered behind shrubs from verandah."

"Where?"

They went out and stood in front of the dining-room windows, and Hardwicke leaned over the low rail and poked the earth with his stick. But the bank sloped, the earth was hard, and broken twigs of the bushes alone showed where the body had been wedged in the narrow space.

"Not so much as a match," Hardwicke muttered.

"He would use a torch."

"You think it was chucked there after dark, then?"

"Can you picture it in broad daylight?"

"No, of course it must have been night. But surely the whole brutal job can't have been done here—the stripping. Eugh!"

He barely suppressed a shudder of disgust. But again Mr. Moh soothed him.

"Such conjectures can be banished from mind owing to fact that whole process would be visible to any casual passer by. Note the altitude of verandah and scantiness of tops of laurels."

"Yes, that's definite," Hardwicke said with relief. "They don't reach much higher than my knees. No one could be insane enough to take a risk of being caught in the act. Hullo, what's that?" They had both caught an animal's shrill yelp of pain, followed by a woman's cry.

In his strung-up state Hardwicke's imagination instantly pictured further horrors happening, at Innisfree. The crowd had drifted away temporarily on the heels of Gorham and Norris, but, disregarding the remark of the policeman on guard, "It's only that little tyke next door, sir," Hardwicke leapt down the steps, out of the gate, and reached that of Innisfree at a run. He pushed it open and entered the garden without ceremony.

Halfway down a broad, flagged walk, flanked by glorious herbaceous borders, a figure that seemed to come back to him out of the past knelt piteously and clasped a bright spaniel in her arms.

A bark from the dog made her look round, and a look of instantaneous recognition and relief flooded her eyes.

"Oh, Lewis, you! Do come to Robin; I'm so distressed!"

"Yes, yes. What's happened to him?" He hurried up. "My word, what a blaze of colour you've got in here! You don't get a hint of it from the road."

But she was oblivious of everything but the dog; even taking his unheralded return after two years' absence as a matter of course. "He was out all night. We were horribly worried. I went to church" (she was wearing a heavy black coat and skirt, and hat, in spite of the brilliancy of the day—the only sombre object in the sunlit scene), "and he must have come back while I was out, but when he ran to meet me and I touched him he screamed, and, look—there is blood on my glove!"

She showed him her hand with the spontaneous gesture of a frightened child, and he stooped and took the dog from her with careful hands.

"I don't fancy there's much wrong with him," he said gently. "But suppose we bathe the cut in warm water."

"Oh yes, come to the kitchen." She trotted ahead of him down a cross-path, round a corner of the low house, to another path paved with red brick, and a rose-hung porch outside the kitchen door. With a journalist's eye for picturesque detail he noted the homely charm of the place. Here was a square of kitchen garden surrounded by a macrocarpa hedge, with fruit trees and bushes, cabbages and parsley and lavender growing beside brick paths in friendly proximity. The porch framed an interior that might have been figured in a Dutch painting, with its gleams of bright copper, square-tiled linoleum, and blue curtains, and in the midst a middle-aged woman in a white cap and print dress who might herself have sat for Van Hoogh. On the hearth was a dog's basket.

She looked up with an eager greeting.

"Oh, madam, you saw Robin has come home!"

"Oh yes, Eliza. I am so thankful. But did you notice that he was hurt? This is Mr. Hardwicke; he is going to look at him."

An odd look, as if she scarcely knew whether she had heard aright, reminded Hardwicke that she was deaf, and he gave her a nod and smile as he stepped forward and laid Robin in his basket. He knelt down, touching the furry body with fingers that looked clumsy but were singularly tender, and even skilful where dogs were concerned, while the two women looked on intently; and somehow his nerves felt soothed by this atmosphere of anxious feminine dependence on male help that encompassed him. It was one to which, with himself as centre, he was wholly unaccustomed.

The dog, with a spaniel's sweet temper, licked his hands, and only emitted a low growl when his side was touched.

"I don't think there's much to worry about, Miss Hyde," Hardwicke said at length. "It looks as if he'd had a nasty kick." He was still exercising Robin's feathered legs, feeling his sides and body. "But there are no ribs broken, and no internal damage, I believe. The side's sore, of course. Keep still, old man, while we clean you up." He looked up into Eliza's face. "Got any warm water and boracic?"

Immediately she fetched a bowl, powder, and sponge, prompted, he felt, by her own common sense, for she gave no sign of having heard what he said. He glanced at something that had scratched his finger through the dog's rug, and slipped it quickly into his pocket.

"Did someone bring him home, Eliza?" Now that her fears were subsiding, Miss Hyde felt slightly ashamed of her undignified display of emotion. And again Hardwicke believed that, seeing her mistress speaking, the woman guessed at rather than heard the question.

"He suddenly ran into the kitchen just a few minutes after you'd gone, madam, that pleased and excited to be back you wouldn't believe. He had a long drink of water and a biscuit out of his tin, and after looking all over the house for you he curled up in his basket and went to sleep till Mr. Hyde came in. He told me to say he stayed at Yorker's last night and was going back there. He only dashed home for his golf things and clubs, and not to expect him tomorrow. I went down to the garage gate to make sure he hadn't left it open again, but he came out quick and drove off again. And Robin went to the other gate to wait for you."

Robin was enjoying this conversation all about himself, and the attention that was being lavished on him. He affected extreme languor, and lay on his back with his paws in the air.

His mistress watched him with anxious eyes, and the amateur vet wondered uneasily whether he had missed some vital injury; but Eliza seemed to understand Robin thoroughly, and said, "Shall we try him with his dinner, sir?" producing a plate of liver the sight of which galvanized him into life.

Hardwicke wiped his hands on a towel Eliza brought him, and chuckled aloud when the invalid swept the plate clean and settled himself for slumber with a tired sigh.

"Not much to worry about there!" he said, and Miss Hyde smiled.

"I'm none the less grateful to you for coming to our rescue," she murmured. "It is absurd of me, but the sight of blood unnerves me ridiculously. And wounded animals always seem so utterly helpless, don't they? Come into the sitting-room."

She led him into a long, low-ceilinged room that had windows at either end, those in the front looking across a tiny terrace down the broad walk with its gorgeous borders, though net curtains were drawn to temper the sunshine, while those at the far end gave cool glimpses of a shady square of turf enclosed in leafy trees. The restful charm of the room, that was full of brown shadows and scent from bowls of roses, seemed strangely appealing to his overstrung nerves, a place of cloistral peace and beauty that one entered from the noisy, jarring, horror-ridden world outside as into a place of sanctuary.

She smiled again as he stammered a banal word of appreciation.

"It is only a cottage, you know, not half the size of your own house next door. Only this room besides the kitchen down here, four rooms upstairs. Mine and Eliza's, and my brother's, and a tiny room that used to be Hilary's."

"That was your jolly little niece!"

"Yes, Laurence, my elder brother's girl. But she is married now, and lives in Kenya. But, Lewis, I have been very remiss. Surely you haven't been long at home? I simply accepted you when you came in as an Act of Providence!"

He laughed, and explained that he had only just arrived, omitting any reference to the ghastly affair that had greeted him.

"Then"—her voice sounded oddly diffident—"if you have nothing prepared, no one to cook for you, won't you lunch here with me? You see, we had expected my brother; it won't make any difference."

He cast a swift thought to Gorham and the rest. It was well on the cards that the police would come here asking questions. Suddenly he felt himself resenting hotly the idea of a police invasion. In any case, she ought to be prepared. He wanted to banish all remembrance of that hideous affair from his mind for a brief space, but it was his plain duty to safeguard this little lady from hearing about it first from the bald statement of a policeman. "I believe I was going to cut out lunch. I'm an old campaigner, you know, used to shifts," he said with rather an awkward laugh. "But if you're sure it wouldn't be a nuisance I'd love to come."

"That's good," she exclaimed. "I'll just tell Eliza you are staying, and then go and change my frock. I shan't be ten minutes."

"All right. I'll go and shut my front door."

Chapter III

Miss Hyde's bedroom was over part of the sitting-room, and of an odd shape, for a narrow recess, with a casement window, ran forward to the front of the house, which was just wide enough to contain a single bed and small table, and nothing more.

The remaining square of space, which was large, was furnished with an austerity rarely to be seen in women's bedrooms.

True, it contained a dressing-table with deep, serviceable drawers, and a roomy wardrobe of the same finely grained mahogany, both period pieces inherited from comfortable Victorian ancestry, but otherwise it might have been a man's study, and a workmanlike study at that.

Low bookshelves ran like a dado round the walls, filled chiefly with books of reference and works referring to Eastern countries, topography, exploration, and travel. A tall filing-cabinet stood in one corner, and in the long, low windows which overlooked the enclosed lawn at the back was a large desk with drawers down one side, on which stood a covered typewriter.

On the desk, too, lay a long envelope containing the story she had typed out on Saturday night, ready for despatch to the editor of the *Fleet Magazine*, which for years had included an L.V.H. tale in its monthly issue. And in the drawers were several other stories, the typed lines disfigured by corrections in her own neat hand, which still awaited their final clean copies.

L.V.H. made no secret of the fact that he hated the drudgery of revision and correction.

"Give me the idea for a yarn and I'll dash it off in record time!" he would admit, grinning. "That's how every really gripping tale has got to be written, in my opinion; dropped hot from the pen, dashed down, and damn all worry about accuracy and style. All that can be seen to afterwards, in cold blood, and that's where my good old sister comes in. She acts as my secretary, you know, dots the 'i's', and corrects my wonky spelling, and even does all the business side for me, too. I tell her she'd make a damn' good agent if I ever get finally dried up. But as she loves the job, and I'm saved the tedious nuisance of it, we're both happy. Makes her feel she's one of the firm, you know."

As Miss Hyde changed her frock her glance rested thoughtfully on the photographs on her dressing-table: the sweet, intelligent face of her mother, and that of her elder brother Laurence, to whom she had been devoted. She felt that life would have taken a different course for her had he lived, for he inherited many of the qualities, but especially the generosity and large-heartedness, of their grandfather, the famous Professor Laurence Vincent, whose name her mother had given to all her children. But his wife and he were killed in an air crash, and two years later her mother had slipped peacefully from the home they had shared together, leaving her alone save for the child, Hilary. Hilary was fourteen when Sidney came back from Assam desperately ill, helpless, and half-blind. Those months of nursing had a horrible nightmare quality. But she got through them, and then, later, when Sidney had grown strong again, other difficulties had arisen. Hilary and her uncle could not get on together. The holidays were scenes of constant friction, and when the child left school it had seemed wise to let her share the home of her best friend in town. She had been happy there, well cared for by the friend's mother, had finally gone out with them both on a visit to Kenya, and married.

Miss Hyde was grateful for the work that gave her occupation, for the garden that was her abiding joy. The girlish over-sensitiveness—caused by a disfiguring birthmark which lay over one cheek—which made her shrink from meeting strangers in those youthful days when friendships are formed lightly and without effort, had become under the stress of prolonged unhappiness a deliberate withdrawal from human contacts.

She had broken through the habit of years this morning when she invited Lewis Hardwicke to luncheon. But Lewis was scarcely a stranger, though she had not exchanged two words with him since he was a boy. He was like a bit of the past come back to life from an earlier scene in which she had played with actors whose dear voices had gone down into silence long ago, and she had loved his sensible, warm-hearted mother.

"It will be a novel experience to entertain a quite distinguished man," she thought with a grim smile, and it would serve to distract her thoughts while the resolve she had reached as she watched him bathing Robin's bruised side took final shape in her mind. The dinner-table was set near the open windows at the end of the shadowy room, and when Lewis Hardwicke sat down opposite the small figure of his hostess, whose high-backed carved chair was placed beyond the glare of daylight in the shade of velvet curtains, he felt again that sudden quietening of his nerves, that sense of restful remoteness from harsh discordancies and struggle that the tranquil atmosphere of the place shut outside.

It was a perfectly cooked, if simple, meal: lamb, new potatoes and beans, a queen pudding, stewed fruit and custard, cheese straws and coffee. Miss Hyde encouraged him to talk about his travels, contributing little herself to the conversation but the interested word necessary to keep him going.

He realized with naive surprise that he was enjoying this interlude, his inner man satisfied with the first homely English meal he had eaten for years, his irritable nerves soothed by her voice, and—he did not shirk the acknowledgment of her interest in himself.

But he also realized that his interlude must soon end. That ghastly business outside could not long be kept at bay.

He began to ask about old acquaintances in the neighbourhood, masking his immediate reason for curiosity behind the natural interest of a returned native.

Miss Hyde had nothing to tell him about the Hubberds at The Burrs. The youngish married couple who had taken the house eight years before on the dispersal of the cheerful family who had lived there in his boyhood. Cousins of Madeline they had been, and it was there that he had first met her, a pig-tailed, long-legged schoolgirl. Somehow that sudden image of her as a pink-cheeked, awkward school-girl of fifteen playing rounders in The Burrs garden with a pack of youngsters, himself among them, seemed infinitely more definite and vivid than that of the later Madeline whom he had nearly married. What the devil was he to do with that houseful of stuff next door, that mawkish sentiment—or was it sheer moral slackness that shirked facing disagreeable facts?—had prevented him from selling at the time?

"I rather liked what I saw of Ted Hubberd," he said aloud, "and Ethel, too, though it struck me that they were both rather out of their element in a country place like Finnet, and he was trying to make the best of a bad job. She couldn't stick the East, where they first met, and made him chuck up his work there and hauled him home. But I believe the chap felt like a fish out of water in England, where he'd neither friends nor interests; and poor old Ethel was bored stiff if one lured him into talking on his own subjects, and shut him up quick. But he'd just started in a job connected with a new race-track at Northbourne when I left England last. Do you know whether he's pulling out at all?"

"I should imagine that money cannot be very plentiful with them still," Miss Hyde answered. "But really I know nothing of their affairs. I did not even know that Mr. Hubberd knew the East," she added with quickened interest. "Surely he isn't one of the great Hubberd family that has produced so many Chinese scholars? Descendants of Edward Pine Hubberd, whose *Letters from Pekin* were in my grandfather's library?"

"I believe he is," Hardwicke said, amused by her awed tone—"one of its mute, inglorious members, that is. But I know he was born in China, and except for a few years at school spent his whole life in commercial jobs in the Far East. And I believe he once mentioned a cousin, Pine Hubberd, living in England at the moment. If you're interested might I bring him along?"

"It is too late now." Miss Hyde repudiated the suggestion stiffly, and, feeling snubbed, he asked with some diffidence how Mrs. Manstead was these days.

"She was troubled by the loss of her last companion, who had been with her for some years, and who married and went to Canada in June. She is away just now. At Littlehampton as usual."

"My word, you don't mean that stout Rosa Dartle sort of soul who giggled and asked questions perpetually has married?"

Miss Hyde assented, and, without change of tone, said that Miss Croft's cheerful interest in trivial things had probably helped to enliven Mrs. Manstead's stay-at-home days, and she hoped that her successor would prove equally useful.

Lewis grinned inwardly and wondered if his hostess were quite as simple as she wished him to believe.

She had changed her heavy black coat and skirt for a filmy frock of a tone between light fawn and grey; the shadow, he thought absurdly, of the down on a very young sparrow's breast, and it gave her a shadowy look, unsubstantial, like a pastel drawing whose outlines melt into its background. The removal of her harsh black hat showed mouse-brown hair smoothed back into a knot, grey eyes, an oval face, thin, severe lips. The ugly birthmark that he remembered was there, across one cheek, yet the whole effect of her was not ugly, but of something remote, withdrawn.

Probably L. V. Hyde dominated the home when he was present. Was her quietude the natural reaction of a gentle nature to her brother's boisterous self-assertion? She had made no reference to him beyond mentioning that when the weather was fine he often spent a long week-end at Yorker's Manor Club, where he played golf with friends.

"Feels the need of exercise, I expect," Lewis Hardwicke said, feeling kindly towards Hyde on account of his absence. "Writing's a sedentary job."

"Yes," said Miss Hyde.

The monosyllable reminded him oddly of the fact that she also was an author of a minor degree, of verses for children, probably pretty little trifles, but such things are notoriously ill-paid. Was it possible that she felt slightly jealous of her brother's literary and financial success?

He did not want to go away, to leave this tranquil room or her unexacting companionship. Yet that beastliness that had happened in his garden next door had got to be faced again. Gorham was a thorough fellow. Probably he had interviewed the half of Finnet by this time, but he certainly would not omit tackling every mortal person by whom that wretched creature had ever been employed. He sat up in his chair. Orders or no orders, he wasn't going to allow this little lady to be tackled unprepared.

"Do you remember a woman who used to live with Mrs. Manstead? Shields her name was . . ." he began, then broke into an irrepressible grin.

"Why, dash it, of course, you were at that foul party years ago, that my mother dragged me to, when she skilfully contrived to empty a whole pot of boiling water over my feet!"

"I certainly remember how well you behaved!" she said, with the first hint of a smile in her eyes that he had seen. "But poor Ellen was horribly distressed!"

"She wasn't the only one," he observed grimly. "I couldn't put boots on for days afterwards, and missed the best soccer match of the season, though it gave me a weapon against my mother's yearning to polish my manners by carting me to tea with her friends that I didn't fail to use, so the effects weren't wholly bad. But have you see anything of her lately? She worked for every house in the Lane at different times, didn't she?"

"Except yours." Miss Hyde smiled. "Your mother was one of the dearest women I ever met, but she could not tolerate what she used to call 'do-lessness'. An odd word that I never heard from anyone else. And Ellen was 'do-less' to a degree—if it means a sort of natural genius for doing things, with the best intentions, in the wrong way. She would spend hours, for instance, in darning a stocking with a different-coloured thread, so that it could never be worn again. When she washed up, cups and vegetable-dishes parted magically from their handles, and when she carried a tray downstairs she either dropped it with a deafening crash or fell herself, arriving amongst fragments of one's china on the mat in a sitting posture so bruised and distressed that one could not be vexed. But it is a shame to laugh at her—poor Ellen. She was tirelessly kind and patient when she helped to nurse Sidney. She waited on him hand and foot in the restless weariness of his convalescence and sometimes lectured him for his good like a kind nurse with a spoilt little boy."

"The last time I met her was after Madeline's death. She started to condole, and I'm afraid I was rather terse."

"That was very natural."

"She meant well, I dare say. But I was feeling a bit raw at the time. Don't know which I barred most, the fools who spoke of it or those who didn't. But what happened to her after she left you?"

"Nothing in particular. The same sort of round. She does odd jobs for me, and spends a week or two occasionally at Mrs. Manstead's. But for quite a long time now she has had regular daily work with your friends the Hubberds.... This interest in Ellen does credit to your warmth of heart, Lewis."

He looked at her ruefully.

"I was trying to be tactful. But I'd better stop trying. The—the fact is, I'm afraid the poor soul has come to a rather miserable end. The police found her body this morning in, of all places, my front garden."

She stared at him with horrified, incredulous eyes.

"Ellen Shields! In your garden! Do you mean she was *dead*!"

"Yes. Ghastly, wasn't it? I turned up there before noon and found the lot of them standing round her. She must have died last night. An—er—unnatural death, too. The police are bound to investigate, it. And probably they'll start by asking a lot of damn' silly questions of everyone who ever employed her. Of course," he hastily corrected himself, "they'll be pure formal inquiries, just to enable them to build up her dossier—quite normal routine in every police case. But I didn't want them to call here before you'd had some sort of warning. Good Lord, you look deathly white! Can I get you anything?" He sprang to his feet. "I ought to be shot for startling you so horribly. Shall I call Eliza?"

"It was horrible news. Ask her to bring me sal volatile," Miss Hyde murmured in a faint tone.

He dashed to the kitchen, where Eliza was wiping plates, and after one glance at his perturbed face she mutely handed him a slate from the mantelpiece. Feeling that he might as well be hanged for a sheep as a lamb, he scribbled his message first and then the news that had so upset her mistress. But if he feared that Eliza might faint he was agreeably disappointed. She read his sentences with scarcely a change of expression, then nodded, put down the slate, and a second later was holding a wineglass to Miss Hyde's white lips.

"What a woman!" thought Lewis, watching the scene.

"Did he tell you? Oh, poor Ellen!" Miss Hyde whispered pitifully, and read comprehension in the woman's eyes. "He says the police may come here. Oh!" She shuddered as a knock at the front door set Robin barking, but collected herself and sat up. "I'm all right now, Eliza. There they are. Bring them here—"

But it was Lewis Hardwicke who, with a gesture, forestalled the servant and marched into the hall.

The Chief Inspector gave him a glance of reproach as he opened the door, and Lewis's blink might have been interpreted as defiance or dazzlement at the blaze of sun-flooded colour revealed behind the stolid forms of Gorham and the sergeant.

"Moh told me you were here, Hardwicke, so I'm taking Innisfree first. You've not tampered too badly with our witnesses, I hope?"

"Don't be an idiot!" Lewis retorted with righteous heat. "Miss Hyde's got nothing to do with this foul affair. She's an old friend of my mother. I told you that. It was only decent to warn her you might come trampling in—break the shock a bit, I mean. She's a delicately brought-up lady, not accustomed to police interviews, so mind your step. She mustn't be treated roughly."

"Thanks for your instructions, Hardwicke. She shall not be treated roughly."

"In here, then, you sarcastic devil."

He led them into the sitting-room and towards the table at the far end by which the two women were grouped, and muttered a sentence of introduction which Miss Hyde acknowledged with dignity, though she did not rise from her chair.

"Pray take a seat, Mr. Gorham," she said.

"Thank you." He drew forward the chair that Lewis had vacated and faced her across the polished surface of the table. Norris, at a second gesture of invitation, collected another chair and seated himself with diffidence beside his leader whose ease of manner he envied.

Lewis Hardwicke lounged against the window, his shoulder half turned, and Eliza remained standing, grimly disapproving the sight of low-born policemen sitting in her mistress's presence.

Gorham studied a paper which contained a list of queries and then looked up.

"No doubt Mr. Hardwicke has already told you about the painful business on which I am employed," he said. "One has to collect one's facts as quickly as possible in such a case as this, and as Miss Shields did not live in Finnet, my simplest method seemed to be a request for any information that they can give about her from ladies who employed her. Mrs. Manstead is unfortunately away—I understand that Miss Shields acted as her companion at one time. And also that she worked for you. Have you known her long?"

"Since she first came to Mrs. Manstead, very many years ago. She only came to me latterly to do odd jobs, such as coming in to air the house at holiday times, or to help with extra cleaning, or for mending. She was with me for six months or so seven years ago—

before my friend and maid Eliza Priest came to me—and so knew the ways of the house."

"I see." The Chief Inspector guessed shrewdly that Ellen Shields' "work" for this self-possessed lady had occurred when she, rather than Miss Hyde, was in need of help. Eliza (friend and maid—a good phrase, that) kept the place like a new pin; every inch of woodwork gave back its reflection of light. "Did she work for other ladies besides those in Pound Lane?"

"At one time, perhaps, but certainly not latterly, for she had regular daily work at the end house, The Burrs."

"Have you seen her yourself at all recently?"

There was a pause.

"I think the last time was about two months ago—in the late spring, at any rate—when I met her in the street," was the quiet reply. "She called next day for a small bundle of things that I then mentioned to her, but I did not see her."

"Could you tell me what sort of impression you formed of her character?"

"I formed the impression that she was honest, or I should scarcely have employed her in my house, Chief Inspector," she answered stiffly.

"Of course, madam; but I meant in other ways. Would she be popular with—er—men, for instance?"

"She was liked, and I hope, respected, by all persons with whom she came into close contact for her real goodness of disposition," she said calmly. "But I should say that she was unlikely to have men friends—certainly no illicit love-affair, which, I suppose, is what you mean."

"I'm told she used to live in Finnet with her mother." Gorham was quite patient. "Can you tell me if she had any other relatives here to whom I could apply for information?"

"I never heard of any, except a younger sister who quarrelled with Ellen after their mother's death. She was married, I believe, and lived in the north. I don't know her name. Ellen herself moved to lodgings in Harlesden when their little flat was given up. Her address was 105 Lavender Road, Harlesden."

"Thank you. Make a note of that, Norris. Then"—he turned again to Miss Hyde, brisking up as if the end of a difficult interview were within sight—"to come to last evening. Did you hear sounds at any time in Pound Lane that struck you as unusual?"

"No."

"Would you object to telling me exactly how your household was employed, say, from seven-thirty onwards? I mean whether you were at home here, whether anyone—who might have noticed something in the Lane—went in or out during the evening?" He spoke diffidently, but Miss Hyde showed no signs of offence.

She reflected.

"I spent the evening in my room above this—the window faces the back like this one—over some typing," she said at length. "My brother went off for the week-end before seven, so he doesn't come into it. I finished at ten and came down here, and Eliza brought my supper-tray at once. Then we both realized that my little dog was missing. He had spent most of the evening with me but asked to be let out, and I thought he had stayed with Eliza. She thought he had come back to me after a run in the garden. We went to look for him and found that my brother had left the garage gates open after driving out, and Robin had escaped. Eliza stayed by that gate, which opens into Chetwynd Avenue, and I by the one in Pound Lane, and we called and called. There wasn't a soul in the Lane, and he didn't come back, and at last, when it was half-past eleven, we had to give it up and go to bed."

Gorham sat up.

"You actually had the road under observation from ten till half past eleven!" he exclaimed. "Did you see anyone about?"

"A few people went by in Chetwynd Avenue, but no one stopped or did anything in the least odd. I saw no one in the Lane at all except Mrs. Hubberd and Mrs. Hughes, about eleven, coming home from the 'flicks' they said. They had walked up West Avenue, and I met them at the corner, by their house. I had gone along to see if Robin could be shut in anywhere. Absurd, of course, because we should have heard him whining. But the gates were all shut except those of The Burrs garage, that were ajar."

"Thank you. That evidence is most useful." Gorham smiled. "Do you think that your maid can add anything—as to the hours before you came downstairs, for instance?"

"You can ask her," Miss Hyde said indifferently. "But she is deaf."

Gorham wrote a couple of questions on a sheet of his notebook and handed them to Eliza with a good-humoured look.

She sniffed, but gave clear replies.

She had sat sewing in her kitchen till her mistress came down and the dog's absence was discovered. After that she went out and called it. No one passed along the Lane while she was there, and the only person she saw was "that fellow" Dent, come round the far corner and go into The Burrs, just before eleven. There was no moon and the Lane was dark, but no one could have walked down it without her or Miss Hyde seeing them, as one of them was in the Lane the whole time till the mistress said they must give up and go in and she'd go to the police if Robin wasn't back by lunch-time tomorrow. Yes, she knew Miss Shields, but she didn't have much to say to her, her voice being indistinct. She'd seen her in the Lane, coming from work at The Burrs, and what she usually wore was a tweed coat over a printed silk dress (a sniff) and an orange wool "Marina" beret with a green Woolworth feather stuck on the top. And she carried an American cloth bag with her apron and working things in it. She hadn't seen her for weeks to speak to, not holding with idle talking. Here she looked straight at Gorham, who laughed and stood up.

The interview had taken longer than it should have, and but for the point about the Lane had been a sheer waste of time. Miss Hyde had given him the least information possible, and Eliza had told her tale in almost the same phrases. Hardwicke had probably coached them both.

He stooped and patted Robin, who, more cordial than his mistress, was standing up against his leg for notice.

"I see this fellow turned up safely again," he remarked, stroking the long brown ears. "This morning, I suppose?"

"Yes; before noon. He has never stayed out all night before, but I suppose the open gate tempted him."

"Quite. My experience with my own young cocker is that this type of dog hates to be away from its own people. Are you coming, Hardwicke? I'll say good afternoon, Miss Hyde."

"Good afternoon. Lewis, please show them out."

"I suppose I ought to be going myself, Miss Hyde. Thanks most awfully for having me," Lewis said boyishly, and her stiffness relaxed in a smile that took years from her age.

"Why not stay on to tea now you're here?" she said. "Have you anything special to do?"

"Not a thing! I'd love to. One second, though." He dashed to the gate. The police officers had gone without waiting for him. They were heading for The Burrs in earnest talk.

Lewis strolled back to the house, frowning.

Chapter IV

THE PAIR went straight to the end house, The Burrs, where Ellen Shields had last been employed.

As they walked up a weed-grown gravel path, Gorham said briefly: "Introduce me here, Norris. And later, if I give you the tip, go and fetch further help. Meantime, I'll do the talking."

"You mean if anything fishy turns up here, sir?"

"Exactly. We'll soon know."

The front door stood open and disclosed an interior once well furnished, but showing every evidence of slovenly neglect.

A carved oak chest was piled with heterogeneous litter; a table with carved legs and rim was laden, in addition to a dead fern in a tarnished brass pot, with circulars, an empty beer-bottle, boot-brushes, and a half-empty jar of marmalade without a cover.

Two good Persian rugs on the tiled floor were stained and thick with dust, and the red-pile stair-carpet looked as if it had not been thoroughly swept for years.

The sergeant's smart rat-tat with the knocker echoed startlingly through the hall, and a mutter of quarrelsome talk which reached them from the back room was interrupted by a soprano voice which ejaculated, "Blast! Visitors!" in accents of disgust.

A tall, good-looking man materialized at the door of this room and stared with a quizzical lift of fine eyebrows across the hall.

Norris stepped forward.

33 | DEATH HAS NO TONGUE

"Can we see Mr. Hubberd for a moment? You know me, I dare say, Mr. Hughes—Sergeant Norris—and this is Chief Inspector Gorham, of the Criminal Investigation Department, Scotland Yard."

Mr. Hughes exclaimed. "The Sacred Works himself!" his mobile features registering exaggerated deference, then stuck his head back into the room and announced them in a shrill cry:

"Ted, you're sunk. Here's the police!"

"If there's one time when you're less amusing than another it is when you're trying to be funny, Charles," came an irritated retort, and Mr. Hubberd appeared.

Beside the striking height and good looks of the actor he seemed plain and insignificant. He had, however, the saving quality of neatness in his appearance. His dark-blue suit, if shabby, was clean, which was more than could be said of Charles Hughes's tennis shirt and shorts.

"'Afternoon, Sergeant. It's about this beastly show at Hardwicke's, I suppose," he said, unamiably but not rudely. "The milkman told my wife. Better come in here. You might shut that front door, will you? We're in a damnable muddle, as usual. And late. Never get a meal on time in this wretched house. Look here, can't you girls clear that table and make the place look reasonably tidy?"

The remains of an ill-served meal lay on the table in the dining-room, among a huddle of papers, ash-trays and bottles, though the time was close on three o'clock, and the air was heavy with the smell of food and stale smoke.

Hubberd, having got Gorham's name, muttered some sort of introduction of which the words "my wife" were just audible.

Mrs. Hubberd was still wearing a cotton overall stained with grease in which, presumably, she had cooked that morning, and her make-up was in bad need of repair. The other woman, Mrs. Hughes, in a Jap silk wrap whose scarlet undertones matched her lips and nails, with eyes heavily darkened under black, arched brows, lounged back in an arm-chair smoking a cigarette in a long green holder, with a generous display of legs that terminated in a pair of soiled satin slippers. Her bold black eyes stared languishingly at the two strange men, but Mrs. Hubbard ignored them, repudiating her husband's suggestion with a snapped:

"Can't you see I'm pouring the blasted coffee? I cooked the beastly grub. Clarice can clear it for a change."

Clarice, stretching like a lazy cat, but otherwise making no move, retorted with bland agreement:

"Beastly's right, darling, after your so-called cooking!" Charles Hughes, with a shrug of his broad shoulders—he stood just under six feet and had an actor's studied elegance of movement and gesture—started to pile up crockery on a tray, crowning a heap of plates with a dish of half-raw, congealed beef, on the hacked remains of which he poised a bowl of lumpy custard.

Then he kicked the third man, who was stretched on a sofa, to his feet with a genial warning: "Now then, Bob, you lazy hound, cart that tray to the kitchen, and don't smash the lot, or we'll stop it out of your beer-money."

"That won't help poor old Ted much, since it's his china, and his money that pays for dear Robert's drinks," Clarice drawled maliciously.

The angry red dyed Ethel Hubberd's cheeks and she darted a venomous glance at the speaker, but Gorham was tired of being a target for sidelong glances from one woman and the studied rudeness of the other. Before Ethel could retort he interrupted the sordid scene. Mr. Hubberd had folded the cloth and bundled it into a sideboard drawer, and with quick, irritable movements was attempting to reduce the room to some semblance of order.

Uninvited, the Chief Inspector drew a chair to the table and sat down with his note-book open before him.

"Now, Mrs. Hubberd, please. I understand you have already heard the reason for my call. A murder has been committed, and the victim identified as a Miss Ellen Shields. Is it true that you employed her?"

His tone compelled a startled attention from the room, and she nodded sullenly.

"When did you last see deceased?"

"Yesterday. She worked here and managed to break my best vegetable-dish, the clumsy idiot."

"At what time did she leave your house?"

"I don't know. I went out about four."

"She was here then?" He turned to Clarice Hughes. "Can you tell me when deceased left?"

"My lor', no. I went to town with my hubby on the 12.5 train. The old trot was mucking about in the passage when we left."

"How did you spend the day, and when did you come home?"

She opened her eyes, with a cackle of laughter.

"You want a lot, don't you? Well, if my movements interest you, we lunched at the Conquest Hotel, Russell Street, with my brother-in-law, who owns the show—lucky dog that he is. Then I did a bit of shop-gazing and had tea with my great pal Edie Vavasour in her dinky little flat in Compton Street; she's in the chorus in *The Airy Maid*, you know, and so full of herself she kept me gossiping till she had to go to the theatre after we'd had a snack together. Then I tooled back to Finnet to the second house at the Odeon, met Mrs. Hubberd, and we saw that creature Bergner! I can't see why they make such a damned fuss of her except it's that hank of hair and her frightful skinny legs that attract them as a change. Well, then we came home. Oh, the old freak from Innisfree was yowling up and down the Lane for her tyke, but no one was murdering old Shields in the road then, if that's what you're trying to get at. We'd be sure to have noticed it, wouldn't we, darling? We passed the time of day—or rather night—with the Freak, and turned straight in to beddibyes."

"What clothes was Miss Shields wearing when you saw her last?"

Clarice gave an affected crow of amusement.

"Hell! It was true, then, that the old thing's body was naked! What an 'orrible sight! Why, she was wearing a ghastly old frock of cheap artificial silk—purple, with pink roses all over it—a washed-out rag of a yellow cardigan, a sacking apron, grey stockings, and bath-shoes that flapped as she walked."

Gorham made a note of the clothes in his book, then turned to Ethel Hubberd, who was fiddling with her coffee-cup.

"Presumably you came home, Mrs. Hubberd, before meeting Mrs. Hughes for the second house, which would begin about 8.30. Had deceased left the house then?"

Unbecoming colour flamed in her cheeks again, and the eyes that glared at him were full of smouldering resentment.

"I tell you I don't know when she left the house, or care a damn either. I went to Ealing to my mother's, and joined Clarice outside the Odeon—straight from the—the station."

Gorham thought: "They were both up to something fishy, or I never heard lying before." Aloud he said:

"What about you, Mr. Hughes? Did you come straight back after your wife left you?"

"Oh, what a naughty, sinister phrase! You wouldn't leave me, darling, would you? For anything short of another fellow, eh? But seriously, no. I saw the poor old blister in the morning, naturally, slopping about with a bucket, when my wife and I went out. We lunched with my brother, as you've heard, and after she trotted off to Edie I stayed chatting with my sister-in-law, and had tea, and maundered about for a bit in town, wishing I wasn't so devilish hard-up, and that, till I finally cleared off to the house of a pal over Harrow way, where we spent the evening hitting it up with a few like-minded spirits, till a neighbour looked in and asked did we know it was Sunday morning? We weren't in any condition to be clear about anything by that time, but at his hint, being strict Sabbatarians, and honest lads in the main, we dispersed the meeting quietly, and a pal gave me a lift to the end of the Lane. All clear on the Pound front, I do assure you, when I toddled in. No female screams rending the air, or anything like that. Not so much as a rabbit abroad, that these eyes beheld. Though, as I admitted," he added reflectively, "owing to the foul nature of the liquor dispensed by Murgatroyd, my eyes weren't in the best trim for observing trifles like rabbits."

Gorham stolidly made a further note, and, with no lightening of his grave expression, looked across at the man who had carried out the tray, who was now perched uneasily against the sofa-head, shuffling his large feet.

As a policeman he recognized the type with difficulty.

In boyhood probably nice-looking, with blue eyes and a weak mouth, at thirty-odd his features were coarsened, his eyes bloodshot, his mouth loose, and, at the moment, sullen.

He started when the Chief Inspector addressed him by name.

"You, Mr. Dent. Did you see deceased yesterday? If so, where and when?"

"I?" He spoke aggressively, scowling. "Of course I saw her yesterday. She was slaving here all day like a good 'un. And when she cried when my sister went for her over that dish I tried to buck her up. And I shifted the kitchen table, that was far too heavy for her to move alone, and gave her a mat to kneel on while she washed the floor, because she told me how damp made her bones ache. I know she made an awful sketch of herself with clothes she made herself, but it's beastly to make game of her, because she was a real good sort really, and tried to influence others for their good."

After the flippancy with which the others had treated the death of a woman who, if in a humble capacity, had been in close contact with their lives, this outburst was as welcome as it was unexpected. But a giggle from Clarice Hughes spoiled its effect. For some reason that giggle exasperated Ethel Hubberd beyond the bounds of control. She sprang up, with blazing eyes, and began to shout:

"You hold your blasted tongue, you! I'm fed up with your sickening airs and your dirty cadging and scheming, and I don't care if you clear out today and take your handsome husband with you! I'm sick of you both, and you can find someone else to stand you free meals and a roof over your heads, for I'm through with you, you snake in the grass! And you"—she flashed round on her husband—"if you'd the pluck of a mouse you'd protect me from that woman's insults! . . ."

"Ethel, that's enough—" Hubberd began. But Hughes took more effectual measures to end the scene.

In two strides he was by her side, his protective arm round her waist, impelling her gently to the door.

"Dear little woman, it's all been too much for you," Gorham heard him whisper tenderly. "But you mustn't lose your pluck. Now trot upstairs and have a hot bath, my dear. When you've put on your best frock and powdered the little nose you'll feel a different creature. I'll make young Clarice toe the line."

He closed the door on the sobbing woman and, his eyes brimming with laughter, advanced on his wife, who uttered a delighted shriek as he picked her up bodily and ran with her across the room, down a flight of iron steps outside the french window, and dropped her, still shrieking with hysterical laughter, on a deckchair in the garden.

Hubberd shut the window and drew a thick curtain across with vigour. He came back to the table.

"Hughes can carry off that cave-man stuff, but I can't," he muttered ruefully. "Comes of stage experience, I suppose. He treats women as if they were irresponsible children, instead of reasonable beings . . ." He stopped, flushed and troubled-looking. "I must apologize for my wife's *crise de nerfs*, Mr. Gorham, but the fact is she is terribly upset over this rotten affair. Absolutely all in. Please finish your job here as quickly as possible. I must go up to her."

Gorham nodded.

"Mr. Dent, when did you last see Miss Shields?" he asked curtly.

"When?—oh, what time, you mean? What time was it when you came in, Ted? I left the house soon after, you remember. About 6.30, wasn't it?" He seemed subdued by the recent scene, nervously anxious to finish his evidence. "It was a perfect evening, you know, so I strolled round to the bowling-green at the 'Fox and Goose'. Fresh air, you know. Then stayed on and had a spot of billiards after it got dark, and a snack at the bar instead of tootling home for grub. Besides, I knew everybody was out. Then I came home and turned in about eleven, or a bit before perhaps. House was dark and I didn't see anybody indoors—or out, for that matter."

"I see. Did you actually see Miss Shields before you went out at 6.30?"

"Oh yes"—readily. "I went to the kitchen on purpose. I saw she was washing dishes in the scullery, so I just called out 'Good night', and she called out 'Good night', and I went out by the side door and the garage gate."

"Thank you. That's all, I think."

Bob Dent was escaping towards the door like a released schoolboy when his brother-in-law stopped him.

"Look here, Bob, go and make a cup of tea for Ethel and take it up to her. Tell her I'll be up presently."

Bob nodded and went, leaving Hubberd and Gorham alone.

"You were apparently the last of your household to see Miss Shields, Mr. Hubberd. Did you speak to her after Mr. Dent went out?"

"Yes." His tone sounded preoccupied. "She came into the hall and I asked were the others out? Something like that. And she said my wife had mentioned going to the cinema as usual, and did I want dinner, because there was nothing in the house. That was nothing unusual." He interrupted himself apparently to excuse his wife's housekeeping. "We usually treat Saturday as an off-night for cooking, going our own ways. I believe I said I wouldn't be back, but I'd got a bit of a head. I told her I shouldn't bother, I was going to bed. Still, while I was looking through my letters she brought me some sandwiches and a beer, and I took them up with me. She said she hadn't finished all her jobs, so I told her to take it easy and get some grub before she left, and I suppose she did. I heard her pottering about for a bit, but I didn't take much notice of the time. She knew the house as well as I did, and often stopped late when she wanted to. I heard the door bang later on. That's all I can tell you."

"You can't make the time closer than that? Would it have been eight?—nine? do you think?"

Hubberd stood frowning.

"Nearer nine than eight, I should think," he said at last. "But, honestly, I can't be sure. I was reading. It was still broad daylight, but I fancy the light was changing, as it does before sunset, you know."

"Sunset is about 9.20 this week. It would be about nine, then. Um! How was she dressed when she left?"

"A sort of blue dress, with staring flowers or something all over it, I think, and a yellow jacket—you know those wool things women make. Clarice—Mrs. Hughes—an orange-red beret. Her usual gear."

"Was she wearing a beret so early in the evening, before she'd finished her work, when she brought your sandwiches," Gorham asked, surprised.

"Well, that's odd. I imagined she was," Hubberd unhappily. "It had a sort of feather. But, as I said, that was her usual head-gear of late. Perhaps I am confusing it with the day before. She made an unholy sketch of herself, poor thing."

"It is important to us to learn what she actually was wearing when she left here," Gorham said slowly. "Our information is that she wore, generally, as you say, an orange beret and a brown tweed coat. Had she on this coat?"

He saw an odd contraction of the man's face, and after a second's pause Hubberd shook his head.

"I think it's hanging in the kitchen now. She must have left it behind. It was too hot, I suppose, and she expected to come back today for a couple of hours. Do you want to see it? Come along, then."

He led the Chief Inspector down a passage to a kitchen which was a scene of slovenly disorder. Unwashed breakfast-things, cooking-utensils, boot-polishing brushes and cloths, remnants of food, and the plates and unappetizing remains of dinner just carried out from the dining-room already covered by swarms of flies, filled the scullery sink and overflowed on to the gas-stove, table dresser, and floor.

While Hubberd stood frowning in sour disgust at the sight Gorham picked his way through the mess and took down a shabby brown coat from the scullery door. One glance through the window had told him that the unkempt garden was empty. The Hughes pair had evidently slipped in by the back entrance and gone to their rooms upstairs. The house was uncannily quiet, giving him a sense of closed doors.

"That's it," Hubberd said. "At least, I'm sure it is."

The coat was heavyweight, its cheap cut dragged out of shape by much use, cuffs and pockets frayed, and the lining in ribbons, past all mending, though it had been patched again and again. It was far too heavy for summer weather, but probably it was the only coat that Ellen Shields possessed for daily use. Possibly it had been left deliberately by its owner on a warm summer night. Gorham looked at Hubberd and caught him listening to the silence.

"I'd better take this," he said civilly, and made a note as to its identity, which Hubberd impatiently initialled.

As the inquisition was apparently complete the two men walked together to the front door, where Norris was already waiting, but on the top step Gorham handed the coat to his subordinate and glanced across at a shabby garage.

"You have a car, I see, Mr. Hubberd. May I see it?"

He crossed over to it without waiting for his assent, and, annoyed, the owner followed.

"I can't see what the devil you can want with my car!"

"We may as well finish the whole job at once," Gorham returned. "It'll save trouble. And there's no harm in telling you that there's a possibility that a car was used in the case."

"Any car that figures in this damned case of yours can't have been mine, because it hasn't been out since Friday," Hubberd grunted sharply. "My wife hasn't passed her test yet, and I only use it on my job. Yesterday I had to go into the City, and went by train. A car is more damn' nuisance in Town than it's worth." He opened the door. "Sorry I didn't have it polished up for your inspection," he added sarcastically to Norris, for the Sergeant was walking round the car, taking deliberate note of its number, make, and condition.

It was a Singer, four years old, shabby, but serviceable yet, in spite of out-of-date lines.

"Friday?" Norris exclaimed, from the far side of the car. "The clay on those wheels looks pretty damp still!"

He gave the vehicle a push, which sent it forward a couple of feet.

But Hubberd did not reply. He was staring at a muddied object that had been under the left rear wheel, but as he bent to snatch it up Gorham's hand covered it.

The Chief Inspector's manner altered to an official gravity. He spread the object over his fist, a beret of orange-red wool, caked with yellow clay and with a jagged hole in one side where a piece roughly V-shaped had been torn out. At the top the broken shaft of a metal ornament.

"You say Ellen Shields was wearing this when you last saw her, Mr. Hubberd? How came it here, in your garage?"

"God knows!" Hubberd's tones were hoarse, his eyes staring. "The feather's broken. She must have been in here—left it behind, like the coat. I tell you I didn't see her when she left the house."

Leaving Norris to search the garage and car, Gorham drew Edward Hubberd outside.

"Mr. Hubberd, you see this is an awkward business. The clay on those wheels is wet still, after a warm night. That car was certainly out last evening. Can Dent or Hughes drive a car?"

"No. At least, not mine," he said grimly.

"Do you wish to add anything to your statement?"

"No."

"You still stick to your story that you were alone in the house all last evening till your wife and Mrs. Hughes came in? That you did not see Ellen Shields after you went upstairs in the early evening?

That you heard her leave about nine? And that you did not take your car out at all yesterday?"

"Yes, I do. It's God's truth. How that thing came there I don't know, as God sees me."

The sergeant emerged from the garage, and Gorham went to meet him, leaving Hubberd standing by the steps.

"Nothing more in there, sir."

"The house will have to be searched. Summon a couple of men from the call-box at the corner. Hardwicke's to be kept right out of it. You'll have to look for her other clothes, her bag, and any sign she was put-out in the house. I'll stay here till you return. One second, though. If he turns rusty we shall want a search warrant."

He went back to where Hubberd was fidgeting with a cigarette and a lighter.

"Well?" he snapped.

"I consider that a further search should be made, as part of deceased's clothing has been found on your premises," Gorham said, with civil ignoring of his scowl. "Have you any objection to my men looking through the house and grounds for a clue to the time and manner of her leaving last night?"

"I've already told you that she left about nine o'clock when I was alone in the house and in bed," Hubberd answered hotly. "I haven't the remotest notion how her beret came to be in my garage."

"The fact that it could have got there without your knowledge suggests that other things may have happened downstairs unknown to you if you were in bed," Gorham pointed out. "Will you consent to an informal search or not?"

"You've got me in a trap, damn you! If I don't consent you'll come with a warrant and leave me no option, I suppose. Oh, all right."

Chapter V

Edward Hubberd fidgeted in his front hall in a state of sullen misery during the sergeant's absence. He had sufficient sense to realize that the Chief Inspector, who employed the interval in adding to his notes in the simplified shorthand he used for private purposes, and mercifully left him alone, would veto any attempt to warn the others of the impending search. He waited in tense expectation of someone coming to look for him, but the time passed and not a sound broke the nerve-racking silence.

When the uniformed police arrived after ten minutes, that seemed like hours, Gorham had a word aside with Norris, then civilly asked Mr. Hubberd to show the sergeant the upper rooms himself.

"Leave your men below while you go up unless you require extra help. You know what to do and will give as little inconvenience as possible," he instructed his subordinate, and, with a nod to his unwilling host, went out. He examined the car inside and out, then went down to his own, which was parked by the gate of Innisfree.

"I don't envy Norris his job when Ethel and Clarice spot what he's up to," he thought with an unfeeling grin. "Hope those she-cats don't scratch his eyes out. Wonder if I'd have got more out of them if I'd taken them one by one? But I'd no ground then for a show of authority. Striking the way Hughes cleared the women out of the way. Picked up that wife of his as if she'd been a feather, and she was no slim kid, either. The brute who carried that body up Hardwicke's steps and dropped it over the railing behind those bushes must be tall and pretty hefty. On that point Hardwicke, Hubberd, Dent, and Hughes are all in the running—Hullo!"

He drew up beside a small figure on the pavement which paused deprecatingly at his yell.

"It was feared that this lowly worm would be unpopular with revered Chief over ruin of Sunday's peace."

"I'd have been sent for, anyhow," Gorham said, with a forgiving sigh. "I deal with all Gray's murders while he's sick, lucky devil. Hop in, Li Moh. Where have you been?"

"Removing traces of devastation in garden of Innisfree," said Mr. Moh, hopping in, "since honoured friend ignored same."

"This fresh beastliness gave me no chance for side issues, old man." He turned and looked keenly at his friend. "You don't think there's any connection, do you?"

"The broken flowers, and a naked body next door?" He shrugged his shoulders. "Ask me something easier Gorham. But I will tell you a queerness that signified little when it happened. While surveying the ruined loveliness of that bank of flowers yesterday with Miss

Hyde I saw deceased peering over the gate devouring that sight with protruding eyes."

At another time Gorham might have pointed out that eyes, however protruding, do not devour. Instead, he asked quickly if Miss Hyde had seen her too.

"No. Her back was to the gate—that into Pound Lane, of course. Shields was craning over elongating already long neck sideways, for only so could she glimpse bank from gate. She drew back head and vanished when she caught my look. But I have recalled since that also, when tulips were laid low, I saw her, actually in the garden that time, bending intently over the bed, and her face was hot and red and excited as she hurried past me to the house."

"You think she was possibly responsible for these senseless acts of destruction?" Gorham said slowly.

Mr. Moh jerked up his hands.

"It had been freshly done—within, say, three hours when I saw it at eleven. She passed the gate on her way to work about nine, generally. It was possible. Miss Hyde breakfasts at eight, but has retired to her typewriter before nine, upstairs, at the back, where I hear the machine go click. The paved walk cannot be seen from the kitchen. Mr. Hyde rarely appears before ten. It could have been."

"I'm on my way to her lodgings now. Harlesden," Gorham said abruptly. "Got to collect more data before trying to form any theory of the crime. Your idea doesn't throw light on the murder, Li Moh."

"Under keen desire to aid admired detective in amassing of general knowledge from which salient facts can be sifted later as basis for logical deductions, I," said Mr. Moh calmly, "contributed my unworthy trifle."

"You mean, she knew both times what had happened *when* she looked at the broken flowers?"

"She displayed excitement, but no surprise. No. She looked at something she expected to see. Yes. And was secretly excited—possibly with feeling of satisfaction. Further than that I don't know."

Gorham frowned.

"Miss Hyde said Shields lived with her once, for six months. Servants see the seamy side of their employers' characters, Li Moh. Could she have guessed that the lady had smashed her own flowers! Look here, Miss Hyde's own reaction to the show is the most suspicious point about it. What does a lady do normally who finds part of her garden wantonly wrecked? She registers distress, surprise, and indignation and forthwith dashes to the police to complain, kicking up the deuce of a fuss. I've handled dozens of cases of she-householders whose plants have been lifted by street hawkers, and, believe me, their fury against the thief, who could rarely be caught, was only less than their rage against the police who'd failed to catch 'em. Yet your Miss H., who, you say, adores her flowers, and calls them all by their pet names, shuts you up with a fantastic yarn about wild dogs, tells you to clear up the mess, and trips on her way singing."

He shook his head. "Even say she guessed it was Shields who, in a moment of cracked spite, smashed the almond tree, and decided on an act of Christian forgiveness, do you suppose, when the thing happened a second and third time, she'd still suffer in silence? She'd realize that a woman subject to crazy impulses like that was a danger to the community, demanding proper restraint."

"And your alternative is Miss Hyde herself, and Shields who guessed and held her tongue," said Mr. Moh, troubled. "Yet to suggest such hideous practices without any evidence seems unjust to her."

"Fair's fair, Moh. It's equally unjust to try to hang it on to Shields, of whom we know nothing except that she was an underdog and has been brutally murdered. And that's a fact in her favour, come to that. Because she didn't murder herself." His genial face looked stern and unforgiving. "I'm on the side of the underdog myself, and if you'd heard those unnatural harpies at The Burrs crabbing her you'd realize that this one got more kicks than ha'pence in her jobs, at any rate. Maybe we'll turn up some clue to your show as we go along," he added consolingly, "but here's one definite point that separates the two cases so far. The only suspects we've got in the flower business are women, and the murder was done by a man, and a tall, hefty man at that. Lavender Road. Here we are. Now perhaps we'll get some solid facts to work on."

No. 105 was a small two-storey villa exactly like its neighbours but the curtains and doorstep were white, and the bell highly polished. It being Sunday afternoon, when the day and Sunday garments demand respect, the street was empty of children, and quiet.

Their ring was answered by a neat little woman in black.

"Is this Miss Shields' house?"

"It's where she lives, yes. But I'm sorry she isn't at home. Ben, here's a gentleman asking for our Ellen."

A man came forward carrying a bicycle pump in his hand.

"Be you friends of Miss Shields?" he inquired in slow tones. "Maybe you've come to say what's come of her, for Mother and me's a bit worried where her's got to."

"There, I expect it's no more than she's stayed with one of her ladies, being one to oblige in sudden illness and such. But not coming home to fetch none of her things this morning—well, what with these road casualties—persons being took to the 'ospital and never a word said—my Ben was just going to bike over to inquire what was keeping her, if only to ease my mind, like, but maybe you've come from her. I'm Mrs. Higgs, and this is my son, Ben 'Iggs."

"Thanks, Mrs. Higgs." Gorham smiled pleasantly. "Well, I'm glad we caught you, Mr. Higgs. Saved you a journey, so to speak. The fact is there has been a—well, accident, and I've come for a bit of information about Miss Shields."

"Better come in, sir." Ben flattened himself against the passage wall to let them pass, at the same time opening the parlour door with a dexterous kick, and slipping a comforting arm round his mother's waist. "You from the police? There, Mum, you keep your pecker up."

In the stiffly furnished but shining parlour the Chief Inspector informed two sober persons that Miss Shields had died last night and the police had only just obtained her address.

"Have you known her long?" he inquired of Ben, to allow Mrs. Higgs, seated on a red-plush chair, holding tightly to her son's hand, time to get over the shock.

"Matter of five year she's lived here," Ben replied briefly. "Never knew her afore. Obliging party she were. Never a wry word so long as she lodged with us—not that mother's one to quarrel with none. So it's both sides, as you might say."

"Did she have many friends to see her here?"

Ben looked dubious.

"Well, I can't say as I know much about her 'abits, but I never seen none. What with me being at the guv'nor's all day, and her

working for these here ladies of hers, only of a Sunday, maybe...."
He stooped over his mother, who was wiping away furtive tears on a clean handkerchief. "Mum, the gentleman wants to know if Ellen had friends here. I never met 'em, but you knowed her better than what I did...."

Mrs. Higgs looked up, red-eyed, but controlling herself.

"I wouldn't say pore Ellen had exactly any friends, sir," she said. "Not on visiting terms, like. She was one to keep herself to herself, though as easy a lodger as you could find, and paid her money regular as regular. And what with me having me scrubbing early mornings, and in the evenings, too, at the Labour Exchange, and Ben at his job, and poor Ellen with her ladies to oblige, we didn't see each other a lot, not to say talk, except Sundays, and then she'd her own things to see to and her church."

"Was she often late coming home?" It was a fixed rule of Gorham to allow witnesses to tell their stories in their own way, with an easy question slipped in here and there to keep them going. His method, he maintained, took longer, but was infinitely more productive of information in the long run than the normal system of barking interrogations at them, which either annoyed or scared them, causing them to shut up like oysters. Mrs Higgs was well under way.

"Well, sir, lately as often as not she was, though her proper time for leaving was six week-days and twelve Saturdays. But she'd often stay on to give the lady what she did for a bit of extra if needed, not being one to be sticking about her times as some are, but more one to be put upon, in a manner of speaking, this Mrs. 'Ubberd not being an easy lady to do for, and inconsiderate in judging what one pair of hands can get through, five in family and a 'elpless lot. Ellen come home so tired sometimes she said she didn't hardly know how to carry on, she was that dis'eartened. Only she couldn't afford to give notice—the work being regular by the week—till she heard of another place."

"I see. Then, as she'd often been late before, you didn't worry when she didn't turn up yesterday afternoon?"

"No, sir. But, you see, what with my being at my cousin May's most of all day yesterday, it being the wedding of May's Beryl, and not coming home till night, I scarcely give her a thought, pore soul."

Gorham curbed an impulse to cut Beryl firmly out of the conversation; instead, he said with patient good humour:

"Did this wedding really go on till night?"

"You might say it did, sir." She brightened involuntarily at remembrance of yesterday's gay doings. "First there was the wedding at the church, then the reception at the bride's mother's house, my own first cousin May, at number 87 down the road—only a step along, and that convenient to give an 'and behind the scenes, what with plates and cups and glasses being wanted over and over, and the little ones to be given their teas to—and then when the guests had left after our May's Beryl had gone off on her honeymoon there was about twelve of the family left with my Ben and me to make up a party for the pictures, and when we come back there was a cold collation, my cousin May having prepared sandwiches in the morning, and then when Uncle and Aunt and their three left to catch the last bus, the men set to and put the furniture back in its places, which had been stacked in the yard to make room and all put about, and not so much as a bed for pore Tom and May to drag theirselves to till we'd made them again, so it was near one in the morning before Ben and me got home. And then it did surprise me to find Ellen not in her room, her often being late, as I said, but never stopping out all night before, not since she's been at Mrs. Hubberd's. But still, I never thought harm could have overtook her, only that she'd stopped because of sudden illness or something. But this morning, when she never come home, seeing I'd got the wind up thinking of these road casualties, Ben said he'd bike over to Finnet after dinner to see she was okay, and just when he was going you come, and pore Ellen did meet with that accident after all!"

Tears flooded her eyes, and Gorham hastily intervened. "That's quite clear, Mrs. Higgs. But when she was late sometimes perhaps she met a friend after leaving her work, went for a walk or to some house—"

"That she never!" Mrs. Higgs flared up. "When she said she'd been kep' at her place she'd been kep'! She wasn't one of those flighty ones to tell a lie as soon as look at you."

"She'd a perfect right to walk out with a friend if she wanted to!" Gorham expostulated, but Mrs. Higgs was roused.

"A course she had, pore soul, but she never did, and when she was late in of an evening she explained she'd been kep' at Mrs. 'Ubberd's, and she'd *bin* kep' at Mrs. 'Ubberd's!"

"Right," said Gorham, giving in. "By the way, you never heard of any quarrel she had? Anyone who might have a grudge against her—might want to do her an injury?"

She shook her head, bewildered.

"How could there be when she never knowed anybody? Well, there were the ladies that belonged to her churches, but church folk aren't like chapel folk, warm-hearted and friends together. If they passed a remark about the weather at one of the meetings they had, or give a smile in the street, it would be all, and as for asking her into their homes for tea, it never dawned in their heads. And as to her own sister, Mrs. Vardon as is, though with a little 'ome and her husband in the green-grocery, never once did that person ask our Ellen up for an 'oliday to Manchester."

"Thank you, Mrs. Higgs. Now, if I might have a word with your son . . ."

"That's right, Mum, suppose you go and make that cup of tea what you was doing when these gents arrived. It'll do you good," Ben said earnestly, and shepherded her into the kitchen.

"Now, mister, what's come to our Ellen?" He shut the door and stood against it. "No call to fret Mum with details."

"Exactly." In a few sentences Gorham gave him the facts. "Now you see what I'm trying to get at. Can you throw any light on her murder from what you know of her life?"

Higgs stood in glum thought.

"No, I can't," he muttered at last. "It was like what Mother said. She didn't have no personal friends, nor no enemies either, I'd have said. She never went to no other places but these church gatherings, services and bazaars for fun. And the people she worked for, of course. It was to be near her pet church she come to live in Harlesden."

"You never heard of her meeting any man on the quiet?"

"No, sir, never. She wasn't that sort. Well, I mean to say . . ." He stopped helplessly, unable to express how utterly Ellen Shields wasn't the sort that men would want to go out with. "You'd only got to look at her, I mean," he added sheepishly. Gorham appeared to grasp his idea.

"Looks aren't everything. Idiots fall for all sorts, and that applies to both sexes. Still, you may be right. But the woman was murdered. By a man. If it wasn't sexual we've got to look for a pretty strong motive elsewhere. For instance, if she'd got across some shady fellow—"

"Don't see where she'd have picked him up, sir," Higgs said, after another pause. "Not likely at these here churches. 'T'ain't as if she'd belonged to the Army, where there's a good few toughs as well as holy blokes. And she didn't hold with pubs. Said females ought to be ashamed to enter them, and she'd die before she'd so demean herself, encouraging men to waste money and time and 'ealth on drink. Her idea was women ought to hold a high standard and influence others for good."

"Did she try to influence you?"

Ben grinned slowly.

"Well, only sideways, like. Mentioning the craving what might arise from me glass of beer Sundays, like a chap in the house she worked at who'd pitched her a tale about how he'd been led away as a ninnocent boy and now had this sort of low shameful passion for nips that he couldn't battle against proper. What I understood was he'd go and sob his heart out to Ellen when he'd got ticked off by the other gents for rolling in tight the night before."

"That," said Gorham thoughtfully, "would be Bob Dent. Unfortunately, he was at his favourite pub all last evening. Can't be connected up with the murder so far. Now, just as a formality, what were you doing yesterday? At this wedding-party all day?"

"Yes, my young lady was one of the bridesmaids. We went to the pictures in the evening, and I seen her home after we'd had this cold grub. Not that it took much seeing, she living at the corner shop, Best's, Tobacconist's and Sweets, which my girl runs with a bit of help from her old dad, to make a home for the old people. Being Best by name and nature, as her dad says, being one for his joke. Then I come back and helped Tom and May cart the furniture back and put up their bed, and Mother and me come in 'ome. What with the wedding and the party, Mother didn't bother a lot about Ellen's bed being not slept in; but by dinner-time she was fair worrying her head off, and I said I'd go over and see what was up."

"All right. Now look at these things." He opened the case he had earned in. "Recognize that coat, or that beret?"

"That coat's hers—Ellen's, I mean. Wore it always. And that beret—that's hers right enough too. Saw her knitting it of an evening for weeks, undoing it half the time. And she'd stuck a Woolworth feather on the top; bright green, some metal stuff, not a real feather. Comic it looked to me, but she'd preen herself in the chimbley glass trying it on, this way and that. It'd have been rude to laugh. But—"

"Don't touch it. The shaft of the feather's missing, and the thing's torn. Know what she got paid at the Hubberds'?"

"A quid a week and an odd sixpence sometimes thrown in. And her fares out of it—six days' work and a couple of hours Sunday as often as not. She paid ten bob a week for her room and breakfast and a bob for meals on Sunday and extras. It was a stiff job for poor pay; but what Mum said was that if she stuck out for more, as like as not they'd sack her for someone less—well—sloppy, if you understand. And she was sort of used to these Finnet ladies, and liked them except when Mrs. H. let fly. Well, she was well-meaning, pore thing, but she'd muck up a place as much as she cleaned it—see? If she was let put coal on the fire she'd drop half and we'd crunch it on the lino till she'd dash off and get a dustpan to sweep it up and then leave the dustpan in the passage for someone to break their necks over. She was a good-natured sort and would laugh herself at her errors. But what I was alluding to was Mrs. H. might have cause for snapping her up. But I can't sort of believe any chap would do pore Ellen in—unless it was in mistake for someone else!"

"Awkward sort of mistake to make," Gorham said drily. "Now let's see her room, and then we'll be getting along." He locked his case, and he and Mr. Moh followed Higgs upstairs to a small bedroom. Like the other rooms in Mrs. Higgs's house, it was clean and comfortably furnished, with a single bed, dressing-chest and washstand, and a hanging curtain for clothes, but here her influence ended and Ellen Shields' began. The place was crowded with odd cardboard boxes, half-mended garments, oddments of all descriptions—rag, tag, and bobtail. Bits of improbable-looking knitting, muddled attempts at blouse-making and fancy-work, parish magazines, manuals of prayer with the covers missing, texts, one "Be Ye Kind One To Another" hung above the bed crookedly.

Higgs dismissed, the two men went rapidly through the accumulation of rubbish, but the search yielded nothing of value except an old letter or two, captious, not to say cattish, in tone, from the sister, Maggie Vardon, from a Manchester address.

The few tattered books, pious verses, and manuals with such exalted titles as *Communion With God* were worn and underlined, suggesting that if Ellen Shields' outward existence were humble, her inward life was nourished on strong spiritual food.

Again, in every receptacle—drawers, boxes, work-bags—were scraps of paper bearing texts or pious axioms scribbled in pencil, often so rubbed as to be scarcely legible. And from beneath the mattress Mr. Moh finally withdrew a black exercise-book which, at a cursory view, appeared to be a sort of religious diary of prayers, daily resolutions, quotations, and general remarks.

"Nothing more in this room concerns you," Mr. Moh remarked, handing over this book. "But these writings, which seem to reveal her idea of herself, may tell something."

"It'll take a solid couple of hours to go through them," Gorham agreed with gloom. "And a good light. We'll cart them with us. Collect the lot into this newspaper; that's finished, I think."

They heard Mrs. Higgs crying in the kitchen and her son murmuring comfort as they went downstairs. He came out as they reached the passage, looking warm and sheepish.

"Just been telling Mum, and she's taking on a bit. Can't seem to believe it. Seen all you want, mister?"

"Yes. I've locked that door upstairs, but I'll return you the key as soon as possible. Look here, you realize you'll be wanted for the inquest, to formally identify the body if we can't get Vardon, the sister, in time? I've got her address; but you'd better come prepared. Probably Tuesday morning. You'll be told time and place."

"Right, sir."

"And if any further fact comes to your knowledge, anything whatever, however trifling it may be, either hand it in at the nearest police station for me or notify me direct; here's my card. John Gorham, Chief Inspector, C.I.D., Scotland Yard. Got all that?"

"Okay, sir. And I can tell Mum you'll communicate with that sister? She's worrying about that."

"Yes, we'll inform her. And one thing more, Higgs. If reporters come here you and your mother had better keep still tongues in your heads till after the inquest, see? You can say Miss Shields lived here and was a pleasant lodger. But more than that you don't know. Understand?"

"That's right, sir."

"That washes out one suspect, at any rate," said Gorham with satisfaction, as they drove away. "That small chap could no more have carried that body up Hardwicke's steps than I could an elephant. I'll have that wedding crowd checked as a matter of form, but their yarn rang true, eh?"

"Unworthy self has ever had indubitable conviction that the criminal was a Finnet man."

"You consider the choice of that garden a deliberate one, not a chance shot?"

"Would a murderer, anxious to unload inconvenient corpse from his car, touring round seeking suitably retired spot, select garden of obviously furnished house simply on strength of windows being shut? Wouldn't he fear outraged proprietor popping out to interrupt nefarious doings of criminal trespasser?"

"Quite, he would," Gorham agreed. "That means someone who knew enough of Hardwicke to know he was away and the house definitely empty. Higgs could have known from Shields' talk, but he has no car. He has a fair alibi, and physically he's incapable of the job. That leaves who?"

"All men inhabiting Pound Lane, visiting tradesboys, husband of caretaker, policeman on beat, and"—Mr. Moh ended with a beaming smile—"me."

"You're out of it for the same reason as Higgs. And you've got a nice alibi as well. If you hadn't been under my own eye at home brooding over our delphiniums at the crucial time it might have gone hardly with you, my lad. Tradesboys we can ignore, the bobby and postman too. You forgot the postman. The caretaker's husband is in hospital with a broken leg. That leaves Hardwicke and the three men at The Burrs, where she worked." He frowned, and began to tell Mr. Moh what had happened at The Burrs.

Chapter VI

Norris, who had just returned when they reached the police station at Finnet, reported tersely that his search at The Burrs, thoroughly carried out, had been negative in result.

"Did they put any difficulties in your way?" Gorham inquired, and the man's good-looking face reddened.

"Mr. Hubberd was stiff, sir, but he made no objection to my doings till I asked to go into his wife's room. Then he damned my officiousness and swore she was asleep, but finally knocked and opened the door when I insisted. This was on the landing outside, intended to prepare her, of course. But the lady hadn't taken the hint. She was lying on the bed on her face, with next to nothing on till Mr. H. threw the eiderdown over her as he bent down and whispered a word. I went through everything as quick as I could. But I suppose she was watching and it made her mad, because she suddenly leapt off the bed and dragged off the sheets, yelling out that I'd better search that too for a b—y spy—"

"You kept your temper, I hope?" Gorham said sharply.

"Yes, sir, I did. I never said a single word, only I handed her her dressing-gown from a chair, and she screamed and slapped my face."

"And then?"

"I walked out of the room, sir, and Mr. Hubberd followed me, and I heard her howling, and he sent her brother to her. I searched Dent's room—on the same landing—while he was out of it, but there was nothing there but his clothes and empty bottles."

"What about the Hughes?"

"They have the three rooms on the top floor. They appeared on the stairs at the noise, both properly dressed, which was a treat, and started laughing and chaffing Mr. H. over his Happy Sunday Afternoon, all merry and carefree. He wasn't amused. And when they realized their own quarters were my next objective Mr. Hughes suddenly went all indignant and high-minded, and asked Mr. Hubberd what the devil he thought he was doing, insulting the girls by allowing this b—y inquisition! He'd not allow it, by George! And the lady called Mr. H. a few choice names for being so unkind to his poor wife. I said all right, I'd go and report their refusal to you. And turned to go down, when Mr. H., who, I will say, had kept a grip on himself till then, took the floor. He ignored the lady, but I thought for a second he was going to tackle Hughes, he looked so white and grim. But he rapped out: 'The sergeant's obeying orders, with my permission. Clear off those stairs, Charles.' And they cleared off, and I went up.

"The men searched downstairs thoroughly, but none of us found a thing we could identify as belonging to deceased, sir. There were plenty of feminine frills lying everywhere in the women's rooms, but the undies looked far too dainty to be hers, and the rose-patterned purple dress and yellow cardigan and American cloth bag definitely weren't in the house. I wouldn't like to take my oath about the bit of green feather, being small, but we couldn't find it, and Brown tipped over the dustbin on the chance. But it had been cleared Saturday morning, and contained nothing but ordinary garbage. Mr. Hubberd saw us off the premises quite civilly, and shut the door behind us. Brown will patrol the road till further orders from you."

"Quite right. Keep a man in the road till after the inquest, at any rate. And you'd better forget that slap in the face, Norris. It was fair exchange for that gesture of yours with the dressing-gown. That seems to have gone right home, but it was Shields' clothes you were there to deal with, not Mrs. Hubberd's lack of them. Now"—he changed the subject—"I've been to deceased's lodgings in Harlesden and seen the landlady and her son. Respectable people named Higgs. They've got a cast-iron alibi for all yesterday till the early hours of this morning, and on that ground alone can be eliminated from the case. The local police will check their story, of course, but I've no doubt myself it's all right. Higgs will appear at the inquest for the formal identification. I've been on to the coroner, and he agreed to Tuesday morning for the inquest. That'll give us time to fetch the sister, Mrs. Maggie Vardon, from Manchester. Otherwise we got nothing new or very helpful from the Higgs. Shields had no friends, and no houses at which she visited except those in Pound Lane where she was employed.

"So far the results of all our inquiries are negative, but Mr. Moh and I have definitely reached the conclusion that the choice of The Laurels garden was deliberate, not a chance that just came off. And that points to a criminal with certain local knowledge. What's your opinion, Norris?"

The sergeant looked taken aback, but gratified.

"That's right, sir. Someone who knew The Laurels was empty, and old Mrs. Manstead's house next door too very likely. An outsider, judging by the curtains in the windows, couldn't be certain there was no one inside either of them."

"That's one point, then. Now the time of the murder. I think we can practically fix it as just before sunset yesterday. Here's the surgeon's report. . . . Um . . . as we said, strangled by hands, probably from front . . . approximate time of death . . . between eight and eleven, say . . ." He put the paper away. "Then Miss Hyde's evidence narrows it down further. The body was hidden behind those bushes either after 11.30 or before ten. Take that with the surgeon's report and we get sunset again."

"Looks to me, sir. much likelier the body was put there late at night when he'd be sure everybody was in bed and no chance of casual passengers along the Lane like what there would be early in the evening when it was barely dark, even if the crime took place then."

"At first sight that's a reasonable view," Gorham said thoughtfully. "But the theory doesn't reckon with two objections. First, the steadily increasing difficulty in carrying the body; second, the murderer's instinct to get quit of it as soon as possible."

"Unless there were two in it. One who did the murder, and an accessory after the fact who helped to hide it up."

Gorham shook his head.

"You're confusing what evidence we have by jumping to the conclusion that the crime took place in a house—The Burrs for choice," he said—"where the murderer could have been discovered with the body by another member of the household, who then was induced to help cover the crime. That postulates Hubberd, who, according to his own story, was alone in the house all evening. Now, where are you going to get your accessory from? You heard the Innisfree evidence. The servant there saw Bob Dent go home 'just before eleven', and Miss Hyde met Mrs. Hubberd and Mrs. Hughes at 'about eleven', a difference of a few minutes probably. That makes four people all ready not only to condone a murder but to incriminate themselves in a capital crime. One accessory might be a remote possibility; three are purely fantastic, eh, Moh?"

57 | DEATH HAS NO TONGUE

"Lacking spirit of friendly co-operation which appeared intensely absent from Sergeant's report," Mr. Moh agreed elliptically, but with a deferential gesture towards Norris that was flattering. "To self, unless accessory theory receives indubitable proof now non-existent, the depositing of victim where found followed almost directly on crime, i.e. before ten o'clock p.m."

"At any rate, we'll take that as a working hypothesis," Gorham said. "But now let's take the clues we've got; the beret first. Found in Hubberd's garage *under* his car, the wheels being thick with wet clay after weeks of drought. . . . What about it?"

"There's only one place about here that clay could have come from," Norris put in eagerly; "that's on the road to Finnet Beeches, which is practically a continuation of Pound Lane. About half a mile away they're laying new sewers to cope with the building that's going on up in the Beech Woods, and the road's in a fair muck with piles of excavated clay and water from the cock they've got for mixing their cement. Hubberd's car must have come down Finnet Beeches road last night and turned straight into the garage by the tracks, because there's not a sign of clay-marks in Pound Lane itself, only by The Burrs corner."

"No, I saw that," Gorham said quietly. "That explains the wetness of the clay." He made a note. "The car was run in on top of the beret, which was already torn and part of its feather missing. And Hubberd denied the car had been out at all. Whoever drove the car in didn't notice the beret."

"If it was Hubberd himself he'd probably turned off his lights to escape notice. He'd know his own garage well enough to run in in the dark; it was run in, not backed in, you remember, sir. He certainly got a shock when he saw it this morning."

"By that time he knew that a murder had been committed, from outside information, so his reaction to the discovery doesn't tell much one way or the other. Your idea is that, having killed her when they were alone in the house, and run the body down to The Laurels, he turned and ran out on this Finnet Beeches Road. But why?"

"To hide the clothes and bag, sir. They weren't in the house. And that way, doing it at the time you said, before ten, but after sunset, he wouldn't need an accessory, and he didn't see he'd dropped the beret. Finnet Beeches would be just the place he'd think of to drop the clothes in, because the woods are still thick in parts in spite of houses being built among them."

"In that case why not drop the body there too, instead of on a neighbour's doorstep? But we're back again at theory, Norris, and this one only accounts for some of the facts, not all."

"It doesn't account for his motive—"

Gorham made a gesture of impatience.

"Motive's like the coat of paint on a new house. You may know what the colour is going to be, but you don't start applying it to the woodwork till the building's finished. Here we don't even know the shade yet. And guesswork is a sheer waste of time. We've got to rely simply on pointers arising from the crime itself, and here are two that don't fit into that theory. Why was the body stripped? And how came the beret to be torn?"

"Couldn't it have been torn in the struggle, sir?" Norris ventured with a touch of sulkiness. This was his first job under Chief Inspector Gorham. He felt that his theory deserved more credit than it had received, for Gorham might be a pleasant-mannered sort of chap, but he hadn't noticed any undue brilliancy about him so far. Gorham would have been horrified if he had.

"There was no struggle," he said quietly. "She was facing the criminal when he seized her by the throat. She was talking to him. He killed her, possibly without premeditation, but certainly with deliberate intention. Beyond that we have no safe ground for theorizing. Where's that beret?"

He unpinned the piece of newspaper, taken from his case, and gently teased the beret into shape, loosening fragments of now dry and crumbling clay on to a clean sheet of notepaper, and finally hung the thing over the massive inkstand on the desk.

The three men stared at it intently, and from it to a lump of clay taken directly from the wheel placed beside it.

"Clay was acquired," said Mr. Moh slowly, "from wheel of car, identified by observant police officer as coming from Finnet Beeches Road. Minute specks of black embedded in wool beneath clay superimposed on same, not appearing in pattern lump, suggest acquisition by beret before wheel rolled on it."

"From the garage floor perhaps?" Gorham bent over the magnifying-glass. "No, you're right, they're mixed into the wool meshes;

don't suggest just casual contact with floor-dust. And the clay was superimposed. I get your point, Moh. They got into the wool before the beret fell on the garage floor or they'd have been on the underside only, and the clay on the upper side where the wheel rested. But they're too small to identify without a microscope. I'll have to have them examined."

He carefully folded the sheet of paper into which he had shaken several of the black specks, labelled it, and set it aside.

"Now about this jagged V-shaped tear in the beret," he said, and again the magnifying-glass passed from hand to hand.

A portion roughly triangular in shape had been torn out, leaving a hole, with a few rows of the knitted band to give an approximate idea of the beret's original size and shape.

"The wool ends are jagged, not cut—"

"It's more as if it had been violently ripped on a nail—"

"Or wire. But then one would expect the wool to be pulled, constricted, and some of the missing bit to be hanging." Gorham's tone was doubtful.

"It is the effect a burn would produce," Mr. Moh said, frowning. "But there is no trace of burning. It looks highly significant to me," he added with provoking calm. "But what of escapes me."

"Same here," Gorham acknowledged, and laid the jacket on the desk.

Once more the three peered, and for a full minute no one spoke.

It was the coat of a lightweight blue suit which had seen considerable wear and was shiny at the seams, and rubbed and frayed at the collar and cuff edges. The name-tab had been cut away, and the buttons were of the type turned out by the million for cheap ready-made suits. It was stock size, but badly out of shape, the soiled lining split as if its wearer had increased in bulk, the cheap cloth pulling under the strain. It was also much creased, as if it had been badly folded away for a considerable time. And the pockets were empty, though in one were dry fragments of some vegetable substance that might have been grasses, which crumbled, in spite of his care, as Gorham gathered them into an envelope. But the jacket possessed one extraordinary feature. Stitched underneath the back of the collar was a white ticket on which "9d." was marked in ink.

"A sale ticket!" Norris exclaimed. "It must have come from a slop-shop. But it's funny there's no name on it." He felt the edge of the ticket. "Or a charity sale more likely. That ticket's amateur work, cut with scissors from a cheap postcard."

Gorham nodded agreement.

"Either that or an old-clo' man. And no big charity organization either, such as the Church Army. They'd have distinctive tickets." He looked at Mr. Moh, but Mr. Moh seemed devoid of ideas.

"Connection between man's jacket and female victim feelingly eludes me," he stated flatly. And as his remark summed up Gorham's mental condition as well as Norris's, the beret and jacket were laid aside.

An examination of the brown tweed coat that had belonged to Ellen Shields added nothing to their knowledge. In the absence of evidence to the contrary, and presuming that she left the house alive, in view of the sultryness of Saturday evening she might clearly have left the coat deliberately behind, intending to reclaim it on Sunday or Monday when she went to work again.

Mr. Moh seemed to have lost interest in the proceedings and sat apart, deep in thought, while Gorham made notes and the sergeant packed up the exhibits.

"Do you often come across murder cases with such a lot of heartlessness in them as this one, sir?" Norris inquired frowningly, as he rose from his knees.

"What?"

"Well, sir, what I mean is, except Dent, those people at The Burrs showed no more feeling about deceased than if she'd been a dog; as if they didn't regard her as a human being at all. In fact I've seen more fuss made over the death of a family cat."

"Um, there was one person who felt a shock—Miss Hyde—"

"Miss Hyde? She seemed pretty cool—"

"Somebody had revived her with sal volatile just before we turned up."

"That was that queer smell? And a wineglass on the table!" he exclaimed. "I looked for a bottle."

"It was on the chimney-piece, behind a silver frame."

Norris stood up.

"Think she knew more than she said, sir?"

"No-o," Gorham replied thoughtfully. "It could have been just human compassion—the emotion so conspicuously lacking from other ladies in the case. Now get down to work on the various local lines at once. Start a strenuous search for the clothes and bag. I'll have Hughes and Hubberd tailed, but you can look into Dent's story. If he was on the premises of the 'Fox and Goose' from 6.30 or so till nearly eleven, as he says, he can be eliminated. Then trace Hubberd's car last night . . . the usual lines of inquiry. That clay give a point to start from. Then find out if Mrs. Hughes and Mrs. Hubberd were actually seen at the cinema, and if so try to get definite times of their arrival and leaving. No need to be too official over these local inquiries. You probably know the cinema attendants, so get the information you want by way of casual chat. Same at the pub. The whole village will be agog about the crime, but it's not to be told what direction the investigation is taking. I'll give you the dope for reporters. Nothing about the beret or jacket is to be published at present. Got all that?"

"Yes, sir, Dent's alibi; clothes and bag; cinema inquiries, and Hubberd's car."

"And anything else that occurs to you. It might be useful to discover whether that milkman got anything beyond the bare fact, and what story he is spreading." He slipped his note-book into his pocket and rose from his chair.

"Know the woman who caretakes for Mr. Hardwicke—Blenkinsop? Husband in hospital with a broken leg. I'd like to know when she last received instructions from Mr. Hardwicke; whether she'd seen him to hand over the keys of the sideboard that he used to get out that whisky. That's the lot. Don't know what experience you've had, Norris. But you understand in the beginning of a job like this it's sheer routine work to collect information about anything and everyone having the thinnest connection with the victim and scene of the crime. Like Mr. Hardwicke, for instance. When we've got the general facts we can judge what's relevant and what isn't. Not before. See? Come on, Mr. Moh."

Sergeant Norris watched Gorham and Li Moh get into the Chief Inspector's car and drive away after this short instruction on the art of crime investigation with the wakening of a new and disagreeable doubt in his mind.

Did Gorham actually suspect Hardwicke, yet hesitate to turn the limelight on him because they were friends? It looked like it. He set himself to think the matter out.

Hardwicke was a bachelor, a man of means, had only reached England on Saturday, and had no visible motive for committing murder the instant he reached his native shores. But—Norris grinned—the Chief himself had lectured him on the unimportance of motive at this stage. What had he said? Motive was like the coat of paint on a new house, only to be applied when the building was finished, though you might know what it was to be. All right; washing out any question of motive, then, and any alibi he might trot out later, Hardwicke could have done the job more easily than anyone. Say he met Shields after she left The Burrs, invited her into his house, killed her while she was talking to him indoors, tidying up after himself carefully before dropping the body over that railing *outside*, and carrying away her clothes to dispose of elsewhere. Then turning up publicly this morning when he had spotted from the end of the road that the police were in possession and discovery made.

He had then behaved naturally enough, chiming in with his recognition of the corpse, but not till Mr. Moh and Brown had named her first, and further silence might seem suspicious. No trace was left in the house. The slight film of dust on polished surfaces in hall and dining-room showed no finger-marks, but it was no more than might have settled during the night if the floors had been brushed to remove footmarks. There had been carpet-dust in the dustbin, as easily left there by Hardwicke in the evening as Mrs. Blenkinsop in the morning. Hello! Hello! He had learned at The Burrs that the ash-cans were cleared on Saturday morning. Yet that soft wad of carpet-dust was there on Sunday.

Blenkinsop had probably bought and put the siphon and bottle of whisky in the sideboard, but the cupboard doors were locked, and Hardwicke had produced that key as well as his latchkey from his pocket. The point was that, whether or no he had collected Mrs. Blenkinsop's keys this morning, he no doubt habitually carried his latchkey, and so had means of access to the house yesterday.

He had a nasty jar—and showed it—when the Chief insisted on that preliminary search of the premises. Was he wondering if he had succeeded in covering all traces while he was detained in the hall during the operation? He was anxious and ill at ease, and immensely relieved when it was over.

Hardwicke was a big, loose-jointed fellow, but physically as hard as nails—which made the jumpiness of his nerves the more noticeable—and capable of carrying through the whole job single-handed. In his case alone no car was necessary, and he could have walked away afterwards, even carrying a suitcase, unnoticed, as he could choose his moment to leave the house.

What other points fitted?

No theory that he had yet manufactured explained the stripping of the body, but the jacket might well be an old one from a wardrobe upstairs, though, again, the sale ticket was a mystery.

The beret? Well, he could have found it at the last moment, just as he was quitting the place . . . a damning piece of evidence against himself . . . and chucked it into Hubberd's garage with an idea of diverting suspicion. . . . Surely—surely it couldn't have been he who temporarily borrowed Hubberd's car for that run out on the Finnet Beeches Road to get rid of the clothes?

Chapter VII

Gorham raised an aching head from the mass of papers that strewed his desk as Li Moh came into his room with a tray at eleven o'clock that night.

"Good! I can do with a drink, old man! Mary gone to bed?"

"Half-an-hour ago. Are you still worrying over those papers from Lavendar Road?"

Gorham nodded gloomily.

"They seem a mere farrago of religious rubbish to me," he said. "But somehow I can't get over the idea that they may have a meaning buried somewhere in them if one could only drag it out."

"Is any name mentioned?"

"Not a name. Nor, what is still more exasperating, a date, among the lot. The entries in the book are the only guide to chronological order among them, and that's muddled because a lot of the scribbles on scraps of paper we collected in that messy room of hers seem to be simply try-outs, that she afterwards copied into this book. I've traced nine so far, simply texts and moral remarks, and the remainder are the same, all beastly worn and rubbed as if she carried them folded in her purse for days. The entries in the book are in ink, thank Heaven; not so deadly to make out. And allowing for the general muddle of her mind, the thoughts in the book—if you can call them thoughts—seem to be the ones she wanted to hold on to."

"Do you expect to find some reflection of the people she knew in them?" Mr. Moh asked, puzzled.

"Scarcely that. Nothing's clear enough, but it's my job to go through them in any case, and"—his tone sounded none too hopeful—"there's just a chance, if they can be sorted out properly, that we might get her reactions to some of these people. Norris was right, you know, Moh—those people she worked for only seemed to regard her as a drudge; only *saw* her in terms of the jobs they wanted done and the hash she made of them. That's what Norris meant by heartlessness. I told you how those women behaved; they made me sick."

He paused, and Mr. Moh waited, for the Chief Inspector seemed to be struggling with some idea that he found difficulty in formulating. "My point is, how did Shields see them? She wasn't a mere domestic robot, though they treated her like one. Dent seemed genuinely upset, though it was maudlin feeling. Hubberd was decent, but no more, and Hughes flippant. They were spitting like angry cats when I interrupted, and the women kept it up, though the men controlled themselves in front of me, and tried to shut them up.

"It struck me that the way Hughes picked his wife up and rushed her off, shrieking with laughter, in his arms, was pure theatre. As if, to get out of a difficult situation, he threw himself into some old comedy role, and she caught her cue and played up. Both of them play-acting all through, before the Hubberds and me. Ethel's rage was the real thing. No acting there. Just plain, tense, crazy, hysterical hatred of everybody."

"But she didn't let out a word that suggested she knew the criminal, eh?"

Gorham looked sober.

"No, she didn't, Moh, and that's a fact."

"Then let us return to the effusions of Shields, my Gorham," Mr. Moh said cheerfully. "Where all is shrouded in dense fog one bit of puzzle is as good as another to worry at."

He bent over the book, turning page after page, while Gorham watched with glum amusement. He read some entries aloud:

"Lord, increase my faith, that in the troubles of this world I may have strength and a right judgment in all things.

"Be kind and patient when others are spiteful and angry, so that they may be influenced by your example into correcting their faults.

"Be ye kind one to another, tender-hearted, forgiving one another."

"That's a text, of course," Gorham observed, "and repeated more than once, as if she had a lot to forgive. My idea is, she'd write down a text like that on any bit of paper that came handy, and carry it about with her as a sort of moral tonic, to be taken when she needed it. But you get my idea. She didn't regard herself as a worthless drudge, but as an equal of the people she slaved for, hoping to influence them by her example. See?"

"Here is another:

"No work is derogatory in itself, for every duty may be ennobled by the spirit in which it is performed.

"That is initialled E.H., Gorham. Why?"

"A lot are. I took it to mean some book she got them from." He peered at the page over Mr. Moh s shoulder. "Here's another 'E.H.':

"Whatsoever thy hand findeth to do, do it with care as to the Lord, and not unto men, not with eye-service, as men-pleasers.

"Hello!" He frowned and slumped back into his chair. "That's signed E.H., but it comes from the Bible."

Mr. Moh stared at him, puzzled.

"Are you sure?"

"Certain. My mother used to rub it into me as a nipper when I'd tried to scamp some little job, doing only the bit that showed." He leaned back to light his pipe, a reminiscent smile on his face.

"Men-pleasers, she said, were the sort who built showy-looking houses without safe foundations, and swept dust under mats, and polished the grate without cleaning the flues, so that the chimneys caught fire, and beetles swarmed in the hidden dirt, and the house fell down and killed the occupants who weren't already dead of diseases. I wish you'd known my mother, Moh. She was a great little woman. Stood about four feet eight, and was the standby of the whole neighbourhood in trouble, and my old Dad too, thought he was outsize. 'Whatsoever ye would that men should do to you, do ye even so to them,' was another of her sayings. My Dad called them her 'whatsoevers.'

"He'd say, chuckling: 'Come on, Johnny, we'd best go and put this here job through properly, or we'll have your Mum down on us with her whatsoevers.' But here's a specimen of Shields' muddling." He bent over the page again and pointed with his pencil. "She's got that text all wrong. Mixed up two of them, I think. Let's see, how does the thing go?" He frowned. "'Whatsoever ye do, do it heartily, as to the Lord, and not unto men'; and the phrase 'not with eye-service, as men-pleasers' comes in the verse before. But what the dickens did she initial it 'E.H.' for?"

"She could have heard it from E.H. Or it might apply to E.H." Mr. Moh suggested. "There are other initials too. 'M.', for instance."

"I know, but none of them are grouped together. I took them to refer to the pious book she got them from. But that one's definitely from the Bible, so I'm wrong. You mean E.H. might be someone alive, whom she knew? Look here, Moh, look them all out and I'll type them on a sheet of paper together. Then we'll see if they make sense."

Half-an-hour later the two men stared blankly at the typed page.

In her tongue is the law of kindness. E.H.
Making many books is a weariness to the flesh. E.H.
There is a man whose labour is in wisdom and knowledge, yet to a man that hath not laboured therein he shall give it for his portion. This is evil. E.H.
Let me love and suffer in silence for this Beloved Friend. E.H.
He that goeth about as a tale-bearer revealeth secrets, and a scorner loveth not one that reproveth. So be silent. E.H.

A noble example of patience teaches one to bear one's burden of silence till God gives the sign. E.H.

Labour, working with our own hands. That is a commandment. If any man will not work, neither shall he eat. The destroyer shall be punished. E.H.

"Silence seems to be the keyword," Gorham said at last. "If there's any meaning there at all, it looks as if she knew something about E.H. that she couldn't tell. As half of it is texts, the pronouns are no guide. E.H. may be a man or woman. Half the people in this case have names that begin with 'H'."

"But not all are E.H. Eliminate the others and who remains?"

"Clarice and Charles Hughes. Hardwicke is Lewis. Ben Higgs, Mrs. Higgs?"

"L. V. Hyde, Miss Hyde—I have heard her brother call her Jane—"

"That leaves both the Hubberds." He pushed away the book. "This is the sort of job that defeats me altogether," he grunted. "Take it E.H. is a real person; they are the only two E.H.'s we know she knew, and that Law of Kindness bit certainly doesn't fit Ethel Hubberd. Anything but. Then this 'making many books' bit. If it were L.V.H. it could be a reference to those futile stories in the *Fleet News*, about girls with blue hair. But E.H.! Besides, it's a text out of Proverbs, I believe. Solomon. He had eight hundred wives and unlimited concubines, and in his spare time wrote books crabbing women he was fed up with, and finally got fed up even with books."

"Laudable knowledge of Holy Writings, while throwing admirable light on early training, is unshared by this totally uneducated person," said Li Moh, firmly checking Gorham's tendency to display his learning. "But suggest that use of symbolism in religious phraseology is apt to confuse significance of plain-seeming words. The point to establish is whether or not E.H. refers to actual person. As a test let us drop E.H. for a moment and use same method with extracts under 'M.', the only other initial vaguely used."

"Right ho," Gorham assented wearily. "Those to E.H. are in the early pages chiefly—all except the last three. M. comes about the middle. And they're a gloomy lot. All about the dead. Read 'em out."

He put a fresh sheet in his typewriter and they began their task. The extracts this time were longer and more conventional in tone. But Gorham's first impression was startlingly confirmed. Read together, they suggested one idea. Bereavement, prayers for comfort in grief, reflections on death, on departed souls, on the feelings of those left behind.

"Some of these are taken from the Burial Service," Gorham said soberly. "The only person we know of Ellen Shields losing by death was her mother. 'M.'—that fits. See here, Li Moh, after the M. extracts no more are initialled."

"The last three E.H.'s come afterwards, the last almost at the end, but no others. You are right, my Gorham. The later entries all seem to refer to the struggles of daily living. A brave and pitiful struggle too. If, as you say, she muddled her texts when she wrote them down, it seems she tried to live by them."

"Those women who made game of her might well have borrowed her standards," Gorham growled. "Miss Hyde was clearer-sighted. Saw something of the real creature beneath the grotesque exterior. But"—he put the papers together in his desk drawer—"we've wasted three hours for nothing, old man. There's nothing here that's useful to our case. Her mother died five years ago, and all the chief E.H. entries were made before that. So if E.H. has some secret that Shields discovered and hated keeping quiet about, it's ancient history, whether it refers to a Hubberd or not. They settled in the Lane eight or nine years ago, so she could have known Ethel. Maybe she liked her before she worked for her!" Grimly, "Lord, I'm dog-tired. Let's go to bed."

Chapter VIII

With the freakishness that governs the acquirement of news value, Ellen Shields, who in life had never roused a spark of human interest in any person with whom she came into daily contact, and to whom, had she been killed in a normal street accident, no one, in all probability, would have given a second thought, in her death became the supreme topic of the week.

The newspapers splashed her name in heavy headlines. People stopped to discuss the murder in the street, hotly arguing their private theories, and Finnet flamed into an unfortunate and disagreeable notoriety.

Communication with the Manchester police produced, on Tuesday morning, a flustered pair who announced themselves as Norman and Maggie Vardon, brother-in-law and sister of deceased.

Mrs. Vardon was a small, neatly made woman with traces of former prettiness in sharpening features and sallow cheeks that had not quite lost the contours of youth.

The husband, a quiet, weak-looking man with a fair complexion and a sandy moustache, was younger than his wife, and possibly under the domination of her quicker temper, though in the presence of the Chief Inspector, and subdued by the official atmosphere of the police station, she deferred to him with becoming meekness. Neither could add to Gorham's knowledge of Ellen's last years, however, for communication between the sisters had latterly been confined to an exchange of cards at Christmas.

When the inquest opened the room was packed with reporters. Evidence of identification was given by Norman Vardon, relative, and Ben Higgs, in whose house deceased had lodged for five years. And when the police had testified to the finding of the body in the front garden of The Laurels, Pound Lane, and medical evidence had established the cause of death as manual strangulation, Edward Hubberd, of The Burrs, Pound Lane, in whose employment deceased had been till her death, and who, apparently, had been the last to see her alive on Saturday evening, was called and subjected to a sharp and damaging examination.

Hubberd's eyes looked tired, and he spoke in a low voice, though with no sign of nervousness. He stuck to the story that he had given the police, but contradicted himself on minor points.

He had come in after six and gone to bed with a headache. No, of course he did not always go to bed when he had a headache; it depended on circumstances. That night everyone was out, it was a broiling hot evening, and it seemed the easiest thing to do.

Yes, he had first spoken to Ellen downstairs, not long after he'd come in. He could not be definite as to whether she was wearing her hat then—not a hat?—well, a woollen thing—beret. He was sure she had it on when she brought sandwiches and ale to his room. What? Sorry, he couldn't remember whether she brought them to him upstairs or not. On second thoughts he believed he had taken them from her in the hall when he was glancing through his letters on the table there and carried them upstairs himself. In fact, he was sure he had. What? How long between his asking for sandwiches and Ellen bringing them? He hadn't asked for food at all. She brought them off her own bat. Time? About an hour, he supposed. What? Of course he hadn't stood in the hall doing nothing for a whole damned hour. He had read his post, circulars, and so on. Probably it had not been anything like an hour in reality. Half, or a quarter, he really couldn't say. He hadn't been watching the time. Why should he be?

At any rate, when she brought the sandwiches to him, either in the hall, or possibly upstairs to his bedroom, deceased had already put on her beret as if she had finished her work and were ready to leave, when, in fact, according to his own assertion, she did not actually leave till nearly nine, two hours later. Did this point strike Mr. Hubberd as peculiar?

There was a red spot in Mr. Hubberd's cheeks by this time, though the rest of his face looked pinched and white.

He hadn't thought about it at all, he said unhappily. He probably was wrong in imagining that he had seen her wearing her beret at all that evening, confusing it with other times when he had noticed it because it had an odd, rather absurd appearance. All he could be sure of was that he saw her for the last time when she brought the sandwiches, and he supposed she left later when he heard the front door slam when he was in bed. His belief was that that was somewhere about nine, possibly before, but he could not swear even to that as he had not looked at his watch.

They let him go at that, not mentioning the finding of the beret in the garage, and he went back to his seat in a silence that was only broken by the rapid scribbling of reporters' pens.

No other witnesses were called, and the inquiry was adjourned for a fortnight.

Lewis Hardwicke followed Hubberd out of the courtroom and walked back with him to Pound Lane.

The two men had known each other in a casual way for years, as neighbours, and occasionally they had called at each other's houses, and played golf together.

After a nod of recognition they went along without speaking till Lewis Hardwicke said gloomily:

"Damned nuisance, this business."

"Filthy."

"Have to sell my house now. Wish I'd done it long ago. Been a white elephant for years; only hung on from sentiment, dislike of making a clean break with the parents' home and that. Tosh, of course. Didn't want to face up to things; now I'll have to pay for shirking. This'll mean a heavy cut in its value." Hubberd nodded. He seemed too full of his own troubles to attend to Hardwicke's. But he made an effort.

"Hard luck. Mine's only rented, luckily. Ethel wanted a flat in Town from the first. Only I couldn't stick the thought of pavements and confined rooms after the East. Didn't realize what decent living cost in England, or the difficulties we'd have over servants—" He stopped abruptly, and for a minute the ghost of the murdered woman rose vividly before them both. Hardwicke said hastily:

"Ever done anything more about your book?"

"Good Lord, no. Dropped it years ago. Used a few of my notes for articles, but expert's stuff is at a discount these days. Not that I'm an expert"—he corrected himself with shocked haste—"or in the same running as my father or old Pine, my cousin, but bright, snappy travel yarns by trippers who've 'done' China in a ten-day Cooks tour—that's the sort of tripe publishers want, illustrated by pretty watercolours done by the author from colour notes at home."

"Authoress, mostly. Tosh by the semi-literate for the semi-educated."

Hubberd nodded, his interest in the subject lapsed. "Remember the Hughes? They've cleared off."

"Gad, they didn't lose much time."

"Damned rats."

"Hughes used to be an amusing bloke. Clarice was always the typical gold-digger, though. Female leech, what? Trouble shows up the seams in one's pals badly, eh?"

"Shows who your friends aren't, at any rate. Damned swine. Come in and have a drink."

They turned into the gate of The Burrs and entered the hall, where dust and disorder added slovenliness to a queer, bleak air of desertion.

Lewis Hardwicke recalled the house as he had first known it, when the Hubberds seemed likely to become a social asset to the neighbourhood; Hubberd's innate taste for good stuff, balancing his wife's love of gay colour, had given the young pair a distinguished setting. He had spent some pleasant evenings here yarning with Ted while Ethel played the accomplished hostess.

Hubberd glanced about with a quick, disgusted look. "Have to get someone to clean up the muck in this place soon. Think the woman you employ would oblige?"

"Blenkinsop? She might. She's got a pack of kids at home; hasn't too much spare time. But I'll ask her if you like."

"She might know someone. The house is far too much for Ethel to manage alone. Ellen wasn't much good, but she was better than no one. Wonder where Ethel is? . . ."

An empty whisky-bottle, standing amidst the littered debris of a meal in the dining-room, promised poorly for their drink. Hubberd picked up a letter that lay on the table, and while he mastered its short sentences the colour left his face. He folded the paper and slipped it into his pocket.

"Sorry, Hardwicke. Ethel has gone over to her mother's. And"— he glanced grimly at the bottle—"as my sweet brother-in-law has obviously got at the whisky it looks as if drinks were off."

"Come into my place instead. I'd ordered stacks in—against a really hilarious homecoming, what? If Ethel has taken Bob along with her she's done a good work, I'd say."

"She hasn't. I mean he wouldn't go home if he were dragged. My ma-in-law is strict T.T. And I don't blame her for putting her foot down, considering the damnable experience she's had with her second venture, and her son. Ethel started a tale that Step-father taught her innocent brother to drink. Bob's mother isn't so credulous. He was a wrong 'un born."

"Can't think how you stuck him so long. He's been asking for a hard kick in the pants since I first saw him. Come on, Hubberd. What you want after all you've gone through this morning is the poison your ma-in-law condemns, and I can do with a quick one myself."

He laid a casual hand on Hubberd's arm, and the touch apparently turned the scale of his hesitation. He followed his leader through the hall on to the steps and slammed the front door behind him. Once in Hardwicke's dining-room, which on the point of cleanliness at any rate was in pleasing contrast with the one they had just left, and, supplied with drinks, the host lounged back in an easy chair opposite to his guest and waited for him to refer to recent events if he wanted to. Presently he did want to.

"Suppose I made an almighty fool of myself before that coroner."

"We-ell. If you're putting up a yarn it's sound policy to be consistent on details, I'd say."

Hubberd nodded.

"Fact was, I'd forgotten the tale I'd told that damn' police inspector when he interviewed me first, on Sunday. Wasn't attending properly to the job. Trying to think out something else while I answered him with half my mind, and it didn't work."

"It wouldn't with Gorham. He wasn't missing anything. He's as shrewd as they're made."

Hubberd glanced across with a sharp frown.

"Hullo! You know the bloke? Not understudying him now, are you?"

Lewis Hardwicke grinned.

"You've told me a fat lot, haven't you? I know Gorham all right. But I don't love him enough to do his dirty work for him. But what you'd better realize is that another interview with him is bound to happen soon, after your ditherings this morning. You'll have to brace yourself to decide what bits of your tale you intend to stick to. It's the details you try to alter that he'll be out to trip you up over."

"What do you suppose the police idea is, Hardwicke?" he said with deepened anxiety. "Do you think they're trying to fasten this murder on to me?"

"The murder happened. It's their job to fasten it on someone—preferably the murderer, of course. For God's sake don't intimate to me you did it, old man. I'd be bound as a citizen to inform the authorities, or risk my precious skin as an accessory."

"Don't be a fool, Hardwicke. I'm not going to intimate to you or anyone else that I murdered the woman. What I want to get at is how I come into the case at all. What the whole filthy show looks like to outsiders at the present time—especially my position in it." He smoothed down his sleek hair with a nervous gesture of both hands, then broke into a sickly grin. "You see, there's been such a hellova row raging at my place ever since Sunday, when those bobbies walked clean into the thick of it, that I've been sort of obsessed—never had time to get abreast of outside thought. You know the police found her cap—or beret, whatever the thing is called—on the floor of my garage, and then asked leave to search the whole premises. Quite civilly. But the iron hand in the velvet glove, eh? Could I refuse?"

"Wouldn't have been the smallest use if you had. They'd have smelt a rat and come back with a search warrant damn' quick, then you'd have had no option."

"Exactly. But could the others see that? The Hughes and Ethel went clean off the deep end over it. Ethel . . ." His face crimsoned in a painful flush. "Oh, well, that doesn't matter. Charles cursed and threw his weight about, till I cut him fairly short, and Clarice called me by every dirty epithet she could think of. Then, when the police cleared off, the girls let fly at each other—kept at it half the night—till it ended in the others packing their traps and sneaking off while I was at the office. I couldn't do a stroke of work, I was so strung up. And when I got home Ethel told me they'd cut and run, and—and—well, we had the father and mother of a row between ourselves, and it ended in Ethel shrieking for Bob to come and protect her from my brutality. You can guess the scene. I told Bob if he was there when I got back I'd knock his head off, and cleared out for a tramp to cool off. When I got home at night Bob had taken my hint, I thought. At any rate, he didn't show up. I didn't see Ethel this morning, before I had to attend that infernal inquest. And, well, there was her note just now." Again he made that harassed gesture with his hands, then jerked his head up. "But you say that bobbie will start questioning me again after the exhibition of idiocy I made of myself in that damned court. And I've simply *got* to understand what the position is before. I haven't even seen a paper. Tell me how the case stands, my dear fellow, if you can."

Hardwicke heaved himself out of his chair and did hospitable things with the glasses.

Hubberd looked as if he were just out of a fever, his eyes bright with anxiety, his face, as he stopped talking, set in haggard lines.

"Gad, he looks as if he hadn't slept for a week—those viragos!" Hardwicke thought. But aloud, as he resumed his seat, he said reflectively: "I see. You want the story as it might be read by a stranger, official or otherwise. Right ho. Here's me, beginning at the beginning, like in Alice. This woman, Ellen Shields, is a native of Finnet, where she lived with a mother and sister before the latter married and went north—you saw her in court this morning, little woman in mourning, with snapping black eyes, sat beside her husband, who gave evidence—and the former died, when Shields went to lodgings at Harlesden. But before she left Finnet she'd formed a roving connection with employers in the place which boiled down eventually to houses in Pound Lane, and was employed still by all of us in turn. How long have you had her?"

"Oh, I don't know." He rubbed his eyes wearily. "She came by fits and starts, when servants left. But she's been coming in daily now for months . . . twelve months or more. I remember her last summer. But does it matter?"

"Only because a fat-headed stranger would want to know. Put it at a year, long enough for her to seem like part of the furniture. She was an ineffectual sort. When you'd summed her up as well-meaning, though, you'd said about the worst of her."

"She was a decent, good-natured woman, and damned religious; a kindly soul, too, and uncomplaining, if she did slop about and make a guy of herself. Get down to brass tacks, Hardwicke; I know what she was like as well as you do. Better."

"Then you'll agree that it wasn't for her sexual attractiveness that she was put out, whatever the motive was," Hardwicke retorted. "So the commonest motive of murder that the normal stranger would suggest is a clean wash-out. Well, here's Saturday evening. She'd worked at your house all day, and left in the evening when everybody else was out, and you were upstairs in bed, about nine o'clock, after pottering about alone downstairs for hours, so you told the police. The Lane is an unfrequented spot. Mrs. Manstead and her fool of a companion are away, so never, like Mrs. Gill, looked out of their windows. My house was empty. Hyde had cleared off to Town in his car about seven, and Miss Hyde and her servant weren't anywhere near the Lane side of Innisfree garden till ten. So there were no observers in the Lane till ten, when Miss Hyde's dog was reported missing. And she and Eliza, the maid, charged up and down, here, there, and everywhere, calling him, till 11.30."

"I heard 'em!" Hubberd broke in impatiently. "But all this is irrelevant, Hardwicke."

"Far from it, old man. Wait and hear. The bobbies found her body hidden behind some bushes in my front garden, damn them, at five to eleven on Sunday morning. She'd been stripped naked, strangled by hands, and a man's jacket stuck on her. Gorham was there. He decided she'd been killed and shoved where she was found almost directly afterwards on Saturday evening. That is, between nine, when she was supposed to have left your house, and ten, when Miss Hyde began to patrol the Lane. Now you see where Miss Hyde comes in. If her dog had not been lost and she had stopped indoors the time could scarcely have been so definitely fixed, see? Wherever she was murdered and stripped—and about that I believe they've nothing still but conjecture to go on—the body must have been conveyed to The Laurels in a car, carried in the gate by the murderer, and dumped behind the bushes, which are fairly thick, and which screened it till morning, when the road was clear, the whole job taking perhaps a couple of minutes.

"But Gorham's certain it was done *before* Miss Hyde appeared on the scene. I needn't go into his reasons, but a man of his experience isn't likely to be wrong when he makes a definite statement like that. So there it is. After nine, and before ten. Say in the first real spot of twilight after 9.30. Because the murderer would want the cover of darkness, and he'd want to get rid of the body out of his car as soon as possible. Why my garden was chosen is open to question. He may have been sailing round looking for a dumping-ground and noticed the house was empty—closed windows and so on. Or he may have known it to be empty and made it his direct objective. What?"

"Oh, well, sorry old man, but couldn't it all have been done on—on your ground?"

"What? Murder! Stripping the whole bag of tricks in a spot of garden in full view of any chance passer-by? I can't take it! Besides, that bright idea occurred to our police friends, and they kindly searched, not only the garden, but my house itself, for signs of the job, and gave it a sweet, clean bill of health, damn their eyes. Well, that's the lot, as far as my knowledge goes. There's an intensive search out already for the woman's clothes, and the strange jacket she was wearing may give them a clue. They wouldn't let me near enough to it to discover if it had any significant marks. Then, you say, her beret was found in your garage?"

"Her coat was in the kitchen too. But they found nothing else. Except the beret under the car-wheel, stained with mud from it."

"Had you had your car out, old man?"

"No. Not on Saturday at all. I told the police so. Unluckily, the mud on the wheels was wet, so they didn't believe me."

"Hell," said Hardwicke, perturbed, "and then you dithered as to whether she was wearing the thing or not when you last spoke to her!"

"I tell you I wasn't attending properly to what I was answering at the time. Besides, he didn't fish up the beret till afterwards, so it didn't seem to matter then. And this morning I couldn't for the life of me remember what I *had* said."

"I suppose you're not really muddled as to when and where you saw her last, or whether she was wearing the thing or not?"

"Good Lord, no. I can see her now, plain as a pikestaff!" Lewis Hardwicke jerked in his chair, but his brows were corrugated in intense thought.

"Can't you suggest some point, however trifling, that would back up your statement that you were in bed at 9.30?" he growled, after a minute of silence so strained that his voice, breaking it, sounded loud and harsh. "Is your room in front? If so, someone could have seen your light. Miss Hyde, for instance, when she came right down the Lane."

"Not a hope. I didn't have one. When it got too dark to read, not that I'd read much—better cut out that bit, old man. Say I lay in the twilight thinking things over. Had a lot to think over."

Hardwicke jerked again, impatiently.

"Which of your crowd came in first—the girls?"

"No, Bob."

"Well, did you speak to him, man? What time was that?"

"Before closing-time," Bob's brother-in-law said grimly. "The hall clock hadn't struck eleven. So he'd probably been kicked out. I certainly didn't speak to him—or see him. To hear him stumbling up the stairs was quite enough. I knew the stage he'd reached by the hymn he was crooning. And I was in no mood to endure maudlin penitence." He paused a moment, then asked uncertainly: "What are the police doing, do you think?"

"Ask me another, old man. I'm not in their confidence." Silence again.

Even after the broad hints he had given, Lewis Hardwicke was doubtful if Hubberd had taken in the extreme seriousness of his position. His face still wore that queer, stupid, withdrawn look of mental preoccupation with some inward problem, as if less than half his attention was to spare for the immediate need. Yet if ever a man wanted all his wits about him at a given moment Hubberd did at this crisis, with Gorham watching out for his slightest slip. And Ethel had chosen today of all days to bolt and leave him alone to face the music. The rot they talked of women's love and loyalty! This woman, whether or no she believed her husband guilty of murder—and it was on the cards that that was the cause of her deserting him—had done her damnedest to confirm police suspicions that he was by bucketing off like that. For all she knew or cared he might be under arrest now, facing trial and a hideous death.

Edward Hubberd put down his untasted glass and stumbled to his feet.

"I see. Well, thanks very much, Hardwicke." He picked up his hat and stick. "Ought to get on to the office, you know. Northbourne. Stacks of work waiting. Langton's had to do my job as well as his own this morning. The Inspector will find me there if he wants me."

Lewis Hardwicke got up and came gloomily to the door with him.

"Anything I can do, you know . . ." he muttered.

Hubberd nodded, and ran down the steps.

The other turned back, almost envying him for having an office that claimed his time. He had completed his contract with his paper when he sent in his last article from Spain, and, sick of his roving, unsettled life in a world where slaughter, hatred, and misery had swamped, as it seemed to his wearied senses, all the sweet fruits that centuries of civilization could have given to humanity, had definitely renounced his job.

He wanted peace and quiet, away from the sound of guns and bombing aeroplanes, and the sight of uniformed battalions of men, organized and drilled, and despatched to the shambles by rival Governments with as little volition of their own, and as helpless to escape their doom, as the beasts driven into the stock-yards at Chicago. He was not ill in body, but he was sick to the depth of his being of the hideous *bouleversement* of modern life, its mad party cries, its emptiness, its crazy distortion or suppression of natural human instincts.

He had come home to find—if not happiness—at least contentment of spirit in England, where individual freedom still existed, where war's destructive powers had not laid waste, and horrors could be forgotten.

And here, at home, in the garden where his mother had pottered about with her trowel and watering-can, in the ancient, shady hat that his father and he chaffed her about and derisively called Gampus from some obscure family jest, this thing had happened. This sordid, brutal, filthy thing. Fouling his own nest. The one decent spot to which his imagination had turned back to find escape and rest. He could never see or think of the place again without the image of that pitiful, unbeautiful, stark form sprawled across the grass out there.

His cherished visions of peace and restfulness had been sheer delusions all; there was no love, no loveliness, no tranquillity anywhere. He might as well be back in Spain, where life was too strenuous to admit of one's sitting down and whining, as he was doing at this moment.

Then suddenly he remembered a long room full of brown shadows. Some of the bitterness faded from his eyes. He would go to Innisfree.

Chapter IX

Chief Inspector Gorham sat at the desk in the police station with a large-scale map of the district spread out before him. He had seen the two men, Hubberd and Hardwicke, walk away together after the inquest proceedings were over, and knew that his next move must be an interview with Edward Hubberd. But first he wanted light on certain minor points, and meantime Hubberd was being trailed. He was probably well aware of the fact by this time, too, and if it fretted or angered him, so much the better. Either emotion, anger, or nervousness might serve to loosen his tongue.

He had been engaged on this case for the best part of three days, and so far progress had been negligible, except that some suspects were eliminated, which narrowed down the field of research but did not otherwise tend to enrich it. Ben Higgs, if he had ever been seriously in the running, was definitely out of it. The wedding-party had made no small stir in Harlesden circles, and Higgs had been present at every successive stage of the festivities barring the actual wedding itself. The mother of the bride had, with little encouragement, poured out a delighted and voluble account of the day's proceedings to an interested young man who called at her house on Monday, beginning with a minute description of the bridesmaids' frocks and concluding with grateful mention of Ben's energetic help in putting up the beds that had been dismantled before he and his mother went home after midnight. By a clinching stroke of luck one of the bridesmaids was an attendant at the cinema to which the party had adjourned at eight o'clock, and the manager had made quite a festive occasion of it, receiving the whole party at the door, and standing a round of ices in the interval at 9.15, when the lights were up, and Ben Higgs, rising to the occasion, had treated every girl to a beribboned box of chocolates.

So much for Ben Higgs.

Bob Dent was also eliminated in a manner less creditable to himself. His story that he had been on the premises of the 'Fox and Goose', in the bar, on the bowling-green, or in the billiard-room was substantiated by several reliable witnesses, but the landlord, drawing Norris aside when he heard him questioning the barman, added a further item that was scarcely for the public ear. The barman had already testified to the fact that Dent seemed unusually flush with cash that night, pulling out a pound note, as well as silver, from his pocket when he paid for his first drink. The man's impecuniousness was well known at the 'Fox and Goose', where his cadging habits formed a perennial subject of jocularity among customers, but when the barman jokingly inquired if he had won the Irish Sweep by any chance he laughed and explained that for once his stingy brother-in-law had been induced to loosen up.

The landlord prefaced his remarks to Norris, whom he knew well, by saying that it was none of his business to criticize his customers as long as they behaved quiet and respectable in his house; Dent was the type that was kept an eye on, and allowed no rope, and on Saturday night, being able to pay for more than he could carry, was firmly put out at 10.30 when he showed a tendency towards making himself a nuisance. He, the landlord, like everyone else in the village, heard about the murder on Sunday before noon, and was sorry, for he had known Mrs. Shields in earlier days, though he didn't remember ever doing more than pass the time of day with Miss Shields when they met in the street. Still, it brought it home, in a manner of speaking, when a lady that you knew by sight got done to death.

Therefore, when the greensman discovered this old purse, with E.S. written in ink under the flap, empty, among some bushes behind a seat by the bowling-green, Monday morning, swearing it hadn't been there Saturday tea-time, because he happened to have weeded some nettles off of the bed then, he had told the chap to shut his mouth about it and intended to bring it round to the Sergeant, only the Sergeant had dropped in first.

"Say," said Norris slowly, looking at the shabby object in his hand, "this could have been hers, left at The Burrs by mistake some time, and picked up by some other member of the household—Mr. Dent, of course, being one of them. Was it certain that it was dropped behind that seat Saturday evening? Could it not as easily have been Sunday?"

All the landlord could say was that Mr. Hubberd never came at all, and though Mr. Hughes played an occasional game, and the ladies had strolled down with him to watch once or twice, none of them had been through the gates of the green Sunday, and only Mr. Dent on Saturday evening. He had done his duty, handing that purse to the sergeant, seeing it was initialled E.S., the circumstances being what they were. But they could easily have been someone else's, neither E. nor S. being uncommon initials—"Smith, Sullivan, Sparrow, Seaton, Simms..."

"Sayers, Soane, Sopwith, Sinclair, Sergeant, Saunders, Soutar—"

"That's right," the landlord enthusiastically returned. "Lots of names beginning with 'S', and with 'E' too: Emmeline, Elsie, Edith, Edwin, Ethel, Esau, Everard, Eric, Ernest . . ."

"Eleazer, Elizabeth, Ephraim, Eustace, Eleanor—and why stop there if time wasn't getting on?" retorted Norris, grinning, and as he walked away he left the other muttering, "Edmund, Eva, Esther, Edward . . ."

He hinted at this possibility to his superior when he handed over the purse and details of its discovery, but Gorham shook his head.

"Everything could almost always be something else," he said lucidly. "But this was Ellen's all right. What's more, it showed she'd been paid, and that swine pinched the purse—out of her bag, or, more probably, off the dresser or somewhere when he went out by the back door. He said he went to the kitchen on purpose to say good night to her, and she was washing dishes in the scullery. That's how it was. The only point is, who paid her? Mrs. Hubberd probably, before she went out. Then"—his tone was thoughtful—"what happened next? She'd miss her purse at once, and know only Dent could have taken it. Did she march straight off to complain to Hubberd? Or wait a bit, brooding—?"

"If she went and accused his wife's brother of stealing her money, doesn't that provide a reason for their quarrelling, sir?"—eagerly.

Gorham looked dubious.

"Did it strike you that Hubberd loved his lout of a brother-in-law so much that he'd want to slay anyone who cast asparagus at his lily reputation?" he demanded. "I'll go so far as to allow she spoke to him about it . . . she had to have money to get home. I think she waited a bit, though, probably feeling upset; oh yes, she had to tell him. When she was ready to go. In her beret. And upstairs, I think. I don't think Hubberd murdered her because of that, though he'd scarcely like it—"

"Come to that, both he and deceased, being daily in the house, must have had a good notion what Dent was capable of," Norris put in. "If he'd descend to pinch the wages of a poor thing like her, he wouldn't stop at lifting a bob or two wherever it lay handy."

"No, there's that."

"Yet he seemed real fond of his sister, and she of him; clung round his neck howling when we left that bedroom. Now you mention it, Mr. Hubberd did look disgusted," said Norris. "But he'd looked as if he were going to be sick all through. This would give a hold on Dent, supposing you wanted to put him through it again, but it can't be pinned down on him."

"No. It's a useful bit of information, but Dent's out of the main case, and so is Higgs. His alibi has been confirmed at every point. Now run through the rest of your report. What about the clothes?"

"Still missing, sir. I've had every inch of Finnet Beeches searched, on the line that Hubberd's car could have picked up that clay when it was run out after the murder to drop the clothes somewhere."

"Um! Look at this map, Norris. Pound Lane lies here, between West Avenue and Chetwynd Avenue. The Burrs at one corner . . . where the Lane carries on to Finnet Beeches, on West Avenue, Innisfree at the southern end of Chetwynd. The garage gate is actually in Chetwynd Avenue, though the garden gate is in the Lane. Behind those four houses there seem to be just market gardens stretching right to the buildings along Harrow Main Road, into which both these avenues lead."

"That's right, sir. The two avenues curve downward to Market Parade—that is, the shopping-centre of New Finnet, where the banks and cinemas are. The Finnet brook divides New Finnet from the old village on the hill, so if you want to reach the church at the top of the old High Street, or the station on London Road that curves round the base of the hill, you've got to cross the bridge."

"Who owns those market gardens?" Gorham asked, his glance still on the map.

"They were really allotments till quite recently, sir, but now I hear Ewings, the market gardener, has bought the land. His old ground was behind the station, but there's a lot of small building going on there, and he's sold his land piecemeal till he's only got his bare cottage left."

"There's not much in point of distance between the two avenues," Gorham murmured. "The Innisfree lot would naturally go down Chetwynd to the shops and church and station, while The Burrs crowd would use West Avenue. I imagine Shields was an exception, and liked walking from the station by Chetwynd Avenue and the Lane, probably to keep a friendly eye on her other employers as she passed their houses. Is Finnet Beeches Road much frequented?"

"Not much, sir. You see, The Beeches is really a private estate, and the road through, being private, is shut in by gates. But it doesn't lead anywhere much except to Finnet Beeches Halt, and not many trains stop there."

Gorham folded the map.

"Now give me your report on Hughes' movements."

"I saw Mr. Murgatroyd, who lives in a semi-detached villa in North Harrow, his mother keeping house for him. He confirmed Mr. Hughes' story that he arrived there on Saturday evening about nine. The mother I did not see. Mr. Murgatroyd was very frank and breezy, described it as a stag party, and referred me to any of his other guests to confirm that 'Good old Charley', as he called him, was the life and soul of the evening, and that two men living in Kew gave him a lift home about 1.30. I had a feeling he'd been got at before I called yesterday evening. He was so pat. But he was definite as to the times.

"Then for the cinema inquiry. I gathered, after a lot of casual chat with the attendants, that Mrs. Hughes was there first. She bought chocs, from a girl who knew her, about 8.15, and was then alone. But later, while the big picture was on—it started at 9.30—the girl noticed she had changed her seat to the side aisle and another woman was beside her. To get that closer, I tackled the commissionaire, who knew Mrs. Hubberd by sight. He stated that she'd run up the steps in a hurry—he couldn't give the time, but it was after the lights were put on, and he fancied she had stepped out of a car farther along the pavement, but, what with a bus stopping in between and a crowd of people getting out and mounting the steps with her, he couldn't be certain. The ticket-girl, who also knew her, said she snatched up her ticket, and looked red in the face, as if she was upset about something. The commissionaire saw both ladies leave together at the end of the show, just before eleven. Do you want me to go further into that, sir?"

"No-o. That's enough for the women. I'd like the time Hughes arrived at that party more closely fixed, though. Give me his address. I'll look him up myself in the City, and you might try to catch the mother when he is out of the way."

He pocketed the slip of paper, glanced at his watch, and rose.

"You know, of course, that the Hughes left Pound Lane yesterday," he said. "They are located at the Conquest Hotel, Russell Street, apparently planted on his brother, who runs it, since they'd made The Burrs too hot to hold them."

The telephone rang, and Gorham picked it up.

"Hullo? Yes, the Chief Inspector, Gorham, speaking. Well?"

"Mrs. Hubberd left The Burrs with a suitcase while the inquest was being held, and has gone to 14 Locust Gardens, Ealing, her mother's house," he said when he put it down. "I must get on to Hubberd at once . . . hullo, hullo!" The instrument rang shrilly again, and he listened impatiently.

"What—with Mr. Hardwicke? Yes, I know that. Where is he now? Went into The Burrs, then out again directly, and both went into The Laurels for half an hour, after which he—where? Northbourne? Oh, his office. Right. Stop where you are till I come along—unless he quits, of course, man. It's your job to keep him tailed up."

"That's Hubberd," he remarked to the sergeant, once more putting down the receiver. "Found his wife had bolted, I suppose. Had a talk with Hardwicke, and is now in his office, where I hope he'll stop till I can reach him. Hardwicke seems to be butting in a good deal—first Miss Hyde, and now Hubberd. Just run through again what you reported on Hardwicke last night. Then I must go."

The Chief Inspector drove to Northbourne and found the office of the new racing-track without difficulty.

The place seemed to be still in course of erection, for building materials and scaffolding were about an uncompleted frontage, and he was shown, first by a workman, then by a girl clerk, through a concrete passage into a temporary office, where Hubberd sat at his desk.

The manager looked even more harassed than he had done at the inquest, but he received Gorham civilly, and without any betrayal of surprise.

"Obviously expected me," thought Gorham. "That's Hardwicke. Damn Hardwicke!" He murmured something about the building. The office was a bare room, plainly furnished with a desk, a file and safe, and a couple of wooden chairs besides the one occupied by

Hubberd, and the boarded walls were adorned with printed bills and advertisements.

"Yes, rather a mess as yet," Hubberd remarked mechanically, as if he had repeated the explanation often before. "But the place is still under construction. It takes time to get a show like this completed, and the public quarters had naturally to have first consideration."

"Quite," said Gorham. "Has it been going long?"

"Three years, and successful beyond our wildest anticipations. I've been with the company from the start. This office is only a temporary building, but we hope to move into our *permanent* quarters next spring. You wanted to see me about something, Mr.—Gorham? I had to take the morning off for that inquest, and I've got a lot of work to get through."

It struck Gorham, from the unnatural tidiness of his desk, that he had done nothing to wipe off arrears before his own appearance; that he had, in fact, been sitting with idle hands, but he nodded acceptance of the hint and came straight to the point.

"It is, of course, in reference to your evidence this morning, Mr. Hubberd. You realize that it is essential to fix the time at which deceased left your house as closely as possible. Your house was shut up this morning, and no answer could be obtained. Is your wife not at home?"

"No"—coolly. "She has gone to stay with her mother till something can be fixed up about domestic help. A house of that size cannot possibly be run without some sort of service. The Hughes left us yesterday, as you probably know already. I'll be glad if you will leave my wife out of it. It was made quite clear to you on Sunday and this morning that she was out of the house the whole evening on Saturday."

"Yes, I understood that. But her absence leaves us solely dependent on your memory to fix those times, you see. Would it help to clarify things to run through your whole day—get it in sequence, so to speak? You were here on Saturday morning?"

"No, I had to go to Town on the company's business. I went straight from Finnet station to Holborn by the 10.30. There, after doing some banking business, I called on our agent who supplies furniture, etcetera, as we need it, and he took me down to various warehouses in Whitechapel, where we were occupied for the rest of the morning. Then we parted. I had a late lunch in the City with a solicitor friend of mine who's been putting through a small job for us, and we lingered to chat a bit. Finally, I went back to Carter's, the agent—whose office is in his flat in Great Compton Street—and worked over the revised figures of an estimate he is drawing out for office furniture. His wife gave us tea; but relatives of hers having turned up in Town unexpectedly, we had to put off the dinner and show we had planned, so I was at a loose end and went home."

"Where, as you were expecting to be out, no dinner was provided," Gorham murmured tentatively.

"Exactly. I'd told my wife I was due to take the Carters out."

"And you're not on the telephone, I see. Then you reached home—when?"

"As I told you, about 6.30. May have been a few minutes before."

"Your brother-in-law was still in the house then, but the others were out?"

"Yes. Ellen said Clarice and Charles had gone off in the morning. My wife had had an early cup of tea and gone over to Ealing."

"How soon after your return would you say that Mr. Dent went out?"

"Just long enough for him to try and fail to touch me for half a quid," Hubberd said grimly. On the subject of his dislike of, and contempt for, his wife's brother he showed no sign of reticence. "He slouched out of the dining-room in the sulks. I heard him speak to Ellen in the kitchen, then he cleared off."

"Then was it before or after he left that you had your first talk with Miss Shields in the hall?"

Hubberd looked startled for a second, then collected himself.

"Oh, after. I told you on Sunday. She came out of the kitchen while I was glancing over the afternoon post on the hall table, and I asked where everyone was and heard what I've just given you. Then she said that there was no preparation for dinner, and I said I'd have some ale and go upstairs, and she was to rake up what supper she could find for herself and go off when she liked. She was upset over some dish she had broken earlier in the day, and looked worried."

"Did you do anything more—any sort of job or that—before going upstairs, do you remember?"

"No—o. I ran through an advertisement catalogue of electrical appliances, I think, then decided I'd go up and change and go out for dinner. It was while I was changing that I decided I'd stop where I was, and lay down."

Gorham thought, exasperated: "Every time one questions the fellow he tells a fresh yarn." But his tone maintained its smooth friendliness as he tried a new gambit.

"About those sandwiches. Do you think she brought them out of sheer thoughtfulness, or to make an excuse for a further chat?"

Hubberd made an uneasy movement, and a gleam of anger showed in his eyes.

"Which do you guess yourself, Chief Inspector?" he asked, with sarcasm that was rather overdone.

"I'd say it was both, Mr. Hubberd," was the calm reply "Did she not make a complaint to you?"

"Well, if you must have it, she did," Hubberd burst out angrily. "But it's no earthly concern of yours. She was upset by something my beautiful brother-in-law had done. I made it all right with her, and that was that?"

"I see. This was in your bedroom, I suppose?"

"Why should you suppose it?"

"You admitted this morning it was possibly upstairs," Gorham said patiently. "She had to make the sandwiches. You said you just ran through the catalogue—leaflet—whatever it was, and went up. What's the object of trying to make a mystery about it? Was there any reason why the woman shouldn't come to your bedroom?"

"What the devil do you mean? Of course there was no reason. And I'm not making a mystery. It simply doesn't seem to me in the least important whether she came upstairs or not."

"Then why are you trying to confuse what is, as you say, a quite simple point? You either went down again yourself or she came up to you. Which was it?"

"All right. She came to my room. Now what? Oh that beret, I suppose. So far as I can remember, she was wearing it—dressed to go. Now are you satisfied?"

"Nearly. You spoke about the sandwiches—"

"Naturally. She said she'd found an end of boiled bacon and cut them from it, and I thanked her."

"You were in bed?"

"On it; in pyjamas."

"Then she broke into her complaint? You can't tell me what it was about?"

"Something she'd mislaid. She thought Bob must have shifted it; at any rate she couldn't find it."

"So you made it up to her. Did you get up?"

"No, she handed me my wallet from the dressing-table—"

He stopped. But Gorham ignored the betrayal.

"You had no doubt of her honesty, Mr. Hubberd?"

"Not a shadow—then or ever." The words rang out with bitter sincerity.

"I see. Now let us get back to these times. Since you spoke to her in the hall you had lingered about downstairs and then undressed—not too quickly perhaps—and she had finished her work, made the sandwiches, and taken off her working apron and dressed to go. How long did all that take, do you suppose?"

"Oh, I don't know," Hubberd growled sullenly. "I'd heard her pottering about for ages, and she didn't go at once when she cleared out of my room. It seemed hours before I heard the door slam. Then I noticed the light was changing. I remembered one evening in Siam. G—d, the summer in London is suffocating! What do you want? The time she left? I can't put it nearer than I did before; somewhere round nine, within half an hour or so of sunset, I suppose."

"Let's try it backwards. Did you look at the time when you had to switch on the light? After the slam of the door, I take it?"

"I didn't switch it on."

"Do you mean you were asleep?"

"No. I mean I didn't have a light at all. When—when it got too dark to—er—read I just lay in the twilight till I suppose I dozed off."

"Was it before, or after, your last interview with Ellen Shields that you heard the car driven in?"

Hubberd stared for a second, then leapt to his feet, his face crimson with fury.

"I never heard the car at all. It never went out on Saturday at any time. Are you trying to set a trap for me, you damned, insolent police spy?"

"Abuse won't help you, Mr. Hubberd." Gorham was grave, untouched by the other's blazing anger. "Your window overlooks the garage. The mud on those wheels was picked up on the Finnet Beeches Road while the stretch they are excavating for sewage operations was still soaking wet from overflow from the cock used by the workmen. The men stopped work at noon Saturday. When I went over the spot on Sunday afternoon late the ground was rapidly drying out. The clay on those wheels was still damp on Sunday at 2.40. The car must have been over that ground on Saturday evening. If, as you maintain, you were in your room the whole evening, not even reading after sunset, you must have heard when the car was driven in. You see the implication? Ellen Shields was already murdered by then. The car was run right over her beret in your garage. Her torn beret." He rose and picked up his hat. The man before him was grey-faced, his eyes glaring. "Have you anything more to say?" Hubberd clutched the back of his chair with whitened knuckles.

"Yes, just this. Clear out before I kick you into the street." Gorham nodded, and quietly, with no undue haste, opened the door. Then, pausing, he turned to ask an apparently crazy question.

"I'm told you've lived in the Far East, Mr. Hubberd. Have you ever gone, or heard of, lion-hunting in China?"

Hubberd, in the midst of his rage, stared as if completely taken aback. Had this stolid-looking police officer taken sudden leave of his senses?

"Lion-hunting? In China? Is this some insolent joke?"

"No. A simple question. Have you?"

"I don't know what you're talking about. Get out, you ignorant bobby. There are no lions in China."

"I thought not. Thanks," the Chief Inspector agreed with a faint smile, and went out, closing the door quietly behind him.

Chapter X

On Tuesday morning, instead of retiring as usual to her desk, Miss Hyde walked out into the garden.

This disturbance of the normal order worried Eliza, and while she cleared the breakfast-table she cast anxious glances through the open windows at the slight figure moving quietly beside the flower-beds.

On the table lay the morning mail, chiefly addressed to L. V. Hyde, Esq. Miss Hyde invariably dealt with his business correspondence, proofs, press-cuttings, letters from agents and editors, but today she had left it untouched.

Eliza, who after years in an author's household could distinguish the various envelopes without difficulty, crossly sorted the mail into piles, advertisements, press-cuttings in their neat brown wrappers, two bundles of proofs, a couple of magazines, a thick envelope, addressed to Miss Ella V. Hyde, from the bank, and carried out her tray.

But Miss Hyde's thoughts were far from the garden, though her eyes noticed the smallest change that had taken place in bud or leaf, so intimate was she with every shrub and plant put in with her own hands, cherished and encouraged through every stage of growth with the patience that is born of skill and knowledge.

She had always employed a man for the rough work in the kitchen garden, for the homely aspect of most vegetables made no appeal to her beauty-loving spirit, but her flowers she had jealously tended herself till a brief attack of lumbago, which made stooping an impossibility, caused her to engage Mr. Moh.

She did not dismiss him when her powers returned, however, because she realized in the odd, quiet, obliging little man exactly her own attitude towards beauty.

She had glimpsed his face, convulsed with anger, before the smashed delphiniums.

She had worked late on Saturday evening in order to forget those mangled flowers, till the loss of Robin supplanted that distress with one still more acute.

Her restless sleep that night was haunted by nightmare visions of the dog struggling in a trap, its paws half torn off, its screams unheard, its wounded, bloodstained little body stiffening at last in helpless death.

Robin was safe, his hurt incomparably less than those her imagination had conjured up. Yet that cut and bruise that Lewis Hardwicke had dressed so skilfully had had the effect of hardening emotion into cold, pitiless resolution.

And now, overshadowing that unchanged resolution, lay the terrible shadow of Ellen Shields' murder.

The horror and pity of it darkened her thoughts, flooding her memory with scenes from those months, years ago, when Ellen had lived in the house through the ghastly period of Sydney's illness, when the hospital nurse had been dispensed with.

He was an exacting patient, but the physical nursing had been nothing beside the untiring demands he made on her spirit. His restless need to be entertained during every waking moment exhausted her vitality almost to the point of extinction.

The very remembrance of the mental strain of that time filled her with shuddering revulsion. And how willing, and kind, and exasperating poor Ellen had been through it all, with her invaluable good temper, her nerve-racking capacity for spilling and upsetting and dropping things, her extraordinarily irritating trick of leaving trays and towels and unsightly utensils on floors and stairs, her habit of crashing about, and mislaying things in the very disorder she created!

And through all had been the pressing need of money for the expenses of the illness. The idea of utilizing his constant, gossipy chatter of life in the East in the framework of the stories had proved an immense source of entertainment to Sydney. But in result it chained her—with her typewriter—to his bedside, and later his sofa, in a perpetual mental and nervous strain that made Ellen's idiosyncrasies seem the final, unendurable straw.

She had been as thankful to pack the poor, faithful creature out of the house (with liberal thanks and pay) as she had been to see Sydney drive away to enjoy the final stages of his convalescence at Brighton.

With Eliza, who came to her soon after those hideous months, in charge in the kitchen, with order restored and a blessed quiet reigning—at least, during Sydney's frequent absences from home, for former harsh experience of human impatience with deafness had taught Eliza to be chary of unnecessary speech—no need had arisen to employ Ellen again in any domestic capacity, nor could she have brought herself to do so had need been never so pressing.

But now, Ellen being dead, she remembered odd, touching acts of affection, sloppy cups of tea brought her at night while she worked by Sydney's bedside when he could neither sleep himself nor endure her leaving him; the human goodness in Ellen's sleep-reddened eyes, the willingness of her kind, inefficient hands.

She passed her fingers across her eyes as if to clear their sight, but today there was no comfort in her flowers.

Mr. Moh, watching her slow progress, noticed that she made none of her usual little intimate gestures towards the plants, stopping here or there to smell a rose, or snip off a dead blossom, or straighten a drooping flower.

When she reached his side at the end of the paved walk she stood in silence while he rose and indicated with a wave of one hand the pots of chrysanthemums that he was sorting on the ground.

"Does Madam agree to the placing of these in a bed now empty of loveliness?" he ventured humbly.

"I saw that you cleared it on Sunday. That was kind of you," she said. Then the gardener in her broke irrepressibly through her preoccupation. "But surely it is too late to plant out chrysanthemums, isn't it?"

"Not if suitable care be taken. In China, as probably Madam knows, such sturdy plants as these are induced with careful processes to carry rosettes of blooms of many shades, each of one stem bearing a quaint and beautifully hued posy. In England that is not done. But these, the cuttings we took last year of red and copper and golden flowers, will give a massed display of colour in September."

"Did you know Ellen Shields, Mr. Moh?"

"By sight only, madam."

"That detective, Gorham, has he found out how she—how she died?"

"Worthless stories are repeated by foolish lips, but nothing is yet known, madam. The inquest opens this morning."

"Will you tell me if anything is discovered, and also when the funeral is to take place?"

"Unless there is unforeseen hindrance the funeral is arranged for tomorrow morning at ten o'clock. I will bring definite word to Madam later; when the inquest is over."

"Thank you." She was turning away. "About those chrysanthemums. If you would like to have any for yourself, take them. Do what you please with the rest."

She hastened towards the house as a car, hooting impatiently, drove up to the garage gate.

Mr. Moh walked thoughtfully along a cross-path and opened the gate in answer to a peremptory shout.

"Hope you took long enough coming!" Mr. Hyde growled, and drove in to the garage entrance, where he got out of the car, carrying his clubs, and strode towards the house without further acknowledgment of the man's services.

When Lewis Hardwicke came to the garden gate of Innisfree, after parting from Hubberd, he was surprised and annoyed to see the celebrated author seated very much at his ease in the flowery enclosure that he had chosen to regard as exclusively the setting of Miss Hyde.

Hyde had selected the prettiest spot in the garden, a circular space in the centre of the paved walk where wings continually fluttered about a bird-bath, for his chair. He evidently imagined himself to be at work, for a sheaf of galley-proofs lay across the table in front of him, which also bore bottles and a glass; but all round his chair were newspapers tossed down, some sheets of which sprawled over the flower borders.

The whole atmosphere—the lovely spell of the place—was, to Lewis' heated imagination, ruined by his presence. He had come, on a sudden, undefined impulse, to seek the peace that had soothed his overstrained nerves on Sunday, and here was a fellow who had changed his sanctuary into the semblance of a cheap beer-garden with his litter of papers and drinks.

He decided to beat a retreat, for, apart from disappointment, Hyde was exactly the type of person he wanted to avoid just now, a part of that noisy, bustling outside world of which he was heartily sick. But he was a second too late. Hyde had turned, and was waving a boisterous welcome.

"Hello! Hello! Come in!" The intruder reluctantly approached, and the other scrutinized him with a look of puzzle that dissolved in doubtful recognition.

"Cheers, old boy! It's Hardwicke, isn't it? Come along and give a poor hard-worked scribbler the news of the Town! G—d!"—he took off his glasses and dropped them on the proofs, feeling his eyes with tender fingers—"this glaring light plays the very deuce with my unlucky eyes."

Hardwicke remembered vaguely that the historic illness that found frequent mention in Hyde's conversation had one effect in temporary blindness. But he looked fit enough now, his long legs stretched out, his skin still walnut in hue from tropical suns; but his big figure slouching at an ungainly angle in his chair, showed, with the curves of cheek and jaw, a weakness for good living that threatened in a few years a demand for slimming restrictions.

His eyes, when he stopped rubbing them, showed themselves to be pale blue and rather prominent, but they beamed on his visitor with the cordiality of a bored man who sees his tedium unexpectedly relieved.

He stretched his arms with a yawn as if he were stiff with the effort of concentration. But as the proofs slithered to the ground Hardwicke's fault-finding mood noted morosely that the page disfigured with corrections in a bold, untidy hand was Number 1.

"'Morning, Hyde," he grunted. "If you've read all those beastly papers you know a damned lot more news than I do, and you've not done much with those proofs either."

Mr. Hyde chuckled and pushed the fallen slips aside with his foot.

"They're hard work, my boy. Jane can run through the rest. I can't be bothered with the silly rot!"

"Rot? Your own immortal effusions? This is a pleasing break into candour!"

Hyde chuckled again, but he looked annoyed.

"One has to pay the penalty for one's place on the permanent shelves that you lucky journalists escape!" he said with a hint of good-humoured patronage. "You can't guess the weariness that proof-reading induces in the creative artist who has to dissect the finely woven texture of nervous prose to pin down a misplaced comma or period—"

"For the Lord's sake, don't waste your periods on me, or your prose either, Hyde," Hardwicke interrupted with more feeling than courtesy. "Keep all that tosh for the half-baked literary neophytes at your next Foyle's luncheon. Is Miss Hyde at home?"

"No, she's in Town, I believe," Hyde murmured rather sulkily. "Want her specially?"

"Oh, I only thought she'd like to hear the result of the inquest."

"Oh yes, you've been having your little local dramas in Finnet."

Mr. Hyde sat up, frowning as if his eyes hurt intolerably; and taking a case from his pocket, and extracting a pair of dark spectacles, he fitted them carefully on.

"I spent the week-end at Yorker's Manor, and so missed the whole show. My word, Hardwicke, they've turned that place into one of the best-run club-houses in England. The food's first class, and besides doing you well—it's as good as an A1 hotel for modern comfort and service—you meet as jolly a crowd of fellows there as you could wish. You must come along with me some time and I'll introduce you to old Talbot, the secretary. He's a great pal of mine."

"Thanks, I don't need an introduction there. I knew Talbot long before he succeeded in turning Yorker's from a decent, exclusive little club into a sort of bloated caravanserai for guzzling guinea-pigs and their fat wives. If you like that type of thing you can take it. Personally, I go to a golf club to play golf."

"So do I. And I don't mind owning I played some of the finest games of my career this week-end!" Hyde retorted. "Personally, I'm thankful to the committee for gingering up the membership a bit, and turning that mouldy old Manor into an up-to-date house where you can sleep in a comfortable bedroom and get a decent dinner. I only got back this morning. But what about this affair here? Have the police arrested anyone yet?"

"Not to my knowledge."

"But if you were at the inquest! What happened there?"

"Only medical evidence was given, and Hubberd's of course, to fix the time she left his house on Saturday evening. He was almost the last person to speak to her."

"Almost?" He spoke sharply. "He *was* the last. At least, I understood so. Who saw her after him?"

"Her murderer."

"Oh, I see." He relaxed into a smile. "You don't think he did it, then?"

"Who says he did?"

"Oh, my dear fellow, do stop jumping down my throat. I didn't say it. I don't know anything about it, naturally, beyond what I've read in the papers. And they don't actually accuse Hubberd—of course they couldn't without authority—but, well, it's the way they put the facts; that she passed the whole evening alone with him in his house; some of her clothes found on the premises; his statement. All the evidence there is as to the alleged time of her leaving. ... And she wasn't seen afterwards. It looked as if it was meant to be suggestive. Of course, I don't know Hubberd except by sight. Don't remember that I ever spoke to him in my life, so I've no idea what sort of chap he is. But did anything fresh come out at the inquest? What was the verdict?"

"Verdict isn't reached. Proceedings adjourned for police inquiries."

"Oh, you don't mean the thing is going to hang on indefinitely! What a nuisance!" he frowned. "I mean, it's going to be putrid for the neighbours here if the police think they've got freedom to come poking into private houses. You know, they actually had the nerve to question my sister! I only wish I'd been at home. It upset her horribly, and no wonder. She ought to have rung me up and referred the fellows to me."

"As you were away all Saturday evening and night I scarcely see what use you'd have been," Lewis Hardwicke grunted. "But I heard you came home Sunday morning. Why didn't you stay then?"

"My dear man, how could I possibly guess there was anything up on Sunday morning? I'm not a prophet! But as I work it out now I realize I must have missed the show by inches! You see, what happened was this. I ran up to Town soon after tea on Saturday evening intending to dine with Noel Strachan at the Burdock and do his show, *The Airy Maid*, with him. However, he didn't turn up, and the club was like a mausoleum. Didn't see a soul there but Donald Levi, and he'd only looked in for letters and said he was clearing off to Yorker's for the week-end. And I said, 'By Jove, I'll come too.'

"However, having ordered my dinner, I stopped to eat it, rang up Talbot to make sure of a room, and when I'd finished dinner I drove straight out. And glad I did, too, for there was the usual amusing crowd there, and a pretty hot lot in the card-room too." He chuckled. "But they had to hand it to little L.V.H. I sat down about ten, and went to bed before midnight, after not much more than two hours' play, with a packet!

"After breakfast, Sunday, I just dashed home to collect my clubs and a change. But I was in such a deuce of a hurry, knowing a man I knew out East was waiting for me, and not wanting to lose our turn, that I wasn't in the house five minutes. Only saw the servant, to leave a message for Jane, who was at church. I came in by the garage gate in Chetwynd Avenue, and left the same way, of course, not touching Pound Lane at all, so, as I say, I must have missed all the police business there by inches. And a bit of luck I did, too, for I played the game of my life when I reached Yorker's again. Absolutely at the top of my form. Old Mack said he'd never seen anything like it. I simply couldn't miss a stroke." He sighed happily, then continued with a change of tone:

"But of course I'd have chucked everything had I known poor Jane was being bothered. Do you think they—the police—are likely to call again? You see, old Mack—MacDonnell, who left Yorker's yesterday—asked me to go down today and join him and his missus at a dinky little cottage they've taken at Frinton for the season. I was going after tiffin—which is overdue now." He looked at his watch. "Hope Jane won't be too long!"

"There's no reason why the police should call again that I know of," Lewis Hardwicke growled. "And if they do they're not likely to do Miss Hyde any personal injury. Please tell her I called, will you? I must be off myself."

He paused to remove a sheet of the *Daily Express* from the birdbath with an irritable gesture. How could any bird come to drink while Hyde was planted here, his beastly papers flapping about all over the path and the flower borders, making the delicious path look like Hampstead Heath after a Bank Holiday?

He nodded and muttered something which Hyde accepted as a farewell, and stalked back to the gate. He noticed chrysanthemums newly planted in a bed at the end of the walk which had looked like a rubbish-heap on Sunday when he passed; but Mr. Moh he did not see, for Mr. Moh stood tensely behind a lilac bush. He had spent a busy morning in the garden and did not wish to be detained from his labours in idle conversation.

Miss Hyde returned soon afterwards, and Mr. Hyde rose, collected his proofs, and went into the house for luncheon.

Mr. Moh trotted quietly into the walk from close by, removed the chair and table to a distance so that the birds could approach their water without fear, and gathered the newspapers into a neat pile which he carried to the kitchen, where Eliza could read the paragraphs about the Finnet murder over her midday dinner.

Mr. Moh received a small weekly wage from Miss Hyde which properly covered two days' work, but in fact he was at liberty to come and go as he pleased. And Eliza privately wondered sometimes how his other clients fared, since of late he had become almost a permanent feature of the Innisfree landscape.

But she knew about the little house at Hammersmith, and his wife and little girl, and guessed that he was not wholly dependent on his earnings as a jobbing gardener. She thought him a simple, kind, efficient little man whom it was pleasant to have trotting about the place, bringing in vegetables, and doing many an odd job for her that did not, strictly, fall within a gardener's business. She approved of his attitude towards her mistress, in which she discerned a fine mixture of deference and protection.

For instance, while those policemen were in the house on Sunday he had cleared away all those poor trampled blooms from that bed that Miss Hyde could not bear to look at, and early on Monday he burned every scrap of them in the incinerator so that her eyes should not be hurt by any reminder of them.

Eliza's heart burned as fiercely as the incinerator at thought of that cruel, wanton act of destruction, and she was grateful to Mr. Moh. But with characteristic reticence they had not exchanged a single word on the subject, though she had helped him cover the pitiful rubbish-heap with sacking on Sunday, in the kitchen plot, and both knew why it had to be covered till it could be burned.

With the same tacit understanding she accepted the papers from him and read them over her dinner; while he, despatching his own swiftly, slipped out again to tie up the luxuriant branches of an Emily Gray against the side wall of the sitting-room.

He was modestly out of sight of the two lunching there together, but scraps of conversation inevitably reached his ears.

"Do you intend to stay long at Frinton?" came in Miss Hyde's calm tones.

"As long as it is amusing, I expect. Mrs. Mack used to be a jolly little woman, a great sport. It'll be great to see her and the old crowd down there! She has the great faculty of gathering lots of old pals together and making them all feel as jolly as sandboys. And Mack's the same, always up to something. Never a dull moment where he and Mrs. Mack are! You don't grudge me a bit of gaiety, now, do you, old girl? This house isn't too cheerful, is it, eh, what?"

"I certainly don't grudge you to your friends, Sydney. In fact, I am going to take a holiday myself."

"You are?"—startled. "Got the work well ahead, eh? Well, well, a few days off ought to freshen you up."

"Yes. It may surprise you to hear it, but I am thinking seriously of giving up work altogether. I, too, scarcely find conditions in this house satisfactory."

"What on earth are you talking about? Surely you're not feeling ratty with me because I stopped away a couple of days without letting you know? It's your own fault, because you refuse to have a telephone here, my dear. Of course, I'd have rung up like a shot! But after all, it couldn't have made much difference in the housekeeping. . . . By the way, this is a top-hole little meal you're giving me now. I always say you are the finest housekeeper ever!"

"Don't forget your Mrs. Mack, Sydney. I don't believe you imagine I am 'ratty' because you stayed away. But I don't want to rush you unduly, and your meeting with Eastern friends may give you a chance to make fresh arrangements. Engage a new secretary, perhaps. These proofs, that I see you have scarcely looked at, are the last I intend to correct."

"Good G—d, Ella! Have you gone crazy?" His tone sounded furious. There was a rustle as chairs were pushed back and a bell rang sharply in the kitchen.

"No, Sydney, just tired of unremitting work to no purpose, and of other things that I need not specify. Yes, Eliza, we have finished. You may clear away."

"Look here, Ella, I'm not going to dash off and leave you feeling wretched, as you apparently do," Hyde's voice broke in, its tone effectually altered by Eliza's presence. "I see you're feeling absolutely out of sorts! I expect you do want a bit of rest, old girl. But look here, what about our going away together for a bit of a spree?

You'd like that, wouldn't you? Think it over this afternoon, my dear. The fact is, you shut yourself up alone in this house too much. No wonder you go all brooding and worried over silly little trifles! You couldn't really think of breaking up the old firm at this time of day! No, no, of course you're only kidding me. But I'll tell you what. I've got to run up to Town this afternoon, and I'll get hold of old Mack and tell him I can't join them till tomorrow. Then tonight we'll talk over things properly, see?"

"Will you come now and see Robin have his dinner, madam?" came an interruption in Eliza's toneless voice.

"Oh, damn the dog!"

Mr. Moh was in the kitchen when the two women came in, Miss Hyde curiously faint and breathless.

"There, madam, you sit down here in this chair. Madam has come to see Robbie ask for his dinner, Mr. Moh. You stop and see how beautiful he begs now. And he always does it better for his missus than for me—there, now, up Robin! Isn't he a picture!"

Chapter XI

Lewis Hardwicke strode away from the gate of Innisfree in a state of temper that vented itself in lively, if silent, disparagement of a popular author. Hyde was exactly the sort of literary man that he could not stick, an empty-headed, conceited, bombastic bounder who swallowed the flattery ladled out to him by the shovelful by self-interested followers and imagined that notoriety was fame and literary achievement could be measured in terms of money. An inflated, mannerless, patronizing snob laying down the law about his insufferable prose rot! At this point it occurred to him that his own manner during the late interview had lacked suavity, and a chuckle escaped him.

Hyde had been on his own ground, and a thick-headed populace might concede that he had a right to sit in his own garden and litter it with sordid newspapers as he pleased. Lewis grudgingly conceded him the right; but what he objected to was the thick-skinned insensitiveness that permitted him to mar the loveliness of the place without being aware of sin.

Lewis wondered what on earth he was to do with an interminable day that stretched before him. He had had a sneaking hope that Miss Hyde would ask him to stay to luncheon.

He would get lunch at the pub, the 'Fox and Goose', put up his house for sale, collect his car from Turner's, and cut his connection with Finnet, at any rate.

A sound meal put him into a better humour with himself and his world, and he turned into the estate agent's office in the High Street in a distinctly more cheerful temper.

Mr. Gale, an old acquaintance, received him cordially, but did his best to diminish his cheerfulness when his errand was made known. He was discouraging about any chance of selling The Laurels. Murder on the premises, he pointed out, or even the discovery of a dead body which had received its death-blow elsewhere, was a misfortune which inevitably marked down the value of property for a time, and could certainly destroy any immediate hope of a sale.

"Last week I could have got you fifteen hundred for the property without difficulty, Mr. Hardwicke," he said sadly. "But now"—he shrugged his shoulders—"people will have these little prejudices!"

"It's damned rough luck on me," Hardwicke assented gloomily. "I've been intending to sell it for some time. A family house like that is a sheer incubus for a bachelor like myself. What I want is some jolly little cottage in the country where I can put up a guest if I want to, and potter about in the garden, grow apple trees in an orchard, and do as I please. Finnet's turning into a fifth-rate suburb with all the cheap building that's going on. Nothing left of the pretty, secluded village it was when my father bought the house and settled there.

"Chetwynd Avenue was a green lane, and West Avenue didn't exist. I didn't bother, being out of England, and so on. And now, when I'd made up my mind finally to break with the associations that held me to the place, you tell me I shan't be able to find a purchaser because of that foul business on Sunday!"

"Well, you see, it was an extraordinary piece of ill-luck that the body should be found on your premises." Mr. Gale sighed. "No one can account for these things. For the matter of that, murder does no place any good. Gives outsiders an idea that it's an undesirable district to live in, and makes the inhabitants restless and keen to move away. I hear the inquest didn't throw much light on the crime, and the police seem pretty well stumped at the moment; though I've just learned that the poor thing's clothes have been found—"

"No! Have they? Where?" Hardwicke demanded, excited. "I was at the inquest. They hadn't been found then."

"No." Mr. Gale seemed mildly pleased to be able to impart news. "It was actually while the inquiry was going on, I believe, or just after. Some boys were fooling about in the Finnet . . . the ditch never runs completely dry, you know; though after all this hot weather there is only a few inches of water, and the pipes draining into it from above are all exposed. Well, these boys were paddling about, and Norris, the police sergeant, happened to be on the bridge—"

"Then it must have been after the inquest. He was in court," Lewis Hardwicke interpolated impatiently. "Go on, man!"

"Well, Norris was peering over, and suddenly one of the boys farther up, in deeper water, gave a yell, and Norris jumped clean in and waded along. And the long and short of it was, there was the bundle of clothes sucked down into a drain where it was wedged under the bank, concealed by a thin spread of water and duckweed. In my opinion, if the police had had any sense they'd have searched the ditch first, it being the obvious spot where the clothes would be hidden, instead of scouring all over Finnet Beeches as they have been doing. Though you wouldn't have thought that that trickle of water would have concealed a dead mouse for three days, would you? Let alone a bundle that the whole division of police are searching for!"

"And no credit to them it's found now," Hardwicke cried. "If it was the kids that spotted it, as you say. If you ask me, I think they're making complete idiots of themselves in the way they're running this show. What was the great idea of searching the Beeches?"

"Well, everyone is saying that they have a clue that leads them to find some connection with Finnet Beeches," Mr. Gale said cautiously. "Clay on the wheels of Mr. Hubberd's car. And that's the only road it could have been picked up on. And they are convinced a car was used to convey the body to—to—well, your premises. . . . It stands to reason the criminal couldn't have carried it—even a few yards—wherever the poor soul was done to death. Still, of course, all that is mere hearsay, Mr. Hardwicke. In my opinion, till they find out for certain where the murder was committed they won't get any convincing proof as to who did it. And without proof they can't make any arrest, however many clues they may talk about." Hardwicke's harsh-featured face was suddenly screwed up in an expression of angry suspicion.

"These damned know-all merchants can always give points to the men in the game," he exclaimed sarcastically. "Who is it they are talking about? I suppose they've got it all cut and dried—who did the murder, how, and why!"

Mr. Gale shook his head with a sad smile.

"You can't prevent people from talking, or forming their own conclusions from known facts. It happens in every murder case, and naturally Finnetonians are seething with bitterness over the delay in arresting the criminal. There's a lot of hysterical feeling getting up. And in my opinion, if steps aren't taken soon it'll end in some nasty sort of demonstration."

"But, man alive, what do you mean by known facts? The devil of the whole situation is that the facts aren't known."

"Not the whole of them, perhaps, but those that are point pretty strongly in one direction, according to the general idea. And the ugliest rumours are going round about the parties concerned—scandalous talk. You know what a small community is for gossip. I'm bound to hear a lot of the conjectures that are going about in my way of business; some say one thing and some another, but they all seem pretty well agreed that there was strong provocation."

"Then they're a pack of idiots, and you're another for believing them, Gale!" Hardwicke burst out explosively. "That poor thing Ellen Shields was too meek to provoke a rabbit!"

"Even the meek can see, and talk about what they see, Mr. Hardwicke. But, dear me, here are our own tongues running on! I wish you had put your property in my hands a year ago."

"I wish I had!" growled Hardwicke. "I wouldn't be in this damned concern now if I had. Look here, Gale, you'll have to do something about it."

"I will do my best, but I can only be honest with you. There's not a hope of a sale that I can see. At any rate till the odium attached to the property has had time to fade a little. And even so its financial value will still be heavily impaired." He considered for a moment. "If I may make a suggestion. To let it at a purely nominal rent—any other is out of the question, but cheapness is always attractive—

would give the best chance to the property to recover something of its value. You don't intend to live there again yourself? That would really be your wisest course."

"No, I don't," said Hardwicke brusquely. "Apart from this filthy business, it would mean a staff of servants, and house-keeping on a scale that I have no earthly use for in a place that has lost all the attractiveness it once had! Suburban life is a compromise between town and country, and, like every other compromise, retains the worst features of both extremes while it absolutely misses the best." He glowered at Gale and stood up. "Do what you can with it, letting, furnished or unfurnished, if selling is impossible. It will keep the place in repair, at least."

"Very good. I can assure you that we will make every effort—"

"Thanks, old man." His smile broke out for a moment, transforming his harsh face. "'Afternoon, then."

His next visit was to Turner's, near the station, where the car that he had bought just before he was sent to the States was laid up. He had liked the model, and, uncertain as to the length of his absence, had obstinately refused to sell then. Another of the things he had let drift, he thought gloomily. Should he sell it now and get something really up-to-date?

Young Turner greeted him cheerily, and while they stood by the car together repeated, with utmost enthusiasm, what Gale had said about the depreciated value of his house.

"You know how it is, Mr. Hardwicke. A model is superseded nowadays practically before it has been on the market a month. Of course you could get a bit on an exchange."

"Damn it, man, if I can't get more than a tenth part of the price I paid for her, where's the sense of exchanging?" Hardwicke exclaimed, exasperated by these rebuffs. "She's in good condition, isn't she? She went like a bird the few times I had her out."

"Oh yes, she's in perfect condition," Turner admitted. "Her line is a bit out-of-date, but when you've said that you've said all. As sound a little bus as a man could want. She's been thoroughly overhauled since you called in Saturday evening. And my brother, who gave her a trial run this morning, said she went as sweet as butter. By the way, a funny thing happened yesterday. A police sergeant turned up and asked a lot of questions about the car. Had it been taken out recently—that sort of thing. And if you'd been down. Luckily the chap he interviewed didn't know you were in here Saturday evening. Said, of course, the car hadn't been out. The sergeant said he'd call again when my brother or I were here. What are we to say?"

Lewis went cold with anger.

"You can say what you damn' well please! You can also hand over my car, and make out my account in full settlement of all charges between us."

"As you please, sir." The young man's tone was civil, but there was veiled impertinence in its very indifference, and in his slight smile. "The sergeant spent some time examining the car, our chap not feeling he had sufficient authority to refuse permission, and he mentioned that you were seen in Finnet by some Nosy Parker on Saturday evening, so my brother told me to inquire what you wanted said. As I mentioned, my brother had her out for a good trial run, so she's fully tanked and ready now, if it's the same to you. Shall we send the bill to your club or to Pound Lane?"

"Make it out now. I'll wait."

So Gorham had got on to his run out here on Saturday evening. All right. If he chose to make inquiries he could make his damned inquiries, and much good they would do him, for there was not a single soul alive who could give him away. And wild horses would not drag an admission out of him. The nuisance was that now that some infuriating chance had dropped this information into Gorham's ears he could not hope to obtain further confidences as to the progress of the case. Yet, after all, what confidences had he received?

Disclosures made on the spot had unavoidably been shared with him, yet even then Gorham had been cautious. And only from Hubberd had he heard of the discovery of the beret. What deductions was Gorham drawing from her beret being found in Hubberd's garage? Why had they searched Finnet Beeches for her clothes? And now they had fished them up out of the Finnet, were they a step more advanced in their hunt for the murderer?

He was restless, angry, apprehensive, not inclined to accept the position of passive outsider that Gorham seemed inclined to thrust on him, yet undecided whether he should risk awkward questioning by thrusting himself on the Chief Inspector's notice.

Young Turner came back with an envelope, which Hardwicke took and casually slipped into his pocket.

"Tell your brother I'll post a cheque tonight," he said brusquely.

"There's no hurry, Mr. Hardwicke," young Turner said. He was not smiling now, but rather subdued. His brother would not be very pleased at losing an old customer. Yet it was not his fault. The chap needn't have flown off the handle like that. . . .

Lewis's mood lightened as he drove out into the road. Turner was right: the car responded to his hands with beautiful ease. He would have been a fool to sell her. Here, at any rate, was something with which he could amuse himself. He would take a long run into the country this afternoon and look about for that cottage of his dreams. At least, that idea would afford an object for many a future run that would fill his empty days.

But he wasn't going to start by running away. To test her paces he had gone straight on down the London Road, past the station, and through the district that he remembered as market gardens fringing woods and charming country, but which cheap and rapid building was swiftly converting into an unsightly warren of lower-class streets. He turned left, shook off the fringe of building, and, by a broad lane he well remembered, mounted the hill and, passing the ancient group of houses and the grey church in its steep graveyard that crowned the brow, ran down the broad, sunny High Street up which he had walked so often as a boy with his father and mother on summer Sundays; they hadn't laid a disfiguring touch here yet, he noticed.

The quaint, irregular rows of shops were exactly the same, though some of the names on the lintels were new. It had been a perfect summer's day when, his mother beside him, her hand in his, he had followed his father's coffin up this street to the church above; sunny again, five years ago, when, alone this time, he had followed hers, to lay her beside her husband in that churchyard.

It was a pouring day in January when Madeline was buried in a bleak London cemetery. He had been exasperated by her sisters' weeping in the carriage: anxious only to get away.

His mind seemed to be running on funerals, he thought bitterly, and stopped the car and went up the steps of the police station.

Gorham, just back from Northbourne, was alone, writing, when Hardwicke was shown in by a constable.

He looked up with a smile.

"Hullo, you, Hardwicke? Just wait a second while I finish this." He scribbled a few more lines on the page, blotted it, slipped it into a folder, then capped his pen and sat back.

"The clothes have turned up. Have you heard?"

"Yes." Lewis Hardwicke was agreeably surprised by this genial opening. "I heard about it in the village. Are they any good to you?"

"Not much. Just her frock and under-linen. Thin, flimsy stuff that, rolled up tightly together, made a very small bundle. They had no identifying marks, but they tally with the description we were given. No doubt they were hers. They'd been slit up with a penknife to hurry the job."

"Then they don't put you any forrader?"

"I won't say that," Gorham replied slowly. "But they tell us nothing we didn't know about the murder, unfortunately. The shopping-bag is still missing. That may be useful—if it ever turns up. What did you think of the evidence this morning?"

Hardwicke moved impatiently.

"Evidence? I heard nothing but repetitions of what we all knew on Saturday!"

Gorham grinned.

"Mr. Hubberd hasn't mastered the art of repetition. He didn't stick to the tale he told me personally on minor points. Did he give you a third version? No, no. I don't expect you to tell me what it was."

"My dear chap, his tale seemed to me perfectly straight-forward. He was thinking about his own affairs—business affairs," he added hastily. "And he couldn't be expected to notice what the slavy was doing all evening—even when she interrupted him. Why should he notice particularly what she was wearing, or when she cleared off? Could he imagine that the police would make it a vital issue next day?"

"He told you about our finding the beret, I see."

Hardwicke looked angry for a second.

"I don't understand why you're making it out to be so damnably important!" he snapped. "Couldn't the woman have dropped it herself?"

Gorham raised his eyebrows.

"In the garage, my dear fellow? And then gone coolly off home wearing no hat at all? Don't tell me that lots of women do. Of course they do, but not Ellen Shields. She put that beret on and went upstairs to tell Hubberd she was going. And that is the last time we hear of her alive—"

"You have Hubberd's word that he heard her slam the front door."

"You mean that for both facts we have only Hubberd's word to go on. That isn't true. I hold corroborative evidence that she must have gone up to interview her employer before she could go home. Nothing to substantiate his statement about the door. And nothing whatever to explain the condition of the beret when we found it." He paused, his face grave. "You might have been of considerable help in this inquiry, knowing the place and the people interested as you do," he added, "if you had chosen."

"Why should I choose?" Hardwicke growled.

"Well, you're an interested party, aren't you? The discovery was made on your ground. You turned up, quite patly, while it was being made, and—don't be offended, old man—you told me a lot of tarradiddles about having landed in England Saturday night, when in point of fact you landed Friday, slept at an hotel, as the Burdock hadn't a spare room till next day, and were actually here in Finnet on Saturday evening, though you were careful not to tell me that."

"I hope that fool of a sergeant enjoyed examining my car!"

"He was quite right to examine it," Gorham said, unperturbed by the other's savage sarcasm, "as soon as he learned you were seen near the station that night; it was a routine job that he couldn't neglect, though in your single case no car would be necessary."

He leaned forward and checked a violent movement from Hardwicke with a firm gesture. "Don't be a fool, man! You understand as well as I do what impression all this leaves on the outsider. Why not clear up the mystery here and now?"

"What mystery are you alluding to?"—shortly.

"Well, why you thought it necessary to feed me a pack of lies, in the first place!" Gorham was growing annoyed.

"If you choose to credit me with lying, you can. I tell you, Gorham, I've no earthly intention of gratifying your unauthorized curiosity as to my business, either now or later!"

"Then you won't tell me what business brought you down here Saturday?"

"No."

"All right; let it rip, then." Gorham got up with a sigh. "It won't be difficult to find out, I expect. But if you find yourself subjected to a certain amount of annoyance during the process you've only yourself to blame. Remember I warned you!"

Chapter XII

When Lewis Hardwicke crashed out of the police station in a flurry of rage the Chief Inspector grinned quietly to himself. As he had indicated, the man's movements had been closely scrutinized since it was discovered that he had landed in London on Friday, a day earlier than he had given out, and actually was seen in Finnet on Saturday evening. He had been less candid about inquiries that were being made for the taxi-driver who had dropped a fare at the Burdock Club, Sackville Street, at 10.35 p.m., Saturday. Meantime, till he appeared by request, Hardwicke would certainly give him a wide berth.

He was dissatisfied with the way that Norris was handling local inquiries, though when he followed up definite directions his results were sound enough. Dent was out of the main case, and the information obtained at the cinema was useful.

The fact that Mrs. Hughes was seen there at 8.15 p.m. fitted her story that she had returned to Finnet and gone straight there after a scratch meal with her actress friend. Mrs. Hubberd's arrival after lighting-up time, the commissionaire's belief that she had got out of a car, the chocolate-seller's evidence that Clarice Hughes, evidently on the look-out for her, had been the one to change her seat, were illuminating points. And the further facts that Ethel Hubberd looked upset, and that, after an evening spent at the pictures in apparent friendliness, Ethel Hubberd was hating Clarice Hughes with virulence next day, were scraps of the puzzle that, to Gorham's satisfaction, fitted without a hitch.

But Norris had overlooked the Finnet as the obvious spot into which the clothes would be dropped—or rather pitched—from a car crossing the bridge, and wasted two days in scouring Finnet Beeches for them. He had also muffed the Murgatroyd interview badly. Of course, Murgatroyd had been got at. But did Norris imagine that it could be left at that?

Gorham decided that, the clothes having been found in the Finnet, the section of the puzzle that concerned Hubberd's car must be finished at once.

Stepping into his car, he drove quickly to Harrow, found Murgatroyd's villa without difficulty, and in a few minutes was interviewing a scared, elderly lady who admitted that she was Mrs. Murgatroyd.

"Your son lives with you here, I understand?" Gorham began, taking a firm line as one empowered with mysterious, illimitable right to demand answers to his questions.

"Well, it isn't exactly like that," she faltered. "You see, it is really my son's house, and I live with him."

"Is he married?"

"Oh no, of course he isn't!" she exclaimed.

"I see; then you were hostess at the party you gave last Saturday evening? I understand that there were complaints made by neighbours of the noise being kept up to an unseemly hour. At what time did the party begin?"

"Oh, it does seem horrid of people to make a fuss over the gramophone going and a little singing!" she cried, almost in tears. "I know that Mr. Smith did come and shout through the window about being kept awake, but he needn't have been so spiteful as to go to the police about it, especially after my son invited him in, and he laughed as much as anybody over Charlie Hughes' imitations of George Robey!"

"What? Was that Charles Hughes, the actor?"

"Yes," she said with eager pride; "my son knows lots of theatrical people. Though he isn't an actor himself, heaps of people think he's quite as clever as any of them! But you know what it is when entertaining men get together like that. They were *perfectly* quiet all evening until they finished playing cards, and then, after Leslie's City friends had gone, they just got singing and laughing. And if Hughes did make rather a noise, there wasn't a bit of harm in it, really there wasn't."

"No, I don't say there was. You were there all the time?"

"Oh no. I wasn't exactly there. I mean I got all the sandwiches and supper ready; just cold things—salad, and cold fowl, and things like that, you know. My son saw to all the drinks himself, but it was what they call a stag party. So I slipped off to sit with a neighbour at half-past nine, and ran up to my room when I came back."

"Didn't you see Mr. Hughes at all, then?" Gorham said, surprised.

"He hadn't arrived when I left, but when the last of them were going I did. When my son called me down to make coffee," she explained guilelessly. "That was after Mr. Smith had gone again; but I do assure you they were all perfectly quiet then, perfectly! Charlie Hughes said what a nice supper I had provided," she added, pleased with the little compliment. "He has such charming manners, hasn't he?"

Gorham laughed. He quite understood why Mrs. Murgatroyd had been kept out of the way when Norris called, after Hughes had 'got at' Murgatroyd to put back the time of his arrival.

"I suppose he has," he said. "Well, it seems fairly obvious that there wasn't much cause for complaint after all, Mrs. Murgatroyd. I don't think you will be bothered again. We get a lot of complaints about wireless and gramophones in the summer, when everybody has the windows open. And, of course, in certain circumstances they are a nuisance—in illness, say, or when different stations are on together in neighbouring houses."

"Oh yes, that is dreadful. But there was no one ill in the street on Saturday, I do assure you."

"No. All right, then; thank you for being so frank about it. Good afternoon. By the way, if your son would kindly ring me up at this number when he comes in I will make it all right with him too."

"Oh, thank you. He will be home about five, because he is going out to tennis afterwards. Good afternoon."

"Five?" Gorham stopped in the hall. "Oh, I'm afraid I shan't be back by that time. It's nearly four now. What is his telephone number? I'll call him at his office."

He stopped at the nearest telephone box and had a brief chat,,
"Yes, Murgatroyd speaking. Who is it?"

"Chief Inspector Gorham. I have just interviewed your mother. About a recent talk of yours with a police officer, Mr. Murgatroyd. I'd like the actual time at which Mr. Charles Hughes arrived at your house last Saturday. The time you then mentioned, nine o'clock p.m., was obviously a mistake."

"Oh dear, was I so definite as all that? I don't remember. Let me see. Some of my guests arrived about nine—"

"I'm not interested in your guests, or in the version Mr. Hughes asked you to put over if inquiries were made. Please oblige me with the actual time as closely as you can remember it."

"Oh, well, you've seen my mother, you say? I've no earthly reason for not telling what you want. He turned up between half-past nine and ten, I believe, or say about the quarter past. Certainly not much later. Yes, about fifteen minutes past ten—that's it. He was almost the last to arrive, and it struck the half-hour as the last fellow blew in."

"Thanks. Good-bye."

That had not taken long. Why Murgatroyd should gather City friends round him in his suburban villa, with the nature of games played, did not concern him, though the later hilarity when those friends had departed suggested that, from the host's point of view, the party had been a success. He was probably explaining to Charlie Hughes at this moment that he had had to throw him over, and Charlie agreeing that police visitations must be discouraged at any cost. But then it was not inquiries from the police that he had provided against, so it did not really matter.

Gorham was satisfied so far. He knew who had taken Hubberd's car out, where it had been and why, and the approximate time at which it had been driven in. The tearing of the beret remained a mystery; in fact the real clues to the murder had not been touched during the investigation yet, but the field was a good deal clearer than it had been of confusing cross-threads, and to his credit side he had three certain facts:

The body had been thrust behind those bushes just before ten o'clock.

Ellen Shields was a censor of morals.

Her clothes had been thrown into the Finnet.

From the first fact he deduced the certainty that Hubberd's was not the car used. It had not been driven beyond its garage after its expedition over the Beeches road. There had been a trace of clay left at the corner by West Avenue as it turned into The Burrs garage. None farther along Pound Lane. Ergo, the clothes had been flung from the bridge—but not from Hubberd's car. Any car crossing the bridge would be going towards London, either by the High Street, over the brow of the hill, or by the lower station road.

Hardwicke, for instance, had he taken his car out and into the Lane, must have returned by that route over the bridge to garage it again at Turner's, which was only a few doors from the station. He had not, however, had out his car, or any other from Turner's, who kept three old taxis, and did all the local station work. The possibility remained that he had driven out in a car hired in London. That point would be cleared up when his taxi-driver was found.

It was an odd point that Shields' belongings had been disposed of in three lots, not all together. The beret, the clothes, and the still missing bag. Was that accident or design? About the beret a startling but entirely unsubstantiated theory had begun to haunt the back of his mind, but he was inclined to believe that the separation of the other two items was accidental.

Leaving aside the hypothesis that Ellen met her death at The Burrs, and a second hypothesis that gave Hardwicke the central role, that she had been murdered where she was found, a third hypothesis—the only other feasible explanation covering the facts— was that after leaving The Burrs, complete with clothes, beret, and bag, she had encountered a third, unnamed man, stopped, or been stopped by him, invited into his car.

How did that work out?

They must have talked. But what about? Could Ellen have held some dangerous secret of the unknown? Considering her limited social opportunities, nothing could be less likely. Gorham's spirits fell. True, he believed that she had just made a highly unpleasant revelation of his family affairs to Hubberd, but her knowledge there had been picked up, so to speak, in his own kitchen. She would probably still be feeling all worked up, sternly moral and righteous. Well, well, well. Skipping motives that he frankly failed to guess at, and which, being only a policeman, and not a novelist, he was incapable of creating to suit his book, how did the rest work out? Talk, anger, but no suspicion of danger on her part—sudden seizure; death in a few seconds; a desperate man, his thoughts racing for means of escape from his crime. The first idea to simulate common assault.

Slitting up her thin clothes with a knife—yes, that was all right. But the car must have been standing in some dark, unfrequented place. Putting on that coat—not his, of course. He would have no overcoat on a hot evening; he couldn't appear after the crime in shirt-sleeves. That would be to court notice.

The coat was an insuperable contradiction of this hypothesis unless it could be conceded that she had it with her, in her bag. Unlikely as the other guess? Quite. But not absolutely impossible. Well, passing rapidly over that difficulty, what next? He would intend to leave her in that dark road, field, whatever it was. Why not? An interruption, of course. Someone about. Fear of imminent discovery with body in his car makes him start it up—go to find some spot more private. Where? He would glance hastily at all remote spots he knew of. Must be close by, though; dangers of interference from police patrols and kindred possibilities of chance discovery growing momentarily more acute. Had he to pass through Pound Lane to reach some place he remembered? Finnet Beeches, say! Gorham chuckled. Why not?

Then the dark Lane, not a soul about. The Laurels and its neighbour, Manstead House, both shut up, deserted.

A bold decision. Two minutes' frenzied action. A bolt back to the car—accomplished without a hitch. A quick dash. The wretched clothes still to get rid of. Another inevitable stop to knot the flimsy things in the frock, tying the sleeves tightly. A glance round to make sure no one was watching, and a hefty throw into the Finnet with scarcely a splash. Then on again—where? Somewhere where a passable alibi could be established. When did he remember that he had omitted to pitch the bag after the clothes? If the bag were ever found, it should give a sure clue to the route taken by that flying car. He would not dare make any real detour to dispose of it for fear of invalidating that essential alibi. Yet seen in his car it would hang him.

At this point Gorham's ideas ceased to flow in a crystal stream. Turning from West Avenue into Pound Lane, the homeward route that he had inevitably taken as the quickest and most familiar, he drew up on the grassy verge opposite The Burrs and lighted his pipe.

Then he glanced about him and realized fully for the first time how utterly unchanged the Lane still was from the rural retreat it had been sixty years ago when those houses were put up, though modern roads closed it at either end.

The bank under which he sat was a tangled beauty of hawthorn bushes and trees which must be a mass of white blossom in late spring, though these lesser brethren were towered over by huge, gnarled elms whose branches, against the hot blue sky, cast a grateful, flickering shade on the roadway. Behind that hedge, he had discovered, lay a strip of waste land that had not yet attracted the ubiquitous builder. A worn asphalt path ran on the opposite side. Gorham took out his note-book, after a prolonged survey of the three houses that faced the bank. Innisfree, at the far end, was represented, above a long and tall fence, by the blossomy tops of shrubs and trees—mays, lilacs, laburnums, hollies, and syringas—that hid the house completely. It was over that white gate, almost at the corner, that Mr. Moh had seen Ellen Shields peering. Could she really have been the person who destroyed that stiff little lady's delphiniums? And had Miss Hyde guessed it was she who had done that wanton piece of mischief—perhaps aware of an unbalanced streak in her nature that only showed up at intervals—and so refused to prosecute? Mr. Moh seemed to believe it possible. True, he had advanced the theory as a means of deflecting blame from Miss Hyde, whom he appeared to reverence; on the other hand, Mr. Moh was generally right.

He read through the notes of his interview with Miss Hyde, then looked thoughtfully at Hubberd's house. The windows were shut, and the garage doors, but the gate had swung open. He had noticed that the latch was defective.

According to Miss Hyde, all the gates in the Lane were closed on Saturday night except those of Mr. Hubberd's garage. Did she mean that outer gate, or the garage doors?

He started his car and slithered to a standstill outside Innisfree.

There was a thrush splashing in the bird-bath as he entered the paved walk, but no other sign of life in the garden.

He kindly gave it a moment to finish its dip, then walked briskly up to the front door, which, before he had time to knock, was opened by Miss Hyde herself.

"I saw you coming from the window," she exclaimed breathlessly. "Did you want me?"

He smiled as cheerfully as he could to reassure her. She was undoubtedly in a state of fluttering nervousness, in spite of a firm effort after self-control.

Except for that catch in her breath her speech was collected, but her eyes had a strained look, and he noticed that her clasped hands were shaking.

"Nothing much, Miss Hyde," he answered. "Only, as I was passing I thought I might look in to clear up a small point. I'm afraid all this has been very distressing for you."

"It has, of course," she said slowly. "I was attached to poor Ellen. But her death was so horrible in any case. Is it—do you know if—if she suffered much?"

"Not at all, beforehand. I mean, the doctors judge death to have been almost instantaneous, and I believe myself she was taken by surprise, for there were no signs of any struggle or resistance."

"Oh, that was merciful, at least." There were sudden tears in her eyes. "It was horrible to think of her terrified, helpless. Poor thing, her life was so hard, so joyless—and that it should end like this."

"But was she an unhappy woman?" he asked quietly. Miss Hyde had led him into the sitting-room, furtively wiping her wet eyes.

She turned at that and gave him a quick look.

"No, she was not. You are quite right. Happiness is a thing of the spirit, and she was generally cheerful. . . ."

"Well, it's said that only the wearer knows how the shoe pinches," he said with a slight smile, "but, on the other hand, I've known folk greatly pitied for disabilities that they scarcely felt at all."

"The uncomfortable-looking shoe does not necessarily pinch so badly as the outsider fears, you mean," she replied with a faint, answering smile. "No, that is very true. Thank you, Mr. Gorham. I should apologize for troubling you with my feelings, but the thought of—it all—haunts me."

"Well, as to that, it's a relief to hear someone speaking feelingly about the poor thing at all," he admitted. "I've run up against a lot of callousness in this case, and it doesn't improve one's opinion of human nature. What I wanted to ask you is only a little thing, but I like to get even small details clear. About Saturday night; you said you walked as far as West Avenue once or twice?"

She nodded.

"And all the gates were shut except that of The Burrs?"

"Yes. That is right. The garage gate."

"I see. Did you notice if the garage itself was shut?"

"Yes. The doors were open."

"And the car inside?"

"Well, it was very dark, and naturally I did not *peer*," she said rather doubtfully, "but I certainly thought the car was there, just inside. Is it important?"

"It is a small detail, but you think the car was there?"

"I am really sure, Mr. Gorham," said with a touch of dignity. "I saw the dark bulk of it a little to one side of the opening." The sudden slam of a door above sounded startlingly loud in the quiet of the house, and it was followed at once by the heavy tread of a man on the staircase, the scuttering of the dog Robin into the room to the shelter of its mistress's skirt, and the entry of a big man who clattered in behind it.

Mr. Hyde stopped abruptly at the unexpected sight of a visitor, and a male one at that, with his sister, but the Chief Inspector was stooping to attract the dog, which came joyously with eagerly licking tongue and wagging tail.

"Hullo, Ella—just came in to tell you I'm off."

Stiffly she made the introduction.

"My brother, Chief Inspector."

Gorham straightened himself, though his hand still caressed the silky head now reared against his knee.

He glanced at Mr. Hyde, smiling genially.

"Interesting to meet you, Mr. Hyde. I was reading one of your stories the other day. One about a girl with hyacinth hair. It made me feel I'd like to see the Far East for myself."

"Ah, yes." For once, L. V. Hyde, who generally welcomed mention of his stories, and expanded freely in an atmosphere of flattery as the hearty literary man whom fame cannot spoil, seemed disconcerted by this tribute.

"Oh, ah, yes. Travel's an amusing thing. Still, tropical climates have their drawbacks, you know. No joke for the white man really. I stuck it out till it all but killed me. Eugh!" He shivered at remembrance of his sufferings. "Eh, Ella?"

"You were very ill when you came home," she agreed calmly.

"Well, London's my beat," Gorham remarked, without visible regret, and made a move towards departure. "Good afternoon, Miss Hyde; thank you. Now, now, young fellow, you'll wag that tail off if you aren't careful!" He patted the dog and stepped into the hall, where Mr. Hyde stood back to let him pass, then, with a quick movement, he turned again to the sister.

"By the by, Miss Hyde, a lot of branches of bushes were carried off from The Laurels last night—by souvenir hunters probably, but we've had complaints from the neighbourhood that undesirable characters are about. I think myself it's just natural nervousness after this affair here, but tonight a policeman will be on guard. You will have no objection if he is stationed in your garden, I suppose? He can see the Lane from there without being seen himself, and of course a whistle will summon him at once if there's an alarm. You won't mind?"

Her face flushed, but there was something oddly like relief in her eyes, though her tone was cool.

"Not at all. In fact, it will give one a sense of safety." Gorham smiled.

"That's the chief idea," he said. "There's nothing really to fear, but a constable's uniform restores confidence. Very good, then. He will report his presence to you at sunset, then you will leave him a free hand, and if you see a man walking about in the garden you will know it is merely a guardian of the law! Good-day, Mr. Hyde, and to you, madam."

Chapter XIII

Mr. Hyde returned to Innisfree on Tuesday evening in a thoroughly disturbed state of mind. He candidly acknowledged in public that, like the majority of authors, he was an essentially lazy person who hated the necessary drudgery of his profession, and therefore the very thought that his sister—good old Plain Jane, as he called her jokingly, on whose patient and loyal co-operation in his arrangements he had depended for years—should declare her activities at an end was enough to upset him profoundly. It meant, if she carried out her threat, the utter *bouleversement* of his life, the absolute finish of his present comfort and ease. But he could not believe that she was serious, that she would stand out against his expressed wishes when he put them forcibly before her. Probably the foul nuisance of this affair at the next house had got on her nerves and upset her mental balance for a time.

Well, he could understand that. No one could wish more than he did that the fuss the newspapers were making could be allowed to die down. How many hundreds of murders happened in England every year over which not a tithe of this shrieking outcry was raised? Dismissed with a couple of lines, most of them; yet over this one, which was so beastly upsetting by its closeness to his interests and home, the papers were spreading themselves as violently as if it were the wife of the Prime Minister who was the victim!

And as if the fact itself weren't bad enough, here were the unsettling results of all this rotten publicity penetrating his home and making Ella—he must drop that nickname if it annoyed her—threaten to break up the established routine of years. But he'd have to take a firm line with Ella, point out that she stood to lose as much as he did by dropping what was practically her sole means of earning her livelihood. He could not let her carry out such a senseless piece of folly. She'd have to be brought to see that. He'd have to make her see that this evening.

But his proposed talk with his sister was not too easy to arrange. While he ate the cold supper that was laid ready for him in the sitting-room Ella stayed in the garden pottering about in the walk with that queer little Chinese gardener who seemed to haunt the premises these days. She was watching him cut those white lilies that she adored so, by Jove! Every mortal stem of them? What on earth for? For a wild second he wondered if Ella's brain were turned! Then a feasible explanation dawned on him, and he chuckled wryly. No doubt there was some festival on at the church and she was sending them down for decoration purposes. Yes, that must be it, for the fellow was trotting away at last, with his arms full of great white sheaves. Now, if Ella would come in. . . . But Eliza entered with his sweets—no use spoiling a perfect meal like this by argument. She had disappeared from the view from the windows, but there was her voice in the kitchen, gossiping with Eliza, no doubt. He finished his coffee, and Eliza cleared the table, and then Ella did come in and sat down in her usual chair. Then, damn it, another interruption. A brisk knock at the door—he had missed the sight of the unwelcome caller coming up the walk—and here was Eliza bounding in to announce that the constable had come! Could Madam speak to him a moment?

Miss Hyde went, of course, and presently was seen giving the man a cup of coffee, Eliza and she positively beaming on him, introducing Robin, who was jumping round him excitedly providing a comfortable chair from the kitchen to lessen the rigours of his night's vigil, as if the stone seat in the walk weren't good enough for a big copper!

When Ella came in at last and he offered her her chair and suggested a little conversation, she shook her head.

"Not tonight, I think, Sydney. I have been sleeping badly, and I am going to bed early. Have you settled to go to your friends at Frinton tomorrow? Eliza wants to go to London to do some shopping, so I'm afraid luncheon will be scanty. She leaves before ten."

He thought a moment.

With that blue uniform outside the windows it was going to be awkward to make her attend properly this evening. But tomorrow, with even Eliza out of the way, not dashing in and out every five minutes, it wouldn't be so difficult. . . .

"All right, old girl. Never mind lunch for me." He smiled genially. "I'll leave here about noon, or a bit earlier, and drive down. That suit you? And we must have a bit of a chat before I go, on that idea of mine of a holiday together somewhere. I might find some nice spot at Frinton perhaps. Eh? Topping air there. What you want to pull you up a bit. At any rate, we'll discuss what you would like after brekker, when old Eliza has gone off on her jaunt."

"Very well, Sydney," she replied quietly, a reflective look in the eyes that rested for a moment on his face. "Good night, then." She left him smoking his eternal cigarettes, and went slowly upstairs, but when she reached her room she looked out of her window in the long, narrow recess that contained her bed, a table, and strip of rug, and nothing else. Among the shadows of shrubs she discerned a darker shadow moving. There was something exceedingly solid and reassuring about an English policeman, diffusing a sense of safety and protectiveness that she had scarcely felt since she was a child. When, a small, nervous girl, she had shivered in bed in the grip of imaginary terrors, just that warm sensation of absolute protection from evils, real or fanciful, had spread over her when her matter-of-fact, good-humoured Nanna came up to bed beside her.

In a flash she realized that it was protection that she craved for. A laying down of responsibilities she had never been fitted to carry and that had worn her out. Sydney was right in one thing. She needed a change; she was run down, exhausted in mind and heart. Her decision did not falter for a second, but the anger that had first steeled it no longer lent her vicarious strength.

Disputes with Sydney made her weak, drained her of vitality. One had threatened all evening, but, thanks to the distraction caused by that pleasant-faced young constable, she had managed to evade it. She patted Robin, curled up in his basket, and the touch of him brought Lewis to her mind. She locked her door.

The fresh air blew through the open casements as she lay down, and she was smiling as she fell asleep.

Mr. Hyde, never an early riser, came down at half-past nine to a well-spread table to find that his sister had already breakfasted. This was in order, and did not disturb him. He leisurely fortified himself with the good things provided; he had got back into the English habit of enjoying a hearty breakfast, and thoroughly appreciated Eliza's coffee and bacon.

The policeman had gone. He felt at peace with the world when he lighted a cigarette and strolled into the garden in search of his sister. Ella, he felt sure in this comfortable mood, would quickly come to heel when he tackled her this morning in an empty house without any chance of outside interference to deflect him from his purpose.

Even the Chinese gardener was absent this morning.

He was on the terrace reading the latest paragraphs about the murder and noting with a grim little smile the scarcely veiled hints as to Hubberd's guilt, coupled with the ominous phrase, "An arrest may shortly be made", when Eliza came out dressed for the street, with Robin on a lead, and behind her his sister carrying a bouquet of roses.

He stared, scarcely comprehending at first that she was daring to defy him. She was dressed in black, as usual, and save for the strong hues of the roses made a sombre figure.

He stepped forward with an angry gesture.

"Look here, Ella. You're not going to avoid me like this. I told you I want a talk with you about that silly statement of yours yesterday. Send Eliza on, and come back into the house," he ordered.

But she stood her ground, and the other woman, farther down the walk, turned to regard them both with anxious eyes.

"I'm sorry, Sydney," Miss Hyde said quietly, "but you must accept what I said as final. Further discussion would be useless—and very painful, I feel. Don't keep me now. I am going to the funeral."

"Funeral?" he cried furiously. "What the devil do you mean?"

Her eyes widened. For a second she thought he was going to lay violent hands on her in spite of the servant's presence, but her face was calm, her voice controlled.

"I am going to poor Ellen's funeral," she said. "Surely you've not forgotten it is today?"

"Forgotten! My God! What have you to do with her?"

The florid colour left his face. He looked grey.

"Oh, Sydney—poor Ellen!" There were tears in her eyes, but he turned abruptly away without answer, and thankfully she walked forward to Eliza's side.

They moved in silence through the sunny street and over the bridge and up the wide High Street. Eliza was to keep Robin outside the churchyard till the sad ceremony was over and his mistress free. She entered the gates, after a word with the constable, and waited near the grave.

A crowd of sightseers had gathered when the small *cortège* reached the churchyard, and a murmur arose, for the coffin was covered with white lilies.

Police held back intruders at the gates and Miss Hyde felt a moment's tremor as she noticed that only men were with her. Gorham, a stranger—Ellen's brother-in-law, no doubt—and, yes, Lewis Hardwicke. He ranged himself at her side when they reached the open grave, and after a second of hesitation she bent and laid her roses on upturned earth at its foot.

Gorham stood a little apart during the reading of the service. He liked Miss Hyde for coming. It must have cost a real effort to one so shy and retiring. The air was sweet with the scent of her lilies and roses. She was the only one of them all to whom that "this our sister" had a human meaning. Decent of Hardwicke to come, too.

He glanced aside and read the man's name on a cross near by. His parents' grave, no doubt. His eyes fell from the names—William Hardwicke—also Mary his wife—and the dates, to moss-rose buds, below—still fresh . . . Saturday had been Mary Hardwicke's birthday.

They walked back to the gates together in thoughtful silence, and without much difficulty Lewis persuaded Miss Hyde to step into his car. She explained that, lost in view in the dense crowd, Eliza was waiting with Robin, and he went to fetch her.

"You stop here," he said, and penetrating briskly through the crowd brought her and Robin back in quick time.

"All those beastly curiosity-mongers had jammed her up against the railings!" he announced, pushing a way clear for her without ceremony. "But she isn't damaged—are you, Eliza? Now where do you both want to go?"

"Eliza would like the station—she is going up to Town for shopping, and only came with me to keep Robin safely," Miss Hyde said. She was seated in front, beside the driver, while Eliza, looking distinctly elated at this cheerful ending to a painful experience, sat primly at the back with Robin equally cheered beside her.

"That's simple."

He honked his horn while two policemen cleared a path for his car and they drove down the High Street, round the curve at the foot of the hill, and pulled up at the station.

"Now where?" he asked, with a friendly look down at the small figure by his side when he came back from despatching Eliza on her way.

"Home, I suppose. But—are you especially busy this morning, Lewis?"

He caught the hesitation in her tone.

"Me? Rather not! Why?"

"Well, I should be—relieved—if you could come in with me," she murmured with difficulty; and then, guessing his surprise, added simply, "Perhaps it is stupid of me, but Sydney, my brother, may still be there—it isn't eleven yet, is it?"

"No. Eliza just caught the 10.45."

"He is going to join some friends at Frinton this morning. But we have had a difference of opinion, and I should like to avoid any more discussion about it. You see? If you are there—"

"I'll act as an effectual extinguisher on private debate! Rather. I'll love to come in."

She nodded, with a faint smile.

"That's nice of you. Lewis, what made you come this morning?"

He flushed guiltily, as one caught doing a good deed.

"That's rather difficult. Gorham told me when it was to be, and—well, she was found on my premises. I felt someone ought to go besides the officials. Rather cold, you know, only the police. I never dreamed for a second you'd turn up!"

"I think I had the same feeling," she admitted gently.

"I forgot to bring a wreath, though. Doubt if I could have got one, in any case, so early in the morning. If someone hadn't sent those lilies there'd have been only that mouldy effort of the sister's, and the laurel wreath from the police—laurels! I ask you! Beside your lovely roses."

She was silent, and suddenly he guessed the truth.

"Lord! You sent the lilies too! My word, that was just like you!"

Her eyes were full of tears.

"She was so forlorn, Lewis. So kind, too. Her clumsiness obscured it at the time. One was irritated, not grateful. But she helped me through a miserable experience. She asked me for advice and guidance in her difficulties, and the very giving helped me to endure mine. I could not encourage her to bear her trials in the finest way and fail myself."

"So you sent her what you loved best, your flowers . . ." he murmured gently, touched by the child-like nature of her confidence; but she shook her head.

"There was no merit in that."

"Look here, why not come for a drive with me till Hyde has had time to clear out?" he suggested. "It's a glorious day. Fresh air will do you all the good in the world, and I'm absolutely at a loose end. It would be sheer kindness to take pity on me!"

He saw that the idea tempted her, but she vetoed it, at any rate as an immediate possibility.

"Not now, Lewis. I have no wish to avoid Sydney—only a renewal of argument between us," she said with a sigh. "And there are proofs that must be corrected and returned today."

"Why on earth don't you make the fellow correct his own proofs, Miss Hyde? You spoil him!" he said angrily.

"Oh, it is part of my job," she answered. "I must finish it properly. But these are practically the last I shall have to do, I think. I warned Sydney yesterday that I was going to drop all such work for a time. But don't speak of it to him. Lewis, are you really free? I am not imposing on your good nature?"

He laughed.

"Terribly. But not more than it can bear."

"You speak as if I were testing thin ice," she said demurely.

They were both smiling when they entered the sitting-room, where Hyde was filling his cigarette-case, his hat and stick laid on the table.

"Hullo, Ella, back already?"

"Mr. Hardwicke kindly drove me home. Eliza caught her train. Can I do anything about your packing?"

"It's done, thanks. Marvellous things, sisters, Hardwicke. Always keen to help when a job's finished. Have a drink?"

"Thanks. It's on the early side yet. Besides, I'm taking your sister for a spin into the country. She had something to do here first, so I'm waiting. Where are you off to?"

"Frinton. Some old pals of mine out East are there. The MacDonnells. Perhaps you've met old Mack at Yorker's?"

"Thought you offered to put me up for Yorker's yesterday," Hardwicke grinned coolly.

"Mack said you were on the committee, you sly old horse!"

"Mack lied, then. I'm not."

"Have it your own way. Taking Ella out, are you? Don't let *me* stand in the way of your pleasures, old girl! I'll clear off at once if it's necessary to see me quit the premises first! I'm staying till Monday, if the information is any use to you."

"You have left an address for letters?" she said evenly.

"Don't know it. The P.O., Frinton, will find me."

"All right."

"Good-bye. And try to be a bit nicer to me when I come back, Ella."

"Good-bye, Sydney."

He gave her one look, then marched out, picking up his suitcase in the hall. Lewis, in order to annoy him as much as possible, followed him officiously to the garage, and shut the gates behind him as he drove out.

When he came back Ella Hyde was standing as he had left her, by the table on which were spread proofs.

He went up behind, and put a gentle arm round her, for tears were rolling down her face.

"What the egregious Sydney wants," he said vigorously, "is a hard kick in the pants. And what you want is to forget all about him for a few hours."

He put out a firm hand and swept all the proofs into a comprehensive bundle. "We'll correct these outside somewhere. Now, do you want to do anything else before we go? Change your clothes, or anything?"

Perhaps she liked the sensation of being taken care of. It was certainly a novel experience to have a man order her about, but, whether she liked the good-natured audacity of Lewis or felt at the moment too weak to resist, she submitted without protest. "I will change into something lighter, I think," she murmured, keeping her face turned from him because of those stupid, weak tears of which she was ashamed. "This coat is very heavy. But I won't be long. Perhaps meanwhile you won't mind seeing that the place is locked up. Eliza is sure to have left it tidy."

"All right, I will."

When she came down she had laid aside her black funereal garments and wore a frock of cloudy grey voile, and a shady hat of some black gauze material more suitable for the summer day. Lewis had thought of her as old, a contemporary of his mother, but in this pretty dress she was not old, her graceful figure and light step were young. He scarcely saw the mark on her cheek in the smile that lighted her sad grey eyes.

She was shy at first and silent, leaving him to choose the subject of conversation, but she listened with that quiet sympathy that he remembered from Sunday while he talked about himself. Their moods fitted admirably. He wanted the relief of expressing the restlessness of mind that threatened destruction of his whole future. It seemed to him that his guiding hopes and ambitions had run down and brought his life to a standstill, yet left him the wretched prey of clamouring inner dissatisfactions.

Miss Hyde, equally at the end of a phase of life as strenuous as it was bitterly unhappy, and equally unable to determine what direction the future must take once the irrevocable decision of this week was carried into action, only wished to lay aside her thoughts for a while, forget her own troubles in considering those of another. She divined quite clearly his craving for sympathy, and even felt the pleasant flattery in his simple seeking of hers. It was only a passing mood in him, of course. He would presently forget her in more amusing companionship, but she could enjoy today, a day of escape.

Lewis told her that he had finished with newspaper work, and had some vague idea of settling in some country cottage; where, he did not know.

"I'm getting rid of The Laurels, of course," he said. "If I hadn't been a lazy hound I'd have done it years ago, when Madeline died. But somehow, then, I couldn't bring myself to effect a clean cut."

"It would have been wiser," she said gravely.

"I know. I let sentiment strangle common sense. It seemed too beastly then to get rid of all the little fal-lals she'd bought with such pride. I just let things drift, and now I feel still more beastly because I don't care."

"You do care for what they once meant, I think," she said gently, "or you would feel nothing. After all, remembrance of a person does not depend on material things."

"No. That's what her father said last night when I went to look them up."

He did not say that that visit to the shabby vicarage that had once been such familiar ground had brought home to him as nothing else had done the remoteness, and, indeed, the thinness, of his past romance. In that house, where everybody was always rushing out to choir practices and parochial clubs and Sunday schools, where the mothers' meeting gathered in the dining-room and classes were prepared for Confirmation in the Vicar's study, where strange ladies were constantly to be met in the passages carrying tea-urns, and inexplicable Scouts wandered about freely, Christianity had been reduced to its practical elements and sentiment was at a discount. They had made him stay to dinner, but the talk had been about the parochial outing. The Vicar asked about Spain, but kept glancing at his magazine notes while he answered; Madeline's mother told him the family news while she did the Jumble accounts; and even Lois, one of the younger girls, worked feverishly at covering ragged hymn-books with brown paper while she told him about her coming marriage to the Curate.

It was not that they had forgotten Madeline, but simply that the busy present absorbed their thoughts and time.

His liking for Madeline might well, in the closer bonds of marriage and affectionate habit, have deepened into love. But, cut short as it had been, his feeling for her had struck no roots in his heart. His one thought as he stepped out of the Vicarage last night was that Lois might provide the solution of the one problem that still weighed heavily on him in that connection. Could he not give her Madeline's furniture as a wedding-present?

Today, as he drove through the sunlit streets, he let the past slip back to where it belonged. He asked his companion if she had any special ideas as to where they should go, and, when she shook her head, suggested Sandwich, which pleased her greatly.

"But isn't it a long way off?" she said doubtfully.

"We've got the whole day before us," he declared cheerfully. "No one is expecting us back."

Chapter XIV

THEY LUNCHED at Canterbury, and after a glimpse of the cathedral drove on through picturesque Kentish villages in a spirit of deep content. The warmth of the afternoon hours drugged thought, and Ella Hyde felt it sufficient rest to watch the changing beauty of the scene without thinking of tomorrow.

They paused for a delightful moment under a signpost that bore the words Ham, Sandwich, in rich proximity.

"Can it possibly be true?" she said, awed.

"I think so. That is—er—Ham; Sandwich is a mile or so beyond." They looked at the signpost and at each other, and laughed and laughed.

"That," said Lewis, as they drove on, "settles it. After sharing a joke like that I can't go on letting you call me Lewis while I have to stick to Miss Hyde."

"Oh, it seemed to come naturally. Your mother always spoke of you as Lewis," she responded with diffident alarm.

"You could scarcely expect her to call me Mr. Hardwicke," he argued. "For the matter of that, she had a funny little pet name for you."

"Elvie?" she murmured, a tinge of colour mounting to her cheeks. "That was my family name—a corruption of Ella Vincent, you see. No one but Sydney latterly ever said 'Ella' *tout court*."

"L. V. or Elvie—which?" he asked, puzzled.

She flushed more deeply still.

"Oh, as it is spelt. It was Mother's pet name first, and then spread to Laurence and the others," she explained hurriedly. "As an untaught infant I naturally imagined—from study of letter blocks, you know—that Ella began with L. So I signed my name L. V. H. on the first Christmas-card I drew for Mother at the age of three, and the boys derided my ignorance, and I wept, till Mother adopted it and comforted me. So as Elf or Elvie it stuck. There is a long explanation of a point not worth explaining," she added with a touch of impatience. "But of course your mother used it."

"Just as she did my Lewis," he said gravely. "We were a commonplace crowd and eschewed pet-names. But I think I ought to follow her usage, don't you think, as you do?"

"That was different. I knew you as a boy of eighteen."

"And you were . . . ? Look here, looking back, and trying to pierce the egotistical fog of youthful memories, I don't believe you were a day more than eighteen then yourself!"

She laughed.

"Not much, perhaps. But I had an old head on young shoulders. . . . Lewis—this is like a city in a fairy-book!"

"Shall we stop here and explore it on foot?"

They left the car near the Town Hall and wandered about the winding streets and finally up on to the ramparts, and here Lewis suddenly remembered and produced the proofs. But Ella Hyde waved them away.

"Oh no. Not now. I won't spoil this perfect hour. There will be time this evening. I don't want to think about work now! Isn't it marvellously still here?" Her eyes were on the green spaces beneath them, her expression rapt, and he stuffed the bundle into a pocket again and lighted a cigarette, and sat contentedly smoking till it was time to go down to Pilgrim House for tea.

On the way home they played the game of choosing a house, and went a long, meandering way round in order to pass through as many hamlets as possible to give plenty of scope for choice. Lewis became absurd, and chose houses in which it was clear he could never hope to live: cottages with crooked doorways and thatch that came down and hid nearly the whole front wall, solid Georgian houses designed for a family of twelve, with unlimited servants and stabling for coach-horses within a red-walled courtyard.

He argued their merits seriously.

"I don't mind living seven miles from a lemon, and twelve from any modern system of sanitation," he explained, "and all these villages look like museum pieces. It would be distinguished to live in a museum piece."

"But do you want to be distinguished? In quite that way, I mean?"

"The general literary man who strolls about the village in old bags and an ancient pipe, and shakes the natives heartily by the hand, and shows them as prize exhibits to parties of actress friends who come down on Sundays in car-loads and sunbathe on his front lawn? I wonder, do I?"

She smiled.

"I can never understand the amazed pride with which that type of author describes his ignorance of the simplest plants," she said. "You know how he rushes out on the dew-wet lawn and flings myriads of bulbs into the brown earth without the remotest notion what they are—"

"Till the rustic henchman warns him in dialect that he's planting them upside down. And he rushed out in pyjamas too—"

"And having flung the bulbs into the beds, and a cheery greeting to the old gnarled man, he dashes back to soak blissfully in a steaming bath till a delicious odour of bacon stealing in calls him to breakfast, marvellously prepared by his house-keeper. He always emphasizes that housekeeper as if it might as well have been prepared by the Vicar or the village postman." He chuckled.

"Old gnarled man is good. And then, when he has devoured the housekeeper's bacon, he tumbles into his old bags, dons the pipe, and dashes in his old tin Lizzie to collect an actress and a couple of Cabinet Ministers from the station for lunch."

"When he makes salad-dressing from a recipe Balzac gave his grandfather. And they all call each other darling while they sit and sunbathe afterwards, and give pound notes to the Vicar's wife when she calls for a subscription to the organ fund, and their bohemian generosity inspires her—if not to emulate—to forgive benevolently their equally bohemian lack of clothes. And sometimes he dashes away in the midst of it to sit with a sick friend in hospital."

"Ah, yes! The beggar is torrid with sweet human impulses! But you're perfectly right, Elvie, I don't know enough actresses to make that sort of stunt really come off!"

"It is only a phase of an old theme," she said soberly, ignoring his daring, "the contrast of city folk and rustic. Goldsmith played with it, and Jane Austen, though their sympathies were with the country people, whom they knew. Benson satirized the provincial who posed as an intellectual. Do you remember Lucia and her Shakespearean flowers? The form it happens to take is a matter simply of reaction against the last popular type, and if this is a cheap and silly style, it is at least harmless."

"I don't believe silliness is ever harmless!" he growled. "The general public is quite idiotic enough by nature without having concentrated drivel fed to it from its libraries."

Something in his remark seemed to hurt her, for she shrank back in her seat, a painful colour dyeing her cheeks.

"Oh, that is harsh. Too harsh, I think," she exclaimed, but with an oddly apologetic note in her voice. "Even if stories aren't really literature, if they help people to find an imaginative escape from the drabness of their lives, that cannot do harm. You see, most people are in bondage to the circumstances of their lives. They can only escape from them in imagination."

He could have kicked himself for his tactlessness, but he dared not let her see that he comprehended the personal significance of her plea.

"There's that, of course," he agreed good-humouredly. "These beggars may well be forgiven for building improbable cottages if their readers can treat them as chateaux in Spain. A private chateau in Spain is an indispensable possession for everyone if they are to remain human beings and not sink to the level of brute beasts. Are you going to be alone all this week?"

"With Eliza. But I am going to be rather busy."

"Oh, come, that doesn't mean I'm to keep away, does it?"

"Why, no, if you want to come again, Lewis. This has been a delightful day for me."

"Me too," he said, and relapsed into silence, which she did not interrupt while he negotiated street traffic.

Eliza beamed on him when she opened the door.

"Supper is laid, madam, and I have only to heat the soup, as I didn't know what time you would be in. Mr. Hardwicke's note said it might be late."

She hurried away.

He grinned at that blatant betrayal. "Couldn't have poor old Eliza worrying," he murmured. "She's a woman in a thousand, and adores you."

"You must stay to supper now," she said, and smiled as she pointed to the two places laid ready at table.

"I say, you must kick me out if I become a nuisance."

She nodded. "I will." But her smile answered his own.

He went away at last with the finished proofs ready for posting in Town. With his quick and experienced assistance the bundle was reduced in no time, and the work which she generally found tiresome was transformed by the presence of this queer, friendly, masculine coadjutor into such a pleasure that she was almost sorry when he handed her the last sheet to initial for the story's author, L. V. H.

She and Eliza went upstairs together, and Eliza stood for a long time in her mistress's bedroom to talk about her adventures among the London shops, and her visit to a married brother's house in Paddington, which had been the real motive of her expedition. Like many people who live lonely lives, she was a voluble talker when she had both a listener and a subject that thrilled her with personal interest.

"What Jessie said was, madam, if you can spare me it couldn't have happened at a better time, her being real low in her mind and never having recovered her strength properly after the birth of their youngest, and her never able to take an hour's rest, what with all the meals to get and the young ones to see off to school. And I will say that for Jessie, however tired she may be, she feeds them all real sensible. A good breakfast before they go, and a nourishing meal for the young ones at midday, and a good hot meal for Bill and Alec in the evening when they come in; and their looks respond to it, in a manner of speaking, for a cheerful healthy pack they are, and Jessie herself the one poor-looking one among them."

"Well, if you are there for a few weeks to lend a helping hand, Jessie will have a chance to pull up her strength a little. And that will relieve Bill's mind about her too."

"That's what they both said, madam. For, fond of his youngsters as he is, he gets the wind up about Jess when she looks as bad as she does now, for he's wrapped up in her, and he'd give the coat off his back to spare her, but he has to get on with his job, same as she has with hers, and what with the washing and cooking and mending needed for a family kept nice as Jess keeps hers, marriage is a full-time job for a woman, and not one I'd care to take on myself, though I dare say I shall enjoy it for a change, knowing it isn't going to last above three weeks; but mind you, madam, if you change your mind and want me back before, you've only to say. I've not said more than the week to Jess and Bill so far, and they understand you're the first consideration."

"Thank you, Eliza," Miss Hyde said gratefully. "It is an immense comfort to know how I can rely on you always. Now I think we must both go to bed, for the man is coming tomorrow to arrange about the moving. And we have a busy week before us. Not anything like a week, in fact, because we must both be ready to leave the house on Saturday at the latest."

"Does Mr. Hyde know yet, madam?"

"No one knows. You are the only person I have taken into my confidence. But Mr. Hyde knows that I am going away, though he does not know that the house is being given up, and he will have no difficulty about living at his club till he has made fresh arrangements for himself."

"You haven't thought about yourself yet, madam?"

"Not yet. I tried to think today, when I was out with Mr. Hardwicke. We had such a lovely drive, Eliza. The beauty and peace of it helped me to nerve myself—for this break. As I told you on Sunday evening, I feel that it has become absolutely necessary. And once that is realized it is best to carry one's resolution out at once. It—it is the only way to do it. But I cannot think beyond it yet. No doubt the way will come, but sufficient for the day is the evil thereof. We must buckle down to all we have to do in the next three days, and it is a comfort to me that you will be safe with Bill and Jessie."

"That," said Eliza, with a grim look, "won't be much comfort to me if I don't know you're safe too. And begging your pardon, madam, I think that is a good deal more important than bothering about what Mr. Hyde is going to do with himself."

"Now, Eliza—"

"Oh, it's all right, madam. I'm not going out of my place to express my thoughts about the goings-on of Mr. Hyde. But it's time you did consider yourself first, and it's a fact, seeing what's been lately, you didn't ought to be left alone. You didn't really, madam. If I wasn't real thankful last night to have that young constable prancing about down there, and me with a whistle under my pillow to blow as soon as look at you!"

Miss Hyde stared, and then broke into a genuine laugh. "Oh, my dear Eliza, living with an author must have affected your imagination! Now run away to bed and sleep soundly, and be sure and call me early in the morning! Good night."

Eliza marched away, and Miss Hyde lay down in bed still smiling, because, though Eliza wasn't to know it, she had slept with a police whistle under her own pillow last night, and but for the presence of that ruddy-faced young policeman among her lilac bushes certainly would not have slept at all.

But it seemed years since last night, even since she said goodbye to Sydney this morning. She was closing the door on the old life today had been an interlude—a peaceful, perfect interlude—between that wretched past that she had desperately put an end to at a blow and the utter blankness of an unknown future.

There were plenty of practical thoughts to fill her mind tonight, for one does not quit a house full of family associations, where one has lived for twenty-five years, in three days, without requiring all the organizing ability one possesses to come into full play. But actually she lay thinking of the nonsense that she had talked that day with Lewis. She had supposed her very power of trivial chatter, never exercised since youthful days, when she and Laurence could be absurd at will together, had atrophied from want of use. If Laurence and his wife had not been killed fifteen years ago in that air-crash tragedy that had darkened her mother's latter years, and shadowed her own young gaiety into staid middle-age before its time, life could never have worked out as it had. Laurence would have intervened and rescued her. But with Laurence dead there was no one to whom she could appeal for help. And circumstances had closed her in; she could make no friends by herself; too shy to venture to call on newcomers to the neighbourhood like the Hubberds, and Sydney had brought no friends home. For that she was thankful, of course, because she could not imagine herself liking, far less finding a congenial spirit among, the fifth-rate sort of people whom Sydney called his 'pals'. Still, it had meant complete isolation, and a paralysing fear had grown upon her lately that unnatural conditions of existence were making her eccentric, a humbling thought for one with little egotism.

Lewis had not, apparently, thought her a freak, but then he was an eccentric himself in many respects, at any rate in his indifference to the opinion of other people. If he came again she would be glad. If he did not, she must endure the disappointment as she had endured harder trials.

He came again on Thursday afternoon, with something less than his usual hardy self-assurance, and armed with excuses for his presence in the neighbourhood.

Miss Hyde was deep in conversation with an elderly man of broad speech who, in both senses of the word, seemed to be a man of weight. Lewis withdrew to the kitchen garden to smoke, and presently saw the pair emerge and begin to pace the grounds, still in earnest conference, and to him it seemed that the elderly man gazed, and paused, and pointed his stick with a proprietorial air.

He engrossed himself in contemplation of a gooseberry bush when they approached his place of refuge, Miss Hyde serenely ignoring his presence after a brief glance in which he imagined he detected a twinkle of amusement at his ostentatious tact. But phrases in the male voice floated to him on the breeze. And did he once catch the words 'title deeds'? "As man to man's the way I prefer to do my business, Miss 'Yde."

" . . . That's right, ma'am, got to employ 'em as a matter of form, of course, and to comply with legal formalities. But I'll see Lawyer Wright has the dockiments all fair and square Saturday morning. As for fittings, well, a fair price . . . we ain't going to quarrel over that. Known each other a matter of some years now, ma'am. Right you are, Miss 'Yde, I'll bring her along tomorrow morning for a squint round. . . ." They faded away.

Miss Hyde explained the mystery over a perfectly leisurely tea.

"Mr. Ewings is a market gardener, and I have dealt with him for years. He has sold his ground by the station for building-land and has bought this house," she announced calmly.

"I'd no idea—"

"Of course you had not," she agreed, still more calmly. "You are the first to be told now. You see, I decided on Sunday last that I would leave Finnet, and as he had hinted broadly a year ago that if I ever contemplated selling he would like first offer, I had a chat with him on Monday morning in his office, and in the afternoon the title deeds were in the hands of his lawyer," she smiled. "Between two sensible people who know their own minds the sale of a house need not be a protracted affair. A mere matter of goods verified and delivered, and payment made."

"You knew all this yesterday, and never said a word?"

"My dear Lewis—"

"Oh, I know I'd no earthly right to special confidence, but that you could be so cool, so detached . . . I thought women always talked. . . ."

"You must remember that for many years I have had no one who wished to listen. Perhaps I have lost the habit of talking. Yesterday was a waiting time. You turned it for me into a holiday from thought."

Her tone was very gentle. "Lewis, you must not think I wanted to shut you out. But we are new acquaintances; do you realize that we only met last Sunday—when you came and helped my Robin—?"

"Time's got nothing on earth to do with it," he burst out. "Look here, surely in a business like this you could have let me help you. I don't want to butt in, to make myself a nuisance. But somehow on Sunday I thought of this place as a refuge from—oh, from the misery, the restlessness, the brutality of the world, a place one could rest in. That's why I hated Gorham and his beastly policemen trampling in—sort of defiling it with the shadow of their sordid business. I suppose it was that that has driven you to this? . . ."

She shook her head.

"No. That had nothing to do with it. Had that tragedy of poor Ellen never happened I should still be leaving now."

They were on the little terrace, and his eyes wandered over the borders before them, massed with vivid colour, though shorn of the glory of the white lilies.

"Won't you hate to leave all this?"

Her answer was evasive.

"The garden was the chief attraction for Mr. Ewings. He bought up the plots behind this some time ago, and he will probably do here what he has done on his present ground—carry on with his trade till he can sell at a profit for building. He will put up glass for tomato-growing, but keep this front as it is for a time—as an advertisement of Ewings' Nurseries." Her smile was rather bitter. "More tea, Lewis?"

"No thanks. It's useless to suggest a drive, I suppose?"

She hesitated.

"The man is coming to see how many vans they will need for the furniture on Saturday. I'm afraid I must stay. Eliza is nervous of interviewing strangers, naturally."

He sprang to his feet.

"Elvie, you don't mean to say you are clearing out of Innisfree this week? The day after tomorrow? Why, Hyde said he wouldn't be home till Monday!"

She stood looking at him, her face grey, the ugly red birth-mark sprawled conspicuously across the bloodless skin of her left cheek.

"I thought you quicker-witted than apparently you are, Lewis," she said with a deadly quiet that scorched like white-hot steel. "You can form what conclusions you like. But if you betray me to Sydney I shall never forgive you—never."

She turned and walked swiftly into the house as a man walked up from the garage gate to the back door.

Presently Eliza came out to collect the tea-things, and she paused to deliver a message.

"Miss Hyde says, sir, she is afraid she will be engaged for some time, but please not to hurry away unless you wish."

Lewis looked at his watch without seeing the time it registered.

"Oh, sorry—my compliments to Miss Hyde, but unluckily I've got an engagement. Afraid it's useless to wait. Tell her that, will you?" He made for the gate, leaving a ten-shilling note in Eliza's hand.

Chapter XV

Edward Hubberd sat behind his desk in his bare office on Thursday morning and looked dumbly at the woman before him.

This was the climax of the most ghastly week he had spent in his life. Its traces showed in his worn face. He supposed he should consider himself fortunate that so far he had escaped arrest, yet the intangible wall of suspicion by which he was surrounded was prison in itself. He was under observation night and day observation of which the police element was perhaps the leaf galling.

Wherever he went he felt himself the target for hostile glances. Men cut him in the street and turned to stare after him. If an acquaintance jumped into the same carriage he would give him a curt greeting and remain buried in his paper till he could change at the first stop. And the papers. In every hand. Each day their columns grew longer, never actually usurping the judge's privilege of condemnation, yet with ever careful, malicious ingenuity of phrase and juxtaposition of sentences pointing to him as the brutal, cowardly murderer of a miserable creature.

He saw her—was haunted by her queer figure as she stood in his bedroom, her earnest face topped by that preposterous cap with that absurd green feather sticking up.

And now this.

The woman before him was not bad-looking. Far prettier and more comely than Ellen, whose sister she said she was. It was true, too, because he remembered her demureness at the inquest in that same neat black coat and skirt, and close black hat, meekly submitting to kindly shepherding by officials. But at this moment, with that greedy look in her hot brown eyes, she was the reverse of attractive. But she was going to be a difficult customer to get rid of—far more difficult than Ellen, whom death had terribly silenced.

How could one suppose that Ellen, who had seemed such a short-sighted, dithering, ineffectual sort of fool in life, not able to carry so much as a cup of tea without slopping it all over the saucer, could actually have prepared this deadly document for use against him? Every secret meeting noted. Times and places carefully set down under their dates in plain, bald words. Words that bore the unmistakable stamp of truth. She must have snooped and spied. Yet was that necessary? They had all underrated her intelligence, her power of observation in ordinary casual matters. So used to the despised slavy that they had treated her as something sub-human, like a domestic animal, a piece of furniture.

When Ethel was quarrelling with Clarice he had tried to quell them sometimes with a reminder of her presence: "Ellen will hear you, girls!" But they turned on him with a contemptuous: "Don't be a fool! That old thing! She doesn't count! . . ."

She did count, though. He had realized how much that evening in his bedroom. And now that she was dead she was going to count supremely, through this harpy who sat in front of him, who had got him by the short hairs.

"Look here, do you realize that this is blackmail?"

Mrs. Vardon gave a snort of sheer contempt her eyes snapping.

"Blackmail? Don't you try to insult me! It's a sister's feelings, that's what it is. My pore sister having her soul smirched by 'aving to live among such dirty goings-on! It's compensation I want as her nearest relation for what that pore dear thing must have borne in silent suffering! And you can make up your mind I'm going to have it, too, mister. I've told you my terms, and I'm giving you first chance—"

"Look here, suppose I say you can take your document to the damn' police!"

She giggled, malicious triumph peeping through the cunning in her eyes. She was certainly cleverer than poor Ellen, who had disclosed her secret with no bargaining at all.

"I don't think! And wouldn't the police like to get it, that's all! *And* won't it be not half useful to them in wiping up the mystery of pore Ellen's death when they do! No reason why such a poor harmless woman should be brutally done to death, the papers say. Not a reason! No! Put that in your pipe and smoke it, Mr. Clever Edward Hubberd! But it's going to be a nice little surprise to a lot of folk when it all comes out in the newspapers, eh? I came here to give you first chance at it, but that's out of kindness, that is! I've already had the reporters after me to give them exclusive stories of my pore sister's life. Think I couldn't get twice the price out of them I'm asking you for permission to print that diary of hers in full? *And* make some people get the shock of their lives into the bargain! *And* give the police all the evidence they want to hang the fellow that murdered her!"

Edward Hubberd felt sick with horror of this respectable, neatly dressed woman before him. Did human nature really produce such crawling, filthy specimens of heartlessness and greed?

She was capitalizing on her sister's murder. That was what her threat amounted to. And he felt too stupid with want of sleep to think up any way to circumvent her simple, devilish scheme.

"If you imagine that any newspaper would dare to print that screed you are letting your ignorance mislead you," he said quietly. "Perhaps you have never heard of penalties for libel? You can take it from me, editors dread them more than they do the devil. Offer it to them and they'll put you where you belong. They aren't too likely to pay for information they daren't use."

For a moment she was daunted by his coolness, but the next, quick as a cornered rat, she called his bluff.

"If they can't use it they'll hand it to the police, and where'll you be then, my fine c—!" she cried sharply. She got up, and leaned her hands on the desk. "You can take or leave my terms, mister! Ten pounds now to keep this evidence back for one week, see? And before it's up you can settle what it's worth to you for me to keep on holding my tongue, see? And if it doesn't suit my ideas, well, I know where to go to get what's due to me, see? And you will be properly in the cart once for all."

She had been cute enough to bring only a copy with her, made in her own illiterate hand. It was damning evidence against her had he dared to risk prosecuting her for blackmail. But to expose her was to expose his own life's disaster naked. He was effectually caught in that simple trap which makes the profession of extortion under threat both easy and lucrative if it be properly set.

Mrs. Vardon took the ten pounds that he dumbly handed to her with a smile of conscious pride. Ten good treasury notes—more money than she had handled together in her life before, and the reward of her own smartness. But when she was about to put in her bag the paper that she had used so cleverly, an unexpected hand filched it from her, and Mr. Hubberd slipped it into his breast pocket.

She was frightened and enraged by that sudden action. "You give that back to me! It is mine!"

"You had better leave it with me for a bit." His tone was cool and even. "I have, as you said, to work out what it—and the original—are worth to me, Mrs. Vardon. I'm not a rich man, you know. Don't you think you could name your final figure now, to give me additional food for thought?"

He met the greedy, hesitating flicker of her eyes with a look so coldly impersonal that for the first time a shiver of genuine fear went down her spine. Ellen had got herself murdered over this very business, and she would have to be careful. But he could not attempt violence here, in a public office, with a clerk within call in the next room. She intended to demand £100, but under that flick of fear her temper multiplied it by five. To the wife of a greengrocer's assistant £500 was an incredible sum, wealth beyond the dreams of avarice, and avarice was her dominating characteristic.

"Quite so." His courteous manner was that of a man dealing with an ordinary business proposition. "Better give your address where I can drop you a line when I've thought it over."

"You can send it to 105 Lavender Road, Harlesden, where my pore sister lived. But mind, don't you try no tricks on me—I'm not living there!"

"No?" He went to the door and opened it to show her out, and the typist in the front office caught the quiet toneless accents that she had grown accustomed to in Mr. Hubberd this week: "Very good, we'll see what can be done. Good morning, Mrs. Vardon. Miss Stacey, kindly, show this lady the way to the street."

The girl who fulfilled this order—Mr. Hubberd having returned to his room again—by pointing an ink-stained thumb in the direction of the entrance, went back to her typewriter with an excited grin. Miss Stacey knew what was coming next to Hubby, if he didn't.

Langton, the boss, was fed up with having that plain-clothes flattie always hanging round outside, and the same old joke callers always made. But she felt real sorry about losing poor old Hubby herself. He might be a mutt and a dumb-bell, but he'd always treated her like a lady. Yet if she couldn't simply believe he'd got the guts to murder anyone, it was sort of exciting to have all sorts of parties dropping in to ask questions. That big, burly chap who came Tuesday, whom she was sure was a Scotland Yard detective, and the reporters that popped in and out chatting to her—why, one had brought her chocs, and another asked her to tea, only she wasn't having any, thank you! Maybe he'd be at the corner now! Well, she wasn't going to waste her one free afternoon waiting much longer. She covered her typewriter—it was just on one—and snatched down her coat from its peg. But she put it on with unnecessary slowness, anxious not to miss the final drama of the week. Not a sound had come from that room behind the partition wall since Hubby's visitor left. There it was! Mr. Langton running downstairs from his office above! She listened intently. He opened poor old Hubby's door and barged straight in without even a tap first! Well, that was a liberty! Even if he was going to give him the sack he might have been polite first!

They'd probably jaw for hours, though. And time was getting on. Silly to waste her one free day to wait for what she'd hear first thing tomorrow. She went out, thrilled with excitement at the jolly eventfulness of life, and left Hubby to his fate.

Edward Hubberd looked up as Langton walked in, and the spurt of irritation he felt at his casualness showed in his eyes.

"D'you mind—as a mere formality—knocking another time, Langton?"

"Didn't I? Don't be so touchy, old man. You don't look as if you were terribly busy!" His manner was so hearty that Hubberd, with sick dismay, realized what was coming.

"I've finished. I was just going to lunch."

"Glad I caught you, then, old man! The fact is, I've got a message from the directors. We've all been feeling a bit worried about you this week—your health, and that, you know." He paused, but Hubberd did not help him out. "Yes. Don't know if you ever study the old phiz in a mirror. P'raps you don't, any more than I do, finding the vision a damned sight too painful to look at more often than I need, ha, ha! But the long and short of it is, you're looking infernally off colour. We've all noticed it, and what we think is it's time you had a bit of a holiday and took care of yourself."

"Am I to be paid during this—holiday?"

"Well, as to that. . . . Look here, Hubberd, don't, please, take all this in the wrong spirit! You've done some pretty good work for our old show in the years we've slogged to get it on its feet, and going strong, and the directors and myself aren't likely to forget it, are we? Damn it, you know we're not! But what we've agreed about is that you need a bit of a let-up, a rest, p'raps a spot of travel or whatever you fancy best to recruit your energies and tone you up generally."

"Has my work called for criticism?"

"Well, old man, what's the sense of making a silly remark like that? You know you could carry your job on your head. But you've got to regard the situation a bit from the office point of view, you know. We all feel sympathetic over the nasty spot of private bother you've been having lately; but look here, you've got to acknowledge it's not frightfully encouraging to our clients, or even the staff and Board. I'll leave myself out of it this time, for I'm damned if it worries me a jot—but there it is, tecs at the door, and so on. Not too good for business, is it? And, after all, we've got to put the Company's interests first. Ahead of our private feelings. Hence our agreement that you take a holiday till things have blown over a bit. Now, be a reasonable fellow, old chap, and—"

"You haven't answered my question yet, Langton."

"Eh, what's that? Oh yes, about pay. Well, you know as well as I do that's practically impossible, old boy, as things are. It's fit to turn our hairs white to screw up profits sufficient to cover official salaries as it is! And we'd have to pay a—a substitute to carry on as manager here in your place. . . . I'm afraid funds won't exactly run to more than that for the present. But, of course, I needn't say, though the directors bade me be sure and emphasize it, we'll be only too glad to see you back in your old chair when things have calmed down a bit, and you're looking fitter and more like your cheery old self again." ('When you're either definitely cleared or hanged, and I'm damned if I care which way your trouble gets finished,' Langton's thoughts added viciously.) But aloud he said: "But about finances, though. You'd have drawn a month's salary in advance, Friday, like the rest of us poor tykes, so that's all right. You'll be able to trot off for your holiday with a free mind as to cash. So so long, old chap, and all the best! Any message for the Board? Some little genial word of appreciation of their thoughtfulness, eh?"

"You can tell the Board that they have behaved exactly as I'd have expected them to," Hubberd said quietly. "And you too, Langton. That's all, I think."

His eyes rested on Langton's face with a bleak stare that roused him to a sense of acute discomfort. A fantastic thought flashed into his not-too-imaginative brain that he told later to his wife.

"I felt my spine go all creepy, sweat trickling down my skin, you know. But it wasn't because I practically knew the chap had murdered one person, and might be jolly well thinking how he could murder me. It was because his eyes looked dead. Like the eyes of a dead man looking out of a living body. I give you my word, I thought to myself: 'Good Lord! Hubberd himself inside that ordinary sort of mug of his and his big frame, is stone, *dead*!'"

"What did you say then, dear?" she asked, interested.

"I don't think I said anything. I just slid off his desk, where I'd been sitting sideways swinging my legs, to make it all seem jolly and matey, you know. He had opened his drawers and was transferring little personal belongings to his pockets, quite quiet and steady, and when I sneaked to the door he said: 'Cheerio', and I said 'Toodle-oo', and I went upstairs and had a stiff whisky, and not before I wanted it."

"I do hope you're not going all psychic, darling! But"—more cheerfully—"it was because you're so awfully kind-hearted. You hated sacking him. Still, you couldn't go on keeping a murderer in the office!"

"Draw it mild, girlie. It hasn't been proved he did it yet!"

"Don't be silly, Len. Of course he did it! Everyone says so. Besides, who else could have? And look at the way the Hugheses cleared off quick and left him, and Ethel Hubberd, too! Of course they knew he was guilty and didn't want to have to stand up in court and help get him hanged! Though they can't make a wife give evidence against her husband if she doesn't want to, can they? I expect in her case it was sheer blind funk, not wanting to stop alone with him in the house and get herself murdered too. But who's going to take on his job at the office, darling?"

"Oh, well, I'm going to run it in with my own for a while, at any rate, with young Tommy to do the donkey-work."

"Now, Leonard, you are not going to be fool enough to do the work of two men without extra pay!"

"Who said I was, sweetheart? As a fact, it's happened at a rather convenient time! We can do with a bit extra just now, with a new car in prospect, eh?"

"Oh, if you're going to draw his salary properly, besides your own, that's all right."

Edward Hubberd cleared the last oddments from his drawers after Langton left him. He had not expected the sack, because he knew that to the unstinted labour and foresight he had put into it the Company owed three parts of its sound present position. But now that it had happened he realized that he might have seen it coming, for Langton's motives were clear; and, besides, it was of a piece with what had occurred to him that morning.

Though Lewis Hardwicke had met him on Tuesday evening, and very decently begged him to join him in rooms he inhabited off and on in Bedford Row, he preferred, as The Burrs was intolerable, to take up quarters in a private hotel near Northbourne. He was in no mood for company, even that of Hardwicke, whose persistent friendliness this week had been its single redeeming feature. Quite civilly this morning, however, the manager had informed him that his room was required.

Gage, the agent, would receive his note giving notice for the Pound Lane house today. Beyond next quarter's rent (if the place were not sublet meantime) he owed nothing. The furniture was Ethel's, bought in her name with his money when, to appease her discontent, he left the East, his natural environment, and settled in England to an alien type of job, and an existence of uncongenial and empty suburban dullness. He drew £25 per month (and, as Langton knew well enough, not in advance). He had sent Ethel a tenner last night, paid his hotel bill, and given a second tenner away this morning. Ethel must raise what she could on the furniture, and that was that.

His life policy must lapse. In any case it would not be honoured. He sorted the contents of his desk into order. His work was up to date, and whoever took over his job would have plain sailing. Langton would no doubt collect the keys left here.

That lazy young devil Stacey was sure to have gone. He slipped a couple of half-crowns in an envelope, on which he wrote her name, "Miss June (God save the mark!) Stacey", to put in her drawer where she would find it tomorrow morning. As Saturday was their busiest day, the typists were given Thursday off.

He was walking out of this office, where he had worked since the building was put up—before that in a wooden hutch, where he and Langton actually nursed the infant show into existence—with less than two quid in his pocket.

He had completely forgotten the detective outside when he reached the road. The man, who was buying a paper from a boy at a little distance, looked up to discover his quarry mounting a bus.

He raced, he shouted, but the vehicle, blandly unconscious of his need of it, moved inexorably on. He leapt back to where his bicycle was leaning against the kerb—as he realized too late he should have done at once—and pursued. But the brief delay proved fatal. When he overtook the bus at the next stopping-place along the country road, having risked his neck dodging about in thick afternoon motor-traffic, Mr. Hubberd, recalled to the present by his own activities, had chosen a convenient moment to drop off in front of a stationary car, pause behind it while the hunt went by, and—walk away into space.

Chapter XVI

"You have the nerve to admit that you stood outside that entrance all morning and then allowed Mr. Hubberd to walk out and coolly mount a bus under your very nose? What do you suppose you were sent there for? To be a street ornament? I suppose it never entered your head that the very fact of a bus halting there demanded extra vigilance on your part? And what was to prevent your jumping on the bus after him? Going to tell me you were suddenly struck down by paralysis and lost the use of your legs?"

The man wilted under the Chief Inspector's lashing tongue.

"I tried, sir. But the conductor was inside and the bus had started and was gathering speed, and I missed it by seconds. Then I nipped back to get my bike and followed it to the next stopping-place. The traffic was awfully thick on the road, but I overtook and boarded it and searched both decks, but he simply wasn't there. He must have dropped off in between—"

"Of course he dropped off—since you let him get on. Did you expect him to sit tamely waiting till you chose to come up with him again? And you didn't spot him in the road when he'd dropped off, either! Upon my word, for an exhibition of sheer, incompetent idiocy this beats anything I've ever experienced. And if this happened at 1.45, why have you waited till nearly five o'clock to report it?"

"I scoured the roads between the two stopping-places first in the hope of picking him up. Then I went back to his office in case he'd returned. The other manager was in Mr. Hubberd's office when I walked straight in—Mr. Langton. He said Mr. Hubberd was out and not expected back today. So—so I came to inform you, sir."

"Give me your morning report before this disaster happened."

"Mr. Hubberd left his hotel at 8.45 a.m. carrying his suitcase, which he deposited at the left-luggage office at Northbourne Station. He walked from there to his office. There were the usual lot of callers there this morning, but only one who asked for him by name. It was a Mrs. Vardon. I got this from the typist, June Stacey, who went off for her half-day at one o'clock. This person, whom I recognized, having seen her at the inquest, was there half an hour, and went just before Stacey did. The girl didn't hear any of their conversation, as she was typing, and she said Mr. Hubberd was quite cool when he called her to show Mrs. Vardon out, but the woman looked 'very bucked' with herself. Stacey also said that Mr. Langton had gone in to speak to Mr. Hubberd. But nothing else happened till he came out himself. . . . I called at the left-luggage office on the way here, but the suitcase was still there. I asked the clerk to 'phone here, to Finnet police station, if anyone came for it, and to hold the man till he got an answer. There was no address on the case, only Mr. Hubberd's full name. That is all, sir."

"You can go."

The man hesitated, his face white with anxiety.

"Are you going to put me on the report, sir? I know I've made an absolute mess of this job. But it means a tremendous lot to me."

"I'll have to think it over. Meantime, report for duty at headquarters tomorrow as usual. At least you offered me no futile excuses."

"A merciful man," thought Gorham grimly, when a chastened detective had gone, "is merciful to his beast. If I'd been broken for my first failure I wouldn't have gone far in the Department. But if Hubberd goes and commits suicide now—at the eleventh hour! Dash it, why couldn't he stay put for one more day till I've completed the case?"

He rang up the manager of the hotel at Northbourne.

"Sorry, Mr. Hubberd left the hotel this morning."

"Chief Inspector Gorham speaking. Was Mr. Hubberd requested to leave?"

"Well, not exactly, sir. Mr. Hubberd only engaged his room from day to day, and this morning the room was unfortunately booked."

"He was requested to leave, then."

"His room was unfortunately engaged, sir."

Gorham rang up Mr. Langton.

"What? Mr. Hubberd? Sorry, he's not here. . . . What? When is he expected back? Well, that's rather difficult to say. To be candid, Mr. Hubberd is temporarily no longer on the staff. Being in bad need of a holiday, he left us this afternoon, to our deep regret. Awfully nice chap, but there it is. Silly to sacrifice one's health when a bit of rest will put one to rights, eh? No, I can't say where the dear old boy is, he didn't mention any plans or leave an address. . . . What? Disagreement? Of course not! A tremendous favourite with everybody, parted on the friendliest terms. I for one'll be only too glad to have him back when he feels up to tackling the old job again. That all I can do? Sorry, then; his absence leaves me with a frightful lot of extra to do. Good-bye."

Gorham rang up Northbourne Station confirming previous instructions and saying he'd send a man down at once to be on the spot in case the luggage was claimed. But gloomily he felt certain that Hubberd would foresee that move and leave his suitcase severely alone. After being kicked out of his hotel, and sacked by that oily brute of a manager, Langton . . . And his tailer had got to select that critical moment, when the man had been driven to the desperate limit of his tether, to let him slip out of sight!

What had that Vardon woman called on him for? For the matter of that, why was she still in London? They had been given their fare home, and Vardon said he was leaving for Manchester directly after the funeral yesterday. Vardon would bear looking into. She had given the Higgs' address in Harlesden. Had Hubberd possibly gone to join his wife at Ealing?

He hesitated for a long time before making this call, for here he was touching on delicate ground. But Hubberd was not the sort to abandon his responsibilities lightly, and the chance existed that he might have communicated his movements to her.

A few seconds later her voice reached him:

"Hullo. Mrs. Hubberd speaking. Yes?"

"Oh, Mrs. Hubberd, can you tell me where I can get in touch with your husband? I have an important communication to make to him. Is he with you?"

"No. I haven't seen him since Tuesday. Who is it speaking?"

"I'll take my oath you didn't see him Tuesday," growled Gorham's thoughts, but aloud he said in urgent tones:

"A friend of your husband. Look here, it is really vital that I should find him. Can you suggest an address?"

"He is probably still at his office. He doesn't leave before six as a rule, and often later. Northbourne, No.—"

He interrupted her as she gave the number.

"Yes, yes, I've got that. But I'm informed he left there today for good, and the hotel where he has put up since Tuesday at Northbourne as well. They could give me no information at the office as to his whereabouts or future plans. And his house in Pound Lane,

Finnet, is shut up. Do you really mean he hasn't rung you up or written to you—"

"He hasn't written me a line, or rung me up! I had an envelope from him this morning, but all it contained was a miserably small bank-note—not a single word with it. Look here, I simply can't believe he has left his job for good! We haven't a single farthing beyond what he earns! Oh, damn, I *must* know who I'm telling all my private affairs to! Who *are* you? I insist on knowing."

"I'm one that's a good deal more decently concerned about your husband than you've appeared to be since you left him to shift for himself last Tuesday. As you can't help me, that's that!"

He had caught the rising panic in her tone, and it gave him grim pleasure to picture her frantically ringing up the office and having his news verified. That 'miserable bank-note' was the last money of her husband's that she was likely to see, if her statement about their finances was true. And he was right in his judgment of Hubberd. He had paid up, the limit of his resources very likely. But the conclusion that he had stripped himself probably of his last pound did not ease his anxiety about Hubberd. He simply could not afford to let the fellow go and commit suicide—driven to desperation by that public load of suspicion which had lost him his job on top of the loss of his home and wife—now, when he only required certainty on three points—the origin of that coat, the cause of that inexplicable hole in the beret, and one other—to reach a point in the case that would justify arrest of the criminal.

In the matter of the coat Mrs. Higgs might be able to help him, and throw light on Maggie Vardon's doings at the same time.

But this complication of Hubberd's disappearance meant annoying delay in clearing up the investigation.

He seemed to have no ties in Finnet or elsewhere, and not a solitary friend to whom he would be likely to turn for help in a crisis, unless Lewis Hardwicke could be counted one, for though Hardwicke had described their former relations as a merely casual acquaintance, their common misfortune this week had certainly brought them together.

Hardwicke had sought Hubberd out late on Tuesday afternoon at his office and accompanied him to his new quarters, apparently to see him installed, and gone to the hotel again on Wednesday night after he left Innisfree, and stayed till midnight.

Perhaps he would be able to clear up the mystery of this disappearance, which could possibly have been discussed between them during these daily conferences.

Pound Lane was still under close, though now unobtrusive, police surveillance, and learning that Innisfree was once more being honoured by a call from Hardwicke, he sent a note asking him to step along to see him at the police station immediately, if he would be so obliging.

Lewis obliged at once, for the messenger just caught him at the gate, though he did not step, but came in his car, in an extremely bad temper slightly lightened by natural curiosity as to what Gorham had discovered about his Saturday-evening doings.

But the Chief Inspector took the wind out of his sails by thanking him with warmth for his promptitude, and plunging at once into the subject of Hubberd.

"You haven't seen him today, have you?"

"No. I thought of rolling along to Northbourne now," Lewis said, startled. "In my opinion, the way that chap has been treated is sheerly iniquitous. Not only the rotten and absolutely baseless hounding that he's getting from the papers, but the incredible insults he's had to put up with from the public—fellows cutting him dead—people staring and whispering. I've seen it myself, even in that potty little hotel, which ought to be thankful to have a chap like that putting up there to give it a bit of tone. In his place I'd have been fighting mad by this time, and turned round and landed them with something that'd have given their ugly mugs fresh food for thought."

Gorham grinned.

"How does he take it?"

"Oh, in a sort of grim silence. Says it's no more than is to be expected; we've all read about murder cases and jumped to conclusions in the same fat-headed way. But it isn't just fat-headedness in this case, it's the streak of vicious herd cruelty showing up in its nastiest form. One of the pack down and the rest hounding it to death. We talk a lot of bunk about civilized man, but the mass instinct of man to tear a wounded fellow to pieces is exactly the same as that of a pack of savage wolves."

"I don't know much about animals. I wasn't even sure that there were no lions in China till Mr. Hubberd told me," Gorham said mildly. "I'm glad to hear he's taking a sensible view of things. But I gather you haven't heard that he's got the sack—"

"What!" Hardwicke sprang to his feet, his eyes blazing with wrath. "Got the sack from that show he sweated like mad to create? That's that swine Langton, for a snip! He was furiously jealous of Ted from the start, only waiting to edge him out when he'd placed the Company on a sound footing. Ted's an amazingly simple sort of fellow in some things. Couldn't realize what that little swine was after. But he's chatted a lot about his job to me because, well, candidly, it was the one topic he was interested in that we could discuss without tripping over the wires, and from things he let drop Langton's attitude was as plain as a pikestaff to me. But look here, Gorham, this show is really beyond the limit. You're not going to tell me seriously that you yourself believe Ted Hubberd guilty?"

"Don't be silly, man. You know I can't commit myself to any definite statements like that till the case is finally cleared up. But I'll own I'm damned worried about Hubberd. That's what I wanted to see you about. Perhaps you'll see daylight where I can't. Now sit down in that pew, and keep still, and I'll tell you where we are."

He related the story of Hubberd's day without disguise.

"So that's how it is, my boy," he finished. "He was turned out of his lodgings, and on top of that out of the job that's been a sort of anchorage to him this week, and to crown it my man had to go and lose sight of him at the very crisis he was planked at his heels to guard against. I've not been blind to the campaign that's been going on against him," he added gravely.

"The papers aren't under my control, and, besides, they've been careful to print nothing that might hit themselves later. But the danger existed that Hubberd might feel goaded into doing something rash. But beyond that, in my view it was never the outside riot, but the domestic mess he was in when we arrived on the scene, that's chiefly worried him. I don't know whether you're in his confidence as to that. Are you?"

Lewis Hardwicke frowned, and fidgeted in his chair.

"I don't see what his private affairs have got to do with you," he growled.

"Need you pretend to be denser than you are?" Gorham exclaimed impatiently. "If there wasn't a blazing domestic row going on at The Burrs on Sunday when I went there first, my name's not John Gorham. They were at high tension, the lot of them, and Hubberd himself was the only one who attempted to decently cover it. My sergeant interrupted a further instalment later in the day, and add to that the fact that Mrs. Hubberd left the house on Tuesday while he was facing the music at the inquest, and—"

"Ted's been treated damnably from first to last," Hardwicke broke in angrily. "He was in a perfectly good job which suited him down to the ground, in Upper Burma. You know, he's a grandson of Edward Hubberd the great Chinese scholar, and various members of his family, including his own father, have been distinguished in the same line. He was born in China and speaks half a dozen Oriental languages by nature, so to speak. But Ethel, whom he met when she was travelling as companion to some elderly female globe-trotter, made him chuck his job and bring her home to England, where he was like a fish out of water, all his training wasted in rotten little jobs that were the best he could pick up.

"They seemed all right when I first knew them at The Burrs, but—well, you know what happens between married folk with utterly incompatible tastes. Ted had the East in his blood, and the East bored his wife stiff. She'd have been in her element, I dare say, with a smart flat in Town, and servants, and a rich dolt of a husband thrown in, and instead she had Ted, who worked like a horse to keep a bare roof over their heads and the rabble she'd planted on him. Do you wonder if there were rows?"

"No," said Gorham thoughtfully. "How much of this is observation and how much did he tell you of the latest, old man?"

"The latest?" Hardwicke stared. "I put two and two together from bits I'd seen and that. He's kept off discussing his wife, if that's what you mean. It was sickening of her to clear off and leave him when he was all worked up by the infernal, silly questions you'd worried him with. But I still don't see that his domestic affairs need interest you."

He looked genuinely disturbed; his ugly face twisted into an expression of worried apprehension as he stood up.

"Look here, I think I'll run over to Ealing and have a word with Ethel. She's at her mother's. Do you know the address?" Gorham scribbled it on a slip of paper and handed it over. "Apart from Mrs. Hubberd, you don't know any relative or friend to whom he might have gone?" he asked.

"Not a soul. He's mentioned one cousin, Pine Hubberd, but I haven't the slightest idea if he is even in England. I may get something out of Ethel, but—" He bristled with sudden aggressiveness—"If I do, you can take it from me, Gorham, you're the last person alive I'd betray him to!"

"If you get him, stick close to him yourself, my boy. That's all I ask," Gorham retorted with a cool grin. "Maybe we'll be having a little chat about your own doings one of these days. Still finding the Burdock comfortable? They go in for very decent grub there, at any rate."

"What do you know about the Burdock?" Hardwicke inquired suspiciously. And Gorham's grin broadened.

"I looked about for you last time one of your fellow members stood me luncheon there—when was it? One day this week. Very interesting chap, pointed out all the celebrities in the room to me. Said he only knew you by sight, but another Finnet man—Mr. Hyde, the author—he'd often met. Well, so long, old man, you mustn't keep me gossiping here all evening. I've got a job to hold down, if you haven't."

He closed the door he had opened for his visitor, and as he heard the clatter of angry footsteps on the uncarpeted passage, followed by the honk of a car, he permitted himself a mild chuckle.

Chapter XVII

Mrs. Higgs invited Mr. Gorham and his friend Mr. Moh into her spotless kitchen.

"We've come along to worry you again, Mrs. Higgs, you see!" Gorham remarked in his friendly way.

"Is it about the little book, sir?" she said eagerly. "I hope I didn't do wrong giving it to Mrs. Vardon, but there, when you was here Sunday I was that moithered with the thought of pore Ellen passing away without preparation, as you might say. I never thought to mention it, and there it stood up be'ind the clock where I'd put it when I picked it up, and never gave it another thought till Mrs. Vardon and her hubby come Tuesday, then, being her sister, what more natural?"

"I'm not sure that I follow, Mrs. Higgs. What book was this?"

"Haven't you seen my Ben?" she cried, looking quite distressed. "There, I made sure when I see you two gents at the door that he'd managed to get along to you about it after all, though he did say, being on this special job Shepherd's Bush way, that he didn't see how he could spare time to go to the station house before seven this evening on his way home!"

"I haven't seen Ben, Mrs. Higgs," said Gorham good-humouredly. "Suppose you explain about this book, and where Ben comes in?"

"It's the bit of a diary that pore Ellen carried in her bag, sir. What I found on the mat when she'd gone Saturday, and put on the mantelpiece to give her back when she come in, only, of course, with her dying and all she never come back," Mrs. Higgs explained, much flurried. "And Ben late on this job all week, though he had to ask off for Tuesday morning, we've hardly had time to talk a word, and my heart almost too full for speech in any case." Sobs threatened to interrupt now, and Gorham hastened to put in a soothing sentence.

"Yes, yes, of course, you must have felt horribly upset all the week, my good soul. I quite understand that. But about this book—"

"Ben says last night, when we was mentioning Mrs. Vardon, and me not caring for her the same as I cared for pore Ellen, nor nothing near, that I'd ought to have let you have the book, and he'd have to do right by his word and mention my giving it to Mrs. Vardon, being her sister and her rightful heir, as she says herself to me. So you won't think as it's Ben's fault, him being at the police station at this identical moment, I shouldn't wonder."

"No, no. I quite see how it happened. But what was the book like? An ordinary diary, like this?"

He produced a small Letts diary from his pocket and showed it to her, but she shook her head.

"It were a cheaper one than that, sir. A Woolworth one, fatted up with bits of paper that she wrote on, with a rubber band to keep it together. When she read a bit of poetry she liked she wrote it down to remember it by, and if she didn't lose the bit of paper first she'd copy it into a bigger book she had. Said it helped her to get through her duties better if she'd a nice bit of poetry to think about. A real good woman our pore Ellen was!" Tears threatened once more and again Gorham intervened.

"Do you know if her ladies ever gave her any old clothes, Mrs. Higgs? Either for herself or to dispose of at jumble sales or the like? I mean, especially, men's things. There's a man's old suit that I believe was given her for a jumble sale at one of her churches that I've heard mentioned."

Mr. Moh, seated on the edge of a chair, glanced at Gorham with an expression of bland interest on his face. He had not been told the reason for their calling a second time on the good Mrs. Higgs. But to her the question seemed a natural one, for had not poor Ellen been practically clothed in cast-off garments bestowed by her ladies?

"Well, of course they give her lots of things, sir. Hats, and a skirt, and maybe a bundle of stockings or suchlike," she answered eagerly. "Why, Mrs. Hubberd gave her that tweed coat she wore last winter but one! And being so industrious, she'd generally find some way to furbish them up however rubbishy they might be, either to wear herself or, as you say, for the jumble at St. Vitus's. The awful old trash they'd be glad of you'd be surprised! Why, once there was an old busted pair of boots of Mr. 'Ubberd's that even pore Ellen was doubtful about taking, but she did, and she told me, as pleased as Punch, they went off like lightning for ninepence to a cobbler's wife what said her husband could patch them up beautiful for her eldest. Ellen attended that jumble herself, and she was ever so pleased. But it was suits you asked about, but I don't remember her bringing home no suits...."

"Well, perhaps not a whole suit, but trousers, or coats?" Mrs. Higgs shook her head doubtfully.

"No trousers, sir, but there was an old coat, dark blue—"

"Did she mention where she got it from?" Gorham asked quietly.

"I think it was from Miss 'Yde's, sir, though it was done up in a separate parcel. The things that come from Miss Hyde were never just rags, like what Mrs. Hubberd's were. She'd put in good, sensible things, stockings and underwear, and sometimes a length of material that Ellen was thankful to have for herself, but this old coat the servant there gave her separate, saying the gentleman had given it her to throw away, tied up in a bit of paper like she gave it to Ellen."

"I see. The servant just handed over the packet without opening it, is that it?"

"That's what I understood, but Ellen said it would do for the jumble when she looked at it."

"Do you remember when this was exactly?"

"I can't lay my mind to the very evening she brought it home, sir. But the jumble was the very Monday after my cousin May came in to tea Saturday, before going into hospital with her bad leg. And Ellen took her bundle round to the hall that evening. I'm sure it was that day because she came down and asked to borrow some cloudy ammonia to sponge the coat with, but my cousin being here, she wouldn't stop for a cup of tea, being never one to intrude. I went with May to the hospital after tea, and that was May 19th."

"Well, thanks very much, Mrs. Higgs, that explains about the coat," Gorham said briskly. "Now, about Mrs. Vardon. Is she staying with you? I understood they were going home after the inquest, on Tuesday."

"Well, about him I can't say. But they never stayed here, sir. But Tuesday afternoon they come here, which was only natural, though I can't say I take to her, and him just a pore yes-man hubby, though polite enough I will say, and she sorted through her pore sister's things like it was her right to do, a policeman having brought back the key saying it wasn't wanted again. And when we was having a cup of tea together she says now she's in London she thought she'd stop on a bit and look at the shops, though he'd have to go home or risk losing his job, and I'd given her the book at once, never thinking, and she asked if any letters came would I keep them till she called, her having given this address at home."

"You don't know where she's staying?"

"No, sir."

"Have any letters come?"

"No, none at all."

"Well, thanks very much for this chat," Gorham said, rising. "Tell Ben it's all right about the book, and I'd rather you didn't mention you spoke to me about it to Mrs. Vardon if she comes again. No need to stir up bother, is there? Come along, Moh, if you've quite finished chattering your head off with Mrs. Higgs! Jolly talkative chap to go about with isn't he, Mrs. Higgs?"

He laughed, and she giggled, though with a deprecating glance at the silent Mr. Moh to make sure that he took no offence at his friend's joke.

But in the car the two men looked at each other.

"To think that that guileless old body had the key to the whole mystery on her mantelpiece last Saturday, Li Moh, and we missed it!"

"Also information re coat."

"That wasn't important then. We both knew where it came from as soon as we looked it over, but it needn't have had any connection with the crime then."

Mr. Moh uttered a flat contradiction.

"It was always at the heart of the crime."

"I didn't arrive at it that way." Gorham stuck to his point. "I have to keep closely to facts, you know, and till Tuesday the other facts of the case tended to eliminate the coat as a clue of central importance. It wasn't till I interviewed Hubberd at the office that I got my first real grip on the case. If I'd got that diary on Sunday it would have saved me wasting two days."

Mr. Moh looked puzzled.

"But she had not the diary with her on Saturday when she was murdered!"

"No, but she'd probably jotted down the points that led up to her death."

"Do you need her notes?"

"No-o. Except as evidence. I've got all five answers to the essential questions, by whom, how, where, and why, though the where is still guesswork."

"I know the others roughly, but the why I have not got,"

Mr. Moh murmured with a troubled frown. "At least—" He paused, and added earnestly: "I am terribly anxious, Gorham; the murder of this meddlesome woman is only a beginning, I feel, a preliminary—scarcely intended till the last moment, perhaps. But the evil impulse that struck her down is conscious of its power now, brooding, meditating..." He shivered. "It is also known that a killer can only be hanged once. Did you know this diary existed before the good Higgs told you?"

"No. But there were those other scribblings, suggesting that she was in the habit—as she had no friends to confide in—of expressing herself on paper. And I was afraid Vardon had got hold of something we'd missed, otherwise why her call on Hubberd? You see, she heard his fishy evidence at the inquest, saw he was under suspicion. Look here, Moh, I've got an idea. I must go and see a Press agent I know, and you've got to come with me. But first I must arrange with the local fellows to have Vardon copped as soon as she shows her nose at Higgs's door. Stay here like a good chap, will you, and keep cave, till I bring a chap along to watch the house?"

Mr. Moh obligingly got out and waited till his friend returned. "That's all right," Gorham said with satisfaction, and jerked his head towards a tall, uniformed figure that strolled past them on the pavement. "If Vardon appears she'll be taken to the station and searched for stolen property, and her lodgings too if the book isn't found on her. After that it depends—on whether the book is innocuous or not, and what use she's made of it if it isn't. Now for Fleet Street. When I've finished my next job I vote we take the rest of the evening off and have a run into the country. I'm rather keen to see that place Yorker's Manor that's cropped up in this Finnet case once or twice. Do you know it?"

"It is the golf club where Mr. Hardwicke plays and Mr. Hyde spent last weekend."

"That's right," Gorham beamed on him. "But the chap who lunched me at the Burdock yesterday, Donald Levi, says it's the most perfect specimen of a Tudor manor house left round London, and only five miles south-west of Harrow, at that. I thought I knew most places in and about London, but I'd never even heard of this one before."

Yorker's Manor, Levi had informed him with an architect's enthusiasm, had rooms and historical associations that dated back to Plantagenet times, and Gorham, who, though ill-informed in

English history, knew London and its environs intimately, felt chagrined that he had missed a place that was evidently famous.

"We've both been obsessed with this case this week. We deserve a few hours off," he insisted when Mr. Moh inquired with some austerity what he thought he was going to do there.

But when they emerged from a humming building just behind St. Bride's Church Mr. Moh's placidity had vanished. Gorham gripped his arm and dragged a limp and wilting form into the car, for he was in a pitiable state of agitation.

"How could this lowly and totally uneducated person dare to attempt such a task?" he wailed. "Only dense ignorance of pitiless and brutal friend could suppose that an unlettered worm could undertake a writing demanding immense linguistic achievements, wide acquaintance with inflections of hugely varying dialects that sage ones steeped from infancy in atmosphere of scholarship may scarcely acquire. Unparalleled presumptiveness of late gruesome perpetration must draw down unmitigated wrathful contempt of all educated fellow countrymen to obliteration of luckless self in ocean of shame."

"Oh, I dare say it won't be as bad as all that, old man," his brutal friend offered cheerful consolation. "In any case, you're a detective, same as me, and we've got to take the kicks with the ha'pence in our job. If that message you translated hits the right eyes, and gets across, you can forget the sage ones, who've probably never done anything half as useful in their mouldy lives. Now let's get a quick meal before we start on our run."

But Mr. Moh remained mournful even when they were in the car again, and driving westward.

"Look here, Moh, don't you want to come?" Gorham demanded at length. Mr. Moh roused himself from a silence that had lasted for fifteen minutes.

"The company of my Gorham is ever sweet to me," he murmured in deprecating accents, "but in strenuousness of recent chasings about metropolis my bike has been laid up at Innisfree, and I feel yearning to regain possession of same this evening."

"All right, I can go round by Finnet if you like and drop you there," he said. "I've got to look in at the station for any messages at nine o'clock, in any case, but I'll leave you at Innisfree first."

They came along the London Road, past the station, and over the bridge and up Chetwynd Avenue.

Turning into Pound Lane, the car stopped at the white gate, and as Mr. Moh got out and opened it Robin came tearing up with a torn yellow duster held high in his mouth. He abandoned it, however, to dance about Mr. Moh in the eager, joyous fashion that is a spaniel's characteristic form of welcome, and the pair disappeared down the walk as Gorham turned his car and went back down the avenue. But to his immense satisfaction a piece of the puzzle which hitherto had baffled his most ingenious efforts to solve clicked suddenly into its place.

A taxi was standing outside the police station when he drove up, and a second later he was interviewing its driver in the office. He was a superior-looking young man, his name Cyril White, and he walked into the room with an air charged with defensive pugnacity that was not lost on Gorham, though he ignored it. He scribbled down the man's name and number, then put a friendly question.

"What made you come so far out of your beat, White, instead of reporting at Scotland Yard?"

"Just taken a fare out to Harrow, Mr. Gorham, and seeing the inquiry come from you, and I've an hour to spare before picking him up again, I rung up here, and as they said you'd be in at nine I came along to save time. Don't make any difference, does it?"

"Guessed I'd be in Finnet, eh?" he chuckled.

"Suppose it's on this Finnet murder case you wanted to see me, sir," White said with a broad grin, "since the inquiry concerned Saturday night."

"You dropped a fare at the Burdock Club in Sackviile Street at 10.35 p.m., Saturday?"

"That's right."

"Give me the history of that fare."

"I was cruising slowly past the Tivoli about 8.40 p.m., having dropped a fare at the Gaiety, when a gent waved his stick from the pavement outside the Strand Stores, and when I reached him asked if I could drive him out to Finnet. He had a bunch of roses in his hand that he just bought from a street barrow. He told me Finnet High Street and got in. We made the place in good time, and when we turned into the High Street from the lower road, and I asked for fresh directions, he said the church on the hill. We mounted the street; he got down at the churchyard, telling me to wait. He was gone a few minutes, and when he comes back without his flowers—"

"Wait a second. Wouldn't the churchyard gates be shut at that time?"

"The main gates probably were. He stopped at the lych gate below the path to the church and walked round to the side of it. Seemed to know his way all right. It's a pretty part, the whole place, and the church lit up with sunset.

"When he came out I said if he'd told me it was the churchyard he wanted I'd have brought him by a shorter way over the hill, and he said, 'All right, take that road now and drop me at the Burdock, Sackville Street,' which I did at 10.35. That all you want to know?"

"It will be, when you've told me the bit you imagined I'd sent for you about," said Gorham.

The defensive look flashed back in a second to the young man's face. He spoke with righteous indignation.

"Look here, sir, I've got nothing to hide, because it was the chap in front that was wrong, and I barely touched him, though it took some doing, I tell you, with him stopping dead like that without a ghost of a signal."

"Have you reported him to the proper quarter? You took his number, I suppose?"

"You can take it I did!" He fished in the pockets of a very smart wallet. "And my fare gave me his card and said he'd speak for me if anything come of it. Here's his card, *and* the blighter's number."

He noticed no change in the eyes of the Chief Inspector as they studied a combination of figures that had become familiar this week, so that verification from his note-book was unnecessary.

"But as there was no accident, due to my care, there was nothing to report."

"Except his bad driving," Gorham said quietly. "Tell me what happened; where you picked up this car."

"I came up with him first on the new London-Finnet Road," White answered readily, keen to make his position clear now that the subject had been brought up. "He was going a fair forty and kept on the crown of the road, so I kept behind. Fact is, I didn't like the way he was handling her a bit—little points, you know, but you can tell easy enough the sort of chaps you'd best give a wide berth to on the roads. So I followed his tail till we reached Finnet Station where the road is not widened yet, me keeping a careful lookout and he still going a fair lick, but both of us close in to the kerb because three lorries parked on the other side gave us only a one-way track. Then, just as he'd passed the third lorry, if he didn't stop dead, without so much as a wiggle to let me know! There was a fleet of cars behind me by that time, nose to tail, so I did the only thing possible to avoid an unholy smash—signalled the man behind and just managed to pull out round his stationary car into the clear road ahead, missing the third lorry by half an inch. Do you follow?"

"I think so. Three lorries in a row narrowing the track, you and other cars following him in a line, when he stopped dead—still abreast of the last lorry—and you swerved to your right and shot between and ahead in front of the lorry."

"That's right, sir. When he stopped dead like that I'd either to chance pulling out as I did or risk being smashed into by the chap behind."

"What happened to the following cars?"

"I was too busy cursing at the moment to worry about their troubles. But with the space I'd quit to spare they'd got room to pull up. I stopped further along outside a garage, and he must have given them another length, because they followed me and passed on, the first chap chucking me a curse—blaming me, mind you, who'd saved the whole blooming situation! There's gratitude for you! My fare, Mr. Hardwicke—he gave me his card then and there—asked me what the hell I supposed drivers like that were permitted on the roads for, and said I'd been damned quick; then, noticing the garage I'd pulled up in front of, he got out and went in to speak to the boss. Got his own car laid up there, he told me when he came back. I was in two minds about going back and telling that bloke what I thought of him, but when you've got a fare rows don't do one any good. And while I was watching him he came forward and turned in the curve beyond the station and went back down the road and disappeared in the turning to the left, the one I'd have taken myself if I'd known first it was the church Mr. Hardwicke wanted."

"That stretch of road by the station wants widening badly," Gorham observed. "And it was gross carelessness permitting lorries to park there. Was this fellow exceeding the thirty-mile limit when all this occurred?"

"No, sir, nor me either," White retorted sharply, as if suspecting a trap. "We'd dropped to an even fifteen, and if he'd given his signal there'd have been no trouble."

"Did you, or your fare, gather what the reason was for his behaving so idiotically?"

"My fare wasn't taking special notice, and only spotted the thing when I suddenly got a move on, and then he tumbled to facts all right. But I told you we were close in by the kerb; I've an idea he stopped to pick up someone and then turned back to take him somewhere, forgetting there were other cars on the road beside his own. What a chap like that wants," he added with extreme bitterness, "is a whopping great auto road in a desert, all to himself, like what Mussolini's built in Africa."

"That's merely a hypothesis, though? I mean, neither you nor your fare actually saw that he stopped to pick up a passenger?"

"No. There was no one on the pavement by me, but his car blocked my view of the pavement ahead of him, and what he did was exactly what he would do if he was hailed by a pal coming towards him. He stayed still long enough to exchange a few remarks, and then moved on and turned and when he was turning—he wasn't more than a hundred yards behind me by then—I felt sure he'd got a passenger on board, because I caught a glimpse of colour through his side window—a sort of staring yellow. Of course, it might have been a cushion or scarf on the back of a seat, but I don't believe it was, or that it was there before he stopped, because I'm sure I'd have noticed it before, through his rear window, when he was ahead of me on the road. I'd take my oath he was alone then."

"Well," said Gorham slowly, "if someone hailed him and he stopped to pick the person up, it explains his action, though it doesn't excuse the omitted signal. And it clears you. With your fare's backing you're pretty safe. By the way, you'd better drop him a line and say you've informed me of your run out here with him. But if you hear anything more report to me. You didn't see the car again when you passed that way going home?"

"No, sir, and he didn't pass me on the hill either, so I concluded he'd turned off where the road forks below the brow of the hill and a lane—it's nothing but a rough track really—curves round the back of the churchyard and comes out somewhere lower down the High Street."

Gorham nodded. He remembered the place, which was merely a footpath, very secluded, running beneath the high walls surrounding old mansions where the aristocracy of Finnet had once resided, and giving them access by their back doors in the walls to the churchyard gates, by which the path came out at the top of the High Street.

"Probably. Now give me a note of times. You picked up your fare in the Strand at 8.40." He scribbled rapidly. "Then—?"

"This turn up by the station happened twenty past nine, or a minute or two before. I noticed the time when my governor came out of the garage before we started again, twenty-five past it was then, and he hadn't been above a few minutes. When we reached the church, sunset was going on a treat. That's right. He stopped there well under ten minutes, I dare say, and I switched on my lights when we were well on the London Road. Then Sackville Street at 10.35."

The Chief Inspector finished his last note and stood up.

"Altogether a very satisfactory run," he said. "I did it myself this evening in five minutes over your time; not too bad."

"It depends on the time of day, sir," White responded. "I'd allow a good hour myself in the afternoon, but eastward-bound traffic slackens off after eight p.m., and of course we get to know the quiet ways where we aren't perpetually held up by the lights. That's where we lose time in London."

"Quite. I'll keep your name and address, and don't forget to let me know if you get a summons. But I think you'll hear no more about it. Now clear off to your job, and thanks."

"Thank you sir. Good evening."

White went off whistling.

Gorham left the police station and resumed his interrupted drive to Yorker's Manor.

Far from taking a holiday, his brain was acutely following out a certain line of the investigation as he reached and drove through Pound Lane. He passed The Laurels, Manstead House, and The Burrs, and crossing West Avenue took the Finnet Beeches Road.

Till recently, as he knew, Finnet Beeches estate, being private property, had been enclosed between gates. But if, with the sewage works that were in progress, the gates were open and he could cut through the private road the distance to Yorker's, nine miles by the main roads, would be shortened by three at least.

Luck was with him.

For the convenience of early-moving lorries bringing road-making material, which was dumped in unsightly mounds at intervals by the wayside, under the trees that gave the estate its name, the first gate stood open, half a mile farther on the second also. He leapt down and made an inquiry at Finnet Beeches Halt, a tiny station where few trains stopped, but without result.

Again at two places on the direct road to the Manor, at Yorker's Station and at a likely-looking road-house where coaches were halted and excursionists ate snacks at green tables in full view of passing traffic, but still without result.

"After all," he thought as he got back into his seat, "it's a thousand chances to one that the bag, if it were discarded here, would have been picked up by some casual person who'd never own up to having pinched it. The landlord would probably have no knowledge of it whatever."

But even after these three failures he was leaving no possible stone unturned; he was looking for some place where a shabby shopping-bag left behind would be a perfectly natural thing, a matter probably of frequent occurrence where herds of women were constantly going out and in; and when, along the road, a few yards past the wrought-iron gates of the Manor, he saw a shelter put up by a considerate omnibus company for its waiting passengers, he climbed out once more and made for it.

It stood at the entrance of a dirty, oil-stained yard, at the side of which was a wooden shed dignified by the sign, "Travel Agent's Office. Enquiries".

To a disillusioned man who passed his existence in this hutch under a bombardment of, for the most part, futile questions fired at him through a *guichet* by an unthinking populace the Chief Inspector, blocking the narrow doorway with his bulky person, put his now stereotyped inquiry.

"When, and description." The man, wearied by the volubility of his clients, had reduced his own speech to skeleton terms.

"Saturday night. Shabby American-cloth shopping-bag, containing female belongings," said Gorham, equally terse.

He waited for the usual denial of knowledge, but instead the man leaned over from his stool (clinging to it precariously with his right leg as it tilted sideways), rummaged behind bundles in a corner, and produced the required article.

"Yours?"

"Rather! Where did you find it?"

"Sunday morning. Under seat." He jerked his thumb in the direction of the shelter outside. "Sign receipt. Bob to pay."

"My name's Gorham, Chief Inspector, C.I.D."—genially. "Give me a duplicate copy of that receipt, old man, with your own name nicely inscribed on it. Two-and-a-tanner wouldn't break me, but if you prefer a bob, say so." He pocketed his copy gratefully.

"Finnet murder? Want me as witness? Found bag eight o'clock, Sunday. Not there nine p.m., Sat., when I quitted. Find me here. Like your manner."

"So do I yours, old man," Gorham replied with feeling, but interpreted the phrase correctly as a specimen of rhyming slang and put down his half-crown. "I'll just see it's O.K.."

He knelt and went through the bag's contents on the floor. A soiled overall, a pair of broken slippers, a new copy of the *Church Times*, a bag of bull's-eyes, a shapeless yellow cardigan, an envelope containing a pound note and ten shillings in silver.... Hubberd had added a *douceur*, then, when he repaid Dent's theft. And over these poor belongings were scattered tiny fragments of brittle vegetable matter that he knew now to be dried tulip leaves. He shook them carefully into the bag before he replaced the other objects. Enough remained for microsopic examination and identification, with fragments from the coat already in his possession, to hang a man.

The agent watched his proceedings in silence and spoke when they were ended.

"Okay?"

"Okay by me, old man. Good night."

"'Night," replied the man, and pocketed his half-crown.

* * * * *

169 | Death Has No Tongue

The Chief Inspector drove up to the Manor and requested a word with the secretary, to whose office he was taken at once.

Mr. Talbot received him with a certain stiffness at first, on learning his official status, but with the introduction of Donald Levi's name, and the disclosure of an earnest desire to see the glories of the ancient house, of which Mr. Talbot was inordinately proud, his manner thawed and a genial conversation ensued.

Gorham told the secretary everything about the Finnet murder that had been published in the daily papers, and in return Mr. Talbot told Gorham that Lewis Hardwicke, on whose premises the body had actually been discovered, was an old friend of his, though they hadn't met for a year or two, and that another member of the club, L. V. Hyde, the author, was a Finnet man, and a neighbour of Hardwicke.

Gorham nodded.

"That's right; I've just met him, that's all. He's got a delightful little place in Pound Lane itself, but he was away from home during my show; here, I believe. Had dinner here and spent the week-end."

"He spent the week-end here; in fact, he stayed on till Tuesday morning," Mr. Talbot agreed. "But you're wrong about his dining here Saturday. In fact, I met him myself in the drive coming in, and that was at twenty past ten, when I was doing my last round. I didn't speak to him then, but later on he told me he'd had dinner at the Burdock Club in Town, from which he'd rung up earlier to ask if we'd a room, and by a fluke we had. Generally we've got a waiting-list a yard long, but that evening the member who had engaged it 'phoned, poor chap, to say that his small son was desperately ill at school, and his wife and he had to go down to Winchester. So Hyde was in luck."

Gorham had looked surprised at the correction, but now his face cleared.

"I remember now, the Burdock is right. And he came on here after dinner—that's right too. But time's getting on, Mr. Talbot—I'd like to get a squint at this moat of yours before the light fades altogether."

Mr. Talbot rose.

"Come along, then. I'm not sure that the old place doesn't look best in the afterglow. It restores the mysterious sort of quality it had, you know, and softens the alterations and additions we were compelled to make. Come out this way, into the sunk garden. I've kept that bit absolutely intact and unspoiled. There, that's pretty good, isn't it?"

They stood in the gloaming with the twisted chimneys of the manor piled up against the sky, the air about them sweet with the scent of stocks, and Gorham felt a deep content, for his case was complete.

Chapter XVIII

Ella Hyde and her faithful Eliza had worked far into the night to prepare for the forerunners of the removal men, who were to come first thing in the morning.

As in every house that has been inhabited for a number of years, an accumulation of possessions, kept for their value or associations, yet left undisturbed perhaps for a long period, was collected in trunks and cupboards, and the sorting of these half-forgotten belongings could be delegated to no one by the mistress of the house.

In addition to personal possessions, there were family relics of which Innisfree had become the sole repository, as they had naturally belonged to old Mrs. Hyde; books and other precious remembrances of her famous father, Professor Laurence Vincent, portraits, letters, old-fashioned, not very valuable, jewellery and plate, as well as those innumerable, valueless, unclassifiable things kept for their personal associations only, of which human affections forbid either the dispersal or destruction.

But, faced with this Herculean task, which she had decided must be carried out within two days, Ella Hyde preserved complete serenity. The details of her task were clear in her mind. The Vincent relics must be packed together, and stored till her own future became less nebulous than it was at present, with the portraits, books, and furniture. She had not, so far, the remotest notion where she should go when she left this roof, which had sheltered her for the best part of her life, nor even where she must sleep on Saturday night when the door of this house closed finally behind her. All that must wait for thought and decision till she had carried through the tremendous business of cutting adrift from the past and freeing herself from a burden that had for years held her down, tied by a thousand Lilliputian bands of family habit and affections, and pity, to endurance of a crushing, unreasoned bondage. Yet, in the end, what seeming trifles had roused her to cut her bonds—a few mutilated flowers, a slight wound on a dog's side—not trifles at all in reality, since they testified that a wrong tamely endured must inevitably grow and strengthen with what it feeds on till it reaches beyond its original victim.

Her first task was to pack her brother's clothes and all his carelessly gathered possessions in the steamer trunks that he had brought home from the Far East, still preserved in the loft. These were locked and left in the bedroom he had occupied. There was a uniform-case that had belonged to Laurence, in which she had long ago placed such poignant relics of him and his wife as she had, and which was set aside for his daughter. Hilary was a dear child when she lived at Innisfree, the light of her grandmother's eyes, and very dear to herself, though, for the girl's happiness, she had sent her away when things became difficult at home, financing her life with a friend in Town till she met and married her adored Rodney and settled down with him in Kenya.

When Sydney's things were finished, she and Eliza had packed a goodly proportion of the more portable family valuables which must be sent to adorn Hilary's pretty bungalow.

Now only ordinary household goods remained, and when she had dealt with boxes of faded letters, and household linen and china, sorting them ready for the men's packing-cases, she would have finished her part in the work, for Eliza could safely be trusted to keep an eagle-eye on kitchen properties.

On Friday morning, feeling a little stiff from her unwonted exertions on the previous evening, she rose early, and presently she and Eliza were cheerfully at work on the china.

Miss Hyde was a little surprised at the cheerfulness of her own mood in circumstances that might well have induced gloom, but she put it down to the firmness with which she had suppressed any natural out-croppings of regret.

"Once one begins looking at old photographs, or being sentimental over cracked cups that are only fit to be thrown away, there'd be no end to it," she said sternly to Eliza when she showed signs of a desire to hoard rubbish. "We must simply be firm with ourselves. Otherwise we shall find ourselves left with a mountain of oddments added to our own luggage."

"I could take this little sauce-boat that's only got a teeny crack in it to Bill's to keep safe for you, ma'am," Eliza murmured weakly.

"My dear soul—a teeny crack! A perfect fissure! No, no, you are not going to load up poor Bill's house with useless crockery, Eliza! Already you will have to deal with all the linen that comes home from the laundry, and you're taking along lots of odd china and saucepans that your unfortunate sister-in-law will probably curse already!" She laughed as she pried the cracked object from Eliza's lingering reluctance and tossed it into the rubbish receptacle.

"I say, I'm awfully relieved to hear you sounding so jolly," came a voice from the doorway, where Lewis Hardwicke stood framed against the morning sunshine. He was by no means certain how he would be received after his abrupt dismissal yesterday, and his ugly face wore a boyish and deprecating expression. He was indeed prepared for advance or retreat in accordance with Miss Hyde's reception of him, but chiefly for advance, for he was progressive by nature.

"I was afraid I'd find you and Eliza frightfully depressed by this upheaval of the *lares and penates*."

"Then you don't know much about women, Lewis. They adore moving; don't they, Eliza?"

"Well, ma'am, it makes a break," she admitted with caution.

And Lewis stepped boldly in. He had caught the flash of pleasure in Miss Hyde's face as she first turned to him, though it was instantly suppressed to an ordinary look of greeting.

They both laughed, and Eliza, beaming discreetly, withdrew to the corner where she was sorting kitchen cups and saucers, and Lewis begged to be allowed to help.

"I'm absolutely at a loose end today," he pleaded. "Can't I be taken on as odd man? I've never moved house, but I've frequently helped to shift refugees—not to speak of myself—at half an hour's notice, packing old people's furniture, clothes, and livestock under bombardment. Whereabouts in the game are you?"

"I'm just finishing here. The men will pack the china now we have gone over it. The silver has to be checked as it is dealt with, and the next job is packing away the linen and smaller breakables that I don't care to trust them with. The stair carpet has to come up, and I must pack the last of my clothes."

"What about this linoleum?"

"Mrs. Ewings may want to take it over, with shelves and fittings. They will be here presently."

"All right, I'll tackle the stair-carpet first."

He proved himself invaluable during the rest of the morning while Miss Hyde interviewed tradesmen and workmen, encouraged the shy Mrs. Ewings to express her wishes as to fittings, and directed two charwomen engaged to scrub each room as it was vacated, besides assisting Eliza and, in addition to her business of filling three trunks with blankets and linen, flitting about to settle innumerable questions with unruffled calmness.

When she came back after a prolonged delay with Mrs. Ewings it was to find Lewis packing the trunks as neatly as, and much more quickly than, she had done, and she paused for a moment to admire his deftness.

"The Ewings have gone at last," she said. "They want to keep the curtain fittings and everything in the kitchen as it is, besides all the electric lights, except a few globes and other things that I prefer to keep. So that saves trouble. The foreman is in charge of the silver and china now, so there's really nothing more for us to do. They are taking the more valuable cases away today, so tomorrow there will be nothing to take but the books and actual furniture. Now Lewis, what about some lunch? Eliza says she can concoct sandwiches. . . . But directly afterwards I must go to Chancery Lane to see my lawyer—"

"I've got a much better proposal than sandwiches," he declared. "Suppose I run you and Eliza into Town for some lunch, then you can see the lawyer afterwards? Those females have finished all they can do while the furniture is standing about; why not pack them off, and"—he added persuasively—"take the rest of the day as a holiday? Old Eliza deserves a sound lunch! She's worked like a navvy since dawn, and you too."

She hesitated. She must go into Chancery Lane, of course, to complete the legal business of the sale of Innisfree, and the suggestion of a few hours away from the dismantled house tempted her. There was, as she had said, little more that she could do, nothing that could not be finished before the men came tomorrow, yet it seemed sinful to go and enjoy oneself in the midst of such a serious business. She compromised by saying that she would consult Eliza, and Lewis closed the lids of the trunks with a sense of profound satisfaction. If he had acted like a fool, and stopped away today, Ella Hyde might have slipped away irretrievably out of his life, and he knew, with unresentful certainty, that, had he let her go, never by any voluntary act of her own would she have attempted to call him back again. On a surface view they were two unattached persons whom circumstances had brought into contact with each other, who had sought and found a certain relief from outside disagreeables in the friendly companionship of the other.

He did not wish to take any other but that surface view for the present. He was content with what he had, a calm and unexacting friend whose soothing influence over his raw nerves he had felt from the first moment, last Sunday, when he stepped into her drawing-room. In the light of that first impression of the atmosphere of her house and garden as a sanctuary of peace enclosed from a restless world there was a touch of irony in the fact that within a week, without the slightest feeling of remorse, he was assisting her to quit her sanctuary, to leave it to the commercial tenderness of a rough old market gardener and his fat spouse.

But his one feeling, dominating every other emotion—surprise at the *bouleversement* of his first conception of her as the gentle, retired genius of her brother's home; disturbance as to the fate of Ted Hubberd; miserable uncertainty as to his own affairs—was satisfaction that she had accepted his return without question. He had identified himself with her interests. What she said went. He did not even worry as to whether the house were hers to sell, whether or not it was a mean trick to play on the egregious Sydney, to break up his home behind his back and leave him without a roof to shelter him. On the face of it an underhand, shady, unpardonable trick for a sister to play on a brother, apart altogether from any question of financial divisions of housekeeping expenses between them, as to which he had no information. She had decided that she wanted to quit, and apparently fed up with Sydney, intended to leave him standing; very well, Lewis was on her side.

And so long as she let him remain with her, sharing her doings, he was not going to press for confidences. He was merely going to stick by her through thick and thin, as a friend should.

This cheerfully defiant attitude on his part combined with an odd mood in Miss Hyde to infuse an absurdly adventurous spirit into a prosaic luncheon at Lyons' popular restaurant in Piccadilly, at which Eliza displayed a mincing party manner that further cheered her companions.

But when the legal business in Chancery Lane had been transacted Lewis argued against an immediate return to Finnet while they stood together on the pavement.

"If you go back this afternoon you can do nothing but potter about in infernal discomfort," he pointed out with a show of reason. "I ought to run out to see a man in a village in Herts, so what's against us all tooling out together?"

But Miss Hyde hesitated.

"I really think that if you have this friend to see, Eliza and I had best go home now by train," she said with a glance towards her henchwoman waiting in the car, "and you go by yourself. Eliza and I have enjoyed ourselves, but—"

"If you won't come, then we'll tool back to Finnet together," Lewis stated with mulish obstinacy. "And my friend will have to rip. But it's a perfectly decent afternoon, and not three yet. Why deprive poor Eliza of a joy-ride? Do come, Elvie! You will? What ho! Hop in in front this time; I've a lot I want to tell you." His interview the evening before with Ethel Hubberd had ended in an angry scene, chiefly conducted by Ethel, who seemed in a state to blame everyone but herself for the predicament in which she found herself, living on sufferance in the house of a parent with whom she had bitterly and repeatedly quarrelled, and deserted by a husband whose long-suffering she had strained beyond decent limits. But Lewis, though he had endured insulting references to himself as a spy prying into affairs that were not his business, in the hope of discovering some clue to Ted's possible bolt-hole, and stood abuse of Ted himself, up to a point, as a fool and a failure, with the same object, lost his temper and rounded on her when by an inadvertent phrase she hinted her belief that he might also be a murderer.

"Look here, Ethel!" He loomed over her in terrifying wrath, and she turned white, realizing that she had gone too far. "Do you mean to tell me definitely that you've lived with Ted for ten years and don't know, as God is over us, that he is utterly incapable of hurting a fly, let alone committing a cruel, wanton, and absolutely beastly crime like the killing of that harmless creature?"

"You men always stick together! He's hurt me often enough—"

"If he'd taken a stick to you it would be no more than you deserve!" Lewis retorted brutally. "You can't get out of it like that! Do you or do you not believe he had a hand in that murder?"

"Oh, do stop shouting at me, you great bully!" But she was scared by his dominating anger, forced back on weak defence. "Look what all the papers are saying!"

"I'm not referring to the papers. The personal equation doesn't affect them. They simply make use of bare outside facts which in this case are completely misleading." He had got a grip on his temper again, but his ugly features were lit up with a strange and impressive earnestness as he leaned towards her. "I'm asking you, his wife, who've lived with him for years, for whom he chucked up his career and everything that made his life worth while."

"That's right!" she broke in passionately. "Make out it's all my fault Ted's a damned failure! What was this marvellous career you're talking so ridiculously about? Living in a camp on a beastly river, bossing a lot of filthy natives, sweating in intolerable heat all day and in a mosquito-net all night. . . ."

"It suited him—"

"Well, it didn't suit me, and he'd have been dead by this time if I hadn't forced him to quit. It was six for me and half a dozen for himself that he came home, if you ask me! And what have I got out of my life with him, do you think? Poked away in a dead-alive hole like Finnet, never a penny to bless myself with, and pinching and scraping and mucking about with pots and saucepans! Do you suppose when I married him I guessed he'd expect me to turn myself into a kitchen drudge?"

"That's dashed unfair, Ethel! You'd made him chuck the only sort of job he was fitted for, and he pulled his full weight and more. You had your own friends—"

"Friends!" A sudden, almost maniacal look blazed in her eyes for a second, and then she burst into a passion of tears, burying her face in her arms on the sofa. "Oh, go away, go away! I can't bear any more!"

Lewis, after a weak "Oh, I say, Ethel—" answered by a frantic gesture of one hand extricated from the cushions to urge dismissal, crept ignominiously to the door, down the stairs, and bolted from the house. Women, he told himself without any startling originality, defeated him altogether.

After a night of restlessness, when in waking intervals he worried about Ted Hubberd and asleep he miserably pursued the receding figure of Miss Hyde through the streets of a Spanish town whose walls, tottering under a rain of bombs from the air, threatened every second to engulf them both in hideous death, he rose feeling utterly jaded, and drank strong coffee at breakfast to brace his nerves while he read his letters and glanced through the *Telegraph*.

The usual paragraph about the Finnet murder contained an unusual feature, a line which at first he took to be the outpouring of a demented compositor, but which, as the name Hubberd was embedded in the midst of unintelligible groups of letters, he decided might be a phrase translated into English type from some Oriental tongue with which he was unacquainted. He also decided that of his two nocturnal worries the Spanish complication was the more immediately pressing, and started at once, after breakfast, for Innisfree. Now it was to visit Mr. Pine Hubberd, the distinguished cousin of his friend, and to clear up that second worry, that he was driving, with Miss Hyde seated calmly beside him.

"What is it, Lewis?" she asked, catching the last of a series of harassed glances cast at her from perturbed blue eyes as they drove up Tottenham Court Road.

"Would you mind frightfully if we spoke of that foul affair for a brief moment?" he asked anxiously. "It's rather important, you see, because—well, because this chap we're going to see has had rather a gruelling over it. It's just occurred to me that I'd like to hear your views . . ."

"My views? About that crime, do you mean? But, Lewis—"

"Haven't you followed the papers?"

She shook her head.

"I saw a paper in the kitchen on Tuesday, and it made me feel so wretched that I haven't touched one since." She flushed at her avowal of such cowardice. "You see, if it could help Ellen . . . but it wouldn't, and . . . oh, I can't explain. Reading about those horrible things is like deliberately dragging one's imagination through a sewer of filthy thoughts. . . . Do you think me very weak and silly?"

"No, I don't."

"Is the—the criminal found yet?"

"No," he said again, then added hesitatingly: "Then you don't know that Hubberd, the fellow at the end house, has been sort of suspected by a lot of fat-headed idiots?"

At her amazed "Mr. Hubberd! My dear Lewis! Why?" he saw that she was genuinely without the slightest notion bred of speculation on the crime, which she seemed to attribute to some vaguely pictured emanation from an underworld, which Ellen's humble life might have touched at some point, as the bare hint that Hubberd, a neighbour, a man actually known to her by sight, could be imagined responsible, gave her a profound shock. "Tell me," she added briefly.

In jerky sentences he gave her a complete description of the general position with regard to Hubberd, and the happenings of the previous day.

She listened in silence, but when he had finished she touched his arm with an impulsive gesture.

"But you Lewis. He is your friend; you don't believe this awful thing of him?"

"I? Good Lord, no!" he returned with vigour. "I'm only telling you where the suspicions of a bone-headed general public have fallen, simply because it's incapable of getting beyond the obvious external fact. The queer thing is, though, that till that little cat of a wife of his actually implied that she believed the preposterous idea I won't swear I hadn't harboured it myself. At the back of my mind, you know, hovering, as a possibility, and liberally allowing for a whole fleet of extenuating circumstances undisclosed—"

"How could there be extenuating circumstances for murder?"

"Well, there are, often," he protested. "Motives and beastly chances. I suppose it was chances my subconscious banked on here," he grinned, giving himself away with brazen frankness.

"If he'd been drunk, for instance, frenzied with drugs, hit her by mistake in a blind fury, then came to himself and realized what he'd done and had to cover his ghastly deed—that sort of thing."

"Was she struck?"—coldly.

"No, I'm only telling you. I wouldn't think out details. Don't you see? Extenuating circumstances were an absolute necessity, so I had to keep 'em muffled up, not submit them to analysis that might have undermined the—the extenuation of their circumstantiality, if you follow me."

"Quite easily. You lacked the courage of your convictions."

He chuckled ruefully at that flick.

"Scarcely convictions. They'd imply an intellectual conclusion, after argument for and against. I've specifically mentioned that I refused to argue. More an instinct, or perhaps a plain hope. Say a hope, and nebulous at that. And Ted wasn't a friend then. Just a fellow I'd known for years and rather liked. But when Ethel put my back up by doubting him, or pretending to doubt him, to whitewash her own behaviour, I realized I was solid for Ted, because—well—during the last few days we've really rather got together."

"But didn't you go into it, talk over the whole thing?" she exclaimed, turning bright, puzzled eyes on his face. Sitting slouched in his low seat beside her, his squarely shaped head under its thick covering of untidy fair hair thrust forward, his eyes on the road ahead, his big, capable hand on the wheel, the nervous restlessness of his loose-limbed body momentarily stilled in the car's vicarious action, she recognized a powerful quality in the man that was intellectual as well as physical, but it was the shyness beneath his rough exterior, the direct, boyish simplicity of him that seemed to appeal to something simple in herself, the child in her that never before had had a playmate.

"If it had not been for poor Ellen's death I'd never have had this," she thought; "I'd still be buried in that dreadful starved loneliness. All that artificial shell I'd built over myself would be cracked just the same, but there'd have been no one to rescue me."

"Naturally we didn't," he answered her question with a broad grin.

"Then what on earth did you talk about?"

"Oh, everything"—casually—"bar the few little subjects we were thinking about, of course. Dash it, Elvie, you understand."

"Do you think that the police inspector actually believes he is the criminal?"

"I don't know." His tone sounded unhappy. "I tried to sound him yesterday, but I couldn't discover whether his worry over Ted's disappearance was due to remorse over hounding him out of his job or dislike of losing an intended victim. He's as close as an oyster when he's on a case. But he certainly was worried."

"Do you know, Lewis, I liked him. I don't believe he would be unjust."

"He's paid to do his job," Lewis grunted. "What he's out for is to arrest the murderer, and if he can get hold of the right fellow he's not going to be too scrupulous about the means he uses."

"I don't believe he would be treacherous," Miss Hyde said firmly. "I thought him an extraordinarily understanding person. And though he looks big and slow, I'm sure nothing escapes him. For instance, when he came in on Tuesday afternoon some of the morning letters, including my pass-book from the bank, were still lying on a side table. I saw his glance rest on them for a second, but I'm certain he read their addresses, knew exactly how many were mine and how many Sydney's. It was only a little thing, of course," she added hastily, "and it reminded me to put the bank-book away when he'd gone. But it gave me a sense of his penetration that I haven't forgotten."

"What did he bother you again for?" he asked angrily.

"Nothing much. A small point he wasn't clear about." She remembered with a touch of apprehension that the question related to Mr. Hubberd's garage, but refrained from saying so. "Have you heard from Mr. Hubberd, Lewis? Why do you think he is down in Fordyk?"

"Oh, didn't I tell you? He dropped me a line this morning. I felt dashed relieved to get it, after the ghastly nightmares I'd had about him last night. I'd have bolted straight down then if I hadn't been terrified I'd find you vanished next. Would you have let me know where you were when you'd left Innisfree?"

"No," she deliberated. "I think not."

"Then I was right to come," he said.

"It was nice of you to come," she admitted, "but I doubt very much whether Mr. Hubberd will want to see strangers just now, Lewis. I didn't realize the position when we discussed it. Suppose, when we reach Fordyk, Eliza and I leave you to pay your visit alone? I shall enjoy exploring the village, and no doubt there is a tea-place somewhere."

But Lewis refused to agree to her sensible suggestion.

"We can drop Eliza, if you like, but I particularly want you to come along. The poor old chap has had a rotten deal, and the more friends he can rally round him the better. We're bound to show him we intend to see him through."

Miss Hyde uttered no comment on that 'we', which implied that Lewis's loyalties must also be hers, and merely said that she would enjoy meeting Mr. Pine Hubberd, with whom his cousin had taken refuge. As a young man he had been one of her grandfather's students, and the signed copy of his first slender book, presented to Professor Laurence Vincent, was still in her library.

"At least, in one of those packing-cases in which I stowed away special books," she said with an involuntary sigh. How long would it be before she had her books round her again? The future was like a blank wall in front of her after she left Innisfree tomorrow. A night or two in Town, perhaps at some quiet hotel, and then. . . . Well, again, sufficient unto the day is the evil thereof.

Fordyk is one of the prettiest villages in England, and the wisteria-clad cottage of Mr. Pine Hubberd, standing beyond the church and off the main highway, matched its setting.

They had deposited Eliza, who was in high feather, by the village inn, with directions to have tea there when she had sufficiently enjoyed the sights, and await their return; and as they entered the wicket gate in a yew hedge that enclosed three acres of perfect garden they glanced around and then at each other.

"Why," said Lewis gloomily, "does one's ideal house always belong to someone else?"

Chapter XIX

But it was impossible, once they met their host, to grudge him his habitation.

He was a tall, thin man with charming manners, his features refined rather than aged by seventy years which had not impaired the spare vigour of his frame.

He greeted his visitors with pleasing simplicity, and sent Lewis to find his cousin indoors, assuring him that Edward had half expected him to turn up and would be delighted to see him. He had just returned from Town and had gone in to change.

Miss Hyde he retained by his side on the lawn, accepting the grand-daughter of his old friend as one of themselves by inherited right. His sincerity set at rest her shyness and the doubt that lingered as to her wisdom in allowing the headstrong Lewis to force her on strangers in the peculiar circumstances, but at first, avoiding intimate subjects, she spoke of the garden. But he disclaimed her praise while he displayed his domain. "I have lived here for five years while I have been at work on a book," he said. "But the garden is an inheritance from my predecessors. I have added little and changed nothing. But that is, I think, as it should be. A garden that is over two hundred years old is like the English Constitution, a thing not to be altered lightly, and then only by careful compromise with ancient good, and a building-up from precedent to precedent."

"You believe that the old is best, then?" she asked smiling. "No. Not always. But the old has been tested and the new is necessarily still in the experimental stage," he said. "In the carefully garnered knowledge of the past there lies the structure of the present and the foundation of the future. What we destroy we lose; what we adapt we have. But I shall not have this place after this week," he added regretfully. "The first portion of the work on which I have been engaged is now completed, even to the last revision of the proofs, and though I had intended to await its appearance in England this crisis in my cousin's affairs has changed my plans. I shall leave for China with him next week, instead of next month, for, though he offered to remain till then out of generous concern for my convenience, such a sacrifice on his part could not be accepted. I have hope that he will remain with me as my secretary, but meanwhile I have assured myself of the pleasure of his company."

"He intends to go abroad, then, at once?"

Privately, Miss Hyde, in view of what Lewis had told her, could not banish a faint doubt as to Chief Inspector Gorham's attitude towards this plan, but Mr. Pine Hubberd's Olympian calm remained untroubled by any such sordid speculation. He had, however, the advantage of having comprehended a mysterious message in his morning paper.

"At once," he agreed serenely. "In my opinion, the sooner my cousin quits a country where he has endured wretched years of self-suppression, and returns to the sort of life for which he is fitted by habit and temperament, the sooner he will recover tone. There is a point beyond which self-suppression becomes mental suicide, and Edward had almost reached it."

"I see that you are not an advocate of self-sacrifice, Mr. Hubberd," Miss Hyde remarked thoughtfully, her eyes fixed on a tall spike of delphinium in whose flowers skyey tints of blue and sunset pink commingled in indescribable colour. "But perhaps they are not the same thing. Self-suppression hurts no-one but the self. . . ."

"While self-sacrifice may have tremendous influences that may be good or incalculably harmful. That is true. One hesitates to pronounce judgment lightly on so far-reaching a subject, but in private life certainly I have seen deplorable results ensue from an attitude that destroys the sane balance of giving and taking that should exist between normal persons."

"The damage done in your cousin's case is, I hope, not irreparable?" she asked with a faint touch of ironical amusement in her dry tone.

"My dear lady, he never took the extreme step of self-sacrifice!" Mr. Pine Hubberd remarked. "He is a young man of singularly unselfish temperament, but he carried unselfishness to the verge of folly when, to satisfy the wish of a quite unappreciative young woman, he threw over the life and work for which he was pre-eminently fitted, to bury himself in a wretched clerical job in England. I don't know whether you have met Mrs. Edward?"

"They were neighbours of mine, and I have exchanged a few words with Mrs. Hubberd in the street occasionally, nothing more."

"You have lost nothing in missing her acquaintance," Mr. Pine Hubberd assured her with quaint vigour. "She struck me, on the few occasions on which we met, as a person of singularly shoddy character. A quite disastrous mate for a man of sensitive feeling and intelligence to have chosen. Once the thing was done, however, no outside interference was to be tolerated. I had to acquiesce in our almost complete severance for a time."

He sighed.

"You are attached to him?" she ventured.

He smiled down at her at that. If his features were austere in repose, his smile lighted them, softened and transformed them.

"I'm afraid I've been boring you unconscionably with my own affairs," he said. "But yes, he and I are the only representatives of our family in England, and we are attached to each other. I believe we are a clannish race. Now come along and have some tea. There are Edward and his friend appearing at last."

She felt a twinge of discomfort as she met the man whose appearance was familiar to her eyes but whom she greeted for the first time in such singular circumstances. But Edward Hubberd treated her as an ordinary guest, betraying neither surprise nor resentment at her appearance in Fordyk, and she noticed that though he bore little resemblance, physically speaking, to his distinguished cousin, their voices were alike, and their unaffected simplicity of manner.

He looked strained and ill, and seemed preoccupied with his thoughts, leaving the heft of the conversation to his cousin and Lewis Hardwicke.

They took tea on the lawn in the shade of a great cedar, deftly waited on by a Chinese servant to whom both the Hubberd men spoke in his own tongue.

The sunshine fell on the low white frontage of the house, on which a twisted branch of wisteria, now past its blossoming time, made a black, intricate pattern; it cut deep shadows across the verandah and woke beautiful purple hues in the clematis with which its pillars were hung. At the edge of the grass was etched the clear-cut shadow of five tall poplars, gradually lengthening, mingled now in one dark patch, but promising to separate later and lie in five black bars across the green turf.

It was a place of immemorial peace.

Doves had murmured in those trees, as they were murmuring now, before she was born or Innisfree thought of, as they would murmur when she had laid this brief life aside and lay herself among the forgotten dead.

The experiment she had made in her toy house of creating a claustral seclusion from which she could shut out grim and sordid reality had broken down, as such experiments must inevitably break down under pressure of forces which human will can neither control nor hold at bay. Innisfree! The name gave the measure of an illusion that in the end had completely betrayed its illusory nature.

"The next cottage I have," she thought grimly, "shall be called Clay. But I shan't have another. I can't endure solitude again. I shall end as a withered spinster in a seaside boarding-house . . ."

Lewis Hardwicke inquired if Mr. Pine Hubberd had found a tenant for his house during his absence; he had heard of their imminent departure from Edward, who had informed him of their plan while they were indoors together.

Mr. Pine Hubberd said that he held the cottage on a lease of which there were five more years to run, but since Edward's arrival yesterday there had scarcely been time to arrange for subletting the place, and, besides, he would scarcely care to entrust such of his stuff as he proposed to leave behind to any stranger of an agent's choosing.

Miss Hyde would have taken this as a gentle hint that no tenants were desired, but Lewis, to whom shyness in normal concerns of life was unknown, promptly offered to take the place off his hands.

"I'd take immense care of your stuff, sir," he said frankly, "and I'd like to take it over exactly as it stands, if that would suit you. Do you, propose a long absence this time?"

"I haven't the remotest idea," was the calm reply. "It might be for six months or it might be for ever. Could you endure my uncertainties? If so, I should be delighted to leave you here. It would be far better for the house than leaving merely a caretaker in charge. But surely Edward told me that you have one house already?"

"Which the beastly affair in Pound Lane had rendered not only unsaleable but uninhabitable!" Lewis retorted. "I'm told if I care to let it at a nominal rent the Y.M.C.A. might consider taking it as a hostel, and I'm inclined to consent—at any rate, till it has purged its contempt—for otherwise it will merely become derelict. But the furniture I've already settled about. It will be removed next week, so that's that. Miss Hyde and I are in the same boat, orphans cast homeless on the wide world. But she's been luckier than I, for at least she's found a purchaser for her topping little house, but all her stuff is packed up, and here we are, not a roof to cover either of us!"

"But this is too distressing!" exclaimed Mr. Pine Hubberd, gazing at his old friend's grand-daughter with deep concern. "But why cannot you both stay here? My dear Miss Hyde, I assure you it would give me the very greatest pleasure! There are spare rooms; the cottage is larger than it appears to be from this aspect. If your things are already packed, why not remain here now, and 'phone for your personal baggage to be brought over? You need not give the slightest thought to domestic conditions here, because my servants are accustomed to preparing for guests at a moment's notice. And though I am taking them both with me, the week's interim would give you ample time to provide yourself with the English servants, whom no doubt you would prefer."

After one hurried glance at Miss Hyde, whose face was flushed pink but looked both touched and amused at the cordiality of their host's invitation, Lewis Hardwicke turned aside to contemplate an arch crimson in its draping of rambler roses, and to hide an unregenerate grin. Did this guileless, elderly gentleman connect him so closely with his afternoon passenger as to imagine them prepared to set up housekeeping together? "And why not?" some detached voice demanded in his brain. "Isn't she exactly the partner who'd suit me best? Don't I feel more at home with her than I've ever felt with any mortal being before? Why else have I haunted her this week, miserable away from her, and only comfy again in her company? Don't we like the same things, and laugh at the same things, and aren't we as damned lonely a pair as you'd find in the Empire? And she does trust me, and perhaps like me a bit besides. At any rate she prefers me to her brother Sydney, with his insufferable manners. . . . 'Jane' indeed . . . I . . . oh, well—better give her a few more hours to get used to me. . . . tomorrow, when she's finished at Innisfree . . ."

He heard her quietly explaining that she must go home to superintend the final removal of her furniture tomorrow, and that after that her plans were uncertain, though business would certainly keep her in Town next week.

"Then we shall be gone," said Mr. Pine Hubberd with genuine regret. "But the gardener and his wife will be caretakers here till you've made your own arrangements, Hardwicke. I'll send you the address of my solicitors; some sort of agreement is a necessity, I suppose, in case of accidents. But don't wait for that, my dear fellow. Come down when you wish."

"I wish we'd known each other when we were neighbours, Miss Hyde," Edward Hubberd murmured as they shook hands. "But it's too late now."

"It's not too late to wish you well in your new life," she said gently, touched by the weariness in his eyes. "This week has been hideous for you. I hope that is past."

"Thank you." His face lit up for a moment in a smile that was like his cousin's. "We all strike bad patches at times, I suppose, but at least they show you who your friends are. Hardwicke is a great fellow."

Miss Hyde was silent till they had picked up Eliza and were started on the return run.

"That man could no more have hurt poor Ellen than you could," she said suddenly. "How could anyone be so foolish as to imagine him capable of such a thing? Yet there is an inflexible strain in both those cousins."

"And Ethel Hubberd is up against it, and serve her damn' well right," Lewis said grimly, and for the rest of the drive they talked of other things.

They stopped by the way for a nondescript meal on which Lewis insisted, though the women would cheerfully have supported Nature till morning on the excellent tea which each had had in Fordyk, and when they reached the dismantled house dusk had fallen. Lewis went in ahead of his companions to snap on lights, and Ella Hyde, standing in the hall, so bleak in its carpetless state, conscious of a sudden, overwhelming rush of nervous dread, had to fight down a longing to beg him not to leave them, to stay and see them safely through this last night in the house where piled-up furniture cast uncanny shadows on bare walls, and steps sounded hideously loud on bare floors.

He would stay gladly—of that she had no doubt whatever; but prosaic considerations in the end helped her to restrain the impulses. Mattresses and blankets were packed up. She and Eliza had kept back only the barest necessities for themselves. There was not even a couch on which he could sleep in reasonable comfort, no material or utensils with which breakfast that would satisfy a hungry man could be prepared.

The idea did not occur to Lewis himself, or was suppressed unformulated.

"I'll be along early in the morning," he said as he came back to her. "You'll go to bed at once and try to get a good night, won't you? You know, you're looking pretty tired." He paused, an anxious frown puckering his brow. "Promise you won't give me the slip, Elvie!"

"Of course not! Why should you think me so ungrateful after your working like a navvy here today?"

"Not ungrateful—that's rot. Elusive. I'm scared of rushing you, but there's an idea—proposition—I want to talk over with you soon—tomorrow perhaps—but we'd better get all this furniture business off our minds first." He chuckled. "Sure you're going to be all right now?"

Her nervous fears were dispelled in his vigorous presence, and she laughed.

"Ridiculous person! Haven't I looked after myself for nearly forty years?"

"Good night, then." He pressed both her hands, restraining with a strong effort a precipitate and untimely desire to take her in his arms and kiss her, and hurried off down the path to the garage gate where he had left his car.

Miss Hyde sighed and, when she heard the engine purring, closed the front door.

She and Eliza drank a cup of tea in the kitchen, the only room that retained a semblance of itself, though the dresser shelves were empty of china and a packing-case stood under the table, and then, after a few small preparations for the morning went up to bed. Eliza fell asleep as soon as her head touched the pillow, with Robin, whose basket was mislaid, rolled snugly up at the foot of her bed.

Ella Hyde slept also, heavily and dreamlessly, till something—a creak?—no, a pressure against the bed—startled her awake with pounding heart.

"Who's that? You, Sydney?"

In the moonless dark she could see nothing, but she felt someone bend over her, felt hands feeling for, clutching her throat. She struggled, remembering with despair that Eliza was deaf; felt herself lifted by those throttling fingers and lost consciousness before her head was crashed down against the mahogany back of the bed.

Chapter XX

WHILE LEWIS HARDWICKE was employed in taking up stair-carpets and otherwise making himself useful at Innisfree, Gorham was briskly engaged in tying up the loose threads of the case before proceeding to the final act.

As soon as he arrived at Finnet police station, where a bucolic-looking sergeant filled the seat of Norris, who since Wednesday had been absent on other duty. Gorham sent for the young constable who had made first discovery of the body.

He had taken the young man's statement at the time, but on one detail, then without significance, and mentioned incidentally only, he required further light.

"What's your name?"

"Brown, sir—Stanley Brown."

"Of the celebrated Brown family?"

"That's right, sir."

"Good. I like my men to be well connected. Makes them self-respecting. Now, about last Saturday morning. You stated you were in Pound Lane to return the Innisfree dog. Tell me every last thing about your finding that dog. Yes, it was Miss Hyde's animal right enough." Impatiently, as Brown hesitated in surprise, "Go on."

"Yes, sir. Proceeding down West Avenue from Harrow Main Road, at the junction of Pound Lane and Finnet Beeches Road, a man coming from the Beeches hailed me, and I saw he was Mr. Jones, stationmaster at Finnet Beeches Halt. He had this brown spaniel with him—"

"Yes? Don't skip any details."

"Mr. Jones said he was bringing the dog to the station, but meeting me like that he asked me to take charge of it and save him a walk. So I noted down particulars and did so. Mr. Jones lives in a small house by the Halt, him and his wife, and they like dogs, but having had two killed they won't keep any more, he said. But Saturday night Mrs. J. kept hearing a dog howling, and so did he, so when he got up to see the 3.30 a.m. express go through he went to find out what was up with it. He said it was tied tight up to a small tree-trunk with a luggage-strap through its collar, scarcely giving it length to stand on its feet. It was just off the road, but not near any house, and he knew it must have been there for hours. It went nearly mad with relief when he loosed it, and he took it home. Next morning, his first free time, he was bringing it to us, as I said, when he saw me."

"Was there any identifying mark on the strap?"

"No, sir. It looked as if it had been bought a good time, but rolled up and not used. I fetched it along here in case of inquiries being made. Shall I get it? Oh, I forgot to say the name disc had been wrenched off the collar, and Jones said he concluded from that that its owner intended deliberately to lose it and tied it up to prevent it following him again."

Gorham nodded. That was a fair inference in the circumstances. Examination of the strap revealed no more than Brown had stated. It was slightly roughened at the edges as if it had been carried for some time in a car pocket, and still showed a tendency to roll up, but otherwise, apart from inside fraying caused by friction against the tree-trunk, had no sign of usage. He put it aside and bade Brown "Carry on."

"Well, sir, I felt sure at once it was Miss Hyde's dog, because I've often seen him in the village with that deaf maid of hers, and he answered to his name 'Robin', and fairly pulled me down Pound Lane towards his home. But he stopped for a second at the gate of The Laurels nosing about, and it was then I noticed something queer behind the bushes. Looking a bit closer, I made sure it was a bit of bare leg, so I didn't waste time taking Robin up to the house, but just slipped off the strap and dropped him over the gate, when he fairly raced down the garden, before 'phoning the station about the body. Then the officers came along, and it wasn't till evening I was able to ask Miss Hyde if she'd got him all right, over her gate."

"Did she question you?"

"No, sir. All I said, seeing her in her garden, was: 'That was your Robin I found this morning and shoved over your gate?' And she said: 'Oh, that was how he come home! I can't thank you enough. He must have slipped out when the garage gate was left open, and he's broken the disc off his collar.' And I said: 'That's all right, then, ma'am'."

"And the sparkling dialogue ceased there. I see. One more point. I saw that dog about two o'clock, and he'd got a bruised place on his side. Did you notice that?"

"I'm certain there was nothing wrong with him in the morning," the man answered with a touch of warmth. "The Joneses had fed him and cosseted him up after his being tied up like that, and he was as lively as a cricket as he come along with me. He's a fair little treat for spirits. That night I spent in their garden he was all over me. He must have bruised himself afterwards."

"I think so," Gorham said thoughtfully. "The place was still very tender. He is going to give us a pretty useful piece of evidence, Brown, because he was carried away from Pound Lane, and tied up where he was found, by the criminal we're after, and that tree near the Halt is conclusive proof of the route he took after he had got rid of the body. And that's a secret you'll keep strictly to yourself for the present, or I'll have the coat off your back, see?"

He smiled at young Brown and instantly received an earnest promise, for that smile on the square, good-humoured face was an extraordinary grim affair. But Brown felt braced by this confidence reposed in him by the great detective.

"That being clear," the Chief Inspector continued, "your next job is to get written statements from the two Jones as to when they first noticed the dog's howls, where the man found him, and so on. I want exact measurements of the distance of that tree from the road, mind. If they're curious, tell them some action may be taken over the theft of the dog from its home, and they may receive a small reward for rescuing it. See? That's right, then. Go to it. And don't forget to be discreet about the real reason for the inquiry. I shall be at the Yard from now on, and all reports are to come to me directly there."

After Brown had gone he repeated these instructions to Norris's bucolic underling, collected such of the exhibits in the case as remained at Finnet station house, and made quick time for his office in the great building that overlooks the Embankment. He ran through his waiting mail, but, that disposed of, and his clerk, Porter, given orders, chiefly of the "communication received and being given careful attention" type, to deal with it, he settled down to the study of reports from Sergeant Norris which bore the Frinton postmark.

But first he made sure that his message, translated by Li Moh, figured in all the leading journals. He could not, of course, himself test its comprehensibility. For that his trust in Mr. Moh was serene. If it reached the eye of the man to whom it was addressed his anxiety should be set at rest. At any rate, he could do no more. The reports from Frinton varied little in character.

Mr. MacDonnell had rented a large furnished house on the cliffs facing the sea, had assembled a staff of temporary servants, and was entertaining a party of friends, chiefly moneyed people like himself (he was the head of a trading concern with huge ramifications in the Far East), but which included a few youngish women and an odd man or two amongst whom was L. V. Hyde, who shared, so to speak, the crumbs which fell unconsidered from the rich man's table.

Good living and laziness seemed to be the order of the day. Bathing, tennis, and a cinema in the evening occupied the few hours of the day left over when full justice had been done to four opulent meals, which were its chief business. Mr. Hyde's modest car was garaged in the town, as Mr. MacDonnell's double garage was full of Rolls-Royces, complete with smart chauffeurs.

Mr. Hyde had shown no disposition to leave the main herd. He sun-bathed in the morning, played or watched tennis in the afternoon with one of the ladies, after tea bathed again with the same lady, Sylvia-something, who called him Sid, and seemed affectionate in manner, and on Thursday evening after dinner had accompanied three ladies and two of the men to the local cinema, where Norris had sat also, combining business with pleasure.

"In fact," Gorham said to himself, putting the paper away at a knock on the door, "a good time is being had by all. Come in."

"Detective-Inspector Johns from Harlesden to see you, sir."

"It's re Mrs. Vardon, sir," the visitor explained, and Gorham nodded and pointed to a chair.

"Have you got her?"

"Yes, and brought her along in a cab in case you wanted to see her yourself."

"Run through your tale first."

To summarize the story, Mrs. Vardon had turned up at No. 105 Lavender Road soon after nine that morning. She asked Mrs. Higgs, who opened the door, if there were a letter for her, and received an answer in the negative. Disappointed, she had seemed inclined to argue the matter and abuse Mrs. Higgs, but, convinced at last, she was turning away from the gate when the police watcher, who was in plain clothes, accosted her with the request that she would accompany him to the station. She tried to bolt, obviously frightened, but did not succeed. At the station she was informed that a charge of theft had been laid against her, and her bag was searched. As it contained the wanted book, no further action was taken, and the woman, furious and very abusive, had been brought along and was now in a waiting-room below.

The book was a cheap pocket-diary, but irregularly entered up, some pages being blank, others filled with close writing.

Gorham turned first to certain dates, then went back and read it straight through, taking notes of some entries as he came to them, and omitting all those of which the sense was doubtful. Not for the first time in this case he cursed the fact that the initial letter 'H' was shared by most of the persons who figured in it. But here, in her private notebook, Ellen Shields had used Christian names with sufficient frequency to make her sentences startlingly clear.

The book told without disguise the sordid story at which Gorham had guessed, and gave also complete confirmation of another theory that he had formed from a few stray straws that had drifted to his hand from various quarters.

When he had finished, his notes stood as under:

(A Jan. date.)
Worried about Ethel. She ought not to have Ch. H. in her room. 2 hrs. today. Others out.

(A March date, scribbled over three spaces.)

That lovely almond tree of dear Miss Hyde's hacked to pieces. What a dreadful shame. She inspires me so much by the wonderful example she sets of goodness and self-sacrifice, yet he can take everything and not even seem grateful. So difficult at Burrs. Cl. H. is a bad woman. Certain she knows Ch. is carrying on with Ethel. Just wants to live there for nothing. Believe she contrived this scheme.

(April date.)

Shall have to leave Burrs. Ethel and that Charles out for hours in Mr. H's car. Clarice in London all day, purposely, I'm sure. Mr. H. ought to be told.

(May date.)

Terribly upset. Went to Innisfree to collect parcel for J. Sale Miss Hyde promised yesterday when we met in street and saw all her lovely tulips ruined. Certain he did it. Saw top of his head in garden this morning as I went to work early. That almond tree too? She ought to put her foot down and stop his silly pretence. She is too good. Such patience with his masquerading while she works to keep him. All those months when she nursed him like a saint and put up with his swearing and tempers and selfishness. Eliza gave me a bundle from him too, that he'd told her to burn. Do for Jumble if I mend the coat a bit. She'd be dreadfully vexed if I spoke out. But shall straight, to him, if he ever behaves so wicked again.

June dates.

Those two kissing.

Mr. H. in Birmingham. Cl. in London. Those two out all yesterday in Mr. H.'s car. And night too, no beds slept in but Dent's. *Must* find another post. So difficult.

The last entry, Friday, the day before her death.

Dreadful day. Those two hugging, then quarrelling. All terribly wrong. Must speak to Mr. H. But worst of anything those lovely delphiniums. It has got to be stopped.

"Book as useful as you expected, sir?" asked Johns, who had waited with cheerful patience while the Chief Inspector studied his paper. But at that moment his clerk brought in a card.

"The gentleman is waiting to see you, sir. Says it's urgent." Gorham looked at the card and nodded.

"Bring him up," he said, and as the man vanished he added to Johns: "Quite useful. I'm not sure whether anything more's to be gained by my seeing Vardon myself. Detain her here for half an hour, and if I don't have her up meantime you can dismiss her. But make her understand she's suspect for not handing this book to the police instantly. May have involved herself in a serious mess. Action may be taken, that sort of thing, understand?"

"Quite, sir."

"You can hint we're considering a further charge besides suppression of vital information. Not specified, of course. I'm inclined to believe she's been trying her hand at a bit of blackmail. If that's a fact, she can be kept guessing as to how much we know."

Detective-Inspector Johns nodded, and departed to deal faithfully with his charge after due delay.

The Chief Inspector was still deep in thought when Edward Hubberd walked into the room. He had not yet collected his suitcase from Northbourne Station, and still wore the shabby office clothes of their last interview. His eyes were sunk deep in his colourless face, and were underscored with heavy lines of sleeplessness, but his manner was more friendly than Gorham had seen it, though it was still cool and grave.

"This is an unexpected visit, Mr. Hubberd."

"Is it? I felt that the reason for that rather enigmatical message of yours in the *Megaphone* this morning wanted clearing up."

"Wasn't it clear?"

"Oh, quite, as far as the meaning went. It conveyed the fact that I'm no longer under suspicion of having murdered that wretched woman. Was that correct?"

"Absolutely." Gorham beamed. "The man who translated it into Chinese was dubious as to his power to convey my meaning properly, but personally I never doubted his skill. He is one of those rare chaps who always knows more than he says."

"But why the dickens did you want it translated into Chinese?" Hubberd ejaculated.

"Well, don't you see—take a seat, won't you? The idea was to reassure you personally. And when you gave my man the slip yesterday you refrained from dropping me a line giving your new address—"

"Your man—and other things—had rather annoyed me."

"Exactly," said Gorham with satisfaction, bestowing a cordial smile on his visitor as one who had exercised common sense and not permitted annoyance to carry him beyond that bourne whence no traveller returns.

"But why Chinese, man?"

"Oh, that? Well, you see, a lot of English people can read French nowadays." As if that were the only alternative to Chinese. "I didn't want to take the public into our confidence just yet. I guessed you'd understand it all right, as I'd gathered you were one of the Hubberd family—Chinese scholars."

"Hmm. A knowledge of Oriental tongues doesn't necessarily run in a family, like red hair or a squint," Edward Hubberd retorted.

"No. But you told me you knew the Far East. And it seemed probable, if you couldn't make out my message yourself, that you'd refer it to your cousin, Mr. Pine Hubberd, who, I understand, is at present in England."

"You seem to understand the deuce of a lot about us," Hubberd grunted. "As a matter of fact, I'm staying with him now. Perhaps you know that already, too. But I didn't need to refer to him. I suppose I ought to be thankful you no longer suspect me of being a murderer, though you've taken your time—or did you ever seriously suspect me? Or have you used me all along as a red herring to draw off the public while you hunted the real Simon Pure?"

Gorham's beam underwent distinct modification.

"You're feeling naturally bitter at the repercussions of this crime on your own affairs, Mr. Hubberd; I know that, or I'd resent keenly that suggestion," he said, his tone betraying anger that he denied. "When I first handled the case you were under suspicion with every other man who'd come into contact with the victim. You especially because on your own showing you'd been the last to see her and—"

"I kept contradicting myself. Yes, I know that."

"Quite." There was a pregnant pause, then Edward Hubberd, who had been studying his fist as if he had never noticed it before, dropped his hands and jerked up his head.

"How did that beret come to be in my garage? Do you know?"

"Yes."

"You know it had nothing to do with me?"

"Yes."

"Damn it, man, you might be a little less monosyllabic!" Hubberd cried, exasperated. "How did it get there?"

"It was carried there while the murderer was disposing of the body. I discovered how only last night, after placing that message for you."

Hubberd drew a long breath of relief.

"She wasn't put out there, then! The fact is, I've been hideously haunted by the fear that she'd been caught on my premises and I'd failed to—er—notice and intervene—"

"If you were in your bedroom all evening, in the front of the house," Gorham observed, his ironical glance fixed on the other's face, "you can scarcely believe a struggle could take place in the garage immediately under your window, and you remain unaware of it!"

"But, as you've guessed, I didn't stop there," Hubberd announced quite calmly. "As soon as I heard the door bang behind the woman I dashed into my clothes again and went downstairs to my desk in the dining-room to check my accounts and write letters. From there I couldn't have heard anything short of a terrific shriek."

"There was no shriek," Gorham said slowly. "She wasn't murdered in Pound Lane, only her body was brought back. If you hadn't selected that very hour to put your private affairs in order there'd have been no mystery at all, because you'd have seen the car she was killed in, and recognized it at once."

Hubberd's face went grey.

"God! You mean it was my car! That swine Charles Hughes had my wife out in it, but he must have dropped her at the cinema before he picked up Ellen. She's spied on them for months. Had it all down in black and white, chapter and verse. He—she must have threatened to show him up to me—or his wife."

"Hadn't she betrayed them to you already?"

"I don't believe she meant it as betrayal," Hubberd growled, his sense of fairness piercing through a welter of feeling in which anger and disgust struggled for predominance among others less easily defined. "She hated to see it going on; wanted it stopped, as you'd want any flagrant indecency stopped, because it was indecent. But she thought of it as sin. She kept speaking of it as sinful, and that was why she told me at last. Not from any nasty desire to get back at Ethel. In fact she defended Ethel, said she was certain the whole thing was a put-up job between the Hughes, the scheme originating with Clarice, who wanted to keep the free quarters they'd got at any price, as long as I'd stick it. They came as paying-guests, but. . . ." He shrugged his shoulders. "Well, they were both out of a job; you can't get blood out of a stone; they hadn't paid a sou for months. I was sick of the sight of them, but they were Ethel's friends. . . . But if Ellen was right that swine of a fellow was simply out to bluff my wife into believing he was in love with her. If so, my wife was deceived all through."

He got up and started pacing about the room.

"But if you're going to accuse him of murder, for God's sake keep my wife's name out of it! She'd no more to do with it, or knowledge of it, than I had, or you either." He halted in front of the Chief Inspector, his hands clenched, his face convulsed with anger.

Gorham interrupted him with a mild word.

"Don't tell me anything you're going to regret afterwards, Mr. Hubberd. You're jumping to conclusions. I haven't accused Charles Hughes."

"Now I've started I'd better finish. You saw plenty for yourself on Sunday. You'd better know the exact truth to prevent further blundering."

It was Gorham's turn to shrug his shoulders.

"As you like. Did you have the whole thing out with your wife between Saturday night and Tuesday morning, when she left your house?"

"No. It was a filthy situation. Clarice Hughes saw her game—if it were her game—was up, and accused Ethel of trying to steal her husband, and Ethel retaliated. Between them they raked up every cause of quarrel they'd ever had. Look here, Chief Inspector, I'm speaking with revolting, indecent frankness, but you've got to be made to realize that my wife—though she seemed callous on Sunday about that ghastly murder—was simply obsessed by this love-affair. If he wasn't in earnest, and the thing began as a sort of amusing game between them—and in these days people go a long way to get what they call amusement"—bitterly—"she ended by liking the cad in dead earnest. The Hughes bolted on Monday morning, but by that time she worked herself into such a state . . . Oh, damn! Well, I won't deny I was not too cool myself by that time. But what I want to make clear to you is that from first to last she never made the slightest allusion to the murder except to hint more than once that I probably knew a good deal more about it than I'd confessed to the police. But the rather raucous fact that she entertained suspicion of me is proof by itself that her knowledge was nil. Do you see my point?"

Gorham nodded.

"Yes, I get that."

"Well, there you are. Leave her out of your case. She can tell you nothing. You will gain nothing by dragging her into the limelight as witness in a murder trial, exposed to the risk of questioning on private subjects that have nothing to do with the crime, yet which, made public, will do her irreparable harm." There was a silence which Gorham did not break.

Hubberd spoke again presently, in another tone.

"I'm preparing to go abroad at once. But if evidence is necessary it's my job to give it." His eyes, clear of anger, met those of the Chief Inspector in a look of mutual understanding. "Yes, you've guessed correctly. She and I are parting. But I owe her so much support first, and as I said, in any case it's my job, as I was the last to see that wretched woman alive."

Gorham sat still, in thought. Hubberd had told him nothing that he did not already know. But there was one detail yet to be cleared up.

"It was a pity that you were not as frank as you've been today when I questioned you before, Mr. Hubberd," he said at length gravely. "Anything private you had told me then—that didn't directly bear on the investigation, I mean—would have been held as confidential. As it is, I've had to clear all this ground for myself, and that being so I can't tie myself by promises. You will have to give evidence if it comes to a trial, I'm afraid. But whether in person or by a properly attested statement on paper I can't say. That part—the preparation of the Crown case—is a matter for the lawyers, beyond my province. In your place I'd consult your solicitor. However, we're anticipating, for no arrest has yet been made, and that part of it I can't possibly discuss. But there's one point you didn't quite clear up. Do you know if Shields left written evidence of her knowledge of your private affairs? You said she had it down in black and white, chapter and verse. To save confusion, let me mention Mrs. Vardon's call at your office."

Edward Hubberd fidgeted restlessly on the chair on to which he had dropped again when his excitement had died away.

"Your damned spy reported that, I suppose," he grunted. "I can't see, as you've washed me out of your rotten case, that my private affairs are any longer your concern, Chief Inspector."

"Put it another way, then," said Gorham patiently. "Have you any ground for charging Mrs. Vardon with attempted blackmail?"

"She lifted ten quid off me," Hubberd replied with a grin. "I suppose I've ground for a charge, but I don't intend to make it. Ellen told me her tale verbally, but she assured me she could give dates. The paper Vardon showed me was only a copy, but it was a copy of a genuine document, I'm sure, for only Ellen Shields could have had the intimate knowledge of our affairs that it betrayed. I mean, Vardon couldn't have made it up herself."

Gorham opened his desk drawer and took out the diary.

"Ever seen this before, Mr. Hubberd?"

The answer was prompt this time.

"Never!" He leaned forward eagerly as if to take up the book to examine it, but a large hand was laid on the open pages. "That's her writing. Is that the original of Vardon's copy? By the by, I kept that copy."

"You did? Then, as we hold this—can't say if it's your original or not, not having seen your document, but it's likely—we've probably drawn her fangs as a would-be blackmailer. She's very unlikely to have made another copy. But if she tries to touch you again, 'phone us, Mr. Hubberd, and on this"—he tapped the diary—"and your copy in her own handwriting, we'll put her where she belongs, and your name needn't appear."

"Mr. X. I see. Thanks very much. If she does I will. But how—"

"Did she get hold of the book at all?" Gorham interrupted a trifle hurriedly. "Oh, that was simple; she got it from Shields' lodgings, where it escaped the first police search, and evidently saw her way to a spot of private advantage before it was handed over, very properly, to our charge. As you refuse to charge her there's no more to be said, unless she tries again." He rose, and his visitor took leave, after giving his cousin's address.

When he had gone, Gorham, immensely relieved that his message had reached the right quarter and that the Hubberd tangle was cleared away, submitted his completed case to his superiors and made preparation for the final act.

Unfortunately for his neat plan, the Hubberds were not the only men in England who could read that message.

Chapter XXI

Sergeant Norris secretly resented being taken off the main case on Wednesday afternoon and sent down to Frinton to keep observation on a man only remotely connected with it by the position of his house in Pound Lane. Miss Hyde herself had vouched for the fact that he had gone off for the week-end before seven on Saturday night, and she was the sort of lady whose word could be implicitly relied on. However, he was not the man to allow his feelings to interfere with his job. His motor-cycle was in readiness at the modest lodgings he had taken opposite the garage where Mr. Hyde had parked his car, and, in addition, he had requested the local police to post a constable at the level-crossing gates, which shut the little town snugly within its exclusive enclosure, with power to stop and detain Mr. Hyde if he attempted to drive out without his tailer.

But, as he reported, on Wednesday evening and Thursday his duties were both easy and pleasant. Mr. and Mrs. MacDonnell's party kept together and followed a regular routine; the weather was warm and sunny, and Sergeant Norris, in a rather natty grey suit, had merely to lounge about on the greensward of the cliffs or on the sands looking as much like a holidaymaker as possible.

In the morning the luxurious little chalet on its reserved strip of foreshore formed a background for the whole party, which bathed in the sea or the sun as taste dictated. Servants arranged chairs, newspapers, and the inevitable refreshments, carried from the house on the cliffs above, and Norris, on a groyne at a discreet distance, could read his paper and keep his quarry in sight with a mind at ease, for Hyde was among the sun-bathing fans, and, minus his clothes, Norris had little fear of his giving him the slip. The rest of the day was scarcely more strenuous, for the herd habit continued. The dining-room windows of the house were never closed or curtained, the tennis courts which claimed the afternoon were open to onlookers, and the cinema that closed the evening presented no difficulties. Thus all went smoothly for the Finnet police officer till Thursday night.

Friday morning, beginning with the usual bathing routine, gave him no indication of the fatigues he was to undergo before nightfall. When he opened his paper on his groyne and turned to the paragraphs on the Finnet murder case he was startled and puzzled by the line in unintelligible writing in which the only recognizable word was *Hubberd*. And keenly watching the distant group in front of the chalet, he saw that they appeared to be equally intrigued by it, pointing it out to one another and to Hyde, but, making nothing of it, apparently losing interest. But only for a time, for when the rotund, white-flannelled form of Mr. MacDonnell, who had stayed behind to deal with his mail, was seen descending the cliffs they collected again and, as soon as he arrived, crowded round the chair into which he plumped himself and thrust the paragraph under his eyes.

Norris cursed the distance he was compelled to keep which made the scene a dumb show.

He saw Hyde lean over his host's shoulder, joking still, but intent, while the others pressed round MacDonnell's knees, chaffing him and one another, and he in return teased them by the maddening deliberation with which he lighted his pipe before he would attend to what they wanted.

It dawned on Norris that they were sure that MacDonnell could interpret the mystery. But he prolonged the suspense, apparently giving preposterous explanations at first which caused shrieks of laughter and some boisterous horse-play among the sun-bathers. Eventually, tiring of the game, he gave the true translation, which was evidently much less exciting than those he had invented, because the general enthusiasm died away and the group broke up. Some of its members drifted towards the sparkling water, and others disposed their plump bodies on the warm sand with feline enjoyment of physical well-being, but without a cat's decency of fur covering, as Norris thought crossly. He would have liked to have heard that interpretation himself.

Hyde was among those who strolled down to the water, but Norris imagined him unusually thoughtful, as if the explanation of the mystery conveyed some meaning to him that was lost on the others. He dressed early, but just when Norris, whom the bracing air made hungry, was eagerly expecting the party to climb the cliffs towards luncheon, he elected to go out on the water with a boatman, and Norris dared not leave the shore till he returned, long after the others had gone.

From then on his movements were so erratic that the watcher was kept in a state of nervous tension, and dared not relax his vigilance even for the half-hour necessary to snatch a meal for himself. There are no snack bars along the Frinton front to encourage the unwanted tripper, and apprehending at length that there might be more behind Mr. Gorham's order than a mere altruistic desire to afford a subordinate a seaside holiday, he suppressed his yearning to eat in one of the expensive hotels.

He was thankful that he had. The celebrated author spent a bare fifteen minutes at the luncheon-table, where his fellow-guests had already reached the sweets stage when he appeared, and immediately afterwards went off to the tennis courts with the woman of the party who was called Sylvia, whose limbs, generously displayed during the morning rites, had the plump, full curves and satiny brown finish of her waved head. A piece of unblemished physical perfection and not much else. Norris's hope of an hour off while they were strenuously employed, rose, but only to be dashed down. Another man of the party strolled up and he and Sylvia paired off, and Hyde, after watching for a time, went off for a walk. He approached the Gates by ways that avoided the main street, Connaught Avenue, where his car and Norris's motor-bike were parked, but in any case a motor-bike is useless in tailing a man on foot.

There are no lanes or byways in that district, which till recently was pasture land scarcely broken by a solitary farm house; and it seemed to the follower that he tramped endless miles of uninteresting highway with the aimlessness of a householder taking the dog for a walk. Was that, perhaps, Hyde's intention? The suspicion braced him to grim plodding. They reached the sleepy little town of Thorpe-le-Soken, and, aware of a station on the main line here, Norris lessened the distance between them, but Hyde merely loitered through the streets, looking into windows of primitive shops, and finally entered a small tea-garden and sat down to a roughly-served tea.

Norris bought chocolate in the shop opposite and read notices of sales of household effects and farming utensils that plastered a wall of an estate agent's farther up the street. He then entered the office and put inquiries about bungalows for sale to a spotty-faced little girl who appeared to be holding the fort during the agent's absence, till Hyde emerged from the tea-garden, when he abruptly left the small girl and again took up the chase.

Hyde, evidently refreshed by his tea, went away at a brisk pace, making, to judge by the signposts, for Colchester; but an hour later, after a long detour, came round by Kirby, passed through the village, and headed for Kirby Cross and the main coastal road.

Norris, with a stick of chocolate between himself and a seven o'clock breakfast, realizing that they were making for Frinton Gates, and the point from which they had started, fought a frantic impulse to leap on his quarry and slay him where he stood.

If the fellow had dragged him all these miles to test a suspicion that he was being tailed, he had confirmed it now without a shadow of doubt. And now what? Home, and the indignant complaint of an innocent man to the authorities? Or was all this the deliberate prelude to a previously planned escape?

Norris quickened his pace, lessening the distance between them, but not enough.

As Hyde came out at Kirby Cross—which is not a monument, but a cross-roads on the main Clacton-Walton coastal road—a car coming from the Frinton direction slithered to a standstill for just sufficient time to enable him to leap on board, then flew on towards Clacton.

Norris stood alone by the telephone-box, which had evidently been the rendezvous—for the car was Hyde's, and driven by Sylvia—and cursed aloud, as a cloud of dust vanished in the distance.

He had been fooled to the top of his bent by a simple trick, perfectly timed. Hyde had realized that his car, behind Frinton Gates, was a trap. He had arranged that Sylvia should fetch it out and meet him at a given spot on the road. The policeman, ready for Hyde, had no authority to prevent the lady, whose papers were in perfect order, from driving where she liked.

Norris did what he could with the telephone, which took time, and started to tramp back to Frinton, thinking bitterly of his useless bike, but too impatient to wait for one of the buses which plied on the road between Clacton and Walton.

The last straw was heaped on his aching back when at quarter past seven he reached the Gates, which were closed to allow a train through, and a familiar voice hailed him from one of the queue of waiting cars.

"Hullo, Norris!"

He went to Chief Inspector Gorham's car and stated the facts in a few bleak sentences.

"I ought to have kept closer, been near enough to tackle him," he ended miserably. "You've come to take him?"

Gorham nodded, There was no time to waste in chat.

"He'd have killed you, probably, if you had. Sheer bad luck MacDonnell being able to read that message. Hyde knew, with Hubberd cleared, he was for it. I came by Clacton and straight out. They must have headed inland—towards Weeley probably. You've warned all roads? Good. One second, though. He can't cross the river Colne before Colchester, or the Stour before Manningtree. London or Harwich, which? We've got him cold, so far. It's now 7.25. Is this woman Sylvia the sort to go gladly without her dinner?"

"It'll be the first time she's missed one of her solid four square meals a day since school-days, if she does," Norris growled.

"Then he probably inveigled her into rescuing his car by a suggestion of dining somewhere. It's quite unlikely he took her into his confidence except as a joke, to slip you. His objective is London, not Harwich, in all probability. But communicate to have him held in case. Listen, Norris; enlist the help of the local police and have him detained if—by a wild chance—he comes back, and 'phone word to Colchester police station. I'll tap that chance first."

Sylvia wasn't enjoying her escapade with the man she had filched from various rivals in the MacDonnell group as much as she had anticipated.

When he scrambled into the back at Kirby Cross he said, rather perfunctorily: "Marvellous, darling! Timed to a split second!" But after he had slipped into her vacated seat behind the wheel, half a mile farther on, he sent the car along in tense silence, avoiding main roads wherever possible and drawing a breath of relief as they cleared every corner where a hold-up might happen, though once, as they waited before the shut gates of a level-crossing, which are too numerous in this part of Essex, he broke into language about these "infernal death-traps" that made her giggle.

But all this dodging took time, and the grim and silent chase ceased after a time to amuse her. "Goodness, Sid, that chap can't have followed us on his flat feet! This isn't my idea of a snappy evening. I'd be laughing a lot more at the pictures in Clacton, where the others are going after dinner. It's a Jessie Matthews film, and I adore Jessie Matthews!" she exclaimed with a hint of peevishness.

Hyde roused himself.

"Just you wait till we're through this blasted town, honey!" He gave the plump hand on his knee a convulsive squeeze that left red marks on it. She gave a squeal, half pain, half pleasure. "Sorry, was I rough? You see, that chap can't have followed us, but he may have warned his pals to stop us if they can!"

"Well, what if he has? It's a free country, isn't it? They've nothing on you really, if they do want you as a witness! Seems to me you couldn't be more nervous if they were after you for the bloody crime itself!"

"It wasn't bloody. Don't be beastly, darling, and do go on being the topping old sport you've shown yourself already. Babs and Wonky'll fairly gnash their teeth with rage when they tumble to it that we're off together for our night out! What!"

"They'll tumble to it when they sit down to dinner," she giggled. "I hope this tavern of yours sports decent grub, though, Siddie boy; I don't mind owning I'm some darned hungry."

"Rather! You don't suppose I'd take you to some potty little hole where they poison you, do you? After the swell *machan* Mrs. Mack dishes up? There, thank God we've passed the last of those lousy streets!" They were through Colchester, and the traffic signs of Lexden fell rapidly behind them. "Now we can let her rip." The car leapt forward in response to his will, and he sat up with a cleared brow. "Tell you what, honey. Did you see what was on at the Regal we passed in Colchester? When we've tucked into all the grub and bubbly we need to brace ourselves at this little place we're coming to we'll drop in and have a spot of Jessie Matthews on the way home, eh? That's the way to tickle Wonky's curiosity properly, eh?"

"That'll be a scream, and we'll swear we saw her at Clacton like the others!" She giggled again.

She liked the impressive exterior of the road-house at which they presently drew up, and after titivating her face before a mirror in a dressing-room she joined her escort and entered a finely decorated though sparsely occupied dining-room in gay spirits. The dinner, as she said in the phraseology of her class, wasn't too bad, and the wine, which they both drank freely, and without much discrimination, enhanced her spirits without improving her mental equipment.

"Sid" had fastened on the idea of seeing the Jessie Matthews film on the way back to Frinton, and as it was not far short of 8.20 when they began their dinner he was inclined to check her tendency to dawdle over each course.

"No earthly good missing the opening of the picture, though we'll give the news stuff a miss," he said, and she agreed, but refused to forgo an ice as the finishing touch.

While it was coming he paid the bill, and filled her glass from the second bottle, and drank off his own.

"Look here, honey," he said, rising, "suppose you wait here and finish your sweets while I go and make sure the mechanics have rectified that spot of trouble I noticed in the engine? Here's your ice—"

"Right ho."

"Good girl. Never do to risk a breakdown, eh?" He winked. "Can't you guess what Wonky would say? Wait here till I fetch you."

While she answered with her habitual giggle, he replenished her glass from the last of the bottle and left her.

In fact, she was not sorry to secure a few minutes more in her chair before attempting to walk down the broad central aisle of the dining-room, though she did not resist the temptation of that final glass. After all, Sid had paid for it; a pity to leave it, and better she had it than Sid, who'd got to do the driving.

There were plenty of empty tables in the room, and she sat watching the going and coming of diners through a blissful haze.

But after fifteen minutes or more the haze cleared slowly and she began to watch the door for the return of her escort.

Every time it swung open she looked for his appearance with rising impatience.

"I'll tell him off properly for making me scuffle through my dinner, risking indigestion, to see the first of that picture, and then make us both late fooling about gossiping with a lot of dirty mechanics," she thought crossly. "Mucking about with his old car. Oh, that's him at last—!"

But it was not. It was a fresh pair of diners. . . . It was a waiter who looked in—at her, she thought, sitting solitary at her table—and went out again . . . it was the hall porter who looked at her and departed. . . . A party leaving. . . . Everyone stared at her by this time. She felt furious. She would have gone off in search of him but for that doubt about her legs wobbling. She didn't want to start ticking him off and have him retort that she was tanked. . . . There he was! . . . Yes—no . . . it was a man who looked as if he were the manager; at least, he wore a black tie and a dinner-jacket, with a big man in a blue suit, and both made straight for her table.

"Pardon me, madam, but are you waiting for someone?" the manager asked civilly. "I think you came with a gentleman?"

"Yes, but you can't be wanting this table, there's plenty vacant," was her uneasy retort. "My friend went out to stoke up the car, but I'd be glad if you'd send and tell him I'm fairly fed up waiting, and we'll miss that picture altogether if he doesn't get a move on quick."

"You were going to a picture-house, eh? In Chelmsford?"

"No, Colchester. We're staying at Frinton, with friends, and thought we'd do the Jessie Matthews picture on the way back, but if Mr. Hyde thinks I'm the sort to hang around waiting his pleasure he's got another, bigger think coming."

"The gentleman's name is Hyde? Is he an old friend of yours?"

"No, he isn't," she snapped. "Though it's no business of yours. I only met him this week at my friends'. As a matter of fact, he's the celebrated author, L. V. Hyde," she added with a smirk. "Though, being all real pals, we call him Sid. Now, if you're quite satisfied, you might go and tell him I'm waiting."

"Will you come to my office? I'm afraid there's been some slight misunderstanding," the manager suggested. "No doubt we can arrange for the use of a car for you, but I'm afraid your friend—Mr. Hyde?—left the place half an hour ago. He drove straight off when he left you. . . ."

Gorham left the manager to deal single-handed with the wretched Sylvia's incredulous wrath.

He had only waited to discover if she knew any vital facts about her late companion, but it was immediately obvious that she had been used as a cat's-paw to get Hyde's car clear out of Frinton.

A minute later he was speeding along the London Road.

In Chelmsford he learned that the car he was following had turned west. That meant that it was heading, via Ongar, towards the north circular. These inquiries involved delay. He followed and got news of it again, still twenty-five minutes ahead. But clearer roads gave the advantage to Gorham's more powerful car till the built-up area, reached after nightfall, evened chances again. Hyde had no doubt chosen the longer route to avoid endless chances of being held up on the direct road. But Gorham was definite that he was making for Finnet and Innisfree. Idiotic on the face of it, but a risk he had got to take, because he had to supply himself with money before he could make a clean bolt out of the country, and his sister was his banker.

Yet, beyond the warning contained in the fact that Hubberd was exonerated, and he himself under police surveillance, which might mean a merely general precaution, he had no reason to believe himself in immediate danger. There had been no police interrogations, nothing to tell him that suspicion was definitely fixed on himself. Had Gorham believed him to be in a state of panic, likely to abandon his car and try to give him the slip, he would have been detained at Chelmsford. It suited him better to take his man in the Metropolitan Police area, Finnet for preference.

He'd be trapped at the gate of his home. The place was surrounded. The little lady was safe. The worst part of cleaning up a case by the arrest of the criminal was the hideous blow dealt to innocent folk by the act. He was powerless to help that side of it. He remembered the little lady beside Shields' grave, the upturned earth covered with her flowers. Had she then known or guessed the identity of the murderer? He did not believe her capable of imagining the appalling truth.

The delays necessitated by interviewing scouts along the route had been made up on the road till the distance between them was lessened to barely ten minutes when he turned from Harrow Main Road into Chetwynd Avenue, where, halfway down, he left his car. At the garage gate of Innisfree he was roughly grabbed by a policeman, who apologized in a flurried whisper as he realized his mistake.

"He hasn't come yet, sir. We'd taken cover in the garridge," he explained.

"Not come? He was well ahead of me at the last point."

"You see for yourself, sir. The house is dark."

Gorham felt thoroughly perturbed. Had he leapt wrongly to the certainty that Innisfree was the fellow's objective? But he could not be wrong. What other aim could he have in this quarter for which he had made like a homing-pigeon since he left Sylvia planted at that dinner-table beyond Chelmsford?

"The other gate is covered?" he whispered. "All right. Stay here. I'm going in to reconnoitre."

As he crept down the path to the kitchen premises he caught the smothered sound of a dog's bark, and in a flash saw how his men had been fooled. Two sides of the garden were accounted for by Chetwynd Avenue and Pound Lane, the third by the boundary wall of The Laurels, but the fourth side lay open to Ewings's newly acquired market gardens, which stretched practically to the backs of buildings in Harrow Road.

To avoid being seen in the street, Hyde had entered the gardens somehow—he must know every inch of the ground in a place where he'd lived for years—and slipped across them and into the house under the very noses of his watchers.

Gorham dashed forward; no care for silence now. An open kitchen window confirmed his worst fears. He heaved and struggled his bulky body through the narrow aperture. The dog's barking above was frantic. He raced through to the hall, stubbing himself against piled furniture in the darkness, and up the stairs. Guided by the row the dog was making, he opened a door and caught a horrible sound of laboured breathing. But immediately there was a thud, a violent scuffling, and then a tremendous impact against his chest that must have thrown him down but for the support of the doorpost against his back.

Legs and one arm entwined round his unseen assailant—the darkness made the whole thing like something out of a first-class nightmare—his right hand felt for the switch behind him, and light flooded the scene—a crash and he found himself kneeling on a man's stomach, the small, limp body of another man on the floor a yard away, and on a bed in a recess another body that he had scarcely time to glance at.

If it had seemed nightmarish in the dark, light contributed extra elements of screaming farce.

Furniture, pulled out of its place, standing about, trunks, an open suitcase, the dog leaping on him hysterically, evidence of a free fight everywhere, the man beneath him writhing and struggling; but if Hyde fought with the strength of savage desperation, Gorham, with the sight of Mr. Moh's limp body before his eyes, retaliated with the fury of a raging demon.

The contest, though fierce, was short.

The room was suddenly full of large forms.

But Eliza, in a snatched-up red flannel dressing-gown, was there first, who, not waiting to ask questions, handed Gorham a luggage-strap which, with her help, he drew viciously tight about his victim's body and elbows. A policeman produced handcuffs, which he snapped on a whimpering creature exhausted and almost as limp as Mr. Moh, and other uniformed men who poured in at the front door, that someone had opened, crowded in.

"One man followed to see you were O.K., sir. And seeing the light go on, and him whistling, we followed." Thus the bucolic sergeant.

"Take that away."

Gorham dragged himself from the prisoner, to drop on his knees by his friend.

"He came across the allotments. Mr. Moh must have interfered while he was murdering her." A hand jerked towards the bed. "Is she dead? Send for a doctor and ambulance, someone."

He left Mr. Moh and went to stand by Eliza, bending over her mistress's still form.

"What do you know of this?"

"That Hyde? He's lived on my lady for years. She had to give up her home to get quit of him."

"Why? Was she afraid of him?"

"Of his being cruel to Robin, and smashing the flowers. She couldn't bear that no more. But I didn't fear he'd try to get in tonight to kill her, because I knew the police were there. I was asleep till I saw the light, but Robin had slipped off my bed to get to her. He must have followed Hyde in."

"Why should he want to kill her?" Gorham asked slowly, his eyes on her grey face.

"Because he was scared she'd show him up. How he never wrote all the stories."

"Good Lord, you knew she was L. V. Hyde all along?" Gorham muttered.

"I knew, but she never said. So I held my tongue."

"Eliza, did Ellen Shields know that?"

"She must have. She lived here six months before I came. That's why I always thought it was him did her in."

"The devil you did!" said Gorham, but not aloud.

P.C. Brown came back, bringing a doctor from Chetwynd Avenue, a middle-aged man with good and intelligent eyes in a face of rugged ugliness.

"I hear Miss Hyde has been attacked. Is she—"

"Not dead, no. All but. A fellow saved her life. Unconscious, though, and for her own sake you'd better keep her out of things as long as possible. I've just arrested her brother for murder."

"What! Not the author, L. V. Hyde?" he exclaimed, shocked, already busied over his patient.

"No. Her brother Sydney, who never wrote a line in his life. That's the author, Ella V. Hyde, lying there, Doctor. And when you've finished with her there's another patient waiting for you in the next room, the chap who hauled her attacker off. . . ." He went back to Li Moh, where he had been tenderly laid on Eliza's bed, and forgot everything in his dogged attempt to hold the flickering flame of life in him from going out altogether.

The prisoner was removed to a cell for the rest of the night. An ambulance presently arrived, and Ella Hyde was carried away from the scene of her trial in a merciful state of unconsciousness, which now owed something to the doctor's skill.

He agreed with Gorham, when he felt the fluttering of her pulses, that the longer she was kept in profound quiet the better. There was a swelling on her head, as if she had been banged against some rounded wooden edge, probably that of the mahogany bed, which gave him more anxiety than the horrible marks of attempted manual strangulation about her throat. He had been one of the medical men summoned to assist in the examination of the body of Ellen Shields, and had seen just such bruisings then. But if he put two and two together, he was a discreet man, and the result made him the more determined that his patient should pass the next few weeks in complete seclusion from a world whose news could only pierce her with deadly pain.

But by the Chief Inspector, once he had issued the necessary directions that fell within his duty, the gradual clearing of the house passed unheeded. The night seemed the longest he had ever experienced, though the summer dawn came early and showed up the bare, uncarpeted state of Eliza's room, and the bandaged figure on her bed.

The sun had been shining for a couple of hours when a hand on the sheet touched his.

"Moh! Li Moh!"

"Is she—?"

"She's as safe as houses, old man. You saved her life."

"And you mine. You copped him?"

Gorham nodded solemnly.

"I nearly bashed the life out of him when I thought he'd done you in. But don't worry. He's alive, under lock and key. Now have a nice cup of tea, old Moh, and go to sleep again."

He went down to the disordered kitchen and helped Eliza make it.

Mr. Moh drank it gratefully, though his lips were swollen and bruised, and Eliza produced an invalid-cup, slightly cracked, from the box of discards, which helped matters.

The last person to drink from that cup had been Sydney Hyde, when Ellen Shields had held it to his lips and poured so much of the contents over his neck that he pushed her hand away, and between them had produced the crack.

But none of the three knew that.

Then Eliza went out and returned dragging a mattress, which she laid on the floor with a pillow and rug.

"It's not much after six, Mr. Gorham. You can get a couple of hours' sleep yourself now Mr. Moh's more like himself," she said.

So that eventful night ended prosaically, with the two friends slumbering in her vacated room till Gorham was roused by the smell of frying bacon, which Eliza, now in quiet command of the situation, had sent the policeman left on guard downstairs to buy for their breakfast.

Chapter XXII

On Sunday afternoon, in the garden of their house at Hammersmith, while the river that flowed below the balustrade at its foot went out as far as it could, the two detectives again slumbered side by side.

Mr. Moh lay on a couch, his face less swollen, but displaying hardly an inch of skin unpatterned by bruises, that were turning all colours of the rainbow, and which indeed extended all over his body. He was clad in a neat tussore sleeping-suit, and covered by a light fawn rug, and while she settled him for his siesta, before taking her daughter to the children's afternoon service, his wife had fixed a Japanese umbrella that shaded his face from the sun.

Gorham, fully dressed, whose beauty had also suffered considerable damage during that frantic fight on Miss Hyde's bedroom floor, slumbered peacefully on two deck-chairs, Feathers, his spaniel, sprawled across his knees.

On to this placid tableau, by the path by the side of the house, walked Captain Tring, Assistant Commissioner at Scotland Yard.

But if he had mischievously hoped to surprise his subordinate, Feathers' enraptured barking frustrated his purpose.

"Well, well! Very restful scene, my dear Gorham. Thought I'd look in and inquire after our heroic friend. No, lie still, Moh. You're quite a picture as you are," he said lightly, gazing with undisguised admiration at their colourful faces. He took a vacant chair and peremptorily waved Gorham back to his.

"It was kind of you to come, sir," said Gorham. But Captain Tring waved again, this time to repudiate undeserved praise.

"The fact is, I was told that you were both well worth seeing," he said frankly. "And I'm bound to admit that my informant was right. How far does the colour-scheme extend, Li Moh? Far below the Plimsoll line?"

"Not an inch is unhued of this lowly worm's unmentionable person," murmured Mr. Moh, gratified by this distinguished interest. "Also, all is of such extreme tenderness, owing to antagonist's method of banging said form against floor in order to extinguish inconvenient vitality, that extensive swathings of cotton-wool dressings applied by skilled surgical attendant forbid wearing of normal clothes."

"Well, that silk suit you've got on is very dressy." The A.C. eyed it critically. "But, man alive, what were your hands doing that you let him slam you about so roughly?"

"Keeping his away from jugular, where recent intensive practice had taught him skill in strangulation that gave me white feet."

"You either mean white liver or cold feet, Moh," Gorham corrected. "You can't have it both ways."

"Pardon flat contradiction, I had all manifestations of blinking timidity there are," Mr. Moh said with dignity. "Only extreme of terror gave tenacity to keep on with scuffle till you arrived to take over."

"What I don't understand is why you were in the house at all," Captain Tring interrupted. "You knew Hyde was in Essex, seventy-five miles away, and under observation at that, even if you did not know that Gorham had gone down to arrest him. You couldn't foresee that he'd get a chance to attack Miss Hyde."

Mr. Moh wriggled unhappily, then stopped as it hurt. "Extreme unaccountableness of human plans working out as per schedule suggested precautionary measure of lurking in tool-shed during critical hours, so slipped over wall from Laurels and lurked in same as soon as Mr. Hardwicke brought ladies home and drove away."

"How long did you lurk?" Tring asked, amused.

"Not long. Light in bedroom above had gone out perhaps half an hour, perhaps less, when shadow stole towards kitchen window of which catch was defective. He knew that. He leapt in and I followed, but he knew upstairs geography, that was new to me, and so reached that innocent lady in dark before I could catch up," he explained sadly, and stimulated exhaustion by firmly closing his eyes.

Captain Tring, taking the hint, turned to Gorham.

"How soon did you hit on Hyde as the criminal? I had scarcely a doubt myself of Hubberd's guilt, especially after he absconded, till I got your statement on Friday."

"You hadn't met Mr. Hubberd," Gorham said unwillingly. "One can't bank on personal impressions, of course, in cases of murder, but . . . well, Hubberd wasn't definitely eliminated till that beret clue, which didn't fit into any theory of the crime I could form, was cleared up suddenly on Thursday evening, though I'd already sent out that all-clear message to the Press on the strength of other facts I'd got about Hyde. You see," he added, with a touch of deprecation in his tone as he met his chief's keen grey eyes, "it was a toss-up in my mind whether, after the break-up of his married life, and the loss of his job, and the general hounding he was getting on all sides, he mightn't be goaded into suicide. I wanted to prevent that—"

"I always said you had a feelin' 'eart, Gorham," Captain Tring jeered.

"Well, I got caught out properly for being too clever over that message. Mr. MacDonnell, who's traded in Chinese goods in the Treaty ports for forty years, translated it straight off to Hyde, the one chap I wanted to keep it dark from, that Hubberd was out of the show. And the second bloomer I made was not having him stopped on the road."

All this with gloomy frankness, to anticipate the acid comments that he knew the A.C. would make sooner or later. He had made plenty himself on that last one since Miss Hyde and Li Moh had nearly lost their lives in consequence of it.

But Captain Tring was nothing if not unexpected.

"I don't agree that you should have stopped him," he said thoughtfully. "The fact that he was caught red-handed in his attempt to murder his sister will strengthen the whole case against him—in fact clinch it. Without it the chain of circumstantial evidence for his murder of Shields could be broken link by link."

"Do you think so, sir?" The Chief Inspector looked troubled. "I always dislike a case that hangs on evidence of time, a few minutes one way or another. The night porter at the Burdock Club, where he dined, swears he did not see him there after he came on duty at eight o'clock; the day porter didn't see him go, but admits he could easily have left when he was away from the hall on various errands during his last half-hour. The table-waiter served his coffee in the dining-room at quarter to eight and says he left the room a few minutes later. He was the last witness there actually to see him. My belief is that he left the building at once, having suddenly decided to go to Yorker's for the week-end, and, remembering the time rules for Sunday, that he'd have to be on the course at a definite time if he wanted a game, decided to cut round by Finnet in order to pick up his clubs and clothes.

"That first part isn't too satisfactory, I know, for the fact that the night porter didn't see him doesn't actually prove he wasn't in the club, as he asserts, till after nine. But to prove he's lying, I've got the taxi-driver, Cyril White, who followed his tail along the last part of the London-Finnet Road and swears he stopped dead outside Finnet Station at 9.20. As you've read his statement, sir, you also know that White asserts he stopped to pick up a passenger, and that he saw a glimpse of what he called 'staring yellow' in the car as Hyde turned to go back into the quiet lane at the back of the hill."

"One moment, Gorham. You're not suggesting there was an appointment between Hyde and Shields at the station?"

"Certainly not. Their meeting was pure accident. She was on her way to take her train home to Harlesden. She was seething with indignation about the plants he had smashed, and when she suddenly saw him close by the kerb she signalled him sharply, and must have made him realize with a word that she intended to expose him. She may have held up the coat—or called that she knew about the delphiniums. That part we can't ever know, unless Hyde confesses. At any rate, he took her aboard—White's 'staring yellow' was her beret, of course—and turned back into a quiet spot to hear what she'd got to say. When he realized she was dangerous he clutched her by the throat, and killed her. Then, when he saw he'd committed murder, his first idea was to strip her and drop her by the hedge-side to suggest assault by some stranger.

"You remember that recent case in the North, where a girl was assaulted and killed quite close by a house wall. That case was obviously clear in his mind. He got her stripped, and rammed her into the old coat that she'd brought on the chance of confronting him with it, to prove he'd previously smashed other of his sister's plants—tulips that time, from fragments in the pockets. Then he was disturbed by the appearance of people in the lane, and in a panic drove on down the lane by what is really a footpath, just wide enough to admit a small car (I tested it), and so round into the High Street. I feel certain he'd decided to make for Finnet Beeches, to drop the body there. As he passed over the bridge he chucked the bundle of clothes into the brook, and made for Pound Lane. But there he got his final bright idea. Not a soul was about. He knew that Hardwicke's house was empty, and the next too. He took a swift decision to decant his burden there, and did so.

"But here an annoyance occurred. His sister's dog had got loose and was trotting about in the Lane. Seeing his master, he ran up as Hyde came out of The Laurels, and he saw that Robin had got the beret in his mouth. The black specks were bits of asphalt from the path. Robin chased into Hubberd's garage, but there, being afraid of Hyde, he dropped it, and Hyde grabbed him and threw him into the car, driving off towards Finnet Beeches, where he knew he could cut through the private road as the gates were standing open. Then he realized he'd been a fool to capture the dog at all. Probably he did it to prevent it barking and rousing someone to discover his presence in the Lane. But he couldn't take it to Yorker's, where he now intended to clinch his time alibi, so, to prevent it following him, he got out and tied it brutally to a tree where the station-master at the Halt found it later and took it home for the night.

"Hyde made quick time for Yorker's, and stated he was seated in the card-room by ten. The men he played with didn't notice the time particularly, but by good luck the secretary actually saw him in the drive coming in at 10.20. So that's another definite point established. But before he'd entered the gates he gave the car a brisk once-over, and finding he'd overlooked Shields' bag when he chucked away the clothes, he deposited it in a public shelter across the road, trusting to luck some woman would pinch it and no questions asked. At any rate, it was the best he could do in the limited time. Do you still think the chain of evidence thin, sir?"

"No. As you put it it covers every point," said Captain Tring, with the hint of a smile in his grey eyes. "But that bit about the dog and the beret—isn't it almost too ingenious?"

"I'm certain that's what happened," Gorham declared. "That tear in the beret gave me more worry than the rest of the case put together. Then on Thursday evening I saw Robin dash across the garden with a gnawed duster in his mouth, and saw in a flash what had happened. That hole could only have been made in that way, by being actually eaten away. The feather must have been snapped at the same time, but the missing bit has never been found."

"Did Hyde leave it in that garage intentionally, to incriminate Hubberd, do you suppose?" Tring asked slowly. But to that Gorham could give no certain answer.

"It was dark at the time. He was in a desperate hurry to get away. When he'd grabbed the dog, perhaps he didn't dare stop to hunt for it. But he didn't regret it afterwards, as it was a pointer towards Hubberd, and away from himself."

Captain Tring sat up with a brisk air.

"But now for the crux of the matter, the point that intrigues me most," he said. "The motive. How on earth did you get on to the fact that this fellow Hyde was sailing under false colours? He's fairly well known in London, you know, but I've never heard a shadow of doubt thrown on his authorship of the L. V. Hyde stories. He stood for it quite openly. Spoke at literary meetings, and so on. It wasn't a case of fathering the work of a paid ghost—which I've always considered a detestable practice—but of cold, deliberate fraud on the public."

"Not so far as the work went, sir. Editors wanted a certain line of stuff, and they got it. The reputation of L. V. Hyde was built up on the genuine popularity of the stories provided. It was that reputation he stole, and masqueraded under. As far as I know, the fraud didn't start till he came to live with his sister. The people he knew out East all called him 'Sid'—his own name, which is Sydney Laurence Hyde—though his sister was writing even then. I've seen a magazine with one of these stories ten years old. One of that bundle you brought home, Moh. I suppose, as his sister never showed up in Town, it began sort of vaguely, with a hint here and there. Till he'd regularly got caught in his own lies and couldn't stop."

"Um, that's a charitable way of looking at it. But one can well believe that, after years of such masquerading, he preferred to murder the person who threatened him with exposure to being made the laughing stock of London. But you haven't answered my question how you first discovered he was an impostor!"

"I got it before I got the case," Gorham said. And Tring stared. "Will you kindly explain how?" he said politely.

"Well, it was this way," Gorham chuckled. "Miss Hyde unloaded a lot of old magazines on Moh, here, one day, and last Saturday—Saturday week, I mean—I read one of these L. V. H. stories. It was about a young woman with hyacinth hair—"

He broke off, but Captain Tring laughed.

"Hyacinth hair's all right, man. That's Poe. Go on."

"Well, if you say so, sir . . ." Gorham accepted his oracle's statement with reluctance. "I didn't take to the description of this young woman myself. But the scene was laid in China, and a lot of jewels came in—sapphire skies, and emerald grass, and amethyst water, and so on, and then this hyacinth young female, to save the silver hairs of an aged parent from the horror of bankruptcy, consented to go with the villain on an expedition to hunt lions."

Tring looked at the good-humoured face of his Chief Inspector with eyes that hid their appreciation behind a screen of amusement.

"Well?"

"Those lions stuck in the back of my head, and when I heard that L. V. Hyde had lived in Assam, and been to Shanghai, I felt there was something fishy somewhere. Then it came to me."

"Well?"

"Well, sir, if the brother was the author, as he claimed to be, he'd have known enough not to grow lions in China. But if the sister, who'd read a lot, of course, but never been out of England in her life, was the author, then it was a natural sort of slip to make, though I bet she discovered her mistake soon enough and felt silly over it. Then she called him Sydney, and her passbook from the bank was addressed to Miss Ella V. Hyde. And there you are. Ella—Ell—L. To make quite sure, I told him in front of her I'd just enjoyed one of his tales, and he turned me off short. And she went as white as a sheet. So I told 'em I was planting a constable in their garden that night on a trumped-up yarn, but to see he didn't do anything nasty to shut her up as he'd done to Ellen Shields. Next day he went to Frinton, to try and wangle a job out East out of MacDonnell probably, because he knew by then he'd driven her forbearance too far, and she was through with him."

"Then that explains partly why he tried to kill the goose that laid the golden eggs," Tring said quietly. "But you realize, I suppose, that the defence will plead insanity? That illness he came home with years ago almost invariably has latent consequences that result in madness eventually. I've been looking up cases, and the interval extended in one to as long as fourteen years; in another only to four. But the final development of the disease was always heralded by attacks of unreasoned destructiveness, going on to homicidal frenzy if roused by opposition, exactly as has happened in the case of Hyde."

"But that man is no more crazy than I am!" cried Gorham, thoroughly roused at this utterly unforeseen piece of information. "Look at the cool care he took in covering his tracks—bluffing it out and behaving as if he hadn't a care in the world at Frinton—the nerve and cunning he displayed in planning his getaway with the woman Sylvia—"

"In my opinion that woman had a lucky escape," Tring remarked, pleased by the way he had turned the tables on his subordinate. "If she'd tried to oppose him she'd have followed Ellen Shields into the Shades. But his final attack on his sister—from whom he could still have got money and help to start in a new country, no doubt—was stark craziness—the act of a man driven by an overmastering impulse to murder. At least," he added, rising, and dropping into his usual, light, half-ironic tone, "that's how I read the case. Fortunately Moh stopped him. I haven't inquired which of you turned up what on this job. Probably you don't know yourselves. It's a highly irregular partnership, you know that? Still, while Moh continues to bring home the bacon, the Chief Commissioner has decided not to interfere."

"In humble avocation of gardener—" Mr. Moh began indignantly. But Captain Tring interrupted him.

"You cultivate laurels. Exactly. Well, you're a pleasure to look at, Moh. I've enjoyed the spectacle immensely."

He looked down with a kind smile, just touched a discoloured hand, and turned away with Gorham in attendance.

"That disease you spoke of, sir; if it's true he's got it"—Gorham had been silent, pondering this new light on the situation—"does it last long?"

"It won't finish him off as quick as the hangman, if that's what you're hoping. Personally, I prefer a natural ending to our problems. But I'm not expert in tropical diseases, man. The authority I consulted gave a year at the outside, once the acute symptoms appeared. But don't quote me. I merely sketched the possible line the defence will take. May be entirely wrong. 'Afternoon."

"Good afternoon, sir."

The car drove off, and Gorham went thoughtfully back to the garden.

"Do you think he was right, Li Moh? That he was simply cracked all through?" he demanded of his friend.

But Mr. Moh's temper was ruffled.

"No risk being taken by this aching worm of being jumped on for casting doubt on infallibility of sacred Police Chief, same unuttered," he said with austere calm.

"You don't agree, then? All right, I'll forgive your peevishness as you're feeling sore, old man." Gorham gave him a large benevolent smile that was crossly ignored. "But say what you like, the A.C. isn't generally wrong. You're annoyed, and don't properly appreciate his kindness in coming this afternoon . . . just to hand out that tip, I believe. The trial won't last ten minutes if that defence is proved. We've to keep the hint to ourselves. But, mark my words, the Chief is sure to be right about the fact. He'd never have been so definite otherwise."

Mr. Moh kept silence.

"The funny thing was," Gorham went on, after a pause given to further intensive thought, "I felt all along as if I were dealing with an irresponsible, dangerous devil, yet at the same time thought he was as smart as they're made. For instance, I didn't see anything cracked, not to say *cracked*, in that chase of his home. I felt it was sheer crazy of him to head for the one place where he was certain to be copped, but kept thinking up good reasons—how he'd got to take the risk to secure cash for his getaway and that. He was so slick. That by itself should have warned me. Honestly, Moh, did you ever think he was mad?"

"No," said Mr. Moh slowly. "Except with hate of his sister, because he had wronged her and owed all he had to her generosity. While she permitted him to make use of her, self-interest kept his desire to stamp on her in check. He did not try to kill the goose of golden eggs, as your Chief said, till she had told him she would lay no more. That, to me, shows logical thinking, no madness."

"Um. You always get logical thinking in madmen, old man. The true dyed-in-the-wool type. They get hold of some cracked idea, and then work it out, regardless. And that's how you discover they're mad. See?" Gorham grinned. "But that's why you stuck to her like a leech, was it—because you said he hated her?"

"And why did you station policemen in her garden?" Mr. Moh retorted. "To adorn the landscape with their fatheaded presences only?"

"I told you I had a hunch that I was dealing with a dangerous lunatic, Li Moh," the Chief Inspector replied with dignity. "Need you rub it in that I didn't face it for what it was till the A.C. gave the key just now? At the time I just wanted to keep that little lady safe and comfy while I got on with the job with a mind at ease. And if my blockheads had used an ounce of gumption on Friday night she'd have been safe to the end. And you wouldn't look like an amateur oil-painting. Still," he added with a sigh, his heat dying down, "if my case has got to go west on a plea of insanity I'll be glad she's spared the final vexation of having her precious brother hanged."

"I too yearn to have her tender heart spared that final horror, my Gorham. Willingly would this unspeakably sore reptile embrace the knees of your beautiful Police Chief if his angelical prophecy of respite may prove true enough to save her that coronation of pain. Much," he added wistfully, "as I should like to have him dead."

"Look on the bright side, old man. The A.C. gave him a year to live at the outside, in any case. After all, she's alive, and you're alive, so things might be worse. And here, at last, are Mary and Molly with the tea-things, so everything in the garden *is* lovely."

Mr. Moh's long-legged young daughter hugged her honorary uncle with warm affection, while his wife fussed gently round her husband. A table was brought out, and laid with a green linen cloth, and cakes that Mary had baked to tempt her invalids' by-no-means-failing appetites. They ate strawberries and cream with pleasure and enjoyed their tea, and from the contented domestic scene the thought of crime was banished.

Chapter XXIII

"I won't pretend to a grief I don't feel, Lewis."

But her tone was heavy with sadness, too deep for expressing, and Lewis attempted no futile consolation.

They were driving back to Fordyk from the funeral of Sydney Hyde, and a dense fog that pressed against the wind-screen, merging now into the early darkness of a February day, made close attention to his task a necessity.

"Are you cold, Elvie?"

"No. Eliza will have blazing fires waiting for us."

"Good old Eliza."

She did not speak again, leaving him free to attend to his driving without distraction; but her mind, intensely awake, reviewed the dragging months that lay between that first drive into Hertfordshire that they had taken together and today.

When she came slowly to herself in that hospital bedroom, in that strange state of detachment from normal realities that illness brings, Lewis was her first visitor. It was he who gave her the bare facts of what had happened, but her mind, moving, it seemed, in strange, mysterious processes of thought while her spirit slept, had already grasped the truth, so his task was made the easier.

They were married the day after she left the hospital, a week before the date fixed for Sydney's trial. The verdict on expert medical evidence, was a foregone conclusion, but she had protested that they should wait till it was given. Lewis refused to listen.

"We are neither of us romantic children," he argued. "We've no one but ourselves to consider. The verdict, whatever it may be, won't make the smallest difference to our marriage. But being married is going to cut out a lot of the difficulties we've both got to contend with over the whole business and our own affairs. We'll stay in Town till after next week, and then go down to Pine Hubberd's cottage for a few months till we know where we stand and what we want to do next. Come, be a reasonable woman, Elvie." He grasped her hands. "We're friends already, aren't we? But friendship gives one no *locus standi* in law. We must have a deed of partnership," he added, with the single burst of feeling that he displayed during his queer courtship. "Gad! I wouldn't go through these last five weeks again for a fortune! Be merciful—"

They spent the week at a hotel. He left her free to deal with her affairs alone. She had an interview with her literary agent, who had loyally kept the confidence reposed in him, and treated her with an odd mixture of indignant sympathy, respect, and disapproval over her intention to give up writing. "Only for a time, I trust, Mrs. Hardwicke, only for a brief time. Your pen is a gold-mine!" he kept repeating.

But he was beside her at the trial. Sydney was self-possessed, even jaunty, oblivious of his position. She only saw him once afterwards. A dreadful interview, when he taunted her with foisting her silly drivel on him—heaped cruel, vicious insults on her, staring at her with shifty, vacant eyes.

The attendant took him away, and Lewis found her in floods of helpless tears.

He visited Sydney alone after that, brought her reports of a clouded mind steadily darkening. . . . And at last the final terrible phase that death had ended.

She had stood by the grave dry-eyed, scarcely believing that the agony was finished.

The fog was thinner on the higher part of Fordyk, and as they stopped at the familiar gate lights from the windows streamed across the garden to welcome them, diffused on the misty air.

She said, as he came to help her down:

"Lewis, without you I couldn't have borne it."

He said, his arms about her for a swift second:

"You have been marvellous, dear one. Thank God I have you safe!"

Tea was set by the blazing fire that Ella Hardwicke had predicted. Eliza received them in the hall and hovered round her mistress with anxious glances, while Robin danced about his new master. Robin was all for his new master, and Eliza was scarcely behind him in her approval of the present arrangement.

Except for a few words to assuage Eliza's discreet concern, they spoke no more of the event of the day till, the tea-things cleared away, they were alone together with Robin between them on the hearthrug, and the flickering lights from the fire playing over their faces.

Lewis had never got over the sense of magic he felt in first possessing a home, but he knew now that it was Ella's presence that gave it; the setting did not matter. He would feel it just the same in a dugout, or a tent in a desert, if she were there.

"Lewis, doesn't it seem strange that poor Ellen Shields, who seemed so utterly insignificant while she lived, could have power by her death to change the whole world she knew?" she said gravely. "And not only that, but to alter radically all our lives. She wouldn't know a single person in Pound Lane now, yet when she came trailing about there it seemed as if the people in it had got into a sort of timeless rut, would go on there for ever. As if nothing short of an earthquake could make us move."

"And she provided the fuse that blew us all up. But most of the material for explosion was present already. You were actually getting out already, though you were secretive and didn't tell me so."

"That's a better simile than my earthquake." She would not be diverted from her theme till she had rounded it off neatly. "I know I didn't tell you, but I didn't know you till that Sunday, and all that week, when you came in and were rather nice. That week did alter our lives, Lewis!" She shivered.

"It did, thank God!" he broke in hastily. "But it was my coming home at the psychological moment that really did the trick, my dear. If I'd waited another month we'd never have met, and you'd have still been to me just that Miss Hyde my mother used to know. But you're right about the Lane. We'd all been there for so long it seemed as if we'd really taken root, yet a week after the poor soul's end we'd every one of us cleared out. My dad bought that house when I was a school-boy—let's see, twenty-seven years ago—"

"And Mother and I came to Innisfree about two years later, but Mrs. Manstead had been there years and years before that, yet even her house is empty now. She never came back from Littlehampton, you know. I had a few lines from her at Christmas explaining that she had decided to stay in her comfortable rooms there for good, and give up housekeeping, as she had not found another companion whom she could rely on. So her house is for sale."

"And likely to be. I suppose I ought to congratulate myself that the Y.M.C.A. bought in mine at a figure Shylock would have been ashamed to offer. They've taken The Burrs, too. That crowd is scattered, and no mistake. Hubberd in China; Ethel the Lord knows where . . ." He fidgeted. He had heard rumours about Ethel, but Elvie hated sordid gossip. Also he wanted to lead her thoughts away from Pound Lane. "Did I tell you I met that rather decent brother of Charles Hughes, who runs a hotel in Bloomsbury, in Oxford Street last week?"

"No. Had he news of them—Charles and his wife, I mean?"

"Yes. He said they're in Hollywood. I shouldn't be surprised if Charles made a hit there; he's got all the physical gifts. But Clarice will get what's coming to her if he turns into a film star, and can make himself independent of her. Dick said Charles had got in with a shifty crowd and was in a blind funk he'd be rounded up with them on a charge of conspiracy to defraud, so Dick had to raise the money for their fares to the U.S.A. He added quite frankly he hoped they'd never make enough to pay them home again."

He stopped to light a pipe.

"He wasn't as callous as he sounded, either," he continued a moment later. "His wife and he work like blacks to keep that place going, and he said things came to a climax when, after the pair had planted themselves on him for weeks, he found they were borrowing right and left from his regular clients. Besides, he's got his mother and invalid sister there already, not to mention their own three youngsters. He took me up to see his mother in the jolly little suite they've given her, and he warned me to be *cave* what I said about Charles as he's the old lady's favourite son! Said it without a shadow of resentment, too. Rather decent of him, I thought. But not so the sister. Frail little thing, all eyes, she was; but it was Dick they smiled on all right. And he smiled back, and Mrs. Dick too. I believe you'd like them, Elvie."

"When we leave here we might put up there for a night," she said quietly. "Mr. Moh says he's ready to take care of Robin while we're away. Would you like that?"

"You wouldn't mind? Then we could hand over poor old Robin to Moh in the evening, and drive down to Dover next morning in plenty of time for the midday boat. Which day shall we say?"

"There's nothing to pack here. Only the silver to send to the bank. The caretakers are ready to come in at any moment. The sooner the better, I think." She was braver than he, for she uttered aloud the thought that was in both their minds. "There is nothing to delay us any longer."

"All right. Suppose we start on Wednesday, the day after to-morrow?" he said casually. "That'll give you and Eliza time to pack a suitcase each. You'd better tell her, and warn old Prout and his missus they've to move in Wednesday, and I'll go down to the post-office and do a bit of 'phoning."

He stooped and patted her shoulder as he passed her chair. She sat still for a few minutes when he was gone.

It seemed selfish to take him from this homely cottage that he liked so much, but he was like a cat in his odd, casual ways; at one moment snugly tucked up by his fireside as if he never intended to leave it, the next strolling out on an expedition that might end at Cannes, or Canton, or the Cape.

They had always known that the sojourn at Mr. Pine Hubberd's cottage marked an interlude. And the motor tour on which they were now free to start, and on which Eliza, to her great glory, was to accompany them, was his decision. Though she was still too tired in spirit to plan for herself, she knew that he was right. Nothing but the definite break with all her previous life that travelling would give could restore resilience to her bruised spirit. She could not, having married Lewis, go on being broken-winged, hampering his life. She must get herself mended, healed, to take up her real share in their partnership, break with the past and go forward to the future that lay before them both.

And her writing. She had not touched a typewriter since that fatal Saturday when Robin was lost. When poor Ellen's body lay within a few feet of her as she paced the Lane, and she did not know it. Was the power crushed out of existence, or in abeyance, like her other gift for growing flowers? In all the long months here, in this lovely, old-world garden, she had watched the old man, Prout, tending the beds, and had never once touched a plant herself. That must come back some time, that deep, instinctive happiness she had once had in growing things. And perhaps the other instinct too must rise and assert itself again; but what she wrote would be different—utterly different.

And, in any case, both could wait; she could bear quite easily to live without what had once been her whole living, because she had Lewis.

She rose and patted Robin. Leaving the dog behind was the one regret she had in going off on this adventure with Lewis that had no time-table, or any plan or limit but their own wishes; but he would be perfectly happy and safe with Mr. Moh.

She went out to the kitchen to tell Eliza that they had decided to go away on Wednesday.

THE END

Printed in Great Britain
by Amazon